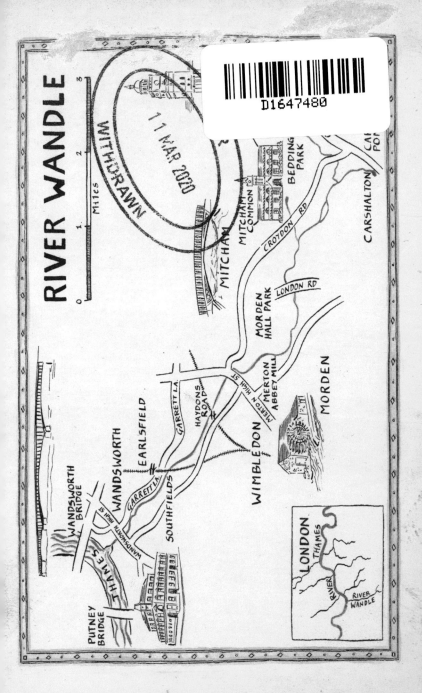

RIVER WANDLE

Miles

0   1   2   3

MITCHAM

Mitcham Common

CROYDON RD

BEDDINGTON PARK

CARSHALTON

CARSHALTON
POND

Morden Hall Park

LONDON RD

MORDEN

Merton Abbey Mill

MERTON HIGH ST

WIMBLEDON

EARLSFIELD

WANDSWORTH

HAYDONS ROAD

GARRETT LA.

GARRETT LA.

SOUTHFIELDS

WANDSWORTH BRIDGE

WANDSWORTH HIGH ST

THAMES

PUTNEY BRIDGE

LONDON

THAMES

RIVER

RIVER WANDLE

PENGUIN BOOKS

WAITING FOR WEDNESDAY

Waiting for Wednesday
A Frieda Klein Novel

NICCI FRENCH

PENGUIN BOOKS

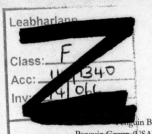

PENGUIN BOOKS

Published by the Penguin Group

Penguin Books Ltd, 80 Strand, London WC2R ORL, England
Penguin Group (USA) Inc., 375 Hudson Street, New York, New York 10014, USA
Penguin Group (Canada), 90 Eglinton Avenue East, Suite 700, Toronto, Ontario, Canada M4P 2Y3
(a division of Pearson Penguin Canada Inc.)
Penguin Ireland, 25 St Stephen's Green, Dublin 2, Ireland (a division of Penguin Books Ltd)
Penguin Group (Australia), 707 Collins Street, Melbourne, Victoria 3008, Australia
(a division of Pearson Australia Group Pty Ltd)
Penguin Books India Pvt Ltd, 11 Community Centre, Panchsheel Park,
New Delhi – 110 017, India
Penguin Group (NZ), 67 Apollo Drive, Rosedale, Auckland 0632, New Zealand
(a division of Pearson New Zealand Ltd)
Penguin Books (South Africa) (Pty) Ltd, Block D, Rosebank Office Park,
181 Jan Smuts Avenue, Parktown North, Gauteng, Johannesburg 2193, South Africa

Penguin Books Ltd, Registered Offices: 80 Strand, London WC2R ORL, England

www.penguin.com

First published by Michael Joseph, 2013
First published in Penguin Books 2014
003

Copyright © Joined-Up Writing, 2013
Map of the River Wandle © Maps Illustrated, 2013

All rights reserved

The moral right of the author has been asserted

Typeset by Palimpsest Book Production Limited, Falkirk, Stirlingshire
Printed in Great Britain by Clays Ltd, St Ives plc

ISBN: 978-0-241-95034-0
OPEN MARKET EDITION ISBN: 978-1-405-91650-9

www.greenpenguin.co.uk

MIX
Paper from
responsible sources
FSC   FSC™ C018179
www.fsc.org

Penguin Books is committed to a sustainable
future for our business, our readers and our planet.
This book is made from Forest Stewardship
Council™ certified paper.

For Pat and John, once more with feeling

ONE

There was no sign that anything was wrong. It was just an ordinary terraced house on an ordinary Wednesday afternoon in April. It had a long, narrow garden, like all the other houses in the road. The one to its left had been neglected for many years. It was overgrown with nettles and brambles; at the far end there was a plastic sandpit full of sludgy water and a child-sized goal that had been tipped over. The garden on the other side was paved and gravelled, with plants in terracotta pots, chairs that the owners folded up in winter to store in their shed, and a barbecue under a black tarpaulin that would be wheeled into the centre of the patio for the summer months.

But this particular garden had a lawn, just cut for the first time this year. White blossom shone on an old, twisted apple. The roses and shrubs in the borders had been pruned back so hard that they were like sticks. There were ranks of orange tulips near the kitchen door. There was a single trainer with its laces still done up under the window, empty flower pots, a bird table with a few seeds scattered on its flat surface, a couple of empty beer bottles by the boot-scraper.

The cat walked up the garden, taking its time and pausing by the door, head lifted as if waiting for something. Then it deftly inserted itself through the cat flap and entered the kitchen, with its tiled floor, its table – big enough for six or more people – and its Welsh dresser, which was really too large for the room and was cluttered with china and odds-and-ends: tubes of dried-out glue, bills in their envelopes, a cookery book opened at a recipe for monkfish with preserved lemon, a balled pair of socks, a five-pound note, a small hairbrush. Pans hung from a steel rail above the cooker. There was a basket of vegetables near the sink, a dozen more cookery books on a small shelf, a vase of flowers that were beginning to droop on the windowsill, a school textbook open spine-down on the table. On the wall was a whiteboard with a 'to-do' list in red felt pen. There was a half-eaten piece of toast, cold, on a plate on one of the surfaces, and a cup of tea beside it.

The cat dipped its head delicately into its bowl on the floor and ate one or two granules of dried cat food, wiped its paw over the side of its face, then continued through the house, out of the kitchen, whose door was always open, past the little lavatory to the left, up the two steps. It sidestepped a broken glass bowl and walked around the leather shoulder-bag lying in the hallway. The bag was upended, its contents scattered over the oak floorboards. Lipstick and face-powder, an opened pack of tissues, car keys, a hairbrush, a small blue diary with a pen attached to it, a packet of paracetamol, a spiral-bound notebook. A bit further on, a black wallet splayed open, a few membership cards dotted around it (AA, British Museum). A framed print from an old Van Gogh exhibition was tipped to one side on the cream wall, and on the floor, its frame cracked, lay a large family portrait: a man, a woman, three children, with broad smiles.

The cat picked its way through the debris and walked into the living room at the front of the house. An arm lay outstretched in the doorway; the hand was plump and firm with nails cut short and a gold band on the fourth finger. The cat sniffed at it, then gave the wrist a cursory lick. It half climbed on to the body, in its sky-blue blouse and its black work trousers, digging its claws purringly into the soft stomach. Wanting attention, it nuzzled against the head of warm brown hair that was greying now and tied back in a loose knot. There were small gold studs in the ear lobes. There was a thin chain and locket round the neck. The skin smelt of roses and something else. The cat rubbed its body against the face and arched its back.

After a while, it gave up and went to sit on the armchair to wash itself, for its coat was matted now and sticky.

Dora Lennox walked slowly back from school. She was tired. It was Wednesday and she had double science last lesson, then swing band in the after-school club. She played the saxophone – badly, splitting notes, but the music teacher didn't seem fussy. She had only agreed to go because her friend Cam had persuaded her, but now Cam didn't seem to be her friend any more, and whispered and giggled with other girls who didn't have braces, weren't skinny and shy but bold and curvy, with black lacy bras and shiny lips and bright eyes.

Dora's rucksack, heavy with books, bumped on her back; her music case swung against her shin; and the plastic carrier bag – bulging with cooking utensils and a tin of scorched scones that she'd made in food tech that morning – was ripped. She was glad to see their car parked near the house. It meant her mother was home. She didn't like coming back to an empty house, with all the lights off and a grey hush to every room. Her mother put life into things: the dishwasher rumbling, maybe a cake in the oven or at least a tin of biscuits laid out ready for her, the kettle boiling for tea, a sense of ordered bustle that Dora found comforting.

As she opened the gate and walked up the short, tiled garden path, she saw that the front door was open. Had she arrived just after her mother? Or her brother, Ted? She could hear a sound as well, a pulsing electronic sound. As she got closer she saw that the small frosted-glass window, just to the side of the door, was broken. There was a hole in the glass and it bulged inwards. As she stood looking at the strange sight, she felt something on her leg and looked down. The cat was rubbing against her, and Dora noticed that she had left a rusty stain on her new jeans. She stepped into the house, letting her bags slide to the floor. There were shards of glass from the window on the mat. That would need to be fixed. At least it hadn't been her. It was probably Ted. He broke things all the time: mugs, glasses, windows. Anything fragile. She could smell something as well. Something burning.

'Mum, I'm home!' she called.

There was more mess on the floor – the big family photograph, her mother's bag, bits and pieces strewn around. It was as if a storm had blown through the house, dislodging objects and tossing them about. Dora briefly saw her reflection in the mirror that hung above the table:

small white face, thin brown plaits. She walked through to the kitchen where the smell was strongest. She opened the door of the oven and smoke poured out like a hot breath, making her cough. She took an oven glove, lifted the baking tray from the top shelf and put it on top of the stove. There were six charred, shrunken black discs on the tray. Utterly ruined. Her mother sometimes made biscuits for her after school. Dora closed the door and switched off the gas. Yes, that was it. The oven had been left on and the biscuits had burned. The alarm and the smoke had scared Mimi and she had run around breaking things. But why had the biscuits burned?

She called out again. She saw the fist on the floor in the doorway, fingers curled, but still she went on calling, not moving. 'Mum, I'm home!'

She walked back out into the hall, still calling. The door to the front room was slightly open. She saw something inside, pushed against the door and stepped into the room.

'Mum?'

At first, stupidly, she saw splashes of red paint on the far wall and the sofa and great daubs of it on the floor. Then her hand flew to her mouth and she heard a small moan coming up her throat, then widening out in the terrible room, becoming a shriek that went on and on and wouldn't stop. She put her hands against her ears to block out the sound but now it was inside her. Not paint, but blood, streams of blood and then a dark, dark lake near the thing lying at her feet. An arm out-flung, a watch on the wrist that still told the time, a comfortable body in a blue shirt and black trousers, one shoe half off. All that she knew. But the face wasn't a face any longer, because one of its eyes was gone and its mouth was shattered and shouted noiselessly at her through a spit of broken teeth. One entire side of the head was caved in and blistered with blood and gristle and bone, as if someone had tried to destroy it.

Two

The house was in Chalk Farm, a couple of streets away from the noise of Camden Lock. There was an ambulance outside and several police cars. A tape had already been put up and a few passers-by had stopped to stare.

Detective Constable Yvette Long ducked under the tape and looked at the house, a late-Victorian semi, with a small front garden and a bay window. She was about to go inside when she saw Detective Chief Inspector Malcolm Karlsson stepping out of a car and waited for him. He seemed serious, preoccupied, until he noticed her and gave a nod.

'Have you been inside yet?'

'I just arrived,' said Yvette. She paused for a moment, then blurted out, 'It's funny seeing you without Frieda.'

Karlsson's expression turned harsh. 'So you're pleased she's not helping us out.'

'I . . . I didn't mean that.'

'I know you had problems with her being around,' said Karlsson, 'but that's been sorted. The chief decided that she was out and she almost got killed in the process. Is that the bit that seemed funny?'

Yvette blushed and didn't reply.

'Have you been to see her?' Karlsson asked.

'I went to the hospital.'

'That's not enough. You should talk to her. But meanwhile . . .'

He gestured towards the house and they walked in. It was full of people in plastic overshoes, wearing overalls and gloves. They spoke in hushed voices or were silent. Karlsson and Yvette pulled on their shoes and gloves and walked down the hall, past a handbag lying on the boards, past a photograph in a smashed frame, past a man dusting for fingerprints, into the living room, where spotlights had been rigged up.

The dead woman lay under the lights as if she was on stage. She was on her back. One arm was flung out, the other lay by her side, the hand in a half-fist. Her hair was brown, going grey. Her mouth was smashed open so it looked like an animal's demented snarl, but from where he stood, gazing down at her, Karlsson could see a filling glinting among the splintered teeth. On one side of her face, the skin was quite smooth, but sometimes death uncreases wrinkles, takes away the marks that life has made and adds its own. Her neck had the wrinkles of middle-age.

Her right eye was open, staring. The left side of the woman's head had been caved in, sticky with liquid and bits of bone. Blood soaked into the beige carpet around her, had dried in splashes all over the floor and sprayed the nearest wall, turning the middle-class living room into an abattoir.

'Someone hit her hard,' murmured Karlsson, straightening up.

'Burglary,' said a voice behind him. Karlsson looked round. A detective was standing at his back, slightly too close. He was very young, pimply, with a slightly uneasy smile on his face.

'What?' said Karlsson. 'Who are you?'

'Riley,' said the officer.

'You said something.'

'Burglary,' said Riley. 'He was caught in the act and he lashed out.'

Riley noticed Karlsson's expression and his smile melted away. 'I was thinking aloud,' he said. 'I was trying to be positive. And proactive.'

'Proactive,' said Karlsson. 'I thought we might examine the crime scene, search for prints, hair and fibres, take some statements before deciding what happened. If that's all right with you.'

'Yes, sir.'

'Good.'

'Boss.' Chris Munster had come into the room. He stood for a moment, gazing at the body.

'What do we know, Chris?'

It took an effort for Munster to shift his attention back to Karlsson. 'You don't get used to it,' he said.

'Try to,' said Karlsson. 'The family don't need you to do their suffering for them.'

'Right,' said Munster, consulting his notebook. 'Her name is Ruth Lennox. She was a health visitor for the local authority. You know, old people, new mothers, that sort of thing. Forty-four years old, married, three kids. The youngest daughter discovered her when she came back from school at about half past five.'

'Is she here?'

'Upstairs, with the father and the other two kids.'

'Any estimate of time of death?'

'After midday, before six o'clock.'

'That's not much use.'

'I'm just repeating what Dr Heath told me. He was saying that it was a heated house, warm day, sun through the window. It's not an exact science.'

'Fine. Murder weapon?'

Munster shrugged. 'Something heavy, Dr Heath said. With a sharp edge but not a blade.'

'All right,' said Karlsson. 'Is someone getting the family's prints?'

'I'll check.'

'Anything stolen?' asked Yvette.

Karlsson glanced at her. It was the first time she'd spoken in the house. Her tone still sounded shaky. He'd probably been too hard on her.

'The husband's in a state of shock,' said Munster. 'But it looks like her wallet's been emptied.'

'I'd better talk to them. Upstairs, you say?'

'In the study. First room you come to up the stairs, next to the bathroom. Melanie Hackett's with them.'

'All right,' said Karlsson. 'There was a detective used to work round here, Harry Curzon. I think he retired. Could you get his number for me? The local police will know him.'

'What do you want him for?'

'He knows the area. He might save us some trouble.'

'I'll do my best.'

'And have a word with young Riley here. He already knows what happened.' Karlsson turned to Yvette and signalled her to follow him up the stairs. At the door he paused and listened. He could hear no sound at all. He hated this bit. Often people blamed him because he was the bearer of bad news and at the same time clung to him because he promised some kind of solution. And this was a whole family. Three kids, Munster had said. Poor sods. She looked like she'd been a nice woman, he thought.

'Ready?'

Yvette nodded and he knocked on the door, three times, then pushed it open.

The father was sitting in a swivel chair, rotating this way and that. He still wore his outdoor jacket and a cotton scarf tied round his neck. His jowly face was white with mottled red patches on his cheeks, as if he'd just come in from the cold, and he kept blinking as if he had dust in his eyes, licking his lips, pulling the lobe of one ear. On the floor at his feet the younger daughter – the one who'd found Ruth Lennox – was curled in a foetal ball. She was hiccuping and retching and snuffling and gulping. Karlsson thought she sounded like a wounded animal. He couldn't see what she looked like, only that she was skinny and had brown hair in unravelling plaits. The father put a helpless hand on her shoulder, then drew it back.

The other daughter, who looked fifteen or sixteen, sat across from them, her legs folded under her and her arms clasped around her body, as though she wanted to make herself as warm and as small as possible. She had chestnut curls and her father's round face, with full red lips and freckles over the bridge of her nose. She had mascara smeared around one of her blue eyes, but not the other, which gave her an artificial look, clown-like, and yet Karlsson could see at once that she had a sultry attractiveness that even the ruined makeup and her chalky pallor couldn't mask. She was wearing maroon shorts over black tights, a T-shirt with a logo he didn't recognize. She stared at Karlsson when he entered, chewing her lower lip furiously.

The boy sat in the corner, his knees pulled sharply up to his chin, his face hidden by a mop of dark blond hair. Every so often he gave a violent shiver but didn't lift his head, even when Karlsson introduced himself.

'I'm so sorry,' Karlsson said. 'But I'm here to help and I'll need to ask some questions.'

'Why?' whispered the father. 'Why would anyone kill Ruth?'

At this, a sound broke from the older girl, a sob.

'Your younger daughter found her,' said Karlsson, gently. 'Is that right?'

'Dora. Yes.' He wiped the back of his hand across his mouth. 'What's that going to do to her?'

'Mr Lennox,' said Yvette, 'there are people who can help you with that . . .'

'Russell. Nobody calls me Mr Lennox.'

'We need to talk to Dora about what she saw.'

The wailing from the small shape on the floor continued. Yvette looked helplessly at Karlsson.

'You can be with your father,' said Karlsson, leaning down towards Dora. 'Or if you'd prefer to speak to a woman, not a man, then . . .'

'She doesn't want to,' said the older sister. 'Didn't you hear?'

'What's your name?' asked Karlsson.

'Judith.'

12

'And how old are you?'

'Fifteen. Does that help?' She glared at Karlsson out of her unnerving blue eyes.

'It's a terrible thing,' said Karlsson. 'But we need to know everything. Then we can find the person who did this.'

The boy suddenly jerked up his head. He struggled to his feet and stood by the door, tall and gangly. He had his mother's grey eyes. 'Is she still there?'

'Sorry?'

'Ted,' said Russell Lennox, in a soothing tone, moving towards him and holding out his hand. 'Ted, it's OK.'

'My mother.' The boy kept his eyes fixed on Karlsson. 'Is she still there?'

'Yes.'

The boy tugged the door open and ran down the stairs. Karlsson raced after him but didn't get there in time. The roar ripped through the house.

'No, no, no,' Ted was shouting. He was on his knees beside his mother's body. Karlsson put his arm round the boy and lifted him up, back and out of the room.

'It's all right, Ted.'

Karlsson turned. A woman had come in through the front door. She was solid, in her late thirties, with short, dark brown hair in an old-fashioned bob and wearing a knee-length tweed skirt; she also had something in a yellow sling around her chest. Karlsson saw that it was a very small baby, its bald head poking out of the top and two tiny feet sticking out at the bottom. The woman looked at Russell, her eyes bright. 'I came at once,' she said. 'What a terrible, terrible thing.'

She walked across to Russell, who had followed his son down the stairs, and gave him a long hug, made awkward and arms' length by the baby wedged in between them. Russell's face stared out over her shoulder, helpless. She looked round at Karlsson.

'I'm Ruth's sister,' she said. The bundle at her chest shifted and gave a whimper; she patted it with a clucking sound.

She had that excited calm that some people get in an emergency. Karlsson had seen it before. Disasters attracted people. Relatives, friends, neighbours gathered to help or give sympathy or just to be part of it in some way, to warm themselves in its terrible glow.

'This is Louise,' said Russell. 'Louise Weller. I rang people in the family. Before they heard it from someone else.'

'We're conducting an interview,' said Karlsson. 'I'm sorry, but I don't think it's appropriate you should be here. This is a crime scene.'

'Nonsense. I'm here to help,' said Louise, firmly. 'This is about my sister.' Her face was pale, except for spots of red on her cheekbones. 'My other two are in the car. I'll get them in a minute and put them somewhere out of the way. But tell me first, what happened?'

Karlsson hesitated a moment, then shrugged. 'I'll give you all a few minutes together. Then, when you're ready, we can talk.'

He guided them up the stairs and gestured to Yvette to follow him out of the room. 'On top of everything else,' he said, 'they'll need to move out for a few days. Can you mention it to them? Tactfully? Maybe there's a neighbour or friends nearby.' He saw Riley coming up the stairs.

'There's someone to see you, sir,' he said. 'He says you know him.'

'Who is he?' said Karlsson.

'Dr Bradshaw,' said Riley. 'He doesn't look like a policeman.'

'He's not,' said Karlsson. 'He's a sort of consultant. Anyway, what does it matter what he looks like? We'd better let him in, give him a chance to earn his money.'

As Karlsson walked down the stairs and saw Hal Bradshaw waiting in the hall, he saw what Riley meant. He didn't look like a detective. He wore a grey suit, with just a speckle of yellowish colour to it, and an open-necked white shirt. Karlsson particularly noticed his fawn suede shoes and his large, heavy-framed spectacles. He gave Karlsson a nod of recognition.

'How did you even hear about this?' Karlsson asked.

'It's a new arrangement. I like to get here when the scene is still fresh. The quicker I get here, the more useful I can be.'

'Nobody told me that,' said Karlsson.

Bradshaw didn't seem to be paying attention. He was looking around thoughtfully. 'Is your friend here?'

'Which friend?'

'Dr Klein,' he said. 'Frieda Klein. I expected to find her here, sniffing around.'

Hal Bradshaw and Frieda had worked on the same case, in which Frieda had very nearly been killed. A man had been found lying naked and decomposing in the flat of a disturbed woman, Michelle Doyce. Bradshaw had been convinced that she had killed the man; Frieda had heard in the woman's meandering words some kind of sense, a distracted straining towards the truth. Gradually she and Karlsson had pieced together the man's identity: he was a con man who had left behind him many victims, each with motives for revenge. Frieda's methods – unorthodox and instinctive – and her actions, which could be obsessive and self-destructive, had led to her dismissal during the last round of cuts. But clearly this wasn't enough for Bradshaw. She had made him look stupid and now he wanted to destroy her. Karlsson thought of all of this. Then he thought of a dead woman lying a few feet away, and a family grieving, and swallowed his angry words.

'Dr Klein's not working for us any more.'

'Oh, yes,' said Bradshaw, cheerfully. 'That's right. Things didn't go very well at the end of that last case.'

'It depends what you mean by "well",' Karlsson said. 'Three murderers were caught.'

Bradshaw pulled a face. 'If the consultant ends up in a knife fight and then spends a month in intensive care, that's not exactly an example of success. In my book, at least.'

Karlsson was on the point of saying something but again he remembered where he was.

'This is hardly the place,' he said coolly. 'A mother has been murdered. Her family are upstairs.'

Bradshaw held up a hand. 'Shall we stop talking and go through?'

'I wasn't the one talking.'

Bradshaw stepped inside and took a deep breath, as if he were appraising the aroma of the room. He moved towards the body of Ruth Lennox, treading delicately to avoid the pool of blood. He looked towards Karlsson.

'You know, blundering into a crime scene and being attacked, doesn't count as solving a crime.'

'Are we talking about Frieda again?' said Karlsson.

'Her mistake is to get emotionally involved,' he said. 'I heard she slept with the man who was arrested.'

'She didn't sleep with him,' said Karlsson, coldly. 'She met him socially. Because she was suspicious of him.'

Bradshaw looked at Karlsson with a half-smile. 'Does that trouble you?'

'I'll tell you what troubles me,' said Karlsson. 'It troubles me that you seem to feel competitive with Frieda Klein.'

'Me? No, no, no. Simply concerned for a colleague who seems to have lost her bearings.' He gave a sympathetic grimace. 'I feel very sorry for her. I hear she's depressed.'

'I thought you'd come to look at a murder scene. If you want to discuss an earlier case, we should go somewhere else.'

Bradshaw shook his head. 'Don't you think this is like a work of art?'

'No, I don't.'

'We need to think, what is he trying to express? What is he telling the world?'

'Maybe I should just leave you to it,' said Karlsson.

'I imagine that you think this is a simple burglary gone wrong.'

'I'm trying to avoid quick conclusions,' said Karlsson. 'We're gathering evidence. Theories can come later.'

Bradshaw shook his head again. 'That's the wrong way round. Without a theory, data is just chaos. You should always be open to your first impressions.'

'So what's your first impression?'

'I'll be delivering a written report,' said Bradshaw, 'but I'll give you a free preview. A burglary isn't just a burglary.'

'You'll have to explain that to me.'

Bradshaw made an expansive gesture. 'Look around you. A burglary is an invasion of a home, a violation, a rape. This man was expressing anger against a whole area of life that was closed to him, an area of property and family ties and social status. And when he encountered this woman, she personified everything that he couldn't have – she was at the same time a well-off woman, a desirable woman, a mother, a wife. He could have run away, he could have struck her a simple blow, but he's left us a message, just as he left *her* a message. The injuries were directed to her face, rather than to her body. Look at the splashes of blood on the wall, so out of proportion to anything that was needed. He was trying to literally wipe an expression off her face, an expression of superiority. He was redecorating the room with her blood. It was almost a kind of love.'

'A strange kind of love,' said Karlsson.

'That's why it had to be so savage,' said Bradshaw. 'If he didn't care, he wouldn't have to do something so extreme. It wouldn't matter. This has an emotional intensity.'

'So who are we looking for?'

Bradshaw closed his eyes before he spoke, as if he was seeing something nobody else could see.

'White,' he said. 'Early to mid-thirties. Strongly built. Unmarried. Of no fixed abode. No steady job, no steady relationship. No family connections.' He took out his phone and pointed it in various directions around the room.

'You need to be careful with those images,' said Karlsson. 'Things have a way of ending up online.'

'I'm cleared for this,' said Bradshaw. 'You should take a look at my contract. I'm a criminal psychologist. This is what I do.'

'All right,' said Karlsson. 'But I think we should leave. The scene-of-crime team need to take over.'

Bradshaw slipped his phone into his jacket pocket. 'That's fine. I'm done. Oh, by the way, give Dr Klein my best. Tell her I've been thinking of her.'

As they left, they met Louise Weller coming back into the house. The baby was still slung round her, but now she was towing a tiny boy by the hand. At her heels stomped a slightly older girl, stocky like her. Even though she was wearing a pink nightgown, and pushing a toy buggy in which a doll was swaddled, she reminded Karlsson of Yvette.

Louise Weller gave him a brisk nod. 'Families should rally round,' she said and, like a general leading a reluctant army, she marched her children into the house.

THREE

At twenty-five past three in the morning, when it was no longer night but not yet day, Frieda Klein woke up. Her heart was racing and her mouth was dry, her forehead beaded with sweat. It was hard to swallow or even to breathe. Everything hurt: her legs, her shoulder, her ribs, her face. Old bruises flowered and throbbed. For a few moments she did not open her eyes, and when she did, the darkness pressed down on her and spread out in all directions. She turned her head towards the window. Waiting for Wednesday to end, for the light to come and the dreams to fade.

The waves came, one after another, each worse than the one before, rising up and crashing over her, pulling her under, then spitting her out ready for the next. They were inside her, thrashing through her body and her mind, and they were outside. As she lay there, greyly awake, memories mixed with fading dreams. Faces gleamed in the darkness, hands reached out to her. Frieda tried to hold on to what Sandy had said, night after night, and to haul herself out of the tumult that had invaded her: *It's over. You're safe. I'm here.*

She stretched her hand out to where he should have been lying. But he had gone back to America. She had accompanied him to the airport, dry-eyed and apparently composed even when he gathered her to him with anguish on his face to say goodbye; had watched him go through into Departures until his tall figure was no longer visible; had never told him how close she had come to asking him to stay, or agreeing to go with him. The intimacy of their last few weeks, when she had let herself be cared for and felt her own weakness, had stirred up feelings in her that she had never before experienced. It would be too easy to let them sink back into the depths. It wasn't the pain of missing that she dreaded but the gradual easing of that pain, busy life filling up the spaces he had left. Sometimes she would sit in her garret-study and sketch his face with a soft-leaded pencil, making herself remember the exact shape of his mouth; the little grooves that time had worn into his skin; the expression in his eyes. Then she would lay down the pencil and let the memory of him wash through her, a slow, deep river inside her.

For a moment, she let herself imagine him beside her – how it would feel to turn her head and see him there. But he was gone, and she was alone in a house that had once felt like a cosy refuge yet, for the last few weeks – since the attack that had nearly killed her – had creaked and whispered. She listened: the pulse of her heart and then, yes, there was a rustle by her door, a faint sound. But it was only the cat, prowling the room. Sometimes, in this pre-dawn limbo, Frieda found it a sinister creature – its two previous owners were dead.

Had something woken her? She had a muffled sense of a sound entering her sleep. Not the distant rumble of traffic that in London never ceases. Something else. Inside the house.

Frieda sat up and listened but heard nothing except the

soft wind outside. She swung her feet to the floor, feeling the cat wind its body round her legs, purring, then stood, still weak and nauseous from the night terrors. There had been something, she was certain, something downstairs. She pulled on tracksuit bottoms and a T-shirt and made her way on to the landing, then, step by step, gripping the banisters, down the stairs, stopping halfway. The house she knew so well had become unfamiliar, full of shadows and secrets. In the hall, she stood and strained to hear but there was nothing, nobody. She turned on the lights, blinking in the sudden dazzle, and then she saw it: a large brown envelope lying on the doormat. She stooped and picked it up. It had her name written in bold letters across it: Frieda Klein. A line slashed underneath diagonally, cutting into the final *n*.

She stared at the handwriting. She recognized it, and now she knew that he was near – in the street outside, close to her home, to her place of refuge.

In a fever, she pulled on a trenchcoat and pushed her bare feet into the boots by the front door. She took the door key from the hook and then was out into the darkness, cool April breeze in her face, the hint of rain. Frieda stared around the unlit little cobbled mews, but there was no one there and as fast as her sore body would go, she half hobbled and half ran out on the street, where the lamps threw long shadows. She looked up and down it. Which way would he have gone: east or west, north or south, towards the river or up into the maze of streets? Or was he standing in a doorway? She turned left and hurried along the damp pavement, swearing under her breath, cursing her inability to move quickly.

Coming out onto a wider road, Frieda saw something in the distance – a bulky shape moving towards her, surely human but larger and stranger than any human could possibly be. It was like a figure from her nightmares and she pressed her hand against her heart and waited as it came closer and closer, and then at last resolved into a man slowly pedalling a bike, with dozens, hundreds, of plastic bags tied to its frame. She knew him, saw him most days. He had a wild beard and glaring eyes and cycled with slow determination. He wavered past, staring blindly through her, like Father Christmas in a bad dream.

It was no use. Dean Reeve, her stalker and her quarry, could be anywhere by now. Sixteen months ago, she had helped unmask him as a child-abductor and murderer, but he had escaped capture and killed himself. Two months ago, she had discovered that he had never died: the man who had hung from a bridge on the canal was in fact his twin, Alan, who had once been Frieda's patient. Dean was still in the world somewhere, watching over her, protective and deadly. It was he who had saved her life when she had been attacked by a disturbed young woman with a knife, though Mary Orton, the old woman Frieda had come to rescue, had died. He had slid out of the shadows, like a creature from her own worst dreams, and hauled her back from the darkness. Now he was telling her that he was still watching over her, a loathed protector. She could feel his eyes on her, from hidden corners, in the twitch of a curtain or the chink in a door. Was this how it would always be?

She made her way back to her house, unlocked the door, and stepped inside. She picked up the envelope once more and went with it into the kitchen. She knew she wouldn't get back to sleep so she made herself tea, and only when it was brewed did she sit at the kitchen table and run her finger under the gummed flap. She drew out the stiff paper inside, and laid it on the table. It was a pencil drawing or, rather, a pattern. It looked a bit like the mathematical rendering of an intricate rose, eight-sided and perfectly symmetrical. The straight lines had obviously been done with a ruler and, examining it more closely, Frieda could see marks where mistakes had been rubbed out.

She sat for some time, staring down at the image that lay in front of her, her expression stern, then she carefully slid the paper back inside the envelope. Rage crackled through her, like fire, and she welcomed it. Better to be burned by anger than drowned by fear. So she sat in its flames, unmoving, until morning came.

Many miles away, Jim Fearby poured himself a glass of whisky. The bottle was less than a third full. Time to buy another. It was like petrol. Never let the tank get less than a quarter full. You might run out. He took the old newspaper clipping from his wallet and flattened it on the desk. It was yellowing and almost disintegrating after all the foldings and unfoldings. He knew it by heart. It was like a talisman. He could see it when he closed his eyes.

MONSTER 'MAY NEVER BE RELEASED'
James Fearby

There were dramatic scenes at Hattonbrook Crown Court yesterday as convicted murderer George Conley was sentenced to life imprisonment for killing Hazel Barton. Justice Lawson told Conley,

31: 'This was an atrocious crime. Despite pleading guilty, you have shown no remorse and it is my belief that you remain a danger to women and may never be safe to be released.'

As Justice Lawson ordered Conley to be taken down, there were shouts from the victim's family in the public gallery. Outside the court, Clive Barton, Hazel's uncle, told reporters: 'Hazel was our beautiful young treasure. She had her whole life in front of her and he took that away from her. I hope he rots in hell.'

Hazel Barton, a blonde eighteen-year-old schoolgirl, was found strangled in May of this year near her home in the village of Dorlbrook. Her body was found by the roadside. George Conley was arrested near the scene. He had left traces on her body and he confessed within days.

Speaking afterwards, Detective Inspector Geoffrey Whitlam offered his condolences to the Barton family: 'We can only guess the living hell they have gone through. I hope that the speedy resolution of this thorough investigation can bring them a measure of closure.' He also paid tribute to his colleagues: 'It is my belief that George Conley is a dangerous sexual predator. He belongs behind bars and I want to thank my team for putting him there.'

It is alleged that Hazel Barton was walking alone because her bus had failed to arrive. A spokeswoman for FastCoach, the local bus operator, commented: 'We offer all condolences to Hazel Barton's family. We are fully committed to maintaining an effective service for our customers.'

Under the headline were two photographs. The first was the mug shot of Conley, released by the police. His large face was blotchy; there was a bruise on his forehead; one eye was askew. The other was a family photo of Hazel

Barton. It must have been taken on holiday because she was wearing a T-shirt and the sea was visible behind her. She was laughing as if the photographer had just made a joke.

Fearby carefully read through his seven-year-old report, running his forefinger along the lines. He sipped his whisky. Almost every word in the report was untrue. FastCoach did not provide an effective service for their customers. And, anyway, they were passengers, not customers. Whitlam's investigation had not been thorough. Even his own byline looked wrong. Only his mother had ever called him James. And the headline – which he hadn't written, and wouldn't have written, even at the time – was the most wrong of all. Poor old Georgie Conley was many things but he wasn't a monster, and now it looked like he was going to be released.

Fearby carefully folded the clipping and replaced it in his wallet, behind his press card. A precious relic.

FOUR

When Sasha arrived at a quarter to nine on Thursday morning, Frieda had just finished watering the plants on her small patio. She was wearing jeans and an oatmeal-coloured pullover, and there were rings under her eyes, which looked darker and fiercer than usual.

'Bad night?' asked Sasha.

'No.'

'I'm not sure I believe you.'

'Would you like a cup of coffee?'

'Do we have time? My car's on a meter for another quarter of an hour, but we need to get to the hospital for half past nine. The traffic's dreadful.'

Sasha had insisted on taking the day off work to bring Frieda to her follow-up appointment with the consultant and then with the physiotherapist.

'We're not going to the hospital.'

'Why? Have they cancelled?'

'No. I have.'

'What made you do that?'

'There's something else I need to do.'

'You have to go to see your doctor, Frieda. And the physio. You've been very ill. You nearly died. You can't just walk away from all the follow-up care.'

'I know what the doctor will say: that I'm making progress but that I mustn't think about going back to work yet, because for the time being, making a good recovery is my work. You know the sort of things we doctors tell our patients.'

'That sounds a bit negative.'

'Anyway, there's something more important I have to do.'

'What could be more important than getting better?'

'I thought I'd show you rather than tell you. Unless you want to go to work after all.'

Sasha sighed. 'I've taken the day off. I'd like to spend it with you. Let's have that coffee.'

The road narrowed into a lane lined with trees that were freshly in bud. Frieda noticed the blackthorn. She stared fixedly: some things change and some things remain the same. But you never remain the same – you look at everything through different eyes so that even the most familiar object takes on a strange and ghostly cast. That small thatched cottage with a muddy pond full of ducks in front of it, that sudden stretch of road winding down over a patchwork of fields, or the farmhouse with its silos and its muddy enclosure of cows, and the line of spindly poplars ahead. Even the way the light fell on this flattened landscape, and the faint tang of the sea.

The graveyard was crowded. Most of the stones were old, green with moss, and it was no longer possible to make out the inscriptions carved there; but some were new and shiny and had flowers on them, dates of the dearly beloved and the sorely missed.

'Crowds of the dead,' said Frieda, more to herself than to Sasha.

'Why are we here?'

'I'll show you.'

She stopped in front of a carved stone and pointed. Sasha, leaning forward, made out the name: Jacob Klein 1943–1988, much missed husband and father.

'Is this your father?' she asked, thinking about Frieda as a teenager, finding him dead, trying to imagine the history of pain that lay behind the simple stone.

Frieda nodded, not taking her eyes off it. 'Yes. That's my father.' She took a small step backwards and said: 'Look at the engraving there, above his name.'

'It's very nice,' said Sasha, lamely, after examining the symmetrical pattern. 'Did you choose it?'

'No.' She reached into her bag and pulled out a piece of thick paper, holding it in front of her, gazing from drawing to engraving and back again. 'What do you see?'

'It's the same,' said Sasha.

'It is, isn't it? Exactly the same.'

'Did you do it?'

'No.'

'Then?'

'Someone sent it to me. This morning.'

'I don't understand.'

'They pushed it through my door in the early hours.'

'Why?'

'That's the question.' Frieda was talking to herself now, rather than Sasha.

'Are you going to tell me what's going on?'

'Dean did it.'

'Dean? Dean Reeve?'

Sasha knew about Dean Reeve, the man who had

abducted a little boy and dragged Frieda unwillingly into the outside world, away from the safety of her consulting room and the strange secrets of the mind. She had even helped Frieda by doing a DNA test that established Dean's wife Terry was in fact the little girl Joanna, who had disappeared into thin air more than two decades previously. Frieda had become convinced that Dean Reeve, whom the police accepted as dead, was still alive. He had become Frieda's invisible stalker. The dead man who watched over her and would never let her go.

'Yes, Dean Reeve. I recognize his handwriting – I saw it once on a statement he made at the police station. But even if I didn't, I'd know it was him. He wants me to understand that he has found out about my family. He knows about the death of my father. He was here, where we are now, where my father is.'

'Your father is buried in a churchyard, but I thought you were Jewish,' Sasha said.

They were in a small café overlooking the sea. The tide was low and long-legged seabirds picked their delicate way over the shining mudflats. Far out, a container ship, as big as a town, was moving across the horizon. There was no one else in the café and no one out on the shingle. Sasha felt as though she'd been taken to the edge of the world.

'Did you?'

'Yes. Aren't you?'

'No.' Frieda hesitated, then, making an obvious effort, said: 'My grandfather was Jewish, but not my grandmother, so his children were no longer Jewish and neither, of course, am I. My mother,' she added drily, 'is most definitely not Jewish.'

'Is she still alive?'

'Unless my brothers forgot to tell me, yes.'

Sasha blinked and leaned forward.

'Brothers?'

'Yes.'

'You've got more than one?'

'I've got two.'

'You've only ever mentioned David. I never knew there was another.'

'It wasn't relevant,' Frieda said.

'Relevant? A brother?'

'You know about David because he's Olivia's ex and Chloë's father.'

'I see,' murmured Sasha, knowing better than to press her and thinking that in the last few hours she had learned more about Frieda than in the whole course of their friendship.

She pierced her poached egg and watched the yolk well up, then ooze on to the plate. 'What are you going to do?' she asked.

'I haven't decided. Anyway, haven't you heard? He's dead.'

Frieda hardly spoke on the way back. When Sasha asked her what she was thinking about, she couldn't answer. 'I don't know,' Frieda said. 'Nothing really.'

'You wouldn't take that as an answer from one of your patients.'

'I've never been a very good patient.'

*

After Sasha had driven away, Frieda let herself into her house. Inside, she fastened the chain and slid the bolt across the front door. She walked upstairs to her bedroom. She took off her jacket and tossed it on to the bed. She would have a long, hot bath and then she would go up to her little study in the garret room and do a drawing: concentrate, yet think of nothing. She thought of the graveyard, the desolate coastline. She pulled her sweater over her head. She started to undo the buttons of her shirt but then she stopped. She had heard something. She wasn't sure whether the noise was inside or a much louder noise outside and far away. She stayed completely still. She didn't even breathe. She heard the noise again, a small scraping sound. It was inside the house and close by, on the same floor. She could feel its vibration. She thought of the front door downstairs, with its bolt and chain. She tried to time it in her head, the scrambling downstairs, the fumbling with the chain. No, she couldn't make it work. She thought of the mobile phone in her pocket. Even if she could whisper a message into it, what good would that do? It would take ten minutes, fifteen minutes, to get here, and then there was the locked, bolted door.

Frieda felt her pulse race. She made herself breathe slowly, one breath after another. She counted slowly to ten. She looked around the room for a hiding place but it was no good. She had made too much noise as she came in. She picked up a hairbrush from her dressing table. It was hopelessly flimsy. She felt in the pocket of her jacket and found a pen. She held it tightly in her fist. At least it was sharp. It seemed like the worst thing in the world, but she edged out of her bedroom on to the landing. It would take just a few seconds. If she could get down the stairs without them creaking, then . . .

There was another scraping sound, louder now, and something else, a sort of whistle. It came from across the landing, in the bathroom. The whistling continued. Frieda listened for a few seconds, then stepped closer and pushed at the door of the bathroom so that it swung open. At first she had a sudden sensation of being in the wrong room or the wrong house. Nothing was where it was supposed to be. There was exposed plaster and pipes and a huge space. The room seemed larger than she'd remembered. And in the corner a figure was bent over, pulling at something to get it loose.

'Josef,' she said weakly. 'What's going on?'

Josef was her friend – a builder from the Ukraine who had entered her life in an unlikely way, falling through her ceiling when she was with a patient. But he had not taken no for an answer, and had a fanatical devotion to her. Now he started, then smiled a bit warily. 'Frieda,' he said. 'I did not hear.'

'What are you doing here? How did you get in?'

'I have the key you give me.'

'But that key was for feeding the cat when I was away, not for this.' She gestured. 'And what is this?'

Josef stood up. He was holding a huge wrench.

'Frieda. You have been not well. I look at you and see you being sad and in pain and it is difficult.' Frieda started to speak but Josef interrupted her. 'No, no, wait. It is difficult to help but I know about you. I know that when you are sad you lie in your very hot bath for hours.'

'Well, not for *hours*,' said Frieda. 'But where is my bath? I was just about to get into it.'

'Your bath is gone away,' said Josef. 'While you were with your friend, Sasha, me and my friend, Stefan, we take your bath away and we take it to the dump. It was a bad plastic bath, and it was small, not good for lying in.'

'It was very good for lying in,' said Frieda.

'No,' said Josef, firmly. 'It is gone. I have great luck. I work on a house in Islington. He spends much, much money. He cut everything out of the house and throw it in four skips and then put new things in. He is throwing out many beautiful things but the most beautiful thing is a big iron bath. I see the bath and I think of you. It is perfect.'

Frieda looked more carefully at the bathroom. Where the bath had once stood, the wall and floor were now exposed. There were cracked tiles, bare floorboards, a gaping pipe. Josef himself was covered in dust, his dark hair speckled with it. 'Josef, you should have asked me.'

Josef spread his arms helplessly. 'If I had asked you, you would have said no.'

'Which is why you should have asked me.'

Josef made a gesture, palm upwards. 'Frieda, you protect all other people and sometimes you get hurt from that. What you must do is let other people help you.' He looked at Frieda more closely. 'Why are you holding your pen like that?'

Frieda glanced down. She was still holding the pen in her fist, like a dagger. 'I thought there was a burglar,' she said. Once more she made herself take a deep breath. It had been well meant, she told herself. 'So, how long will it take to put my old bath back just the way it was?'

Josef looked thoughtful. 'That is problem,' he said. 'When we took the bath from the wall and the pipe and the brackets, there were big cracks from that. That bath was just all crap. And, anyway, it is now at the dump.'

'This is probably some sort of crime, what you've done, but anyway, what happens now?'

'The beautiful bath is now in the workshop of another friend called Klaus. That is no problem. But here . . .' He gestured with his wrench at the damage and gave a sigh. 'That is problem.'

'What do you mean a problem?' said Frieda. '*You* did it.'

'No, no,' said Josef. 'This is . . .' He said something in his own language. It sounded contemptuous. 'The pipe connecting here is very bad. Very bad.'

'It always worked fine.'

'It was just being lucky. One movement of the bath and . . .' He made an eloquent gesture signifying a chaotic and destructive flood. 'I will put a proper pipe here and make the wall good and tiles on the floor. It will be my gift to you and you will have a bath that will be your place to be happy.'

'When?' said Frieda.

'I will do what must be done,' said Josef.

'Yes, but when will you do it?'

'It will be a few days. Only a very few.'

'I was going to have a bath now. All the way home I had an idea in my head of having it and what it was going to be like and how much I needed it.'

'It will be worth the waiting for.'

My very dearest Frieda, I'm sitting in my office, thinking of you. Whatever I do, whoever I meet, I think of you. I can give a lecture, and all the time I'm talking, the words coming quite fluently from me, part of my mind is occupied with you. I can hold a conversation, cut up an onion, walk across Brooklyn Bridge, and you're there. It's like an ache that won't go away, and that I do not want to go away. I was going to say I haven't felt like this since I was a teenager, but I never felt like this as a teenager! I ask myself why I'm here, when my life's work is to make you happy. I can hear you say that happiness isn't the point, that you don't know the meaning of the word – but I know the meaning of the word: happiness for me is being loved by Frieda Klein.

You sounded a bit distracted on the phone this evening. Please tell me why. Tell me everything. Remember our river walk. Remember me. Sandy xxxxxxx

FIVE

Commissioner Crawford frowned. 'Make this quick,' he said. 'I've got a meeting.'

'Is it a problem?' said Karlsson. 'I rang ahead before I came over.'

'We're all doing more with less at the moment.'

'Which is why I wanted to talk to you about Bradshaw.'

The commissioner's frown darkened still further. He got up, walked to the window and looked out over St James's Park. He turned to Karlsson. 'What do you think of the view?'

'Very striking,' said Karlsson.

'It's one of the rewards of the job,' said the commissioner. He brushed a few specks of dust off the sleeve of his uniform. 'You should come here more often. It might clarify your mind.'

'About what?'

'About running a tight ship,' said the commissioner. 'About being a team player.'

'I thought it was about solving crimes.'

The commissioner took a step away from the window towards Karlsson, who was still standing beside the large wooden desk. 'Don't come that with me,' he said. 'A police force is about political influence, and it always has been. If I can't get up the home secretary's arse and get you the funding that you're pissing away, you won't be in a position to solve your crimes, any of you. I know things are tough, Mal, but these are tough times and we all have to make sacrifices.'

'In that case, I'm willing to sacrifice Dr Hal Bradshaw.'

The commissioner looked at him sharply. 'You mentioned him on the phone. Has he done something wrong?'

'I met him at the Chalk Farm murder scene. He just turned up.'

'That's the arrangement,' said the commissioner. 'I know the way he works. The quicker he can get on the scene, the more use he can be to us.'

'I think he's a distraction,' said Karlsson.

'Does this have anything to do with that Dr Klein?'

'Why should it?'

'Dr Klein and Dr Bradshaw were treading on each other's toes. One of them had to go. We went through a full consultation process. The fact is that your Dr Klein is not trained in the forensic field.'

Karlsson paused for a few seconds. 'In my opinion,' he said, 'Dr Bradshaw does not represent good value for money.'

'Wait,' said the commissioner. He strode across to his desk and pressed a button. He leaned down. 'Send him in.'

'What is this?' said Karlsson.

'I don't believe in being underhand,' said the commissioner. 'Things like this should be dealt with face to face.'

Karlsson turned as a young uniformed officer opened the door and Hal Bradshaw walked in. Karlsson felt his cheeks flush with anger and hoped it didn't show. When he saw the hint of a smile on Bradshaw's face, he had to look away.

'Mal,' said the commissioner. 'I don't believe in going behind people's backs. Tell Dr Bradshaw what you've just told me.'

The three men were now standing in an awkward triangle in the middle of the commissioner's office. Karlsson had the feeling that he'd walked into a trap.

'I didn't realize that talking to my boss was going behind people's backs,' he said, 'but I'm happy to be clear about things.' He turned to Bradshaw. 'I don't believe that your presence is helpful to the inquiry.'

'Based on what?'

'Based on the fact that I'm running it.'

'That's not enough,' said the commissioner. 'Dr Bradshaw's got a track record. He appears on the *Today* programme.'

'I don't think he represents a proper use of public money.'

Bradshaw turned to the commissioner and gave a sigh. 'I think this is a problem that you need to sort out between yourselves,' he said.

'No,' said the commissioner. 'I want it sorted out here and now.'

'I think my track record speaks for itself,' said Bradshaw. 'The real problem seems to be Mr Karlsson's belief that a psychotherapist he happened to run into could be effective doing profiling work as sort of hobby.'

'Shall we stick to your track record?' said Karlsson.

'Absolutely,' said Bradshaw. 'I'm here because Commissioner Crawford knew my work and appointed me personally. If you have any objection to that, then now is the time to say it.'

'All right,' said Karlsson. 'I experienced your profiling skills on the Michelle Doyce case. Your analysis of the crime scene was misleading. Your identification of the murderer was completely mistaken and would have derailed the entire course of the investigation, if it hadn't been for Frieda Klein.'

'It's not an exact science,' said Bradshaw.

'Not the way you do it,' said Karlsson. 'Frieda Klein didn't just get it right, she almost got killed doing it. And that was after being effectively fired from the investigation.'

Bradshaw give a sniff. 'From what I heard, Klein's mishap came from the failings of your own officers. I may have my failings, but I've never stabbed a mental patient to death.' He stepped back quickly when he saw that Karlsson had raised his right hand.

'Steady, Mal,' said the commissioner.

'Frieda was fighting for her life,' said Karlsson. 'And she showed you up for the idiot you are.' He turned to Crawford. 'He talks about his track record. Just check it out. From what I've seen, Bradshaw is terrific at profiling criminals after they've been caught. Frieda Klein was more useful when we were still searching for them.'

Crawford looked at the two of them.

'I'm sorry, Mal, but I want Dr Bradshaw to stay on the case. Just find a way to work together. That's all.'

Karlsson and Bradshaw walked out of the commissioner's office together. Without speaking they reached the lift, waited for it, got in and rode to the ground floor. As they stepped out, Bradshaw spoke. 'Was it Frieda who put you up to this?' he said.

'What are you talking about?'

'If she's going to damage me,' he said, 'she'll need to be better at it than that.'

They could all see that Karlsson was in a thoroughly bad mood. It didn't help that the principal operations room in the police station was being painted. The desks were covered with sheets. Karlsson glanced into the various conference rooms but they were already being used by other officers or had been filled with displaced furniture and computers. In the end he led Yvette, Munster and Riley down some stairs and into the canteen. Riley dumped a pile of files on a table, then they all queued for coffees and teas. Munster and Riley bought a bun each, covered with white icing. Karlsson looked disapproving.

'While we're here,' said Munster.

'I missed breakfast,' added Riley.

'As long as you don't get the files sticky,' said Karlsson.

'We'd better get used to this,' said Yvette, as they settled at their table in a corner of the canteen by a window. 'When the cuts take effect, those of us who're left will be fighting for office space.'

'Hot desking,' said Riley.

'What?' Karlsson frowned.

'It's the modern kind of office. Nobody has their own desk. The idea is that you only occupy space when you need it.'

'What about your stuff?' said Munster. 'Your paper clips and coffee mug.'

'You keep them all in a locker. It's a bit like school.'

'Not like my school,' said Munster. 'If you left anything in your locker there, it got broken into and nicked.'

'If you're quite ready,' Karlsson interrupted.

'Hang on,' said Munster. 'Is Bradshaw coming?'

'He's busy today,' said Karlsson.

'Probably appearing on TV,' said Yvette, and Karlsson gave her a look.

'You go first,' he said.

'The situation is pretty much what you saw at the scene. We've had officers taking statements up and down the road. Plus we sent a couple of them to spend time there for the next two or three afternoons, just in case there were people who walked there at that time of day. There's nothing that leaps out.'

'Fingerprints?' said Karlsson.

'They've got dozens of them,' said Yvette. 'But this was a family house, people in and out all the time. They've started to eliminate family prints, but it's hopeless until we can narrow it down.'

'Weapon?' said Karlsson.

'We haven't found one.'

'Have you searched?'

'Within reason.'

'There was a bin collection the next morning,' said Munster. 'A few officers had made a preliminary search the previous afternoon. But we didn't have the men.'

'I don't even know why I'm bothering,' said Karlsson. 'But I'll say it anyway: CCTV?'

'Nothing in the road itself,' said Yvette. 'It's residential. It doesn't have them. We've got the footage from a couple of cameras on Chalk Farm Road. But we haven't been through it yet.'

'Why not?'

'We've got a window of three or four hours and crowds of people wandering down to Camden Lock and we don't know what we're looking for.'

There was a pause. Karlsson noticed a smile on Riley's face. 'Is something funny?' he asked.

'Not really,' Riley said. 'It's different from what I expected.'

'Is this your first?'

'You mean murder? I dealt with a death near the Elephant and Castle. But they caught the guy at the scene.'

'Where's the fun in that?' said Karlsson. He turned back to Yvette. 'The woman, Ruth Lennox. Why was she at home?'

'It was her afternoon off. Her husband said it's a day she normally goes shopping or does things around the house.'

'Meets friends?'

'Sometimes.'

'That day?'

Yvette shook her head. 'He showed us her diary. There was nothing in it for that day.'

'How are the family?' asked Karlsson.

'In shock. When I interviewed them they seemed stunned. They're staying with friends a few doors up from their house.'

'What about the husband?'

'He's not the demonstrative type,' said Yvette, 'but he seems devastated.'

'Have you asked him where he was at the time of his wife's murder?'

'He told us he had a four o'clock meeting with a Ms Lorraine Crawley, an accountant for the company where he works. I rang her and she confirmed it. It lasted about half an hour, forty minutes. Which makes it very unlikely that he could have got back to his house in time to kill his wife and leave before the daughter came home from school.'

'Unlikely?' said Karlsson. 'That's not good enough. I'll talk to him again myself.'

'You suspect him?' said Riley.

'If a woman is killed and there's a husband or a boyfriend around, then that's something to be be taken into consideration.'

'But look,' said Munster. 'As you saw yourself, the little girl found broken glass next to the front door and the door open.'

'Was the door usually double-locked?' said Karlsson.

'Not when they were at home,' said Yvette. 'According to the husband.'

'And?'

'Also according to the husband, when he'd calmed down and looked around, a set of silver cutlery had been stolen from a drawer in the kitchen dresser. Also a Georgian silver teapot that was on a shelf in the dresser. Plus the money from her wallet, of course.'

'Anything else taken?'

'Not that we know of,' said Yvette. 'She had jewellery upstairs, but it wasn't touched.'

'And –' Riley began, then stopped.

44

'What?' said Karlsson.

'Nothing.'

Karlsson forced himself to adopt a gentler tone. 'Go on,' he said. 'If you've got an idea, just say it. I want to hear everything.'

'I was going to say that when I saw the body, she had nice earrings on and a necklace.'

'That's right,' said Karlsson. 'Good.' He looked back at Yvette. 'So? What are we thinking?'

'I'm not saying you shouldn't talk to the husband,' said Yvette, 'but the state of the scene seems consistent with a burglary that was interrupted. The burglar goes to the kitchen, takes the silver. Then he encounters Mrs Lennox in the living room. There's a scuffle. She receives a fatal blow. He flees in panic.'

'Or,' said Karlsson, 'someone who knows Mrs Lennox kills her and stages the burglary.'

'That's possible,' said Yvette, woodenly.

'But not very likely. You're right. So there we are: an apparent burglary, a dead woman, no witnesses, no finger-prints as yet, no forensics.'

'What about your old detective?' said Munster.

'I think we need him,' said Karlsson.

Standing on the pavement outside the Lennoxes' house, Harry Curzon looked like a golfer who'd taken a wrong turning. He was dressed in a red windcheater over a checked sweater, light grey chinos and brown suede shoes. He was overweight and wore thick, heavy-framed spectacles.

'So, how's retirement?' said Karlsson.

'I don't know what kept me,' said Curzon. 'How far away are you? Seven, eight years?'

'A bit more than that.'

'You need to see the writing on the wall. It's all productivity and pen-pushing now. Look at me. Fifty-six years old and a full pension. When you called me I was heading up to the River Lea for a day's fishing.'

'Sounds good.'

'It is good. So, before I head off and you go back to your office, what can I do for you?'

'There's been a murder,' said Karlsson. 'But there's also been a burglary. You worked here.'

'Eighteen years,' said Curzon.

'I thought you could give me some advice.'

As Karlsson showed Curzon around the house, the older man talked and talked and talked. Karlsson wondered whether he was really enjoying his days of fishing and golf as much as he'd said he was.

'It's gone out of fashion,' said Curzon.

'What?'

'Burglary.'

'Back in the seventies it was TV sets and cameras and watches and clocks. In the eighties in was video players and stereos, and in the nineties it was DVD players and computers. It took them a few years but then the burglars suddenly woke up. A DVD player costs about the same as a DVD, and people are walking around in the streets with a phone and an iPod and probably a laptop that's worth more than anything they've got at home. What's the point of breaking in and getting a couple of extra years inside when you can mug them in the street and get something you can sell?'

'What indeed?' said Karlsson.

'Try going to a dodgy second-hand dealer and offering them a DVD player and they'll laugh in your face. Garden equipment, though, that's saleable. There's always a market for a hedge-trimmer.'

'Not really relevant in this case,' said Karlsson. 'So, you don't think this was a burglary?'

'Looks like a burglary to me,' said Curzon.

'But couldn't it have been staged?'

'You could say that about anything. But if you were doing that, I reckon you'd break a window at the back. You're less likely to be spotted by a nosy neighbour. And you'd take some stuff from the room where the body was.'

'That's basically what we've been thinking,' said Karlsson. 'So we're looking for a burglar and you know about burglars.'

Curzon grimaced. 'I'll give you some names. But these burglaries are mainly about drugs, and the junkies come and go. It's not like the old days.'

'When you had your trusty local burglar?' Karlsson smiled.

'Don't knock it. We all knew our place.'

'What I hoped,' said Karlsson, 'is that you'd be able to look at this crime scene and identify the burglar by his style. Doesn't every burglar have his own trademark?'

Curzon pulled another face. 'There's no trademark to this. He broke the window, opened the door and let himself in. You can't get more basic than that. The only trademark in this scene was the trademark of a basic idiot. They're the worst kind, except when you catch them in the act.' He paused. 'But I've had a thought. There's a couple of local shops, trinkets, cheap stuff mostly but not always. There's Tandy's up on the corner of Rubens Road and there's Burgess and Son over on the Crescent. Let's say that if someone goes in there and offers them some silverware, they don't ask too many questions. Get someone to look in the window over the next few days. They might see something. You could take it from there.'

Karlsson was doubtful. 'If you've killed someone, you're not exactly going to take your swag to the local jeweller, are you?'

Curzon shrugged. 'These clowns are addicts, not bank managers. Burgess and Son is a bit further away. That might be his idea of being clever. It's worth a try, anyway.'

'Thanks,' said Karlsson.

On the way out of the house Curzon put his hand on Karlsson's sleeve. 'Can I get you out on the course? Show you what you're missing out on?'

'I'm not really a golfer. In fact, not a golfer at all.'

'Or come and get a little fishing in. You wouldn't believe how peaceful it is.'

'Yes.' Karlsson nodded. He didn't like fishing either. 'Yes, that would be good. Maybe when the case is over. We can celebrate.'

'I almost feel guilty,' said Curzon. 'Showing you what you're missing.'

'Go there with Russell Lennox, if he feels up to it,' said Karlsson to Yvette. 'See if he recognizes anything.'

'All right.'

'Take young Riley with you.'

'Fine.' Yvette hesitated, then, as Karlsson turned to go, blurted out, 'Can I ask you something?'

'Sure.'

'Do you blame me?'

'Blame you? For what?' He knew what, of course – ever since Frieda had been found lying on the floor of Mary Orton's house, in that scene of carnage, Yvette had wanted his forgiveness, his reassurance that it wasn't really her fault.

'For not taking her concerns seriously. All that.' Yvette gulped. Her face had turned very red.

'This isn't really the right time, Yvette.'

'But . . .'

'It isn't appropriate,' he said. His gentleness was worse than anger. She felt like a small child facing a kind, stern adult.

'No. Sorry. Tandy's and Burgess and Son.'

'That's right.'

Frieda took the phone out of its holster and considered it. Her eyes itched with tiredness, and her body felt hollow yet enormously heavy. The grave in Suffolk seemed like a dream now – a neglected patch of soil where the bones of a sad man lay. She thought of him, the father she had not been able to rescue. If she let herself go back, she could remember the way his hand had felt, holding hers, or breathe in his smell of tobacco and the cloves from his aftershave. His hopelessness. His heavy posture. And Dean Reeve had sat over him, with that smile.

The cat clattered through the cat flap and she looked down at it, the two of them staring at each other. Then, still holding the phone, she walked slowly up the stairs – stairs were still hard for her – and sat on her bed, gazing out of the window at the soft grey evening that was settling over the city, making it mysterious again. At last she lifted the phone and keyed in the numbers.

'Hello,' she said.

'Frieda!' There was no mistaking the warmth of his voice.

'Hello.'

'I've been thinking of you.'

'Where are you now?'

'In my office. Five hours behind you.'

'What are you wearing?'

'A grey suit. A white shirt. You?'

Frieda looked down at her clothes. 'Jeans and a creamy-brown jumper.'

'Where are you?'

'Sitting on my bed.'

'I wish I was sitting on your bed too.'

'Did you sleep well?'

'Yes. I dreamed I was ice-skating. Did you?'

'Dream I was ice-skating?'

'Sleep well.'

'All right.'

'So you didn't.'

'Sandy?' She wanted to tell him about her day but the words wouldn't come. He was too far away.

'Yes, my very darling Frieda.'

'I hate this.'

'This?'

'All of it.'

'Feeling weak, you mean?'

'That too.'

'Me being here?' There was a pause. 'What's that noise? Is there a thunderstorm going on?'

'What?' Frieda looked around and then realized. She'd almost stopped hearing the sound herself. 'There's a new bath being put in.'

'A new bath?'

'It wasn't exactly my idea. In fact, it wasn't my idea at all. It's a present from Josef.'

'That sounds good.'

'The bath hasn't arrived yet. So far there's just lots of banging and drilling going on. There's dust everywhere. Including on several shirts – you left them here.'

'I know.'

'And some kitchen stuff, and a few books by the bed.'

'That's because I'm coming back.'

'Right.'

'Frieda, I'm coming back.'

SIX

'Is that Detective Chief Inspector Karlsson?'

'Speaking.'

'Constable Fogle from Camden. I've a Mr Russell Lennox with me.'

'Russell Lennox?' Karlsson blinked. 'Why on earth?'

'He's been involved in an affray.'

'I don't understand. Why would he be involved in an affray? The poor man's wife's just been murdered.'

'He seems to have caused some criminal damage. At a Burgess and Son.'

'Ah.'

He broke a window, not to mention several pieces of china that the owner seems to think might be worth a good deal, and was also somewhat threatening.'

'I'm on my way. Treat him gently, will you?'

Russell Lennox was in a small interview room, sitting with his hands plaited together on the table and staring ahead, blinking every so often as if to clear his vision. When Karlsson came in with the uniformed officer who had called him, Lennox turned his head. For a few moments it seemed that he didn't recognize the detective.

'I've come to take you home,' said Karlsson, lowering himself into the chair opposite. 'You know that you could be prosecuted for affray, assault, whatever?'

'I don't care.'

'Would that help your children?'

Lennox just stared at the table surface and didn't reply.

'So you went back to Burgess and Son?'

Lennox gave a faint nod. 'I couldn't get it out of my head. Anyway, what else am I supposed to do with my time? Ruth's sister Louise is with the children and they don't want to see me upset on top of everything else. So, I walked over there, just to check. I saw this fork.'

'One fork?' said Karlsson, doubtfully.

'Ruth's godmother gave them to us when we got married. I didn't care about them or notice them, really, but this one had a bent spike. That's how I recognized it. Judith used to get angry if she was given it at meals. She said it stabbed her gums. I went inside and asked to see it. Then things got out of hand.' He looked up at Karlsson. 'I'm not a violent man.'

'I think there might be some argument about that,' said Karlsson.

Jeremy Burgess, the owner of Burgess and Son, was small, skinny, with the wariness of someone who had spent years never quite getting anything pinned on him. Karlsson was leaning over a glass counter crammed with medals, old necklaces, cigarette cases, dented snuff boxes, thimbles and small silver boxes, glittery clip-on earrings and oversized cuff links. He took the fork with its crooked tine and laid it on the glass.

'Where did this come from?' he asked.

Burgess gestured helplessly. 'I just pay in cash for little things like that.'

'I need to know, Mr Burgess.'

'I'm the one who was attacked. What's happening about that? I'm just trying to run a business.'

'Shut up,' said Karlsson. 'I know about your business. If the local police aren't bothered, that's their affair. But this is evidence in a murder inquiry, and if you don't co-operate, then I will make your life very difficult indeed.'

Burgess glanced uneasily at two women on the other side of the shop who were poring over a tray of rings. He leaned forward and spoke in a lower tone. 'I'm just a businessman,' he said.

'Give me a name and I'll go away. Otherwise I'll send some officers round here to go through this piece by piece.'

'Billy.'

'Billy who?'

'Billy. Young, dark-haired, thin. That's all I know.'

Curzon's voice kept coming and going. He explained that the reception was bad out there on the river. 'Hunt,' he said. 'Billy Hunt.'

'You know him?'

'We all know Billy.'

'Does he have a record?'

'Robbery, possession, this and that.'

'Violence?'

'He's a bit of wimp, our Billy,' said Curzon, 'but he may have gone downhill. I mean even further downhill.'

Karlsson put Riley on to it. Curzon didn't have an address or a number for Billy Hunt but there were a couple of officers who'd been dealing with the local drug scene. They'd probably know, said Curzon. They hadn't seen Hunt for some time but one of them remembered he'd once worked on a stall in Camden Lock. Selling implements made out of wire. Candlesticks. Little dogs for the mantelpiece. The stall was gone but a woman who'd worked on it was now at the other end of the market, near the canal, selling hot soup. She didn't know Billy but the guy who used to run the wire stall lived in a flat in Summertown. He was out at night mostly and slept during the day. It took repeated banging at the front door (the knocker was missing and the bell didn't seem to make a sound) before a woman appeared and, at their request, went to wake him up. He hadn't seen Billy for a couple of weeks, but he used to drop by a café in the high street or the pub next to it when he had any money.

Nobody seemed to know him in the café, but when Riley showed his badge to the pale young woman behind the bar in the pub, she pointed him to two men sitting drinking at a table. Yes, they knew Billy Hunt. Yes, one of them had seen him today. What had they talked about? Nothing much. Just to say hello. Where was he? That other pub. Which other one? The one up Kentish Town Road, the goth one, the one with the skulls.

Riley walked up Camden High Street and found Munster parked outside Camden Town tube station. He got into the car beside him.

'What's the plan?' he said.

'Plan?' said Munster. 'Find him. And then talk to him.'

'Are we bringing him in?'

'We'll talk to him first.'

The car pulled up before reaching the pub. Munster gazed up at the black façade and shook his head with distaste.

'I used to like heavy metal when I was a kid,' said Riley. 'I'd have loved this place.'

'When you were a kid?' said Munster. 'Right. Do we know what he looks like?'

Two young women, dressed from head to foot in black leather, both with shaved heads and multiple piercings, were seated at a table outside.

'Well, they're not Billy Hunt,' said Riley, cheerfully. 'Unless Billy's a girl's name.'

At the other table a man was sitting alone, with a half-drunk pint of beer and a cigarette. He was thin and pale, with tufted dark hair, wearing black jeans and a rumpled grey jacket.

'That might be him,' said Munster.

They got out of the car and approached him. He didn't notice them until they were a few feet away.

'We're looking for a William Hunt,' said Munster.

'Only my mum calls me William,' the man replied. 'And then only when she's angry with me.'

The two detectives sat at the table.

'Billy, then,' Munster said. 'We've been talking to a man named Jeremy Burgess. He runs a jewellery store just up the road from here.'

Hunt stubbed his cigarette out on the table, took another from a packet and lit it with almost feverish concentration. 'I don't know him.'

'William,' said Munster. 'Now *I'm* getting angry with you.' He took a printout from his pocket and spread it on the table. 'He told us that you came in with this and he bought it from you.'

Hunt turned the paper around and looked at it. Munster saw that even his hands, even his long fingers, were thin and pale. The nails were bitten short but even so they were dirty and stained. 'I don't know,' he said.

'What do you mean, you don't know?' said Munster. 'Is all this Georgian silver becoming a bit of blur?'

'Are you going to buy me a drink?'

'No, I'm not going to buy you a drink. What do you think this is?'

'If you're looking for information, there should be something in it for me.'

Munster turned to Riley, then back to Hunt. Riley was smiling. Munster wasn't. 'You're not a potential inform-ant. You're a suspect. If you don't answer questions, we can take you straight into custody.'

Hunt ruffled his hair so that it stood up even more than before. 'Every time there's some bit of property goes missing,' he said, in a whine, 'people like you come and hassle me about it. Have you ever heard the expression about giving a dog a bad name?'

Munster looked at him in disbelief. 'Is this the dog that keeps being put in prison for hitting people and selling things that other people have stolen? And while we're on the subject, these bits of property don't just go missing on their own. People like you nick them. Don't mess us around, Billy. We've heard about you. You've got a drug habit and you steal to pay for it.'

Hunt took a gulp of beer, followed by a deep drag on his cigarette. He looked at Riley, who was grinning. 'I don't know what's so funny,' he said. 'I only got started when I was inside. There's more gak inside than there is on the streets. And that wanker, Burgess. Everyone comes round and bothers me and there's Burgess with his fucking shop. Why does everyone let him carry on?'

'Billy,' said Munster. 'Shut up. Where did you get the silver?'

Hunt paused. 'There was a guy. He had some bits and pieces, bits of silver. He was desperate for cash, so I gave him some and passed it on to Burgess. End of story.'

'Did you ask him where he got it?'

'No, I didn't. I'm not the *Antiques* fucking *Roadshow*.'

'What's his name?'

'I don't know. Dave, I think.'

'Dave,' said Munster. 'Dave what?'

'I don't know. I don't really know him.'

'Where does he live?'

'South of the river, I think. But I'm not sure.'

'Dave. South London,' said Munster. 'Possibly. Do you know how to get in touch with him?'

'It doesn't really work like that. You run into people. See them around. You know how it is.'

'Yeah, I know,' said Munster. 'And while we're at it, could you tell me where you were on Wednesday?'

'When? The one just gone?'

'Yes. The sixth.'

'I was out of London. I was down in Brighton. Had a few days away.'

'Is there anyone who can confirm that?'

'I was down with a friend.'

'What's his name?'

'His name?' said Hunt. Quite slowly, he stubbed his cigarette out and lit another. 'Ian.'

'Second name?'

'He was always just Ian.'

'But you can tell us his address?'

Hunt looked doubtful. 'I've got it written down somewhere. Or I did have. It was at a friend of Ian's. Ian won't be there. He moves around a lot.'

'Arranging work for people,' said Munster.

'For his friends.'

'I can't believe I'm actually bothering to say this out loud,' said Munster, 'but have you got Ian's phone number?'

'It was on my phone. I'm not completely sure where my phone is.'

'You realize what we're asking?' said Munster. 'You've been here before. We want you to point us in the direction of someone who will say to us: "Yes, Billy Hunt was with me in Brighton on Wednesday." Is there such a person?'

'This isn't right,' said Hunt. 'This is a matter of . . . What this is about is . . . is . . . that I'm not like you. Or you,' he added, looking at Riley, who seemed bemused. 'You've got your nice homes and all your insurance and your water bills with your names on them.'

'My water bill?' said Munster.

'And you've got all your nice friends and you go out to dinner with them. You all look out for each other and – and you can just prove where you were all the time and you've got a job and a pension and paid holidays.'

'What the fuck are you talking about?'

'We're not all like you. Don't you read the papers? Some of us are having to struggle to get by.'

'Will you shut up?' said Munster. 'I don't care about any of this. But I'm finding it a bit difficult to pin anything down. Do you have an address?'

'You see, that's just what I'm talking about. People like you, you always have an address.' Hunt drew imaginary quotation marks with his fingers around the word 'address'.

'All right. Let's make it simple. Where did you sleep last night?'

'Last night?' said Hunt, thoughtfully. 'I don't know. I stay with different people, with friends. I'm looking for somewhere permanent.'

'Like you're looking for a job?' said Munster.

'Like that.'

'One more thing,' said Munster. 'And this is just a formality, so that my colleague can write it in his notebook.'

'What?'

'It wasn't by any chance you who stole the silver from sixty-three Margaretting Street?'

'No, it wasn't.'

'All right,' said Munster.

'So we're done?' said Hunt.

'No, we're not. I've had enough of this. You're coming with us.'

'What for?'

'Well, just for a start, you've already admitted receiving and selling stolen goods.'

'I didn't know they were stolen.'

'Which, if you read the terms of the Act, is not relevant.'

'I've told you everything I know.' Hunt's voice rose in indignation. 'If you need any more information, just get in touch with me.'

'Except that we've established you don't have an address and you've mislaid your phone.'

'Just give me your card,' said Hunt. 'I'll get in touch with you.'

'I would,' said Munster. 'It's just that I've got a feeling that you might go the way of your friends Dave and Ian and be a bit difficult to track down. So are you willing to come, or do we have to arrest you?'

'I'll come. Haven't I been co-operating? Haven't I answered all your questions? I just want to finish my drink. And then go to the toilet.'

'We'll come with you.'

'I can go later,' said Hunt. He sipped his beer. 'Don't you like sitting outside? It's global warming, isn't it? We can sit out on the pavement in London drinking. It's like being by the Med.'

'With skulls,' said Riley.

Hunt peered up at them. 'I don't like the skulls. They're depressing.'

SEVEN

'No drugs,' said Olivia. 'Obviously no drugs.'

'Mum,' said Chloë.

'And no spirits. You've told everybody no spirits? If anyone brings spirits, they"ll be confiscated and their parents can collect them.'

'You've said this about a million times.'

'Have you got a list of everyone who's coming?' said Olivia. 'Then Frieda's friend can cross them off as they arrive.'

'I haven't got a list.'

'How do you know who's coming, then?'

'It's not like that, Mum,' said Chloë. 'For God's sake.'

'But you must know how many people are coming.' There was a pause. 'Well?'

'Sort of.'

'Well, sort of how many? Ten? Fifty? A thousand?'

'We've talked about this. We've talked about it a million times.'

'This isn't a joke, Chloë. Did you hear about the teenage party in Hart Street last year? The father tried to deal with some gatecrashers and one of them pulled a knife. He lost a kidney, Chloë.'

'What's all this about? You said I could have the party. If I can't have it, then just say so and we'll cancel it. Will that make you happy?'

'I want you to have a party,' said Olivia. 'It's your birthday. But I want you to enjoy it. You won't enjoy it if people are being sick and there are fights and the house is being vandalized.'

'It won't be like that.'

'And no sex.'

'Mum!'

'What?'

'This is just embarrassing.'

Olivia reached forward and touched Chloë's cheek. 'You look lovely, by the way.'

Chloë blushed and mumbled something.

'There are crisps and nuts and cartons and cartons of juice,' said Olivia. 'What I'm trying to get across to you, Chloë, is that you'll all have a better time if you don't get falling-over drunk. You can talk to each other and – and dance and things . . .'

'Oh, Mum . . .'

'But nobody enjoys being really drunk and falling over and being sick. That's not a good time. I mean, Frieda, back me up over this. Am I being a wet blanket?'

Frieda was standing by the window, gazing out into the garden. There were unlit candles in jam jars along the gravel path. There was a ring at the door.

'Oh, God,' said Olivia. 'Already?'

'I'll get it,' said Frieda.

She went to the front door and opened it. 'Josef! You're just in time.'

Josef wasn't alone. Next to him was a man who was even taller and bulkier. He was wearing jeans and a leather jacket. He had long curly hair, tied at the back of his head in a ponytail.

'This is Stefan,' said Josef. 'And he is from Russia but we will be pleasant to him in any case.'

Frieda shook Stefan's hand and he gave her a slow smile. 'You are Frieda? I have heard. You are going to have a beautiful bath. It is big and made of iron, like in an old film.'

'Yes, I've heard of you too,' said Frieda. 'You helped Josef take my nice old bath away.'

'It was a bad bath,' said Stefan. 'Cheap rubbish. It cracked like that' – he snapped his fingers – 'when we took it.'

'Well, thank you both for doing this. Although I'm worried that while you're doing it, my bathroom still doesn't have a bath.'

Josef looked concerned. 'Yes, Frieda, I must talk with you. There is a small problem.'

'What problem?'

'More problem with the pipes. But we talk later. I sort it.'

'You know, I had to have a shower here,' said Frieda. 'While they were preparing for the party. I have to carry a towel round with me.' She stopped herself. 'But it's good of you to do this. You'd better come in. Can I get you something to drink?'

'Now we will have juice.' Josef tapped the pocket of his coat. Evidently there was a bottle in there. 'At the end of the night we will celebrate together.'

Olivia gave Josef and Stefan a variety of instructions, constantly adjusted and added to. Meanwhile the doorbell rang intermittently and young people began to drift in.

Frieda stood to one side and watched the scene, as if it was a piece of theatre or an exotic tribe. Suddenly she saw a face she recognized and gave a start. 'Jack! What are you doing here?'

Jack was training to be a psychotherapist and Frieda was his supervisor. She knew him well, but seeing him in this context was a surprise. He, too, seemed taken aback and blushed a deep, unbecoming red. Even by his own standards, he was wearing bizarre and mismatched clothes – a pink and green hooped rugby shirt, with an ancient, moth-eaten tuxedo over the top, and baggy brown cords.

'Chloë invited me,' he said. 'I thought it might be fun. I didn't expect to see you, though.'

'I'm on my way out.'

'Is that Josef I can see?'

'He's the bouncer for the evening.'

After a minute or two Josef looked at her, over Olivia's shoulder, with a faint smile that was a plea for help. Frieda walked across the room and tapped Olivia on the arm. 'Let's go and get our meal.'

'I just need to check on a few things.'

'No, you don't.'

Frieda led Olivia, still protesting, into the hallway, put her coat on for her and pulled her out of the front door. As they went down the steps, Olivia stared around anxiously. 'I can't help feeling that I'm locking *in* the people I ought to be locking *out*.'

'No,' said Olivia, to the waiter. 'I don't need to taste it. Just pour it most of the way up. Thanks, and leave the bottle.' She picked up the glass. 'Cheers.' She took a gulp. 'Christ, I

65

needed that. Did you see them all hugging each other as they arrived? It was as if they'd returned from a round-the-world trip. And as soon as they've finished hugging and shrieking they're on their mobile phones. They're at a party but somehow they instantly need to talk to the people who're not at the party or who're on their way to the party, or maybe they're checking whether there's a better party somewhere else.' She took another gulp. 'They're probably sending out a general call to the youth of north London to trash the house.' She prodded Frieda. 'At this point you're supposed to say, "No, no, it'll be fine."'

'It'll be fine,' said Frieda.

Olivia gesticulated towards the waiter. 'Why don't we order lots of little dishes?' she said. 'Then we can just pick at them.'

'You choose.'

Olivia ordered enough for three or four hearty eaters and another bottle of wine. 'I'm a big hypocrite, really,' she said, when the waiter had gone. 'My real worry about a party like this is that Chloë will do half of what I did when I was her age. Younger than her age. She's seventeen. When I think of parties when I was fifteen, fourteen . . . It was technically illegal. People could have gone to prison. I'm sure it was the same with you. David told me one or two things.'

Frieda's expression became fixed. She took a sip of wine but didn't speak.

'When I think of some of the things I got up to . . .' Olivia continued. 'At least people weren't filming me on their mobile phones and putting it on the Internet. That's the difference. When we were teenagers, you could do things and they were done, gone, in the past. Now they get filmed and sent by phone and put on Facebook. People don't realize they're stuck with their actions for ever. It wasn't like that with us.'

'That's not true,' said Frieda. 'People got hurt. People got pregnant.'

'I wasn't going to get pregnant,' said Olivia. 'Mummy put me on the Pill at about the time I learned to walk. I'm not saying I was a complete wild child, it's just that . . . When I look at some of the decisions I made, well, I'd like to see Chloë choose better than that.' She topped up her wine glass. Frieda held her hand over her own glass. 'But in some ways, I think Chloë is more mature than I was at her age. Now, I know what you're going to say.'

'What am I going to say?'

'You're going to say that if I was less mature than Chloë, I must have been a truly epic fuck-up.'

'That's not what I was going to say,' said Frieda.

'Then what?'

'I was going to say that it was a good thing to say about your daughter.'

'We'll see,' snorted Olivia. 'Meanwhile the house is probably being reduced to its constituent parts.'

'I'm sure you don't need to worry.'

'I don't know what parties you went to,' said Olivia. 'I was once at this party. I was up in the parents' bedroom with Nick Yates and by the time we were finished for the second time the people downstairs had carried the upright piano out into the garden and started to play it, then forgotten about it and it had started to rain. God. Nick Yates.'

A faraway expression came to Olivia's face. Then the food arrived.

'I'm so sorry.' Olivia filled her plate from the different dishes. 'Try this shrimp, by the way. It's to die for. I've been talking solidly about myself and my problems and my wicked past. I haven't even asked about how you're feeling. I know it's all been so terrible. How are you feeling? Does it still hurt?'

'It's not too bad.'

'Are you still being treated?'

'Just check-ups,' said Frieda. 'From time to time.'

'It was the most terrible, terrible thing,' said Olivia. 'At first I thought we were going to lose you. You know, a couple of days ago I had a nightmare about it. I woke up and I was crying. Literally crying.'

'I think it was worse for other people than it was for me.'

'I bet it wasn't,' said Olivia. 'But they say that when really terrible things happen, it stops feeling real, like it's happening to someone else.'

'No,' said Frieda, slowly. 'It felt like it was happening to me.'

On the way back to the house, Olivia was walking unsteadily and Frieda took her arm.

'I'm looking for smoke,' Olivia said. 'Can you see smoke?'

'What?'

'If the house was literally on fire,' said Olivia, 'we'd be seeing smoke by now, wouldn't we? Over the roofs. And there'd be fire engines and sirens.'

As they turned the corner into Olivia's road, they saw the front door open, people milling around. There was a loud electronic beat, a low throb. There were flashing lights. As they got closer, Frieda saw a group sitting on the front steps smoking. One of them looked up and smiled.

'It is Frieda, no?'

'Stefan, right?'

'Yes,' he said, as if the idea amused him. 'Frieda, you like a cigarette?'

Olivia gave an indistinct yell, brushed through the crowd on the steps and ran into the house.

'No, thanks,' said Frieda. 'How has it been?'

Stefan gave a shrug. 'Okay, I think. A quiet party.'

One of the boys sitting next to him laughed. 'They were great, him and Josef.'

'Like how?' Frieda sat on the step beside them.

'This gang of kids came. Chloë didn't know them. They started jostling people. But Josef and Stefan made them go away.'

Frieda glanced at Stefan, who was lighting a new cigarette from the old one. 'You made them go away?'

'It was no big thing,' said Stefan.

'It was a big thing,' said one of the other boys. 'It was a very big thing.'

They laughed, and one said something to Stefan in a language she couldn't understand, and he said something back, then looked at her.

'He is learning a funny Russian in his school,' he said. 'I am teaching him.'

'Where's Josef?'

'He is with a boy,' said Stefan. 'A boy is not well.'

'What do you mean "not well"? Where are they?'

'The toilet on the upstairs,' said Stefan. 'He was sick. Very sick.'

Frieda ran into the house. The hall was sticky under her feet and there was a smell of smoke and beer. She pushed her way past some girls. There was a group outside the closed door of the bathroom.

'Is he in there?' Frieda asked them in general.

Suddenly Chloë was there. She had been crying. Mascara was running down her face. Jack was hovering behind her, his hair sticking up in peaks and his face blotchy.

'They couldn't wake him,' she said.

Frieda tried the door. It was locked. She knocked at it. 'Josef, it's me,' said Frieda. 'Let me in.'

There was a click and the door opened. He was with a boy who was leaning over the lavatory. Josef turned around with an apologetic smile. 'He was like this when he come almost,' he said.

'Is he responsive?' said Frieda. Josef looked puzzled. 'I mean, can he speak? Can he see you?'

'Yes, yes, fine. Just sick. Very, very sick. Teenage sick.'

Frieda turned to Chloë. 'He's all right,' she said.

Chloë shook her head. 'Ted's not all right,' she said. 'He's not. His mother's dead. She was murdered.'

I tell you what, let's go away somewhere this summer – somewhere neither of us has ever been. Though I can't really imagine you anywhere except London. That's where I met you and that's the only place I've known you. Do you ever go anywhere else? The furthest afield I've seen you is Heathrow, which must be your idea of a kind of man-made hell. You hate planes, and you

70

don't like beaches. But we could get a train to Paris, or go walking in Scotland. You love walking the streets at night – but do you like other kinds of walking, where you have a map and a picnic? I know you – but there are so many things I don't know about you. That's what I've been thinking. But we've got lots of time to find things now, haven't we, Frieda? Call me soon – Sandy xxxxxx

Eight

'Can I have a cup of tea?' said Billy Hunt. 'I want a cup of tea and I want a lawyer. Tea with milk and two sugars, and a lawyer sitting next to me for every moment that you're interviewing me.'

Munster turned to Riley. 'Hear that?' he said.

Riley left the interview room.

'And a lawyer,' said Hunt.

'Wait.'

They sat in silence until Riley returned. He placed the polystyrene cup on the table in front of Hunt, with two sachets of sugar and a plastic stirrer. Slowly, and with great concentration, Hunt tore the sachets open, tipped their contents into the tea and stirred them. He sipped the tea.

'And a lawyer,' he repeated.

There was a digital recorder on the table. Munster leaned forward to switch it on. As he spoke the day's date and identified the people in the room he looked at the device to check that the light was flashing. There was always the worry that it wasn't working properly. Cases collapsed because of details like that.

'We're interviewing you on suspicion of handling stolen property. I'm going to caution you that you don't have to say anything, but that anything you say can be used in evidence. Also, if you remain silent, that fact can be presented to the court.'

'Are you sure?' said Hunt.

'Yes, I'm sure,' said Munster. 'And I probably do this sort of thing even more often than you do.'

Hunt drummed his fingers on the table. 'I guess I can't smoke.'

'No, you can't.'

'I can't think when I don't smoke.'

'You don't need to think. You just need to answer some questions.'

'And what about my lawyer?'

'I was about to inform you that you are entitled to legal representation, and that if you don't have representation of your own, we can arrange it for you.'

'Of course I don't have fucking legal representation of my own. So, yeah, get me one. I want a lawyer sitting here beside me.'

'It doesn't work like that any more,' said Munster. 'Money's tight. That's what they're telling us. We can bring you a phone and a phone number.'

'Is that it?' Hunt seemed baffled. 'No cigs and no lawyers?'

'You can talk to one on the phone.'

'All right,' said Hunt. 'Get a phone.'

It was twenty minutes before Billy Hunt had finished on the phone, Munster and Riley were back in the room and the recorder was on again.

'So,' Munster began. 'You've talked to your lawyer.'

'It was a bad line,' said Hunt. 'I couldn't make out most of what she was saying. She had an accent as well. I don't reckon English is her first language.'

'But she gave you legal advice?'

73

'Is that what you call legal advice? Why can't I get a real lawyer?'

'If you've got a problem, you can take it up with your MP. But that's the way the system works now.'

'Why is that window all boarded up?'

'Because someone threw a brick at it.'

'Can't you get it mended?'

'I don't really think that's your problem.'

'And the room at the front – it's like a building site. You'll be next,' he said. 'You'll be out looking for a real job like the rest of us.'

'You've now officially got legal representation,' said Munster. 'Take a look at this.' He slid a piece of paper across the table.

Hunt examined it with a puzzled expression. 'What's this?' he said.

'An inventory.'

'What's that?'

'A list of what was stolen. Including, as you'll see, the silver forks you sold. Is there anything else there you remember?'

He shook his head. 'Sorry,' he said. 'Those forks were all I got.'

'From Dave,' said Munster.

'That's right.'

'So,' Munster went on, 'the items we retrieved were part of a larger haul, but you never saw the rest.'

'That's right.'

'And your link to this theft was Dave, whose second name you don't know, who you think lives south of the river, and who you have no means of contacting.'

Hunt shifted awkwardly in his seat. 'You know the way things are,' he said.

'And your only alibi for the day of the burglary would be provided by a man called Ian, also with no second name, now currently on his travels. And uncontactable.'

'Sorry about that,' said Hunt.

'In other words,' said Munster, 'you can't tell us anything we can check, apart from what we already know.'

'You're police,' said Hunt. 'I don't know what you can check and what you can't check.'

'Of course, if you were to put us in touch with whoever passed that silver to you, we'd seriously consider dropping the charge against you.'

'Then I wish I could put you in touch with him.'

'Dave?'

'Yeah. But I can't.'

'Is there anything at all you can tell us?'

'I don't know,' said Hunt. 'Just ask.'

'Where did you spend last night? At least you can tell us that.'

'I've been moving around,' said Hunt. 'I haven't got anywhere regular.'

'You can only sleep in one place at a time. Where did you sleep last night?'

'It's in these flats, down near Chalk Farm. There's this friend of mine, friend of a friend. He's away. He lets me doss down there.'

'What's the address?'

'I can't remember.'

'Then take us there.'

It was a short drive, then the three of them – Munster,

Riley and Hunt – walked into the courtyard of the battered, dishevelled estate and up a staircase. On the third floor, Munster stopped and leaned on the balcony railing, looking across at the William Morris building. They were in the John Ruskin building. Beyond were houses that, even now, were worth more than a million pounds, but here one in every three or four flats was boarded up, waiting for a renovation that had probably been put on hold until someone was ready to pay for it. Hunt walked along the balcony and stopped. He took out a key from his jacket pocket and unlocked a front door.

'Stop,' Munster said. 'Don't go in. You wait out here with DC Riley.'

He stepped inside and immediately was reminded of his early days in the force when he had spent much of his time in places like this. It was a smell of mustiness, damp, some food going off somewhere. It was the smell of not bothering, of giving up. He recognized it all. The grubby linoleum, the dirty sofas and chairs in the living room, everything grubby and old, except the large new flat-screen TV. In the kitchen, the sink was full of dishes; there was a greasy frying pan on the hob. He was seeking something that didn't fit, something different from the usual crap, and it didn't seem as if he was going to find it. Had Hunt got rid of everything? He should probably send some officers round for a proper search, if he could get them. Because Hunt was right. Legal aid had been cut and now it was the police's turn. But then he went into the bathroom and there, finally, was something. He pulled on his plastic gloves. It was too big for an evidence bag. He called Riley and Hunt inside.

'What's that doing here?'

'It's a cog,' said Riley. 'It looks like it should be in some big old machine.'

There was a pause.

'Why shouldn't it be in a bathroom?' said Hunt. 'It looks nice. Shiny. It's a decoration.'

'You weren't admiring its shininess,' said Munster. 'You were washing it. Where did you get a thing like this from? It's hardly usual.'

'It was from that guy.'

'Dave?'

'That's right.'

'Why didn't you mention it?'

'It wasn't on your list.'

'Why were you washing it?'

'So that it would be nice and shiny when I sold it.'

'We'll see,' said Munster.

Karlsson, when Munster returned with the cog, held it for a moment, turning it over, feeling its heft and weight. Then he went to see Russell Lennox, who was sitting slack and passive in an armchair, staring ahead with bloodshot eyes.

'Mr Lennox,' he said, holding the cog, which was cold in his gloved hands. 'Do you recognize this object?'

Russell Lennox gazed at the cog for several seconds without speaking. His lips were bloodless.

'Is that –' He stopped and pressed the bridge of his nose between forefinger and thumb. 'Is that what she was killed with?'

'We believe so. Yes. But you didn't mention it among the items that were stolen.'

'No. I didn't notice it was gone. It was just a thing we had on our mantelpiece. Ruth picked it up from some skip a couple of years ago. She said it would scrub up nicely, unlike me and Ted.' His face worked and he made a visible effort to control his emotions. 'You're sure?'

'Your wife's blood was on it.'

'I see.' Russell Lennox turned away. 'I don't want to look at it any more.'

Munster restarted the recorder. 'We've been busy,' he said. 'Things have changed. Now, this is your last chance to co-operate. Where did you get the cog?'

Hunt's eyes flickered between him and Riley. 'I said. From Dave.'

'All right. That's enough of this crap.' Munster stood up and left the room.

Hunt looked at Riley. 'What did I say?'

'He's cross,' said Riley. 'You don't want to make him cross.'

'Fucking shut up,' said Hunt. 'So is this some trick so I suddenly think you're my friend?'

'I was just saying.'

A few moments later Munster came back into the room with Karlsson. He pulled a chair across and the two of them sat down. Munster placed a closed brown cardboard file on the table and looked across at Hunt. 'Let it be noted that DCI Karlsson has joined the interview,' he said. 'William Hunt, the next time you want to wash blood off a murder weapon, I'd pop it in the dishwasher. If you rinse it under the tap, you always leave a bit. As you did.'

'I don't know what you're talking about.'

'Russell Lennox has identified it. They kept it on their mantelpiece as a sort of work of art. A dense and heavy work of art. Three days ago it was used to fatally assault one Ruth Lennox. You've been identified disposing of articles that were taken from the murder scene. The murder weapon has been found at a flat where you were staying. You've admitted attempting to clean it. It has your fingerprints on it. We are about to charge you with the murder of Ruth Lennox and with the burglary. Now, Mr Hunt, have you got anything to say? It'll make it a great deal easier for all of us if you just admit what you did, write out a statement and the judge will regard you with some degree of sympathy.'

There was a long pause.

'There wasn't anyone called Dave,' said Hunt.

'Of course there wasn't anyone called Dave,' said Munster. 'And?'

'All right,' he said. 'I did the burglary.'

Another pause.

'And? What about Ruth Lennox?'

'You won't believe me,' said Hunt.

'Believe you?' said Munster. 'You've been lying solidly ever since we met you. Just own up.'

There was another, even longer, pause. To Riley it appeared that Hunt was doing a complicated mental calculation.

'I did the burglary,' he said finally. 'But I didn't kill her. I admit, I broke in, I took the stuff from the kitchen. But I was only there for a minute. The alarm was going so I was in a rush. I went into the other room and she was on the floor. I just ran.'

'You didn't just run,' said Munster. 'We found you with the object that was used to kill her.'

'I picked it up. On the way out.'

Karlsson stood up. 'We've got you at the scene. And you've been lying all the way along the line. You're going away for this one.' He nodded at Munster. 'Just get the paperwork ready.'

NINE

The drilling had stopped but it was replaced by a hammering that wasn't just loud but shook the house. Frieda made tea for Josef so the noise would stop for a few minutes. Josef sat on the stairs and cradled his mug in his large, dirty hands.

'Under everything, this is a good house,' he said. 'The walls are good, fine bricks. Give me six months to rip away all the rubbish, all the plasterboard and –'

'No, no, don't even say that!'

'What?'

'Six months. Those words are very frightening to me.'

'I was talking. Just talking.'

'All right, and while we're just talking, I thought you said you were going to put a new bath in. I hear lots of banging and the bathroom looks like it's been demolished and there's no sign of a bath.'

'It is all fine. I do everything, I sort everything perfectly. Then, at the end, put the bath in. Click click. Just like that.'

Suddenly there was a jangling electronic tone of an old pop song that Frieda couldn't quite place. Josef's phone was on the table beside her. She picked it up. There was a name – Nina – flashing on the screen. She handed it to him but he saw the name and shook his head.

'Is she someone you're avoiding?' said Frieda.

Josef was flustered. 'Someone I see a bit. But she ring and ring.'

'It's usually best to tell people what you feel,' said Frieda. 'But I'm not going to give you advice on anything except finishing this bathroom.'

'All right, all right,' said Josef. He handed his mug to Frieda and went back upstairs.

When she was alone, Frieda swallowed two paracetamol with water. Then she turned to her work email. Most messages she deleted or simply ignored. But there was one from Paz at the clinic she regularly worked for. She asked if Frieda could call her. And there was another she hesitated over. It was from a woman called Marta, who was writing on behalf of her old friend and Frieda's patient Joe Franklin. She was apologetic: Joe didn't know she was writing and she felt bad about doing so – but did Frieda have any idea when she would be returning to work? Joe wouldn't see the therapist she had recommended, and he was in a bad way. He hadn't got out of bed for several days.

Frieda thought of her doctor and her friends, who were all insistent that she shouldn't return to work for several weeks yet. She thought of Joe Franklin sitting in her consulting room with his head in his hands, tears seeping through his fingers. She frowned and wrote an email: 'Dear Joe, I can see you at the usual time tomorrow, Tuesday, if that would suit you. Let me know and best wishes, Frieda Klein.'

Then she picked up the phone and called the Warehouse, as the clinic was called. Paz answered and immediately questioned her about how things were going and her health, the way everyone did nowadays. It was like an obstacle she had to get past over and over again.

'Reuben is worried about you,' said Paz. 'We all are.'

Reuben was the man who had founded the Warehouse. As a young man, he had been a charismatic spokeperson for a new kind of therapy, and had been Frieda's supervisor. These days he was rather battered and disillusioned.

'And?'

'I wanted to see how you were. Someone contacted us. He wanted to see you. I mean as a patient. I said you weren't well.'

'For God's sake, Paz, could you stop handing out my medical details?'

'But he pleaded. He sounded desperate.'

'I'll call him.'

'You're sure about this, Frieda?'

'It's not-working that's the problem.'

He was called Seamus Dunne. When Frieda dialled his number he answered instantly. She introduced herself. 'Is it a good time to talk?'

'Yes. It's fine.' He sounded suddenly tense.

'You want to come and see me?'

'Yes. I do. I think – I feel it's urgent. I would like it to be as soon as possible.'

'How did you find my name?'

'A friend of a friend recommended you,' said Seamus. 'Very highly.'

'We can meet for an assessment session,' said Frieda.

Then you can decide if I'm the right person for you, and I can decide if I think I can help you. All right?'

'Good.'

'Can you make eleven o'clock tomorrow morning?'

'Yes.' There was a pause. 'I think you'll find me a very interesting person.'

A nasty little headache screwed its way up Frieda's temple. Cockiness. It wasn't a good start.

Seamus Dunne was a young man, slim and neat, with even features and shiny brown hair, slicked back. He was wearing a dark, tailored jacket, black cords and a purple shirt that shimmered under the light. Frieda wondered how long he had taken to get ready for their meeting. He had a firm though slightly damp handshake and a clipped, emphatic way of speaking. His smile, when he produced it, seemed disconnected from what he was saying. He used her name slightly too often.

'So, Frieda, how do we do this?' he asked, after he had taken a seat opposite her and put his hands, palms down, on his knees.

'I'd like to know a few details about you and then I'd like you to tell me why you're here.'

'Details. Right. Age, occupation, things you put on a form?'

'All right.'

'I'm twenty-seven. I'm in sales and marketing, and very good at it. I get people to buy things they didn't even know they wanted. Perhaps you disapprove of that, Frieda, but, really, it's how the world works. You don't find out what people need and give it to them. You create the need in them and then you fulfil it.'

'Do you live in London?'

'Yes. Harrow.'

'Tell me something about your family.'

'My father died when I was seventeen. I didn't mind. He was useless anyway and he always had it in for me. I was glad when he went. My mum, she's another story. She adores me. I'm the baby of the family. I've got two older sisters and then there's a gap and there's me. She still does my washing for me, would you believe? And I go there every Sunday for lunch. Just me and her.'

'Do you live alone?'

'On and off. I like living by myself. I don't get lonely and I have lots of friends.' He paused, looked up, flashed her a smile and then looked down at his hands again. 'And girlfriends. Women seem to like me. I know how to make them happy.'

'And do you?'

'What?' He was momentarily startled.

'Make them happy.'

'Yes. I was saying. For a while, but I don't want to be tied down, you see. I'm not a faithful sort of man. I want variety, excitement. I like feeling my heart pound. I used to steal when I was a kid for the thrill of it. Are you shocked by that?'

'Should I be shocked?'

'I don't know. Anyway, it's the same with women. I like the beginning of things, the chase. That's why I'm good at my job too. I get a kick out of persuading people to buy things they don't need. I get a kick out of making women want me. It's only with my mum that I'm calm and ordinary.'

Frieda scrutinized him. There were beads of sweat on his forehead although the room was quite cool. 'If you like your life so much, why are you here, with me?'

Seamus sat up straighter and took a breath. 'I like having power over people.' She could see him swallow and when he spoke it was more slowly, as if he was considering every word. 'I remember, when I was a boy, I used to cut my father's hair. My father was a big man, much bigger than I am, and solid. He had a thick neck and broad shoulders and beside him I felt very small. But every so often I would be holding these sharp scissors and he would shut his eyes and let me snip his hair off.' He paused for a moment, as if recollecting something. 'I can remember the dampness of the hair and the smell of it. Pushing my fingers into it, feeling the skin underneath. It smelt of him. When he let me touch his hair, I knew he was giving me power over him. I can still hear the sound of the blades. I could have killed him with those scissors. I had power over him, and that made me feel strong and tender at the same time. Looking after him with something that could wound him.'

He forced his eyes up and met Frieda's gaze. He faltered slightly. 'I'm sorry, is something wrong?'

'Why do you say that?'

'You look, I don't know, puzzled?'

'Go on,' she said. 'What were you going to say?'

'I used to hurt animals,' he said. 'That gave me the same

feeling. Mostly little things, birds and insects. But some-times cats, a dog once. And now women.'

'You like hurting women?'

'They like it too. Mostly.'

'You mean, hurting them sexually?'

'Of course. It's all part of sex, isn't it – hurting, pleasing, causing pain and pleasure, showing who's master? But now – well, now there's this woman I've met. Danielle. She says I've gone too far. I frightened her with what I did. She says she won't see me any more unless I get help.'

'You mean you're here because Danielle told you to come?'

'Yes.'

'Really?'

'Don't you believe me?'

'I'm interested by the way you describe yourself as someone who likes to have power over people. But you've listened to Danielle, you've responded to her concern and you've acted on it.'

'She thinks I could do something – well, something that could get me into trouble. Not just killing a cat. And she's right. I think so too.'

'You're telling me that you're worried you could seri-ously hurt someone?'

'Yes.'

'And is that all you have to tell me?'

'*All?* Isn't that enough?'

'Apart from Danielle's worries, which you share, are there other things that are troubling you?'

'Well.' He shifted in his chair, glanced away and then back again. 'I'm not great at sleeping.'

'Go on.'

'I go to sleep all right but then I wake and sometimes that's fine and sometimes I just know I won't go back to sleep. I lie there and think about stuff.'

'Stuff?'

'You know. Little things seem big at three in the morning. But everyone goes through patches of not sleeping. And I've lost my appetite a bit.'

'You don't eat properly?'

'That's not why I'm here.' He seemed suddenly angry. 'I'm here because of my violent feelings. I want you to help me.'

Frieda sat quite straight in her red armchair. The sun poured through the window, ran like a river through the room where she told patients who made their way to her that they could tell her anything, anything at all. Her ribs hurt and her leg ached.

'No,' she said at last.

'I'm sorry?'

'I can't help you.'

'I don't understand. I come here telling you I might seriously harm someone and you tell me you can't help me.'

'That's right. I'm not the proper person.'

'Why? You specialize in things like this – I've heard about you. You know about people like me.'

Frieda thought about Dean Reeve, the man who had stolen a little girl and turned her into his submissive wife, who had stolen a little boy and tried to make him into his son, who through Frieda's carelessness had snatched a young woman and murdered her just because she got in his way, who was still alive somewhere with his soft smile and his watching eyes. She thought of the knife slashing at her.

'What are people like you like?' she said.

'You know – people who do bad things.'

'Have you done bad things?'

'Not yet. But I can feel them inside me. I don't want to let them out.'

'There is a paradox here,' said Frieda.

'What?'

'The fact of asking me for help might suggest that you don't really need it.'

'I don't know what you mean.'

'You're worried about being violent, about a lack of empathy. But you listened to Danielle. And you're asking for help. That shows insight.'

'But what about torturing animals?'

'You shouldn't do that. But you said it was a long time ago. So: don't do it again.'

There was a pause. He looked confused. 'I don't know what to say.'

'What about "goodbye"?' said Frieda.

Seamus left and Frieda went and stood by her window, her eyes resting on the site across the street. Once there had been houses there, before a wrecking ball had swung through their walls, smashing them into dust, and diggers and cranes had moved in among the rubble. For a while, it had been a construction site, with Portakabins and men in hard hats drinking tea. Boards had gone up round the perimeter, announcing the imminent arrival of a brand new office block. But then work had stopped: this was a

89

recession after all. The men had left with their diggers, though one stumpy crane still stood in the middle of the space. Weeds and shrubs had grown up where the rubble had been. Now it was a wild place. Children played there; homeless people sometimes slept there. Frieda occasionally saw foxes roaming through the brambles. Perhaps it would stay like that, she thought, reminding people that even in a great city like London some things have to remain uncontrolled, unpredictable, sending up nettles and wild flowers and even a few stray vegetables, the stubborn survivors of gardens that had been demolished.

No. She couldn't help Seamus Dunne, although the image of him cutting his father's hair remained with her, the bright blades opening and closing in her mind.

Dearest Frieda, I do understand that you can't make any plans just now. Just don't make plans without me, OK? I went to see some very purple paintings today. And I bought some pots of herbs for the balcony – though I don't know if they will survive the cold wind that cuts through this city like a knife. I think you could grow to love it here. You could certainly lose yourself in the crowds and the strangeness. There are days when I fancy I glimpse your face among the crowds. A certain lift of your chin. A red scarf. My heart turns over. Surrounded by people I like, I am lonely here without you. My love, Sandy xxxxx

TEN

Jim Fearby never gave up: his doggedness was his gift and his curse. He couldn't help it, he was made that way.

When he was ten and on a school trip, he had seen a demonstration of how to light a fire without a match. It looked simple the way the man in the combat jacket did it – a board with a notch cut into it, a long stick, a handful of dry grass and bark, a minute or so of rolling the spindle between his two palms, and there was an ember catching at the tinder nest, which he gently blew into a flame. One by one the class tried to do the same, and one by one they failed. When Fearby got back home, he spent hours rolling a stick between his palms until they were sore and blistered. Day after day he squatted in their small garden, his neck aching and his hands throbbing, and one day an ember glowed beneath the tip of his stick.

Fearby's mother, who was now long dead, had always declared rather proudly that her son was more stubborn than anyone she had ever met. His wife called it bloody-mindedness. 'You're like a dog with a bone,' she would say. 'You can never let go.' Fellow journalists said the same, sometimes admiringly, sometimes with incredulity or even contempt, and recently with that shake of the head: old Jim Fearby and his notions. Fearby didn't care what they thought. He just rolled his spindle, waited for the ember to catch and grow into a flame.

It had been like that with George Conley. No one else had cared about Conley, barely thought of him as a fellow human being, but he had struck a spark in Fearby, who had sat through every single day of his trial. It was his passivity that touched him: Conley was like a beaten dog just waiting for the next blow. He didn't understand what was happening to him but neither was he surprised by it. He'd probably been bullied and jeered at all his life; he no longer had the hope in him to fight back. Fearby never used words like 'justice' – they were too grandiose for an old hack like him – but it didn't seem fair that this sad lump of a man should have no one to fight his corner.

The first time Jim Fearby had visited George Conley in prison, way back in 2005, the experience had given him nightmares. HMP Mortlemere, down in Kent on the Thames Estuary, wasn't such a bad place and Fearby wasn't sure what it was that had particularly got to him. There were the resigned, tired faces of the women and children in the waiting room. He had listened to their accents. Some of them had come from across the country. There was the smell of damp and disinfectant, and he had kept wondering about the smells the disinfectant was covering up. But, almost embarrassingly, it was mainly the locks and the bars and the high walls and the barbed wire. He had felt like a child who had never properly understood what a prison was. The real punishment is that the doors are locked and you can't go out when you want to.

During the trial, pathetic little Conley had been bemused, almost numb, in the face of so much attention. When Fearby had met him for the first time in prison, he was pale and utterly defeated. 'This is just the beginning,'

Fearby had told him but he seemed barely to be paying attention.

Fearby had seen on his road map that Mortlemere was next to a bird sanctuary. Afterwards he had parked his car and walked along a path by the water, mainly so that the cold northerly wind could blow the rank prison smell off him. But even so he couldn't seem to shake away the stench, and that night and for many nights afterwards, he had dreamed of doors and steel bars and locks and lost keys, of being shut in, of trying to look out at the world through glass so thick that nothing was visible except blurry shapes.

In the years since, in the course of writing articles and finally his book, *Blind Justice*, he had visited Conley in prisons all over England, up in Sunderland, down in Devon, off the M25. Now, visiting him at HMP Haston, in the Midlands, Fearby hardly noticed his surroundings. The parking, the registration, the entrance through multiple doors, had become routine, irritating rather than traumatic. The prison officers knew him, they knew why he was there and mainly they were sympathetic to him – to Fearby and to Conley.

Over the years Fearby had heard of inmates who had used prison as a sort of school. They had learned to read; they had studied for A levels and degrees. But Conley had only got fatter, paler, sadder, more defeated. His dark hair was greasy and lank, he had a long ragged scar down from the corner of one eye, the result of an attack while he was queuing for lunch one day. That had been early in his sentence, when he was the subject of constant threats and abuse. He was jostled in the corridor; his food was interfered with. Finally he was confined to solitary for his own protection. But gradually things changed, as questions were raised, as the campaign began, largely inspired and then sustained by Jim Fearby. Fellow prisoners started to leave him alone and then became positively friendly. In recent years, even the prison officers had softened.

Fearby sat opposite Conley as he had so many times before. Conley had become so fat that his bloodshot eyes almost disappeared in the fleshy slits in his face. He compulsively scratched at the top of his left hand. Fearby made himself smile. Everything was good. They were winning. They should both be happy.

'Did Diana come to see you?' he asked.

Diana McKerrow was the solicitor who had taken over Conley's case for the latest appeal. At first Fearby had worked closely with her. After all, he had known more about the case than anyone else in the world. He knew the weak links, all the people involved. But as the case had proceeded, she had stopped phoning him. She had been harder to reach. Fearby tried not to mind. What mattered was the result, wasn't it? That was what he told himself.

'She phoned,' said Conley, never quite looking Fearby in the face.

'Did she tell you about the appeal?' Fearby spoke slowly, separating each word, as if he was talking to a small child.

'Yeah, I think so.'

'It's all good news,' said Fearby. 'They've got the details of the illegal interview.' Conley's expression didn't change. 'When the police picked you up, they didn't interview you properly. They didn't warn you. They didn't explain things the way they should have done. They didn't pay attention

94

to your . . .' Fearby paused. At the next table a man and a woman were facing each other, not speaking. 'Your special needs,' said Fearby. 'That's enough on its own to quash the conviction. But added to the details of your alibi that the prosecution suppressed . . .'

Fearby stopped. He could see from the blank look in Conley's eyes that he had lost his attention.

'You don't need to get bogged down in the details,' said Fearby. 'I just wanted to come and say to you that I know what you've gone through all these years. All that stuff, all that shit. I don't know how you did it. But you just need to hang on a bit longer, be strong, and it'll all come right. You hear what I'm saying?'

'Coming right,' said Conley.

'There's something else,' said Fearby. 'I wanted to say that it's good, but it'll be hard as well. When someone gets paroled, they prepare them for months. They take you out on visits, you know, walks in the park, trips to the seaside. Then, when you're on the outside, you get to stay in a halfway house and they check up on you. You've heard that, haven't you?' Conley nodded. Fearby couldn't make out if he was really following what he was saying. 'But it won't be like that for you. If the appeal court quashes your conviction, you'll just walk free that minute, straight out the door. It'll be difficult. You should be prepared for that.'

Fearby waited for a reaction, but Conley just seemed puzzled. 'I just came up here today to tell you that I'm your friend. Like I've always been. When you're out, you might want to tell your story. A lot of people would be interested in what you've been through. It's an old-fashioned tragedy-and-triumph story. I know about these things and you'll want to put your own side of the story because if you don't people will do it for you. I can help you with that. I've been telling your story right from the beginning, when no one else would believe you. I'm your friend, George. If you want help telling your story, I can do that for you.' Fearby paused, but the reaction still didn't come. 'Are you all right for things at the moment? Anything I can get you?'

Conley shrugged. Fearby said goodbye and that he'd be in touch. In the old days he would have driven home however late it was, but since his wife had left him and the children had gone, he usually made a day of it. People joked about the hotels at motorway service stations, but they suited him. He'd got a cheap deal at this one. Thirty-two pounds fifty. Free parking. Coffee and tea in the room. A colour TV. Clean. Except for the paper flap across the toilet bowl, there was no sign that anyone else had ever been in there.

He had the usual luggage. His little suitcase. His laptop. And the bag with the files. The real files were back at home. They filled most of his office. These were the ones he needed for reference: the basic names and numbers and facts, a few photos and statements. As always, his first action was to take the purple pending file from the bag and open it on the little desk next to the colour TV. While the miniature white plastic kettle was starting to heat up, he took a new sheet of lined paper, wrote the date and time of the meeting at the top and noted everything that had been said.

When he had finished, he made himself a cup of

instant coffee and removed a biscuit from its plastic wrapping. It was then that he remembered his first visit to Conley at Mortlemere. 'This is the beginning,' he'd said, 'not the end.' He looked at the file. He thought of the room full of files at home. He thought of his marriage, the squabbles, the silences and then the ending. It had seemed sudden, but it turned out that Sandra had been planning it for months, finding a new flat, talking to a solicitor. 'What will you do when it ends?' she had said – referring not to their marriage but to this case, in the days when they still talked of such things. It was more like an accusation than a question. Because there never really were endings. He'd been thinking he could produce a new edition of his book if Conley was released. But it felt wrong now. The book was just negatives: why this hadn't happened, why that wasn't true, why this was misleading.

The question now was different and new: if George Conley hadn't killed Hazel Barton, who had?

Eleven

'Northern countries,' said Josef. 'They all drink the same.'

'What do you mean, drink the same?'

Josef was driving Frieda in his old van. They were on the way to Islington because Olivia had rung in a near-hysterical state to say that the washbasin in the upstairs bathroom had been ripped off the wall during the party and she needed it repaired. Urgently. And she was never, ever going to have teenagers in her house again. Josef had agreed to abandon the bathroom briefly to help Olivia. Frieda felt strangely torn in her emotional reaction. There was Josef taking a break from doing up her bathroom for nothing in order to help her sister-in-law. Not for nothing: Frieda would insist on that, if she had to pay for it herself. At the same time he was constantly in her house, which had stopped being her own. And each time she looked at what had once been her bathroom, its state seemed to be getting worse rather than better.

'In the south, they drink wine and stay upright. In the north they drink clear liquid and fall down.'

'You mean they drink to get drunk.'

'Forget cares, lose sorrow, escape darkness.'

Josef swerved to avoid a man who stepped blithely out into the road, his ears encased in giant yellow headphones.

'So, at this party, were there lots of people drinking clear liquid and falling down?'

'They learn too young.' Josef gave a huge, sentimental sigh. 'The recovery position.'

'That sounds ominous.'

'No. no. This is just life. People fight, people dance, people kiss and hold, people talk about dreams, people break things, people are sick.'

'All in a few hours.'

'Chloë, she did not have such a good time.'

'Really?'

'She kept trying to clear the mess. No one should clear the mess before the party is over. Except for broken glass.'

Josef drew up outside Olivia's house and they got out of the van. Olivia opened the door before Frieda rang. She was wearing a man's dressing gown and her face was tragic.

'I just had to go to bed,' she said. 'Everything's such a mess.'

'It was quite a mess before,' said Frieda. 'You said you wouldn't notice a bit extra.'

'I was wrong. It's not only the washbasin. My blue lamp is broken. My wheelbarrow is broken because they tried to see how many people could fit in it and still be moved – that, apparently, was your friend Jack's idea. How old is he? I thought he was an adult, not a toddler. And my nice coat has disappeared, Kieran's favourite hat he left before he went away has a cigarette burn in the crown.' Kieran was her mild and patient boyfriend – or perhaps her ex. 'The neighbours have complained about all the bottles dumped in their gardens and the noise, and someone has peed into my ornamental orange tree in the hall.'

99

'I will fix the washbasin anyway,' said Josef. 'And perhaps the wheelbarrow too.'

'Thank you,' said Olivia, fervently.

'Don't let him take the washbasin away,' said Frieda.

'What?'

'Is a joke,' said Josef. 'Is a joke against me by Frieda.'

'I'm sorry, Josef, I didn't mean that.' She looked at the wheelbarrow. 'How many did it hold?'

Olivia gave a shaky giggle. 'Something ludicrous, like seven. Standing up. It's lucky nobody got themselves killed.'

Although it was days later, the floor was still sticky underfoot. Pictures hung lopsidedly on the wall. There was the sweet smell of alcohol in the air, and Frieda saw dirty smudges on the paintwork and grime on the stair carpets.

'It's like one of those children's picture books: spot the hidden object,' said Olivia, pointing at a glass inside a shoe. 'I keep finding unspeakable things.'

'You mean condoms?' asked Josef.

'No! Oh, God, what happened that I don't know about?'

'No, no, is all right. I go on up.' He bounded up the stairs, carrying his bag.

'Let's have something to drink,' said Olivia, leading the way into the kitchen. 'Sorry! I didn't know you were back from school.'

Chloë was sitting at the table, and opposite her was a gangly, dishevelled figure: a mop of greasy, dark-blond hair, feet in trainers with the laces undone, jeans sliding down his skinny frame. He turned his head and Frieda saw a thin, pallid face, hollow eyes. He looked bruised and wrung-out. Ted: the boy she had last seen retching over the toilet bowl. The boy who had just lost his mother. He met her gaze and a hectic blush mottled his cheeks. He muttered something incoherent and slumped further over the table with his face half hidden by one hand. Nails bitten to the quick. A little tattoo – or probably an ink drawing – on his thin wrist.

'Hello, Frieda,' said Chloë. 'I wasn't expecting you. It's not chemistry today, you know.'

'I'm here with Josef.'

'The washbasin.'

'Yes.'

'It must have been loose anyway. It just came away.'

'Because two people sat on it!' Olivia lowered her voice. 'Aren't you going to introduce me to your friend?'

Chloë looked embarrassed. 'This is Ted. Ted, my mum.'

Ted squinted up at Olivia and managed a hello. Olivia marched up to him, grabbed his limp, unwilling hand and shook it firmly. 'I'm so pleased to meet you,' she said. 'I keep telling Chloë she should bring friends home. Especially handsome young men like you.'

'Mum! That's why I don't.'

'Ted doesn't mind. Do you, Ted?'

'And this is Frieda,' said Chloë, hastily. 'She's my aunt.' She cast a beseeching glance at Frieda.

'Hello.' Frieda nodded at him. If it were possible, he turned even more crimson and stuttered something incoherent. She could see that he wanted to run and hide from the woman who'd seen him vomiting – weeping too.

'Shall we go to my room?' Chloë asked Ted, and he slid

off the chair, a raw-boned, awkward, self-conscious young man, all angles and sharp edges.

'I heard about your mother,' Frieda said. 'I'm very sorry for your loss.'

She felt Olivia stiffen. Ted stared at her, his pupils enormous. Chloë picked up one of his hands and held it between her own to comfort him. For a moment he seemed stranded in his emotions, unable to move or speak.

'Thank you,' he said at last. 'It's just . . . Thanks.'

'I hope you're all receiving proper help.'

'What?' hissed Olivia, as Chloë led Ted from the room, glancing back over her shoulder with bright eyes. 'Is that –'

'Her friend whose mother was killed. Yes.'

Olivia's hand flew to her mouth. 'I didn't make the connection. Poor boy. Poor, poor boy. What a dreadful thing. He's quite attractive, isn't he, in a grungy kind of way? Do you think Chloë's in love with him? What a calamity. I mean what happened to him. At such an age, too. Just think of it! Let's have that drink.'

Billy Hunt stared up at Karlsson. His eyes were bloodshot and he was twitchier and thinner than ever, but he wasn't budging.

Karlsson sighed. 'You're making life hard for us and hard for yourself. You've admitted breaking and entering; the stolen items have been traced back to you; the murder weapon with your prints all over it, and Mrs Lennox's blood, has been found. Just admit what you did.'

'Unless I didn't do it.'

'The jury won't believe you.' Karlsson stood up. His head felt tight with weariness and irritation. Now his team would have to trawl through the evidence to put a watertight case together. The time he wanted to be spending with his children, Bella and Mikey, would be spent instead examining statements, going through the house again, talking to expert witnesses, making sure the correct procedures had been followed.

'Wait.'

'What now?'

'I wanted to say – there is somewhere I went just before.'

'Before?'

'Before . . . you know.'

'Tell me anyway.'

'Before I went to the house, where she was.'

'Mrs Lennox.'

'Right. I went to another place first.'

'Which you haven't told us about?'

'Right.' Billy bobbed his head up and down. 'You'll see why.'

'Hang on, Billy. If you're going to change your statement, we need to do this officially. I'll come back.'

In the corridor, he met Riley.

'Hey,' said Riley.

'What?'

'I've just come from Margaretting Street,' said Riley. 'We found something. Under the mat. In fact, I found it. Munster thought you'd want to know.'

'What is it?'

Riley held up a transparent evidence sachet. Inside was

a used envelope on which was scrawled a message, written with a blunt pencil.

Karlsson took it and held it up: 'Hello, Ruth, I'm here but where are you? Maybe in the bath. Give us a call when you read this, and we can have our tea.' At the end there was what looked like two interlocking initials or perhaps a signature. 'What's this?'

'Munster thinks it's a "D" and an "M" but I think it's "O" and "N".'

'It might have been there for months. Who's following it up?'

'DC Long, sir, and Munster. But I'm going back there later. It's probably not so important, though, is it, even if it is recent? I mean, if Billy killed her, it doesn't really matter what time exactly she died, right?'

'No, it could be important,' said Karlsson, thoughtfully.

'You're welcome, then,' said Riley, with a cheerful smile.

Karlsson raised his eyebrows. 'Just get back to Margaretting Street,' he said.

Yvette Long showed the note to Russell Lennox, who stared at it, then shook his head. 'I don't recognize the writing.'

'What about the initials?'

'Are those initials? Is that a "G"?'

'A "G"?'

'Or maybe it says Gail.'

'Do you know a Gail?'

'I don't think so. Or it could be Delia, or even Dell. I don't know a Delia either, or a Dell. Or it could just be a squiggle.'

'Which of your wife's friends used to pop round during the day?'

'Oh.' Russell Lennox frowned. 'Lots. I don't know. She knew almost everyone in our neighbourhood. There are her friends and then people she's friendly with – and she helps organize the street party every year, which means people are always coming in and out. And then there are her friends who aren't so local. She was very popular, my wife. I was always amazed at how many people she kept in contact with. You should see her Christmas card list.' He stared at Yvette and shook his head slowly from side to side. 'I can't believe I'm already using the past tense,' he said. 'Was. She was. As if it happened years ago.'

'We've got her address book on her computer,' said Yvette. 'We can look through that. But if you think of anyone in the meantime –'

'I thought you'd got the guy who did it?'

'We're just crossing the 't's,' said Yvette.

'I've been trying to remember the last thing we said to each other. I think I said I'd be back a bit later than usual, and then she reminded me not to forget my cousin's birthday.'

'Well,' Yvette said awkwardly.

'At first I thought that was too prosaic. But it's typical of her. She always remembered birthdays and anniversaries and stuff like that.'

'Mr Lennox –'

'I did forget my cousin's birthday, of course. It was yesterday and I didn't remember until now.'

'That's understandable.'

'I suppose so.' His tone was dull.

*

Jennifer Wall said that Ruth had been the perfect neighbour, friendly without being nosy, always ready to lend eggs or sugar or milk, even nice when one of her boys had kicked a football through the Lennoxes' kitchen window.

Sue Leadbetter remembered the time, not long ago, when Ruth had taken care of her while she'd had flu – bringing Lemsip and loo paper to the house, even getting papers and magazines for her.

Gaby Ford said she used to meet Ruth almost every morning when they both left for work. They would greet each other and sometimes exchange a few words. Ruth had a way, she said, of putting one arm on her shoulder for a few minutes, which she had always appreciated. She was often in a bit of a rush but she was always cheerful, and it was no different during the days leading to her death. She'd never known her down in the dumps or hungover. They were such a nice family. A close family. You didn't come across that so much nowadays.

Jodie Daniels, one of her oldest friends, had seen her at the weekend. They had gone to the garden centre together and then had coffee. Ruth was just normal – unaffected, interested in other people, a bit concerned that Judith wasn't working properly for her GCSEs. They had talked about whether or not she should dye her hair now that it was rapidly turning grey and Ruth had decided she wouldn't. She had said she wanted to grow old gracefully. Oh, God.

Graham Walters had bumped into Ruth's car, two days before she died, and scraped it. She had been incredibly understanding, which was typical. That was the last time he had seen her.

She had bent down and stroked Elspeth Weaver's dog the morning of her death, then got into her car.

She had reversed down the road to make way for Robert Morgan, driving in the opposite direction.

She had phoned that morning from work and told Juliet Melchett that she and Russell would love to come to the Melchetts' party.

At eleven a.m., also from work, she had ordered a bunch of flowers from John Lewis to be sent to Russell's aunt, who had broken her hip.

But none of those people had gone round there and pushed a note through the door.

However, with Dawn Wilmer, who lived two streets away and whose eldest son was in the same class as Ruth's youngest daughter, they finally struck lucky. She recognized the note as hers.

'You pushed this through her door?'

'Yes.'

'On the day she died.'

'Wednesday. Yes. Should I have said? I mean, I spoke to an officer and said I hadn't seen anything suspicious, and I thought I said I was round by her house earlier, but perhaps I didn't. I mean, I didn't go in or anything. I didn't see anything strange or suspicious.'

'What time would this have been?'

'I don't know, just after four. Before four thirty, anyway. I'm sure of that because Danny – that's my son – comes home late that day and I knew Dora did as well. That was why Ruth suggested I go round for tea – we didn't know each other that well. I'm quite new in the neighbourhood and my son's only just started at the school. It was nice of her.'

'So – you went round for tea, as arranged, and she wasn't there.'

'She was there. She just didn't come to the door.'

'Why do you say that?'

'Her car was there. All the lights were on.'

'Did you wait for a long time?'

'A minute or so, no more. I knocked and rang the bell – I even shouted through the letterbox. I didn't have my phone with me so I couldn't call her and that was why I pushed the note through.'

'Between four and half past four, you say?'

'After four and before four thirty.' The woman's face wrinkled anxiously. 'Do you think – is it possible – that she was in there dead?'

'We're just trying to establish timings,' said Yvette, neutrally. 'You're sure you didn't see anything unusual?'

'Nothing.'

'And you stood at the door for about a minute?'

'Yes.'

'You saw no broken window? Next to the front door.'

'No. I'm sure I would have noticed that.'

'All right. Thank you very much for your help.'

Billy Hunt dragged the back of his hand against his nose. 'I was somewhere else.'

'Before you went to the house in Margaretting Street?'

'That's right. I just want to say that this sounds worse than it was. There weren't any kids there.'

'Where?'

'There's this nursery school. But it was empty. It's not finished yet.'

'Why did you go there?'

'Why d'you think?'

'All right, what did you take?'

'Nothing,' said Hunt, holding out his palms as if to prove it. 'It was empty.'

'Did you break in?'

'Through the back. I broke one pane of glass and that was all it took. They need to tighten their security before they open. Cut my hand, though.'

'What was the name of this nursery?'

'Busy Bees.'

'And where is it?'

'Over in Islington, just up from the Caledonian Road.'

'What time?'

'I don't know. About four maybe.'

'So at about four o'clock last Wednesday you claim you were breaking into a children's nursery in Islington. What did you do then?'

'I was going to walk back home along the canal but it started to rain. I saw a bus and jumped on it. The one five three. It took me to Camden. I was having a smoke so they threw me off and I walked up from there. I was just going along the road and ringing on a few doorbells until I found one where they didn't answer.'

'What then?'

'I told you all that before. I broke the window, opened the door. The alarm was going, so I was in a rush. There were alarms everywhere. There was one in the hallway and one in the room where . . . you know, she was. I just grabbed a few things and headed off.' He shook his head. 'It's not my fault. If it hadn't been raining, I wouldn't have caught the bus and I wouldn't have been there.'

Karlsson switched off the recorder. 'And Mrs Lennox would still have been alive.'

'No,' said Hunt. 'That's not what I said. Put the tape back on.'

'Forget about the bloody tape.'

TWELVE

As Frieda approached her front door, key in hand, she saw that it was already open. She couldn't see at first what was happening but then saw there was a man at one end of a large, undeniably impressive bath, and then she saw that the man was Josef's friend, Stefan, and that Josef was at the other end. The second thing Frieda noticed was that the bath was almost too wide for the doorway. She could see that by the grey scraping marks on the doorpost. The third thing she noticed was that they were carrying the bath outwards rather than inwards.

'Frieda,' said Stefan, panting slightly. 'I can't shake hands.'

'Are you having trouble getting it in?'

'No,' said Josef, from the other end. 'We take in fine and upstairs. But problem. Now we take it out and back.'

'What do you mean "back"?' said Frieda.

'Wait.'

With much groaning and a suppressed scream when Josef got his fingers trapped between the bath and the doorway, they got it outside and laid it down on the cobblestones.

'That bath is fucking heavy,' said Stefan, then looked at Frieda guiltily. 'Sorry. It is big, though.'

'But why are you taking it out?'

'Is heavy,' said Josef. 'Hard for floor, I think. We check it now. Probably need joist.'

Frieda heard the phone ringing inside. 'You mean a steel girder?' she said.

'So you don't fall through floor in bath.'

'Well, you'd know about that,' said Frieda. 'Are you sure?'

Stefan smiled. 'We are sure.'

'What do you mean?' said Frieda. The phone was still ringing. 'Hang on.' She pushed past them, but before she could reach the phone, it had stopped. It was almost a relief, something that didn't have to be dealt with, someone who didn't have to be talked to. She stood still for a moment, watching Josef and Stefan pushing the bath back into Josef's van. It seemed to sag under the weight of it. And then the phone rang again, insistently, like a person jabbing at her. She picked it up and heard a woman's voice.

'Can I speak to Dr Frieda Klein, please?'

'Who is this?'

'My name's Jilly Freeman. I'm calling from the *Sunday Sketch*.' There was a pause. 'I'm sorry. Are you still there?'

'Yes,' said Frieda.

'We're running a story in tomorrow's paper and we'd like to hear your comments on it.'

'Why?'

'Because it concerns you.'

Frieda felt a stab of dread and at the same time a numbness, as if she was receiving a blow on a part of her body that had been hit before and then had partially healed. She felt an impulse to smash the phone rather than continue the conversation. Was it something to do with the attack? Were the police reconsidering it? Were the press trying to sniff something out?

'What is it?' she said.

'You've seen a patient called Seamus Dunne.'

This was so unexpected that Frieda had to think, just to recall the name. At the same time, Josef stepped into her line of sight and gestured that they were leaving.

'We need to talk,' she said to him.

'Soon.' Josef backed away.

'What?' said the woman on the phone.

'I was talking to someone else. How do you know about Seamus Dunne?'

'Dr Klein, it might be better if I could come round to your house and conduct a proper interview in person.'

Frieda took a deep breath and, as she did so, caught a glimpse of her reflection in the glass of a picture on the wall. Was that person really her? The thought of someone else, anyone else, coming round to her house made her feel sick. 'Just tell me what this is about.'

'All we're doing is reporting on some new psychological research which we think is really important. As you know, some people think that psychoanalysts aren't sufficiently accountable to the public.' Jilly Freeman left a silence that Frieda didn't break. 'Well, anyway, there's this academic called Hal Bradshaw who has been conducting research. Do you know him?'

'Yes,' said Frieda. 'I do.'

'Well, what he's done is to select some prominent analysts – and you're one of them. And then he sent people to see these analysts with instructions to show the identical classic symptoms of a person who was an imminent danger to the public, to see how the analyst responded.' There was another pause and Frieda didn't speak. 'So I was ringing to ask if you had any comment.'

'You haven't asked me a question.'

'From what I understand,' said Jilly Freeman, 'this patient, Seamus Dunne . . .'

'You said he was pretending to be a patient.'

'Yes, as part of this research project, and he displayed what are the clear, accepted signs of being a violent psychopath.'

'Which are?' said Frieda.

'Um . . .' said Jilly Freeman. There was a pause and Frieda heard pages being turned. 'Yes, here it is. Each of the supposed patients were to talk of having been violent towards animals in their childhood and then to have vivid fantasies of attacking women and to talk about putting these into practice. Did Seamus Dunne talk about that?'

'I don't discuss what my patients say in their sessions.'

'But he wasn't a real patient. And he's talked about it. He gave me an interview.'

'As part of the research project?' said Frieda.

She looked around for a chair and sat down. Suddenly she felt utterly exhausted, as if she might go to sleep even while she was talking. It was as if she had locked the door and blocked the windows and they'd still managed to get in through a gap she'd missed.

'What we want to know for our piece on the research is whether you reported any concerns to the authorities.'

There was a ring at the door.

'Wait a minute,' said Frieda. 'I've got to let someone in.'

She opened the door. It was Reuben.

'Frieda, I just —' he began, but she held up her hand to silence him and waved him inside. She noticed that he seemed dishevelled and distracted. He walked past her and disappeared into the kitchen.

'What were you saying?' said Frieda.

'I wanted to ask you if you'd reported any concerns to the authorities.'

Frieda was distracted by the sound of clinking from the kitchen. Reuben reappeared with a can of beer.

'No,' said Frieda. 'I didn't.'

Reuben mouthed something at her, then took a large gulp of beer from the can.

'From what we've been informed,' continued Jilly Freeman, 'this experiment was designed to present various therapists with a patient who was a clear, present danger to the community. The patient was a psychopath and it was your duty — in fact, it was your legal responsibility — to report him to the police. Could you comment on that?'

'But he wasn't a psychopath,' said Frieda.

'Is it her?' said Reuben. 'Is it fucking her?'

'What are you talking about?' Frieda hissed.

'What?' said Jilly Freeman.

'I'm not talking to you.' Frieda angrily waved Reuben away. 'You've said yourself that he wasn't a psychopath. There was no need to report him. I may have had some concerns about this particular man, but I wouldn't discuss that with anyone but him.'

'I'm sorry,' said Jilly Freeman, 'but this experiment was to test how therapists respond when they are confronted with a patient who shows the classic signs, established by research over the years, of being a psychopath. The public will want to know whether they are being protected.'

'I'm going to talk to you for one more minute,' said Frieda, 'and then I'm putting the phone down. You've told me that he wasn't actually a psychopath. He was just saying psychopathic things.'

'Don't psychopaths say psychopathic things? What else do you have to go on, apart from what patients say to you?'

'And second, as I said to Seamus Dunne himself, psychopaths don't ask for help. He was talking about lack of empathy but he wasn't displaying it. That's my answer.'

'And you trusted yourself to ignore the classic signs of a psychopath?'

'Your minute's up,' said Frieda, and ended the call.

She looked at Reuben. 'What are you doing here?' she said.

'I just saw Josef driving away.'

'He's working on my bathroom.'

'I guess that's why I can't track him down.' His expression hardened. 'It was her, wasn't it? It was that journalist, what's her name?'

'It was a woman called Jilly Freeman,' said Frieda.

'That's it, that's the one.'

'How do you know?'

Reuben emptied his glass. 'Because they've done it to me as well,' he said. 'They've fucked me the way they've fucked you. Jilly rang me up and broke the news to me, and in the middle of our conversation she mentioned your name as well. I tried to ring you but there was no answer.'

'I've been out,' said Frieda.

'I thought I'd better come straight round. Jesus, I need a cigarette. Can we go outside?'

He fetched another can of beer from the kitchen, then opened the door and stepped outside onto the street. Frieda followed him. He handed her the beer while he lit his cigarette. He took a succession of deep drags on it. 'This young man,' said Reuben. 'He said he wanted to talk to me. He'd heard such good things about me. He was worried about himself. He'd been cruel to animals as a child, he had fantasies of hurting women. Blah blah, you know the rest.'

'What did you say to him?'

'I said I'd see him for a bit. And then Ms Jilly rings me up and tells me that I'm going to be on the front page for letting a psychopath loose on the streets.'

'What did you say to her?'

He took another deep drag on his cigarette. 'I should have said what you said. That sounded good. I lost it. I just shouted at her and slammed the phone down.' He jabbed a finger at Frieda. 'We're going to sue them. That fucker Hal Bradshaw and that fucking journalist and her paper. We're going to take them down.'

'What for?' said Frieda.

Reuben banged his fist against the wall of the house. 'For deception,' he said. 'And violating our privacy. And for libel.'

'We're not going to sue them,' said Frieda.

'I was going to say that it's all right for you,' said Reuben. 'But you're in a state of distress. You're recovering from injury. They can't do this to us.'

Frieda put a hand on his shoulder. 'We should just leave it,' she said.

Reuben turned to Frieda and something in his look alarmed her, fierce and defeated at the same time. 'I know, I know,' he said. 'I should just shrug it off. Ten years ago I would have laughed it off. I would almost have welcomed it. But I feel I've had it. That journalist. I'll show her fantasies about hurting women.'

People had been gathering since midday, but there had been minor delays, the last spasms of a clogged bureaucratic system that had kept George Conley in prison for months after it had become clear he would have to be released. It was nearly three o'clock in the afternoon when he eventually emerged from Haston Prison into watery sunlight, clutching one plastic bag and wearing an overcoat that was too tight and much too thick for a spring day. There were beads of sweat on his pale, fleshy face.

Most of the people waiting for him were journalists and photographers. His local MP was there as well, although Fearby knew how little he had done for Conley, only joining the campaign when it was clear it would be successful. A small group from a revolutionary organization had come with banners proclaiming the bigotry of the police force in general. But there were no relatives waiting for Conley. His mother had died while he was in prison and his sister hadn't been to see him since he was arrested. She had told Fearby that she was glad she was married and had taken the name of her husband, because his name made her feel sick. She wanted nothing to do with him. And there were no friends either: he had always been a lonely figure in the small town where he had lived, someone who stood on the edge, looking in baffled wistfulness at life going on. After he was arrested, neighbours said that they had always known he was odd, creepy. It hadn't surprised them at all. Apart from Fearby, he had had no visitors in prison until the last few weeks.

Diana McKerrow, Conley's solicitor, stood near the gates holding a bottle of sparkling wine in readiness. She spoke to the press on behalf of her client, reading from a piece of paper that she pulled out of her jacket pocket: words about the scandal of the police investigation, the lost years that Conley would never recover, the faith of a few good souls who had never ceased to believe in his innocence. She didn't mention Fearby by name, and Fearby himself stood apart from the small crowd. He didn't know what he'd been expecting. After so many years of working towards this moment, it felt thin and dreary. One overweight man shuffling anxiously out of the gates, wincing as the cameras flashed.

The journalists surged forward. Microphones were held out to him.

'How does it feel to be free?'

'Are you going to sue?'

'What are your plans now, Mr Conley?'

'Where will you go?'

'What's the first thing you'll do?'

'Are you angry?'

'What have you missed?'

'Can you tell us your thoughts about the police?'

Fearby was certain that some of them had chequebooks ready. They wanted his story now. All these years he'd been vilified and then forgotten; now he was a hero – except he didn't fit the role of hero. His replies came out in mumbles, half-sentences: 'I dunno,' he said. 'What d'you mean?' He glanced from side to side anxiously. Diana McKerrow put one arm under his elbow. His MP arranged himself on the other side, smiling for the cameras.

Fearby knew that they would all soon forget about Conley again. He would be left in peace, in his little room in a house full of other misfits and loners, passive and defeated. He felt a pang of simultaneous guilt followed at once by resentment: was he going to have to be Conley's only friend even now? Visit him and take him out for a drink, try to find him an occupation? Was this his reward for freeing him into the world?

He inched his way through the crush and touched Conley on the arm. 'Hello, George,' he said. 'Congratulations.'

'Hello,' said Conley. He smelt unwashed; his skin had a grey prison-pallor and his hair was thinning.

'You're going to be busy for the rest of the day. I just wanted to say hello and give you my phone number. When you want, give me a call and I'll come and see you.' He forced enthusiasm into his voice. 'We can have a meal, go for a drink, a walk.' He hesitated. 'You might find all this attention hard, but it'll die down soon. You'll need to think about what you're going to do next.'

'Next?'

'I'll come and see you.'

Conley stared at him, his lower lip hanging loose. He was like a small, fat child, thought Fearby. It didn't feel like a happy ending.

*

Later, at the press conference, the officer in charge of the investigation read out a statement. He wished to be candid about the fact that mistakes had been made. George Conley's confession to the murder of Hazel Barton had been obtained – here he coughed, grimaced – without following the proper procedures.

'You mean illegally,' someone shouted from the back.

Steps had been taken, the officer continued. Reprimands delivered. Procedures tightened. The same mistakes would not be made again.

'What about Mr Conley?' asked a young woman in the front row.

'I'm sorry?'

'He's been in prison since 2005.'

'And we're sorry for the mistakes that were made.'

'Has anyone been fired?' called a voice.

The inspector's face tightened. 'As I say, we have looked very carefully at the way the investigation was conducted. Individual officers have been reprimanded. But it would not be in anyone's interest to make a scapegoat out of . . .'

Fearby thought that the message was very clear. The police believed that Conley was the killer but had got off on a technicality. What was more, they were making sure that everyone else in the room understood that. He felt anger rise in him.

'Excuse me,' he called out, in a loud voice. 'I have a question for you.'

Heads turned. There he was, Jim Fearby, the one who'd been obsessed with the case for years. A journalist who'd been around for decades, one of the old breed who got hold of a story and wouldn't let go. He was in his sixties now, stooped and silver-haired. He looked a bit like a bird of prey, with his beaked nose and pale eyes, wind-blown and weather-blasted.

'Mr Fearby,' said the inspector, smiling with no warmth. 'Yes?'

'Now that George Conley has been released, an innocent man . . .' he paused to let the words fill the room '. . . can you tell us what steps you will be taking to find out the real perpetrator? After all, a young woman was brutally murdered.'

The inspector coughed again, a hard and hacking sound to give him time to prepare his answer. 'At present, there are no new leads,' he said eventually.

'At present?'

'As I said. Any more questions?'

Fearby drove home through the gathering dusk. Conley's last prison, unlike his previous ones, had been quite close to where he lived – in a small town just outside Birmingham. When Sandra had left him, he'd thought he would perhaps go somewhere different – the Lake District, perhaps, or even further north, where cold, clean winds blew off the hills. He could begin again. But in the end he'd stayed, surrounded by his files, his books, his pictures, his DVDs of old films. It didn't matter so much where he lived; it was just a place to sleep, to think.

He went into his study and gazed at the piles of notebooks and folders that were filled with the evidence of his obsession: police reports, legal reports, letters sent and received, petitions . . . He poured himself a large slug of gin because he'd run out of whisky and added water because he'd run out of tonic. What sailors used to drink, he thought – a sad, solitary drink to get you through the hours. He must have fallen asleep in his chair, because when the phone rang it felt at first like part of a dream.

'Is that Jim Fearby?'

'Who is it?'

'I saw you at the press conference. Are you still writing about the case?'

'What's it matter?' Fearby still felt only half awake.

'I want to meet you.'

'Why?'

'You know a pub called the Philip Sidney?'

'No.'

'You can find it. I'll be there at five tomorrow evening.'

I tried to call you. When we see each other, I'm going to give you a short lesson in how to use your mobile! (Mainly, leave it turned on and have it with you.) Now it's probably too late to try again. You'll be asleep. Or perhaps you'll be stalking the streets of London with that frown on your face. Speak soon and until then, take care of your dear self. S xxxxx

Thirteen

Karlsson sat opposite Billy Hunt. 'You must be the world's worst burglar,' he said.

'So you saw I was telling the truth?'

'Busy Bees,' said Karlsson. 'Apart from the fact that it's a nursery school that is being built for little children, and that stealing from them doesn't seem right, what the hell did you expect to get from them? Stuffed toys?'

'There was building work going on,' said Hunt. 'I thought there might be some tools around.'

'But there weren't.'

'No. I didn't find anything.'

'On the bright side,' said Karlsson, 'it was a building site, which meant there were plenty of CCTV cameras and I saw the best images I've ever seen. You could have used some of them for your passport photo.'

'I told you I was there.'

'But, as we know, you were also at the murder scene. You need to tell us about that.'

Hunt bit the side of his thumb. 'If I tell you everything, will you drop the burglary charge?'

'Oh, shut up,' said Karlsson. 'I'm not even sure we're dropping the murder charge. Just tell us everything and stop messing me about.'

Hunt thought.

'I needed some cash,' he said. 'I owed someone. Look, I've told you all this before.'

'Tell me again.'

'I ended up on Margaretting Street. I rang on a few doorbells, and when someone answered, I asked if Steve was in and then said I must have the wrong address. I got to that house. There was no answer. I got in.'

'How?'

'I picked half a brick off a skip and smashed the window next to the front door. Then I opened it.'

'Weren't you surprised it wasn't double-locked?' said Karlsson. 'Or locked on a chain?'

'If it had been double-locked, I wouldn't have been able to get in.'

'But if it isn't double-locked,' said Karlsson, 'that suggests someone is at home.'

'But I'd already tried the doorbell.'

'Forget it. Go on, then.'

'I went in. Took some stuff from the kitchen. Then I went into the other room and . . . you know.'

'What?'

'She was lying there.'

'What did you do?'

'I don't know,' said Hunt. 'I was in shock.'

'Why didn't you call an ambulance?'

Hunt shook his head. 'The alarm was going off. I just got out.'

'Except you took the cog.'

'That's right.'

'Although it had been used as the murder weapon and was covered with her blood.'

'I had a couple of plastic shopping bags from the kitchen.'

'Why didn't you call the police?' said Karlsson.

'Because I was being a burglar,' said Hunt. 'I mean, I'm not a burglar but at that moment I was in the middle of taking things. Anyway, I wasn't thinking straight.'

'So what did you do?'

'I got out. Ran away.'

'And then?'

'I had this stuff to sell. I told you, I needed cash.'

'So you sold all the silver?'

'Right.'

'Except the cog?'

'It needed, you know . . .'

'The blood cleaning off it?'

'I felt bad about it,' said Hunt. 'Seeing her there. What was I meant to do?'

Karlsson stood up. 'I don't know, Billy. I wouldn't know where to begin.'

FOURTEEN

'Frieda?'

'Hello, Chloë.' Frieda walked through to the living room with the phone and eased her sore body into the armchair by the hearth where in the winter she lit a fire every day. Now that it was spring and the weather was balmy, the sky a delicate washed blue, it stood empty. 'Are you OK?'

'I need to see you.'

'Before Friday?' Friday was the day that Frieda taught her chemistry, which Chloë loathed with a scowling intensity.

'Now.'

'Why?'

'I wouldn't ask if it wasn't important.'

It was nearly six o'clock. Frieda thought of the pot of tea, the slice of quiche she'd bought from Number 9 for her supper, the quiet evening in the dimly lit cocoon of her house that she'd planned, sitting in her study with her soft-leaded pencils and her thick-grained paper, the answering machine turned on and no demands on her, then the softness of her pillows and the sealing darkness. Maybe no dreams, just oblivion. She could say no.

'I'll be there in half an hour.'

'I'm not at home. I'm in a café near the Roundhouse. You can't miss it. It's got this giant upside-down aeroplane hanging outside and it's an alternative art gallery as well.'

'Hang on, Chloë –'

'Thanks, Frieda!' Chloë interrupted enthusiastically, then ended the call before Frieda could change her mind.

The café was named, for no obvious reason, Joe's Malt House, and there was indeed a large upside-down plane nose-diving down its outside wall. Frieda pushed open the door and went into a long, dark room cluttered with tables and mismatched chairs, the walls hung with paintings she could barely make out in the gloom. People were sitting at tables and milling about at the bar that cut across the middle of the room. Music played, throbbing and insistent; the air was thick with the smell of beer, coffee and incense.

'Do you need a table?' asked a young woman dressed in shredded black, with a lightning streak tattooed down her cheek. Her accent was upper-class Estuary. Her boots were like the Terminator's.

Frieda heard her name and squinted up the room. She made out Chloë at the far end, waving her arms in the air to attract her attention.

'This had better be important.'

'Beer?'

'No, thank you.'

'Or tea. They do herbal teas here.'

'What's this about?'

'I had to get you here. It's Ted.'

'Ted? You mean the young man?'

'He needs help.'

'I'm sure he does.'

'But the thing is, he won't do anything about it. He just gets angry when people tell him, so I thought I'd have to do it for him.'

'I can give you names, Chloë, but he's got to want to –'

'I don't need names, Frieda. I've got you.'

'Oh no you don't.'

'You have to help.'

'I don't. This is not the way to do it.'

'Please. You don't understand. I really like him and he's so messed up.' She grabbed Frieda's hand. 'Oh, fuck, he's here already. He's just come in.'

'You haven't done what I think you've done?'

'I had to,' hissed Chloë, leaning forward. 'You wouldn't have come if I'd told you and neither would Ted.'

'Exactly.'

'You can make him better.'

'His mother's been killed, Chloë. How can I make him better?'

Frieda stood up, and as she did, Ted stumbled past the bar and saw them both. He stopped and stared. He was in the same dishevelled, undone state as before – clothes flapping, trousers slipping down, laces trailing, hair falling over his pale face, the hectic blotches on his cheeks. He stared from Chloë to Frieda, then back again.

'You?' he said. 'What's going on?'

Chloë scrambled to her feet and went over to him. 'Ted,' she said. 'Listen.'

'What's she doing here? You *tricked* me.'

'I wanted to help you,' said Chloë, desperately. For a moment Frieda felt very sorry for her niece. 'I thought if you two could just talk a bit . . .'

'I don't need help. You should see my sisters. They're the ones who need help. I'm not a little kid any more.' He looked at Chloë. 'I thought you were my friend.'

'That's not fair,' said Frieda, sharply. He turned his wretched, sneering face towards her. 'I agree Chloë acted wrongly. But she did it because she *is* your friend and she cares. Don't lash out at her. You need your friends.'

'I'm not going to lie on your fucking couch.'

'Of course you're not.'

'And I'm not going to cry and say my life is over now I don't have a mother.' But his voice rose dangerously high as he stared at her defiantly.

'No. And it isn't. Maybe we can just get out of here, the three of us, and have some tea or a mug of hot chocolate or something in the little place across the road, which is quiet and doesn't have dreadful paintings on the wall, and then we can all go back to our separate homes, and no real harm done.'

Chloë sniffed and gazed pleadingly at him.

'All right,' he said. 'I haven't had hot chocolate for years. Not since I was a kid.' As if he was a middle-aged man.

'Sorry.' Chloë's voice was small.

'It's all right, I guess.'

'Good,' said Frieda. 'Now can we get out of here?'

Chloë and Ted had a mug of hot chocolate each and Frieda had a glass of water.

'I don't think it makes things better,' said Ted, 'just because you talk about them.'

'It depends,' said Frieda.

'I think it makes things worse, like jabbing a wound to keep it bleeding. *Wanting* it to bleed.'

'I'm not here to make you see someone you don't want to see. I just think you should drink your hot chocolate.'

'Don't you get sick of spending your days with rich, narcissistic wankers going on about childhood traumas, endlessly fascinated by all their noble, manufactured suffering?'

'Your suffering isn't manufactured, though, is it?'

Ted glared at her. His face had a peeled look, as if even the air would sting him. 'It'll pass,' he said. 'That's what my mum would have said. One fucking day at a time.'

'That's one of the sad things about people dying,' said Frieda. 'We talk about them in the past tense. We say what they would have done. But if that's what she would have said, it's not stupid. Time does pass. Things change.' She stood up. 'And now I think we're done,' she said.

Chloë drained her mug. 'We're finished as well,' she said.

When they were outside, Frieda was ready to say goodbye but Chloë seemed reluctant to let her go. 'Which way are you going?'

'I'll walk back through the park.'

'You're going in the same direction as us. Past Ted's house. Except he's not staying there. They're staying with neighbours.'

'I can speak for myself,' said Ted.

'All right,' said Frieda, and they started walking, an uneasy trio, with Chloë in the middle.

'I'm sorry,' Chloë said. 'This is all my fault. I shouldn't have done this. I've embarrassed you both.'

'You can't force help on people,' said Frieda. 'But that's all right.'

'Frieda walks everywhere. She's like a taxi driver. You could name any two places in London and she could walk between them.' Chloë was talking as if she was frightened by the idea of a moment's silence. 'And she's really critical of it as well. She thinks it all went wrong after the Elizabethan age or the Great Fire of London. This is Ted's road. This is where it all happened. I'm sorry, I don't want to start it up all over again. I've done enough damage. This is actually his house, I mean his parents' house, but I'm going along the road with him to say goodbye and sorry and then . . .' She turned to Frieda, who had suddenly stopped. 'Frieda, are you all right?'

Frieda had been about to make way for a group of people – two men and a woman – getting out of a car, but she had recognized them at the very moment they recognized her.

'Frieda . . .' Karlsson seemed too surprised to say anything else.

The other man appeared more contemptuously amused than surprised. 'You can't stay away, can you?' said Hal Bradshaw. 'Is that some sort of syndrome?'

'I don't know what you mean,' said Frieda.

'I was going to ask how you are,' Bradshaw continued. 'But I think I already know.'

'Yes. Your journalist rang me up.'

Bradshaw smiled. He had very white teeth. 'Perhaps I should have warned you. But it would have spoiled things.'

'What's this?' asked Karlsson. He seemed both uncomfortable and distressed.

'You don't need to know.' Frieda didn't want anyone to know, and particularly not Karlsson, but she supposed that soon enough they all would, and the gossip, the glee, the happy, whispering pity would begin all over again.

The woman was Yvette Long.

'Frieda. What are you doing here?'

'I've been having cocoa with my niece, Chloë. And this is Ted.'

'Yes,' said Bradshaw, still smiling. 'We do know Ted Lennox. Are you coming inside? I assume that's what you want.'

'No.' Frieda was about to deny any connection, when she looked at the clenched, haunted figure of Ted standing with Chloë. It would have sounded like a betrayal. 'I was on my way home.'

'She can go where she pleases, can't she?' said Yvette, fiercely, turning her brown-eyed glare on Hal Bradshaw, who seemed unperturbed.

Frieda had to stop herself smiling at the novelty of Yvette defending her. And defending her from what?

Yvette and Bradshaw walked up the steps to the house but Karlsson stayed on the pavement, hovering awkwardly.

'Are you involved in this somehow?' he asked.

'Chloë knows Ted,' Frieda said. 'She wanted me to have a word with him. That's all.'

Karlsson muttered something to himself. 'I'm glad to see you anyway,' he said. 'You look all right.'

'Good,' said Frieda.

'I've been meaning to talk to you. To see you. But now I've got to . . .' He gestured at the house.

'That's fine,' said Frieda. She nodded goodbye to Chloë, turned and walked away in the direction of Primrose Hill.

Karlsson watched Frieda's progress, then went with the others into the house. Munster and Riley were already inside. They followed Munster through into the kitchen. Yvette was taking folders from her bag and arranging them on the table. They all sat down. Karlsson thought of the Lennoxes sitting there, rowdy Sunday lunches, then tried not to. He looked at Bradshaw. 'What was it that Frieda was saying to you?'

'Just shop talk,' said Bradshaw.

'Right,' said Karlsson. 'Let's sort out where we are.'

'Are we really not charging Billy Hunt?' said Munster.

'It should be him,' said Yvette. 'It really should. But the CCTV puts him in Islington at just after four. The neighbour knocked on the door at four thirty and she didn't answer.'

'She might have been in the bath,' said Munster. 'She might have had headphones on.'

'What do the forensics say about the time of death?' said Karlsson, his eyes on Riley, whose expression was blank.

Yvette picked up a file and thumbed through the papers. 'It's not much use,' she said. 'She could have died any time between half an hour and three hours before she was found. But, look, we're not taking the word of someone like Billy Hunt, are we? I mean, nothing about his statement makes sense. For example, he says he set off the alarm. If he didn't kill her, then why didn't the person who did kill her set it off?'

'Because she let him in,' said Bradshaw. 'Psychopaths are plausible, convincing.'

'You said before that he was expressing rage against women.'

'I stand by that.'

'Why was the alarm on?' said Yvette.

'What do you mean?' said Karlsson.

'Why would the burglar alarm be switched on if she was home?'

'That's a good question.' Karlsson stood up and walked to the front door. He opened it and stepped outside. Then he returned to the kitchen. 'This house doesn't have a fucking burglar alarm,' he said. 'We're being idiots.'

'There we are,' said Yvette. 'So Billy Hunt was lying. Again.'

Karlsson drummed his fingers on the table. 'Why would he lie about that?'

'Because he's a psychopath,' said Bradshaw.

'He's a thieving layabout,' said Karlsson, 'but he wasn't lying.'

'What do you mean?' said Yvette.

'Look,' said Karlsson, pointing at the ceiling. 'There's a smoke alarm.'

'How could Hunt set off a smoke alarm?'

'He didn't,' said Karlsson. 'Look at the scene-of-crime file. Riley, what will I find in the file?'

Riley's eyes flickered nervously. 'Do you mean, like, one thing in particular?' he said.

'Yes, one thing in particular. Oh, never mind. As far as

I remember, there was a tray of burned something or other on top of the cooker. That's what set off the alarm.'

Yvette flicked through the file. 'That's right,' she said.

'Are you saying Billy Hunt broke into the house and took some burned cakes out of the oven?' Munster asked dubiously.

Karlsson shook his head. 'You should talk to the little girl again, but I know what she'll say. She came home, smelled burning, took the tray out of the oven. Then she found her mother. Check the smoke alarm in the living room, Chris. Hunt said there was an alarm in there as well.'

Munster left the room.

'All right,' said Yvette. 'So that explains the alarm. It doesn't help us with the time.'

'Hang on,' said Karlsson.

Munster came back into the kitchen. 'There isn't one,' he said.

'What?' said Karlsson. 'Are you sure?'

'There's one in the hallway. That must be the other one he heard.'

Karlsson thought hard. 'No,' he said at last. 'Anyway, if smoke sets off the smoke alarm, you don't talk about alarms. You think of them as one alarm.'

'Really?' said Yvette.

'Are Ruth Lennox's effects here or at the station?'

'At the station.'

'All right,' said Karlsson. 'Give me a moment. I need to make a call.'

He stepped outside. After a long pause, Yvette spoke to Bradshaw. 'Is something up with you and Frieda?'

'Have you talked about it with her?' he said.

'What do you mean, "it"?'

'Your involvement with her incident, accident, whatever you call it.'

'Sorry, I don't understand what you mean.'

'It's just that I hope you don't feel guilty about it.'

'Look –' Yvette began fiercely, and was interrupted by Karlsson coming back into the kitchen.

'I just talked to the woman in Storage,' he said. 'And I found what I expected to find. What Hunt heard in the living room was Ruth Lennox's phone. It had an alarm on it. It was set to go off at ten past four in the afternoon. That was the other alarm that Billy Hunt heard.'

'It may have been,' said Yvette.

'It was,' said Karlsson. 'Put everything together. Look what we've got. Biscuits or cakes burning in the oven. A smoke sensor. And a phone alarm set for ten past four. It's reasonable to suggest that the alarm was to remind her that they were ready.'

'Possible.'

'It's also reasonable to suggest that when the alarm went off, Mrs Lennox was no longer able to respond to it. So she was dead by ten past four, at the very latest.'

There was a silence around the table.

'Fuck,' said Yvette.

Fifteen

She was expecting him. She glanced at herself in the mirror to make sure she was looking in control and reasonably healthy – she couldn't stand the thought of anyone's pity, and certainly not his – then ate the slice of quiche standing by the kitchen window, with the cat at her feet, rubbing its flank against her calves. The house was quiet now after a day of terrible bangs and tearing sounds and drilling. Stefan had been there again as he and Josef had carried two industrial-looking beams into the house. But they were gone now. Frieda didn't know what she actually wanted, but she did know that she felt suddenly more alert and less jangled, as if a knob had been turned very slightly and her world had come into clearer focus.

The doorbell rang at ten minutes past nine.

'Hello, Frieda,' said Karlsson. He held out a bunch of red tulips wrapped in damp paper. 'I should have brought these to you weeks ago.'

'Weeks ago I had far too many flowers. They all died at the same time. This is better.'

'Can I come in?'

In the living room, he took one of the chairs by the empty grate. 'I always think of you sitting by a fire,' he said.

'You've only really known me in the winter.'

There was a silence: they were both remembering the work they'd done together, and the way it had ended so violently.

'Frieda . . .' he began.

'You don't need to.'

'I do. I really do. I haven't been to see you since you left hospital because I felt so bad about what had happened that I went into a kind of lockdown about it. You helped us – more than that, you rescued us. And in return we got rid of you and then we nearly got you killed.'

'*You* didn't get rid of me and *you* didn't nearly get me killed.'

'Me. My team. Us. That's how it works. I was responsible and I let you down.'

'But I wasn't killed. Look at me.' She lifted her chin, squared her shoulders, smiled. 'I'm fine.'

Karlsson shut his eyes for a moment. 'In this job you have to develop a thick skin or you'd go mad. But you can't have a thick skin when it involves a friend.'

Silence settled around the word. Images of Karlsson flitted through Frieda's mind: Karlsson at his desk, calm and in control; Karlsson striding along a road with a tight face; Karlsson sitting by the bed of a little boy who, they thought, was perhaps dying; Karlsson standing up to the commissioner for her; Karlsson with his daughter wrapped around his body like a frightened koala; Karlsson sitting beside her fire and smiling at her.

'It's good to see you,' said Frieda.

'That means a lot.'

'Have your children left yet?' she asked.

'No. They go very soon, though. I was supposed to be spending lots of time with them. Then this case came up.'

'Hard.'

'Like a toothache that won't go away. Are you really OK?'

'I'm fine. I need a bit of time.'

'I don't mean just physically.' Karlsson flushed and Frieda was almost amused.

'You mean am I in a state of trauma?'

'You *were* attacked with a knife.'

'I dream about it sometimes.' Frieda considered. 'And I need to tell you that I also think about Dean Reeve. Something happened a few days ago that you should know. Don't look anxious, I don't want to talk about it now.'

There was a silence. Karlsson seemed to be weighing something up in his mind. To speak or not to speak.

'Listen,' he said finally. 'That boy Ted.'

'I'm sorry about that.'

'That's not what I wanted to say. You know about the case?'

'I know his mother was killed.'

'She was a nice woman, with a decent husband, close family, good friends, neighbours who liked her. We thought we'd got the man who did it, all simple and straightforward. It turns out that he couldn't have and we're back where we started. Except that it makes even less sense.'

'I'm sorry,' Frieda said neutrally.

'Dr Bradshaw has a theory.'

'I don't want to hear it,' Frieda said quickly. 'That's one of the perks of being pushed out.'

Karlsson looked suspicious. 'Is there some problem with Bradshaw?'

'Does it matter?' Frieda didn't say anything further, just waited.

'You wouldn't come to the house with me, would you? Just once? I'd like to discuss it with someone I trust.'

'What about Yvette?' asked Frieda, although she already knew she was going to say yes.

'Yvette's terrific – apart from the fact that she let you get nearly murdered, of course. She's my trusted colleague, as well as my attack dog. But if I want someone to look at a house, just to get the smell of it, have a thought or two, I'd ask you – I *am* asking you.'

'As a friend.'

'Yes. As a friend.'

'When?'

'Tomorrow morning, when the house is empty?'

'That would suit me fine.'

'Are you serious? I mean, that's great. Shall I send a car?'

'I'll make my own way.'

I met a neuroscientist called Gloria today, who I think you'd like a lot (you see, I'm making friends for you out here). We talked about free will – does it exist etc. She was arguing that with everything we know now about the brain, it's impossible to believe there is such a thing, and yet it's impossible not to believe in it at the same time and to live our life as if we have choices. A necessary delusion.

It's a beautiful evening, with a full moon shining on the river. I wonder what it's like in London – but, of course, it's nearly morning for you now. You're asleep. At least I hope you are.

Sandy xxxx

Sixteen

So it was that the very next day Frieda once more walked past the Roundhouse, past the little café where Ted and Chloë had drunk hot chocolate the evening before and the larger one where an aeroplane nose-dived down the wall and music throbbed, into Margaretting Street. Karlsson was already outside, drinking coffee from a paper mug that he raised in salute as she came towards him. He noticed that she walked more slowly than she used to, and with a slight limp.

'You came.'

'I said I would.'

'I'm glad.'

'As long as you're sure no one's in?'

'I'm certain. The family has been staying with neighbours. The house is still officially a crime scene.'

'And Hal Bradshaw?'

'Fuck him.' The vehemence of Karlsson's response surprised her.

Frieda followed Karlsson through the front door. Although the window was still broken, the barriers had been cleared away and the forensic team had gone. But the house had the special emptiness of an abandoned place, already neglected and musty from disuse – and, of course, it was the place where a woman (a wife, a mother, a good neighbour, Karlsson had said) had recently been murdered. As Frieda stood in the silent hallway, she felt that the house somehow knew it and felt abandoned.

A large photograph, the frame cracked and the glass smashed, was propped against the wall and she bent down to look at it.

'The happy family,' said Karlsson. 'But it's usually the husband, you know.'

Official family photographs that are framed and hung in the hall are always happy. Everyone has to stand close together and smile: there was Ted, not as gangly and dishevelled as she'd seen him, with the smooth face of youth; there was the elder of the girls, her arresting pale eyes and nimbus of coppery curls; the younger daughter, skinny and anxious, but grinning despite her train-track braces, her head tipped slightly towards her mother's shoulder. There was the husband and father, as proud and protective as a husband and father is meant to look when he's standing with his family grouped around him for the picture that will represent them – he had greying brown hair, jowly cheeks, his elder daughter's eyes, eyebrows that tilted at a comic angle, a face that was made to be cheerful.

And there she was, standing in the centre with her husband – in a flecked sweater, her soft hair tied back loosely, her candid face smiling out of the picture. One hand on the shoulder of her elder daughter, who sat in front of her, and one against her husband's hip. It was a touching gesture for the official portrait, thought Frieda, casual and intimate. She bent closer and stared into the dead woman's eyes. Grey. No makeup that she could see. Small signs of age drawing down her mouth and creasing her brow. Smile marks and frown marks, the map of our days.

'Tell me about her. Describe her,' she said to Karlsson.

'Her name is Ruth Lennox. Forty-four years old. A health visitor, and has been since her younger daughter started school; she had several years out when the children were small. Married to Russell Lennox,' Karlsson pointed to the man in the photo, 'happily, from all accounts, for twenty-three years. He's an executive in a small charity for children with learning difficulties. Three kids, as you see – your Ted, Judith, who's fifteen, and Dora, thirteen. All at the local comp. Has a dragon of a sister who lives in London. Both her parents are dead. On the PTA. Good citizen. Not rich, but comfortable, two modest but stable incomes and no big outgoings. Three thousand pounds in her current account, thirteen thousand in her savings account. Healthy enough pension pot. Donates to various charities by standing order. No criminal record. Clean driving licence. I'm using the present tense but, of course, last Wednesday she sustained a catastrophic injury to the head and would have died instantly.'

'Who did you think it was, before you discovered it couldn't be?'

'A local druggie with a record, but it turns out that he has a rock-solid alibi. He was caught on CCTV somewhere else at the time of her death. He admitted to breaking in, stealing some stuff, finding her body and fleeing the scene. We didn't believe him, but for once in his life he was telling the truth.'

'So the broken window was him?'

'And the burglary. There was no sign of a break-in when a neighbour came round earlier – we know Ruth Lennox must have been already dead. Obviously the implication is that she let the killer in herself.'

'Someone she knew.'

'Or someone who seemed safe.'

'Where did she die?'

'In here.' Karlsson led her into the living room, where everything was tidy and in its proper place (cushions on the sofa, newspapers and magazines in the rack, books lining the walls, tulips in a vase on the mantelpiece), but a dark bloodstain still flowered on the beige carpet and daubs of blood decorated the near wall.

'Violent,' said Frieda.

'Hal Bradshaw believes it was the work of an extremely angry sociopath with a record of violence.'

'And you think it's more likely to be the husband.'

'That's not a matter of evidence, just the way of the world. The most likely person to kill a wife is her husband. The husband, however, has a reasonably satisfactory alibi.'

Frieda looked round at him. 'We're taught to beware of strangers,' she said. 'It's our friends most of us should worry about.'

'I wouldn't go that far,' said Karlsson.

They went through to the kitchen and Frieda stood in the middle of the room, looking from the tidily cluttered dresser to the drawings and photos stuck to the fridge with magnets, the book splayed open on the table. Then, upstairs, the bedroom: a king-sized bed covered with a striped duvet, a gilt-framed photo of Ruth and Russell on their wedding day twenty-three years ago, several smaller-framed photos of her children at different ages, a wardrobe in which hung dresses, skirts and shirts – nothing flamboyant, Frieda noticed, some things obviously old but well looked-after. Shoes, flat or with small heels; one pair of black leather boots, slightly scuffed. Drawers in which T-shirts were neatly rolled, not folded; underwear drawer with sensible knickers and bras, 34C. A small amount of makeup on the dressing table, and one bottle of perfume, Chanel. A novel by her side of the bed, *Wives and Daughters* by Elizabeth Gaskell, with a bookmark sticking out, and under it a book about small gardens. A pair of reading glasses, folded, to one side.

In the bathroom: a bar of unscented soap, apple hand-wash, electric toothbrush – his and hers – and dental floss, shaving cream, razors, tweezers, a canister of deodorant, face wipes, moisturizing face cream, two large towels and one hand towel, two matching flannels hung on the side of the bath, with the tap in the middle, a set of scales pushed against the wall, a medicine cabinet containing paracetamol, aspirin, plasters of various sizes, cough medicine, out-of-date ointment for thrush, a tube of eye drops, anti-indigestion tablets . . . Frieda shut the cabinet.

'No contraceptives?'

'That's what Yvette asked. She had an IUD – the Mirena coil, apparently.'

In the filing cabinet set aside for her use in her husband's small study, there were three folders for work, and most of the others related to her children: academic qualifications, child benefit slips, medical records, reports, on single pieces of paper or in small books, dating back to their first years at primary school, certificates commemorating their ability to swim a hundred metres, their participation in the egg-and-spoon race or the cycling proficiency course.

In the shabby trunk beside the filing cabinet: hundreds and hundreds of pieces of creativity the children had brought back from school over the years. Splashy paintings in bright colours of figures with legs attached to the wobbly circle of the head and hair sprouting like exclamation marks, scraps of material puckered with running stitch and cross stitch and chain stitch, a tiny home-made clock without a battery, a small box studded with overglued sea shells, a blue-painted clay pot, and you could still see the finger marks pressed into its asymmetrical rim.

'There are also several bin bags full of old baby clothes in the loft,' said Karlsson, as she closed the lid. 'We haven't got to them yet. It takes a long time to go through a house like this. Nothing was thrown away.'

'Photo albums?'

'A whole shelf given over to them. She wrote the date and occasion under each. She didn't do motherhood by halves.'

'No.'

Frieda went to stand by the window that overlooked the garden. There were drifts of blossom around the fruit tree, and a cat sat in a patch of sunlight. 'There's nothing here she wouldn't want to be seen,' she said.

'What do you mean?'

'I always think that nobody's life can tolerate a spotlight shone into its corners.'

'But?'

'But from everything you tell me and everything I've seen, hers seems entirely ready for the spotlight, don't you think? As if this house was a stage.'

'A stage for what?'

'For a play about being good.'

'I'm supposed to be the cynical one. Do you mean you think nobody can be that good?'

'I'm a therapist, Karlsson. Of course that's what I think. Where are Ruth Lennox's secrets?'

But of course, she thought, several hours later and sitting at Number 9 – her friends' café near where she lived – real secrets aren't found in objects, in schedules, in the words we speak or the expressions we put on our faces, in underwear drawers and filing cabinets, deleted texts, and diaries pushed to the bottom of the bag. They are lodged far deeper, unguessable even to ourselves. She was thinking about this as she faced Jack Dargan, whom she supervised and, even during her convalescence, met at least once a week to track his progress and listen to his doubts. And Jack was a thorny ball of doubt. But he never doubted Frieda: she was the constant in his life, his single point of faith.

'I have a favour to ask,' Jack was saying animatedly. 'Don't look anxious – I'm not going to let down my patients or anything. Especially not Carrie.' Since discovering that her husband Alan had not left her but had been murdered by his twin, Dean Reeve, Carrie had been seeing Jack twice a week and he seemed to have done better than even Frieda, who believed in him, had expected. He laid aside his self-conscious pessimism and his awkwardness and concentrated on the woman in distress.

'What is this favour?'

'I've written a paper on trauma and before I send it out I wanted you to look at it.'

Frieda hesitated. Trauma felt too close for her to review it dispassionately. She looked at Jack's flushed face, his tufty hair and ridiculous clothes (today he was wearing brown, balding jeans, a second-hand yellow-and-orange shirt that clashed with his colouring and his hair, and a green waterproof even though the sky was cloudless). In his confusion, he reminded her of Ted Lennox, of so many other raw and self-conscious young men.

'All right,' she said reluctantly.

'Really?'

'Yes.'

'Can I ask you something?'

'You can always ask.'

'But you won't always answer. I know.' Jack avoided her eyes. 'I'm only asking because the others won't and –'

'What others?' Frieda interrupted.

'Oh, you know. The usual suspects.'

'Am I that scary? Go on, then.'

'Are you all right?'

'That's what you – they – wanted to ask?'

'Yes.'

'The paper you've written was just an excuse?'

'Well, yes. Kind of – though I have written it. And I would like you to look at it if you have time.'

'And I'm assuming that you're asking me because you're worried that I'm not.'

'No – well, yes. You seem –' He stopped.

'Go on.'

'Brittle. Like an eggshell. More unpredictable than you usually are. Sorry. I don't mean to offend you. But maybe you aren't taking your recovery seriously enough.'

'Is that what you think?'

'Yes.'

'All of you?'

'Well – yes.'

'Tell everyone – whoever takes it upon themselves to be worried for me – that I'm fine.'

'You're angry.'

'I don't like the thought that you've been discussing me behind my back.'

'Only because we're concerned.'

'Thank you for your concern, but I'm fine.'

Later that afternoon, Frieda had a visitor she wasn't expecting who brought the recent past flooding back. She opened her door to find Lorna Kersey standing on the doorstep, and before Frieda had time to say anything, she had stepped inside and closed the door behind her with a bang.

'This won't take long,' she said, in a voice high and cracked with rage.

'I won't pretend I don't know why you're here.'

'Good.'

'I'm very sorry for your loss, Mrs Kersey.'

'You killed my daughter and now you say you're sorry for my loss.'

Lorna Kersey's daughter, Beth, had been an unhappy

and dysfunctional young woman who suffered from paranoid delusions and who had killed Mary Orton. Frieda had got to the house too late to stop her. The vividness of the flashbacks in which she remembered Beth standing over her with a knife, and re-experienced the blade slicing through her, still woke her in the night, drenched in sweat. She had known that she was dying, felt herself sliding into darkness and oblivion – yet she had survived and Beth Kersey had not. The police had called it self-defence and even Karlsson hadn't believed Frieda when she insisted that it was Dean Reeve who had killed Beth and saved her life.

'Yes, I'm sorry,' said Frieda, steadily. It would do no good to tell Lorna Kersey she hadn't killed her daughter. She wouldn't believe her, and even if she did, what did that matter? Beth, poor lonely Beth, was dead, and a mother's anguish was etched into Lorna Kersey's face.

'You came to me and you got me to tell you things about Beth we never told anyone. I trusted you. You said you would help find her. You made me a promise. And then you killed her. Do you know what it feels like to bury a child?'

'No.'

'No. Of course you don't. How can you bear to get up in the morning?'

Frieda thought of saying that Beth had been very ill, that in her frantic sickness of the mind she had slaughtered an old woman and would have killed her, Frieda, as well. But of course Lorna Kersey knew all of that. She wanted someone to blame and who more obvious than Frieda?

'I wish there was something I could say or do that would –'

'But there isn't. There's nothing. My child's dead and now she'll never be all right. And you did that. In the name of helping people, you destroy them. I'll never forgive you. Never.'

Frieda – you sounded a bit distracted today. I know that something is up but in spite of everything that's passed between us, you're not very good at confiding in me, are you? Why? Are you scared of being beholden – as if I'll have some hold over you? I think you feel you have to deal with things by yourself, as if it's some kind of moral obligation. Or maybe you don't trust other people to help you. I guess what I'm saying is that you should – can – trust me, Sandy xxx

Seventeen

The Sir Philip Sidney was a pub on the side of a busy road. It looked lost and abandoned between a petrol station and a furniture store. When Fearby walked in he recognized his man immediately and he knew at the same moment that he was a policeman, or an ex-policeman. Grey suit, white shirt, striped tie, black shoes. Slightly overweight. Fearby sat down beside him.

'Drink?' he said.

'I was just leaving,' said the man.

'What's your name?'

'You don't need to know,' said the man, 'because we're never going to meet again. You know, we all got pretty sick of you. On the force.'

'They got pretty sick of me on my paper as well,' said Fearby.

'So you must be feeling chuffed with yourself.'

'Is that what you've dragged me out here to tell me?'

'Are you finished with the story?'

'I don't know,' said Fearby. 'Conley didn't kill Hazel Barton. Which means someone else did.'

'The police are not currently pursuing other leads. As you know.'

'Yes,' said Fearby. 'Is that it?'

'I was wondering if you had any avenues of enquiry?'

'Avenues of enquiry?' said Fearby. 'I've got a room full of files.'

'I was having a drink once,' said the man, in a casual tone, 'and someone told me that on the morning of the Hazel Barton murder, a few miles away in Cottingham, another girl was approached. But she got away. That's all. It was just something I heard.'

'Why wasn't this given to the defence?'

'It wasn't thought relevant. It didn't fit the pattern. Something like that.'

'So why are you telling me now?'

'I wanted to know if you were interested.'

'That's no good to me,' said Fearby. 'That's just pub chat. I need a name. I need a number.'

The man got up. 'It's one of those things that irritate you, that won't let you go,' he said. 'You know, like a little stone in your shoe. I'll see what I can do. But that will be it. One call and then you won't hear from me again.'

'You were the one who called me.'

'Don't make me regret it.'

Frieda ordered a black coffee for herself, a latte and a Danish for Sasha. She sat at the table and opened the newspaper. She turned page after page until she reached the article she was looking for. Just a few minutes earlier Reuben had been shouting down the phone at her about it, so she was prepared. She skimmed it quickly.

'Oh,' she said, suddenly, as if she'd been jabbed. There was a detail she hadn't expected.

'What's happening with your home improvement?'

Sasha asked. 'I knew that Josef was giving you a new bath. I didn't realize it would take so long.'

'I've almost forgotten what my old bathroom was like,' said Frieda. 'Or what it was like to *have* a bathroom.'

'He probably thought of it as a kind of therapy for you,' Sasha said. 'Maybe a hot bath is the one experience you allow yourself that's a complete indulgence with no redeeming moral features. So he thought you'd better have a good one.'

'You make me sound . . . bleak.'

'I think it was also therapy for Josef.'

Frieda was puzzled. 'Why would it be therapy for Josef?'

'I know that you were there when Mary Orton was killed. I know how terrible it was for you. But Josef knew her as well. He looked after her, repaired her house. And she looked after him. Her Ukrainian son. Better than her English sons.'

'That's true,' said Frieda.

'When that happened to her and to you, it hit him hard. I have the feeling that when something bad happens to him, he doesn't talk about it. He gets drunk or he makes something for someone.'

'Maybe,' said Frieda. 'I just wish his therapy wasn't so messy. And so loud.'

'And now you're getting written about in the papers again. Do you ever get sick of being picked on?'

Frieda let a few moments go by. 'It's not that,' she said. 'I didn't know about this, but there's something you should know.'

'What do you mean?'

'These researchers targeted four psychotherapists. I'm one, of course. Reuben's another. One of them is Geraldine Fliess. They probably chose her because she's written about extreme mental disorders. And the other is James Rundell.'

Neither of the women spoke immediately and they didn't need to.

'Who brought us together, I suppose,' said Sasha.

'And got me arrested.'

Rundell had been Sasha's therapist. When Frieda had discovered that he had slept with Sasha while she was his patient, she had not only confronted Rundell but attacked him in a restaurant and been taken to a police cell, from which Karlsson had rescued her.

'Does the article mention me?' said Sasha. 'Sorry. I know that sounds selfish. I didn't mean that.'

'It doesn't mention you,' said Frieda. 'So far as I can see.'

'You don't need to worry, you know. I am better. That's all in the past. It doesn't have power over me any more.'

'I'm glad.'

'In fact . . .' Sasha paused, and Frieda looked at her enquiringly. 'In fact, I've been meaning to tell you but there didn't seem to be a right time. I've met someone.'

'Really? Who is he?'

'His name's Frank Manning.' Her face took on a soft and dreamy expression.

'You have to tell me more than that! What does he do?'

'He's a barrister – a criminal barrister. I only met him a few weeks ago. It all happened so quickly.'

'And is it . . .' She hesitated. She wanted to ask Sasha if this Frank was single and free or, like several of Sasha's previous relationships, there were complications. She feared for her beautiful young friend.

'You want to know if he's married? No. He's divorced and he has a young son. Don't look at me like that, Frieda! I trust him. If you met him you'd know what I mean. He's honourable.'

'I want to meet him.' Frieda took Sasha's hand in hers and pressed it. 'I'm very glad. I should have guessed – you're looking very radiant.'

'I'm just happy – I wake up in the morning and I feel alive! I haven't felt like this for so long. I'd almost forgotten how lovely it is.'

'And he feels the same.'

'Yes. He does. I know he does.'

'I have to meet him. See if he's good enough for you.'

'I'll arrange it. But, Frieda, you, Reuben, him, all in the article. Is that just a coincidence?'

'The man running the research project is a psychologist called Hal Bradshaw. He works with the police and we were on the case that nearly got me killed. '

'And you didn't get on?'

'We disagreed about various aspects.'

'Do you mind if I have a look at the article?'

Frieda pushed the newspaper across the table. Sasha leaned over and peered at it, not reading it through but seeing it in flashes. She took in the headline:

SILENT WITNESSES

She saw a row of photographs. A picture of Frieda that had been in another press report, a photograph of her taken in the street, caught unawares. There was a picture of James Rundell, more youthful than when she'd been involved with him, and a much older picture of Reuben. He looked like a psychoanalyst in a French New Wave movie.

She read the intro: 'A disturbing new report suggests that therapists are failing to protect the public from potential rapists and murderers.'

She moved her finger down the page, searching for Frieda's name.

When confronted with a patient showing the classic signs of a murderous psychopath, Dr Frieda Klein offered no treatment and made no attempt to report him to the authorities. When questioned about why she had failed to report a psychopath to the police, Dr Klein responded that she had 'had some concerns' about the patient but that she 'wouldn't discuss them with anyone but him'. In fact, Dr Klein had refused to treat the patient.

Frieda Klein, a 38-year-old brunette, hit the headlines earlier this year when she was involved in a shocking incident in which two women were knifed to death and Klein herself was hospitalized. An eighty-year-old woman, Mary Orton, was killed in a crazed attack by a knife-wielding schizophrenic, Beth Kersey. Police accepted Klein's explanation that she killed Kersey in self-defence.

The leader of the research project, Dr Hal Bradshaw, commented: 'While it is understandable to feel sympathy for what Dr Klein has gone through . . .'

*

'That's nice of him,' said Sasha.

'Of who?' said Frieda.

'Bloody Hal Bradshaw.' She turned back to the paper.

'While it is understandable to feel sympathy for what Dr Klein has gone through, I think there is a serious question of whether she is a risk both to her patients and to the public at large.'

Dr Bradshaw spoke of the urgent issues that his research has raised. 'It brings me no pleasure to expose the failings in the analytic community. We tested the responses of four psychoanalysts and of those only one acted responsibly and called the authorities. The other three failed in their responsibilities both as healers and as protectors of the public.

'When he talked to me, one of the patients in the study, Seamus Dunne, is still angry about his experience: "I was told that Dr Klein was a top expert, but when I gave her the story that showed I was a psychopath, she didn't react at all. She just asked irrelevant questions about food and sleeping and things like that. She seemed like her mind was on other things."'

Sasha threw down the paper. 'I know I'm supposed to say something comforting to you, but I literally don't know how you can bear this. You've become this object out in the world that people kick around and throw things at and tell lies about. The idea of this guy coming to you and saying he was in need and asking for your help and it was all a trick – don't you feel violated?'

Frieda took a sip of her coffee. 'Sasha, if it wasn't

you, I'd say it wasn't a problem and that it comes with the territory. And I'd say it was all quite interesting if it wasn't happening to me.'

'But it is me, and it is happening to you.'

Frieda smiled at her friend. 'You know, sometimes I wish I wasn't doing this job at all. I'd like to be a potter, that's what I'd like. I'd have a lump of clay on my wheel and it wouldn't matter what I was feeling or what anybody was feeling. At the end of it, I'd have a pot. Or a cup. Or a bowl.'

'If you were a potter,' said Sasha, 'I'd be lost or worse. And you don't want to be a potter anyway.'

'That's nice of you to say, but you would have got better on your own. People usually do, you know.'

Frieda pulled the newspaper back to her side of the table and glanced at it again.

'Are you going to do anything about it?' Sasha asked.

Frieda took a notebook from her bag and flipped through it until she found the page she wanted. 'You know people who are good with technical things, don't you? Finding things on the Internet.'

'Yes,' said Sasha, warily.

'I want to see Seamus Dunne. I've got his phone number but I don't know where he lives. There must be ways of finding out.'

'I'm not sure that's a good idea,' said Sasha. 'If you're going to get into a fight again and get arrested, Karlsson may not be able to get you out again.'

'It's nothing like that,' said Frieda. 'I just need to talk to him. In person. Can that be done?'

Sasha looked at the notebook. 'I suppose so,' she said.

She took her phone from the table and punched the number into it.

'What are you doing?' Frieda asked, but Sasha just held up her hand.

'Hello,' she said, into the phone, in a nasal tone quite different from her own. 'Is that Mr Seamus Dunne? Yes? We're actually trying to make a delivery to you and our driver seems to have the wrong address. Can you confirm it for me?' She picked up a pen and started writing in Frieda's notebook. 'Yes . . . Yes . . . Yes . . . Thank you so much, we'll be right with you.' She pushed the notebook across to Frieda.

'That wasn't quite what I meant when I said I needed technical help.'

'No violence, please.'

'I'll do my best.'

Eighteen

'No,' said Seamus Dunne, when he saw Frieda. 'No way. And how do you even know where I live?'

She peered over his shoulder. Student house. Bare boards. Bikes in the hall. Still-packed boxes.

'I just want to talk to you.'

'Talk to the newspaper. Or Bradshaw. It wasn't my responsibility.'

'I'm not interested in any of that,' said Frieda. 'Or the article. It was just something you said.'

Dunne's eyes narrowed in suspicion. 'Is this a trick?'

Frieda almost laughed at that. 'You mean, am I coming to see you under false pretences?'

Dunne shook his head nervously. 'Bradshaw said we were all in the clear. It was completely legal.'

'I told you,' said Frieda. 'I don't care. I'm here to say two things. Let me in and I'll say them. Then I'll go.'

Dunne seemed in an agony of indecision. Finally he opened the door and let her in. She walked through the hall to the kitchen. It looked as if a rugby team had had a takeaway and not cleared up, then had a party and not cleared up, had got up the next morning, had had break-fast and not cleared up. And then left. Seamus Dunne was a bit old for this.

He noticed her expression. 'You look shocked,' he said. 'If I'd known you were coming, I'd have tidied.'

'No,' she said. 'It reminds me of being a student.'

'Well, I'm still a student,' he said. 'It may not look like much, but it's better than the alternative. So, I guess you've come to shout at me.'

'Do you think you deserve to be shouted at?'

Dunne leaned back on the counter, almost dislodging a pile of plates topped by a saucepan containing two mugs. 'Dr Bradshaw told us about an experiment where a researcher sent some students to different psychiatrists and they just had to say they had heard a thud inside their heads. Every single one of them was diagnosed with schizophrenia and admitted to a psychiatric hospital.'

'Yes, I know the experiment,' said Frieda. 'It wouldn't be allowed today.'

'Maybe that's a pity,' said Dunne, 'because it was pretty revealing, don't you think? But you don't want to hear that.'

'The way I see it,' said Frieda, 'people who weren't really psychopaths were sent to therapists and only one of them made the mistake of taking them seriously.'

'So what were the two things you wanted to say?'

'I was interested in what you said in the article.'

'I thought so.'

'No, not the way you think. You said I asked you about irrelevant things, food, sleeping. By the way, how is your sleeping?'

'Fine.'

'No, really. Do you sleep through the night? Or do you still wake up?'

'I wake up a bit. Like most people.'

'And what do you think about?'

'Stuff, you know. I go over things.'

'And your appetite?'

He shrugged and there was a pause. 'Why are you looking at me like that?'

'Do you know what I think?'

'You're probably about to tell me.'

'When you came to see me, pretending to be looking for help, I think you subconsciously used that as an excuse to really ask for help.'

'That's just Freudian rubbish. You're trying to catch me out.'

'You're not sleeping properly, you're not eating properly. There's this.' She gestured at the kitchen.

'That's just a student kitchen.'

'I've seen student kitchens,' said Frieda. 'I've lived in student kitchens. This is a bit different. And, anyway, you're – what? Twenty-five, twenty-six? I think you're slightly depressed and finding it difficult to admit it to anyone or even yourself.'

Dunne went very red. 'If it's subconscious and you think I don't want to admit it even to myself, then how do I disprove it?'

'Just think about it,' said Frieda. 'And you might want to talk to someone about it. Not to me.'

There was another pause. Dunne picked up a dirty spoon and tapped it against a stained mug. 'What was the other thing?' he said.

'That story you told me.'

'Which? The whole thing was a story.'

'No. About cutting your father's hair and feeling a mixture of tenderness and power.'

'Oh, that.'

'It felt distinct from everything else, like an authentic memory.'

'Sorry to disappoint you. It was just something I said.'

'It wasn't your memory?'

'I learned it.'

'Who told you to say it?"

'It was in my pack – I don't know. Dr Bradshaw, maybe, or whoever made up our characters.'

'Who actually gave you your instructions?'

'One of the other researchers. Oh – you want his name?'

'Yes, please.'

'Why? So you can go and make him feel guilty as well?'

'Is that what I made you feel?'

'If you want to know, I felt really nervous, coming to you like that. A bit sick. It wasn't easy.' He glared at Frieda. 'His name's Duncan Bailey.'

'Where does he live?'

'You want his address as well?'

'If you have it.'

Seamus Dunne muttered something, but then tore off the top of an empty cereal box that was lying on the floor and scribbled on it before handing it to Frieda.

'Thank you,' she said. 'And remember what I said about talking to someone.'

'Are you going now?' Seamus Dunne seemed taken aback.

'Yes.'

'You mean that's the end of it?'

'I'm not quite sure it's the end, Seamus.'

*

Jim Fearby had gone back through his files to make sure he had all the facts in his head. He always made notes first in the shorthand he had learned when he'd joined the local newspaper in Coventry as a junior reporter, more than forty years ago. Nobody learned shorthand now, but he liked the hieroglyphic squiggles, like a secret code. Then, on the same day if possible, he would copy them into his notebook. Only later would he put it all on to his computer.

Hazel Barton had been strangled in July 2004; her body had been found lying by a roadside not many miles from where she lived. Apparently she had been walking home from the bus stop, after the bus had failed to arrive. She was eighteen years old, fresh-faced and pretty, with three older brothers, and parents who had indulged and adored her. She had planned to become a physiotherapist. Her face smiled radiantly from the newspapers and TV screens for weeks after her death. George Conley had been seen standing over her body. He had been arrested at once and charged soon after. He was the local weirdo, the blubbery, unemployed, slow-witted loner, who lurked in parks and outside playgrounds: of course he did it. And then he confessed and everyone was happy, except Jim Fearby, who was a stickler for detail and never took anyone else's word for things that happened. He had to read the police reports, had to rake through the files, thumb through law books.

He was sitting in front of the TV, not really watching it, when the phone rang.

'Have you got a pen?'

'Who is this?'

'Philip Sidney.'

Fearby fumbled for a pen.

'Yes?'

'Vanessa Dale,' said the voice, then gave a phone number and made Fearby read it back to him. Fearby started to ask something but the line was already dead.

Frieda poured two whiskies and handed one to Josef. 'How's it going?' she said.

'The joist is good. It is strong. But now after I take the floor up, I think it is better to do tiles. Tiles on the floor. Then new floor make wall look old and bad. So maybe tiles for the wall as well. You should choose.'

Josef seemed to have forgotten about his glass, so Frieda clinked hers against his to remind him. They both drank.

'When I asked, "How's it going?" I was asking about you, not just the bathroom. But I want to say that I'm going to start paying for all of this. You can't afford it.'

'Is fine.'

'It's not fine. I've been thinking about myself too much. I know that you were close to Mary Orton. It was very sad for you, I know, what happened.'

'I dream of her,' said Josef. 'Two times maybe four times. It's funny.'

'What do you dream?'

Josef smiled. 'She was living in Ukraine. In my old home. I tell her I'm surprised to see her living. She talk to me in my own language. Stupid, no?'

'Yes. Very stupid. But not stupid at all.'

Darling Frieda – It's too late to phone you. I've just checked out the link you sent me. Who is this fucking Hal Bradshaw anyway? Can we do something about this? One of my oldest friends is a lawyer. Should I have a word with her?

But I hope you know how highly you're regarded by all the people who matter – your friends, your colleagues, your patients. This story is just a vicious charade that makes no difference to that.

I've had an idea for the summer – we can hire a longboat on the Canal du Midi. You'd like that. I went on one before and they're very cosy (some people would find them oppressive; not you. They are a bit like your house, except they move). We could drift along the waterways and stop for picnics and in the evenings go to little brasseries. Of course, in my mind it's very sunny and you're wearing a sundress and drinking white wine and you've even got a bit of a tan. Say yes! Xxxx

Nineteen

'We were all so shocked,' said the woman sitting opposite Munster and Riley. 'I can't quite believe it. I mean, Ruth was so . . .' She stopped and searched for a word. Her face screwed up. 'Down to earth,' she supplied eventually. 'Cheerful. Practical. I don't know – not someone who things like this happen to. I realize how stupid that sounds.'

They were in the low-rise modern building from which Ruth Lennox had worked as a health visitor, sitting in a small room off the open-plan office with her line manager, Nadine Salter.

'It doesn't sound stupid,' said Chris Munster, after Riley had failed to respond. He looked a bit dazed this morning: his face was creased as if he had only just woken up. 'It's what most people say about her. That she was a friendly, straightforward woman. How long had she worked here?'

'About ten years. Mostly she was out, seeing people, not here in the office.'

'Can you show us her desk?'

'Of course.'

They went into the large room, past desks of avidly curious people pretending to work. Ruth Lennox's desk was scrupulously tidy, which was what Munster and Riley had come to expect – her folders, her notebooks, her work diary, her correspondence and her stationery had been put away in the drawers. Apart from the rather old computer, the only things on the surface were a small jug of pens, a little pot of paper slips and staplers, and a framed photo of her three children.

'We're going to have to remove her computer and her correspondence,' said Munster. 'For now, we're just interested in the Wednesday she died. April the sixth. Was she here?'

'Yes. But just for the half-day. She always had Wednesday afternoon off. We have a general staff meeting in the morning, at about eleven, and then she leaves after that.'

'So she was in the office that day, not out on visits?'

'That's right. She came in at about nine, and left again at midday.'

'Was there anything different about her that day?'

'We've been talking about that. She was just her normal self.'

'She didn't mention anything that was troubling her?'

'Not at all. We talked about how awful it is for young people trying to find jobs, but just in a general way – her kids are too young for that to worry her. Poor things. And she gave me a recipe.'

'Did you see her go?'

'No. But Vicky, over there, was having a cigarette outside. She saw her getting into a cab.'

'A black taxi?'

'No. As I said, a cab.'

'Do you know which firm?'

'No, I don't.'

'Hang on,' said Riley.

He walked over to Ruth Lennox's desk and came back

with a small card, which he handed to Munster. 'This was pinned to her board,' he said.

Munster looked at the card. C & R Taxis. He showed it to Nadine Salter.

'Would she travel by cab on her visits?' he asked.

Her face took on a disapproving expression. 'Not on our budget.'

C & R Taxis was based in a tiny room with smeary windows next to a betting shop on Camden High Street. An old man was sitting asleep on a sofa. A portly man was sitting at a desk with three phones in front of him and a laptop. He looked up at the two detectives when Munster asked about Ruth Lennox.

'Ruth Lennox? Last Wednesday?' He scrolled down his computer screen with a deft, stubby finger. 'Yeah, we took her last Wednesday. Ahmed drove her. Where to?'

They waited for him to say that Ahmed had driven Ruth Lennox home to Margaretting Street. He didn't.

'Shawcross Street, SE17, number thirty-seven. No, we didn't collect her.' One of the phones rang loudly. 'I should get that.'

Out in the street, Munster and Riley looked at each other.

'Shawcross Street,' Munster said.

The road they needed was one-way, so they parked beside an enormous block of flats, built in the thirties. It was being prepared for demolition and the windows and doors were sealed with sheet metal.

'I wonder what Ruth Lennox was doing round here,' said Munster, climbing out of the car.

'Isn't that what a health visitor does?' said Riley. 'Visit people?'

'This isn't her patch.'

They walked round the corner into Shawcross Street. At one end there was a row of large, semi-detached Victorian houses, but thirty-seven wasn't one of these. It was a fifties-style, flat-fronted, dilapidated building, with metal-framed windows, that had been divided into three flats, although the top flat looked empty. One of its windows was smashed and a tatty red curtain blew out of it.

Munster rang the bottom bell and waited. Then he rang the middle one. Just as they were turning to go, the entrance door opened and a small, dark-skinned woman peered out suspiciously. 'What is it?' she asked.

Chris Munster held up his ID. 'Could we come in?'

She stood aside and let them into the communal hallway.

'We want to check on the residents of this building. Do you live here?'

'Yes.'

'Alone?'

'No. With my husband, who's in bed, and my two sons, who are at school, if that's what you were going to ask. What is this?'

'Is your husband ill?' asked Riley.

'He lost his job.' The woman glared, her face tight. 'He's on disability. I've got all the forms.'

'We don't care about that,' said Munster. 'Do you know a woman called Ruth Lennox?'

'I've never heard of her. Why?'

'She came to this address last Wednesday.'

He took the photograph of Ruth out of his pocket and held it out. 'Do you recognize her?'

She examined the picture, wrinkling her face. 'I don't take much notice of people who come and go,' she said.

'She's been the victim of a crime. We think she came here on the day she died.'

'Died? What are you suggesting?'

'Nothing. Really nothing. We just want to find out if she was here that day, and why.'

'Well, she wasn't in our place at any rate. I don't know any Ruth Lennox. I don't know this woman.' She jabbed the photo. 'And we're law-abiding citizens, which can be hard enough these days.'

'Do you know who lives in the other flats?'

'There's nobody above. They moved out months ago. And I don't know about downstairs.'

'But somebody lives there?'

'I wouldn't say *lives*. Somebody rents it but I don't see them.'

'Them?'

'Them. Him. Her. I don't know.' She relented. 'I hear a radio sometimes. During the day.'

'Thank you. And last Wednesday, did you see anyone there?'

'No. But I wasn't looking.'

'Perhaps your husband might have seen something if he's here during the day?'

She looked from one face to the other, then gave a small, weary shrug. 'He sleeps a lot, or sort of sleeps, because of his pills.'

'No. That's all right. Can you tell me who your landlord is?'

'You don't see him round here.'

'What's his name?'

'Mr Reader. Michael Reader. Maybe you've heard of him. You see his boards up everywhere. His grandfather bought up loads of these houses after the war. He's the real criminal.'

TWENTY

Duncan Bailey lived in Romford, in a concrete, brutalist apartment block. It was built on a grand scale, with chilly corridors and high ceilings, large windows that overlooked a tumble of buildings and tangled ribbons of roads.

Frieda knew that he would be there, because after some thought she had rung his mobile and made an appointment to see him. He hadn't sounded flustered, or even surprised, but relaxed and almost amused, and he had agreed to see her at half past five that afternoon, when he returned from the library. He was a psychology graduate student at Cardinal College where Hal Bradshaw was a visiting lecturer.

She walked up the stairs to the third floor, then along the broad corridor. Would Bailey think she was out for revenge? No, it wasn't for revenge that Frieda was there but something odder, more formless. She couldn't see it, couldn't hear it, couldn't smell or touch it, but some vague and shadowy shape shifted and stirred in her mind.

Duncan Bailey was an unusually small young man. He seemed out of place and almost comical in the cavernous living room. He had light brown hair and a neat goatee, lively blue eyes, a thin and mobile face. His manner was genial and mischievous. It was hard to tell if he was being sincere or sarcastic.

'Thank you for agreeing to see me,' said Frieda.

'No problem. I've heard so much about you.'

'I just wanted to ask you a couple of questions. It's about the experiment we both took part in.'

'No hard feelings, I hope,' he said, with a smile.

'Why would there be?'

'Some people might feel they'd been humiliated. But it's all in the cause of science. Anyway, Dr Bradshaw said you might not see it that way.'

'He should know,' said Frieda. 'But, as I understand it, you all had to pretend to be the same case study, describe the same symptoms, is that right?'

'Dr Bradshaw said we could go off script as much as we wanted as long as we smuggled in the vital ingredients.'

'So, things like the story about cutting the father's hair: that was in your story too?'

'Yes. Did you like it?'

'Did Dr Bradshaw create the case study himself?'

'He signed off on it, but it was put together by one of the other researchers. We never met as a group. I came into it rather late, as a favour.'

'Who were they?'

'You want me to give you their names?'

'Out of interest.'

'So you can visit them too?'

'Maybe.'

'You're going to a lot of effort. Romford seems a long way to come just to ask a simple question. I would have told you over the phone. Especially after you've been so ill.'

Frieda didn't say anything, just looked at him.

'Don't you want to know which one I went to see?'

'Not particularly.'

'It was your friend.'

Poor Reuben, thought Frieda. He wouldn't have stood a chance with someone like Duncan Bailey.

'James Rundell.' He looked at her enquiringly, head cocked to one side. 'I can see why someone would want to punch him.'

Frieda suppressed a smile at the thought of James Rundell meeting this sharp, cynical, bright-eyed young man.

'But you can't just go around thinking you can control people,' Duncan Bailey continued. 'I mean, it's very nice to meet you, of course, but someone more sensitive than me might be intimidated by your visit, Dr Klein. Do you see what I mean?'

'I just want the names.'

Bailey thought for a moment. 'Why not? They'll be in the psychology journal soon enough. Shall I write them down for you? I can give you their addresses if that would help. Save you going to any trouble.' He uncurled himself from his chair with the agility of a cat and padded lightly across the room.

Five and a half hours later, Frieda was on a plane. The last-minute flight had been eyewateringly expensive; she was going for a ridiculously short time; above all, she was scared of flying and for nearly a decade had avoided it. She sat in an aisle seat and ordered a tomato juice. The woman next to her snored gently. Frieda sat upright, burning with fear: because she was flying, because Dean Reeve was still alive, because she knew what it felt like to die, because she was so glad she would be seeing Sandy and because caring so much was dangerous. It was safer to be alone.

When Fearby phoned Vanessa Dale, she said she'd moved away years earlier. Now she lived in Leeds. She worked in a chemist's. Fearby said that was fine. He could come and see her. Did she have a break? Oh, and one other thing. Did she have a photograph of herself? From that time? Could she bring it with her?

He met her outside on the pavement and walked with her to a coffee shop a few doors along. He ordered tea for himself and for her a kind of coffee with an exotic name. Although it was the smallest size, the foamy concoction looked enough for four people. Vanessa Dale was dressed in a dark red skirt over thick tights, ankle boots and a brightly patterned shirt. He noticed she had a badge with her name on just above her left breast. He took out his pen and his notebook. You think you'll remember things, but you don't. That was why he wrote everything down, transcribed it, put the date beside each entry.

'Thank you for taking the time,' he said.

'That's all right,' she said.

'Did you manage to find an old picture?'

She opened her purse and took out two passport pictures, snipped from a set of four. He looked at it, then at her. The older Vanessa was plumper in the face, the hair long and dark. 'Can I keep this?' he said.

'I'm not bothered,' she said.

'Someone rang me,' said Fearby. 'Someone from the police. He said that you contacted them on the thirteenth of July 2004. Is that right?'

'I did contact the police once, years ago. I don't remember the date.'

'Why did you ring them?'

'Someone gave me a fright. I called the police about it.'

'Could you tell me what happened?'

Vanessa looked suspicious. 'What's this about?'

'I told you, I'm writing a story. But your name won't come into it.'

'It seems stupid now,' said Vanessa, 'but it was really creepy. I was walking back from the shops near where my parents lived. There was a bit of scrubland. There's a Tesco's there now. And a car pulled up. A man asked for directions. He got out of the car and then he made a grab at me. He got me round the throat. I hit out and screamed at him, then ran away. My mum made me phone the police. A couple of them came round and talked to me about it. That was it.'

'And it didn't feature in the trial.'

'What trial?'

'The trial of George Conley.'

She looked blank.

'Do you remember the murder of Hazel Barton?'

'No.'

Fearby thought for a moment. Was this just another wrong turn? 'What do you remember about your attack?'

'It was years ago.'

'But a man tried to kidnap you,' said Fearby. 'It must have been a memorable experience.'

'It was really weird,' said Vanessa. 'When it happened it was like a dream. You know when you have a really scary dream and then you wake up and you can hardly remember anything about it? I remember a man in a suit.'

'Was he old? Young?'

'I don't know. He wasn't a teenager. And he wasn't an old man. He was quite strong.'

'Big? Little?'

'Sort of average. Maybe a bit bigger than me. But I'm not sure.'

'What about his car? Do you remember its colour, its make?'

She screwed up her face in concentration. 'Silver, I think. But I might be saying that because most cars are silver. Honestly, I can't remember anything, really. I'm sorry.'

'Nothing?'

'I'm sorry, it was just a blur even then and now it's seven years ago. I remember the man and the feeling of his hand on my throat and the car revving and revving, and that's all.'

Fearby wrote everything – such as it was – in his notebook.

'And he didn't say anything?'

'He asked for directions, like I said. He may have said things when he was grabbing me. I don't remember.'

'And you never heard back from the police?'

'I didn't expect to.'

Fearby closed his notebook. 'Well done,' he said.

She looked puzzled. 'What do you mean?'

'You fought him off.'

'It wasn't like that,' she said. 'It didn't feel like me. It was like watching myself on TV.' She picked up her phone. 'I've got to get back.'

TWENTY-ONE

Frieda didn't know New York: it was an abstract to her, a city of shadows and symbols, of steam rising from drains; a place of arrivals and scatterings.

She liked flying in when it was still dark, though dawn showed in a ribbon of light, so that everything was partially hidden from her, just a shifting pattern of massed buildings and pulsing lights, life glimpsed through windows. Soon she would see it laid out clear before her, its mystery resolving into plainness.

She hadn't told Sandy she was coming because she hadn't known that she was. It was early morning and he would still be in bed, so she did what she always did when she felt uncertain: she walked, following the map she had bought, until at last she was on Brooklyn Bridge, looking back at the skyline of Manhattan, which was at once familiar and alien. Frieda thought of her own narrow little house, surrounded by a network of small streets. There, she knew when a shop's shutters had been newly painted, or a plane tree had been pruned. She thought she could have found her way blind to her front door. Suddenly she felt almost homesick and could barely comprehend the instinct that had sent her there.

By seven o'clock she was in Sandy's neighbourhood, but she hesitated to wake him yet. The day was cool and cloudy, with a blustery wind that threatened rain. Even the air smelt different there. She made her way up the street to a small café, where she ordered a coffee, taking it to one of the metal tables by the window that looked out on to the street. She was cold, tired and full of a thick and mysterious trouble. She couldn't work out if this came from the events of the past weeks, or from being there, of being about to see Sandy again. She had missed him so, yet now she couldn't imagine seeing him. What would they say to each other and what could possibly match the intensity of their separation? It occurred to her, with a force that made her flinch, as if she'd been hit hard in the stomach and winded, that perhaps she had come to end things with Sandy. Once the thought had occurred to her, it settled like lead in her stomach. Was that it, then?

The little room filled up with people. Outside, it began to drizzle, spattering the window so the shapes in the street outside wavered and blurred. She felt far from herself – there but not there, alone in a teeming city, invisible. The grey sky made her feel as if she was underwater; the journey made time into a kaleidoscope. Maybe she should leave before anything happened, pretend she had never been there.

Sandy, walking past the deli on his way back from the bakery on the corner where he always bought freshly baked rolls for breakfast, glanced briefly at the window of the café, then away again. But with a corner of his vision he had caught sight of a face that reminded him of someone – and he looked back again, and through the raindrops on the glass he saw her. She was sitting with her chin resting in one hand, gazing straight ahead. For a moment, he wondered if he was dreaming. Then, as if she could feel his eyes on her, she turned her head. Their eyes met. She gave the smallest smile, drained her coffee, stood up and left the café, emerging on to the street. He saw how she still limped; how tired she looked. His heart turned over. She had a leather satchel slung over her shoulder, but no other luggage.

'Christ. What are you doing here?'

'I've come to see you, obviously.'

'Christ,' he repeated.

'I was about to call you. I didn't want to wake you.'

'You know me.' He rubbed his unshaven cheek and stared at her. 'Early riser. What time is it for you?'

'I don't know. No time. Now.'

'So you've just been sitting here, waiting?'

'Yes. What's in the bag?'

'Breakfast. Do you want some?'

'That would be nice.'

'But, Frieda —'

'What? Is there some other woman in your flat?'

Sandy gave a shaky laugh. 'No. No other woman in my flat just now.'

He untied the belt of her raincoat and took it off her, hanging it on the hook beside his own coat. She liked the way he took such care. He unzipped her boots and took them off, pairing them against the wall. He led her to his bedroom and closed the thin brown curtains, so the light became dim and murky. The window was slightly open and she could hear the sounds of the street; the day beginning. Her body felt soft and slack – desire and fatigue and dread plaited loosely together until she couldn't tell them apart. He peeled off her clothes and folded them, putting them on the wooden chair, then unclasped the thin necklace she was wearing and trickled it on to the window-sill. He ran his fingers over her scars, over her tired, stale, jetlagged body. All the while she looked at him steadily, almost curiously, as if she was making up her mind about something. He wanted to close his eyes to her scrutiny, but couldn't.

Later, she had a shower while he made her coffee, strong and hot, and she drank it in bed with the thin sheet pulled over her.

'Why did you suddenly decide to come?'

'I don't know.'

'When are you here until?'

'Tomorrow afternoon.'

'Tomorrow!'

'Yes.'

'Then we have to make the most of the time we have.'

Frieda slept, but shallowly, so that she heard Sandy make calls in the other room cancelling arrangements, while the sounds of the street entered her dreams. They walked through the neighbourhood and bought cooking utensils for Sandy's flat and ate a late lunch in a deli. Sandy talked about work, people he'd met, Brooklyn, their summer plans. He mimicked colleagues, acted out scenarios, and she remembered the first time they'd met. She had thought him another of those doctors – maybe a surgeon, he had a surgeon's hands — self-possessed, amiable, charming when he wanted to be with maybe a touch of the ladies' man about him. Not of interest to her. But then she'd heard his buoyant gust of laughter and seen how his smile could be wolfish, sardonic. He could be detached sometimes, anger made him mild and aloof, but at others he was almost womanly. He cooked meals for her with a delicate attention to detail; had a relish for gossip; tucked the sheet under the mattress with a hospital corner, the way his mother must have taught him while he was still little and, by his own account, fiercely shy.

Only when Frieda was more relaxed did he ask her any questions. Frieda told him about the Lennox family, gave him news of her friends. They were both conscious that something lay ahead of them, some subject to be broached, and now they circled it cautiously, waiting.

'And that news story?' he asked.

'I don't want to talk about it.'

'But I do. You're here for twenty-four hours. We have to talk about things like that.'

'Have to?'

'You can't intimidate me with that voice, Dr Frieda Klein.'

'I didn't like it. Is that what you want to hear?'

'Did you feel humiliated?'

'I felt exposed.'

'When you want always to be invisible. Were you angry?'

'Not like Reuben.' She smiled at the memory. 'Now he was angry. Still is.'

'And did you feel that you acted improperly at all?'

Frieda scowled at him and he waited patiently.

'I don't think so,' she said eventually. 'But maybe I have to feel justified, or it would be too painful. But I really don't believe so. The man who came to me was a charlatan. He wasn't a psychopath, just acting out the part. Why should I have taken him seriously?'

'Did you know that at the time?'

'In a way. But that isn't really the point.'

'What is the point?'

'The point is that what happened has set me off on something.'

'What does that mean, set you off?'

'The man who came to me told me a story.'

'I know that.'

'No,' Frieda said impatiently. 'There was a story within the story and I felt . . .' She stopped, considered. 'I felt summoned.'

'That's an odd word.'

'I know.'

'You have to explain.'

'I can't.'

'What was the story?'

'About cutting someone's hair. A feeling of power and tenderness. Something sinister and sexual. Everything else was sham, phoney, but this felt authentic.'

'And it summoned you?' Sandy was staring at her with a worried expression on his face that Frieda found infuriating. She looked away.

'That's right.'

'But to *what*?'

'You wouldn't understand.'

'Try me.'

'Not now, Sandy.'

They ate in a small fish restaurant a short walk from the flat. The rain had stopped and the wind had died down. The air smelt fresher. Frieda wore a shirt of Sandy's over her linen trousers. There was a candle between them, a bottle of dry white wine, hunks of bread and olive oil. Sandy told Frieda about his first marriage – how it had become an aridly competent affair by the end. How they had wanted different things.

'Which were?'

'We imagined the future differently,' said Sandy. He looked to one side.

Frieda examined him. 'You wanted children?'

'Yes.'

A small, weighty silence wedged itself between them.

'And now?' she asked.

'Now I want you. Now I imagine a future with you.'

At three in the morning, when it was as dark and as quiet as a great city ever gets, Frieda put a hand on Sandy's shoulder.

'What?' he murmured, turning towards her.

'There's something I should say.'

'Shall I turn the light on?'

'No. It's better in the dark. I've asked myself if we should end this.'

There was a moment of silence. Then he said, almost angrily: 'So at the moment of most love and trust between us, you think of leaving?'

She didn't say anything.

'I never had you down for a coward,' he said.

Still Frieda lay against him in silence. Words seemed futile.

'And what have you answered yourself?' he asked, after a while.

'I haven't.'

'Why, Frieda?'

'Because I'm no good for anyone.'

'Let me decide that.'

'I am chock full of unease.'

'Yes.' His voice was soft again in the darkness, his hand warm on her hip. She could feel his breath in her hair.

'Dean's still out there. He's been to my father's grave –'

'What? How do you know?'

'Never mind that now. I know. He wants me to know.'

'You're sure that –' She made an impatient movement and he stopped.

'Yes, I'm certain.'

'That's horrible and incredibly disturbing. But Dean can't get between the two of us. Why should you want to end things with us because of a psychopath?'

'When I said I felt summoned –'

'Yes.'

'It feels a bit like going into the underworld.'

'Whose underworld? Yours?'

'I don't know.'

'Then, Frieda, don't go there. It was just a stupid story. It's your mood talking, the trauma you've been through. It's not rational. You're mistaking depression for reality.'

'That's too easy to say.'

'Can I ask you something without you closing down on me?'

'Go on.'

'When your father killed himself and you found him . . .' he felt her stiffen '. . . you were fifteen. Did you ever talk to anyone about it?'

'No.'

'And since then?'

'Not as such.'

'Not as such. Don't you think that all this,' he made an invisible gesture, 'all this about Dean, about your work with the police, this new idea you've got about some story summoning you – all of this is just about you as a teenage girl finding your father hanging from a beam? Not saving him? And that's what you should be thinking of, rather than charging off on another rescue mission?'

'Thank you, Doctor. But Dean is real. Ruth Lennox was real. And this other thing . . .' She turned her body so that now she was lying on her back, gazing up at the ceiling. 'I don't know what it is,' she admitted.

'Stop all that you're doing. Stay here. Stay with me.'

'You should be with someone who's happy.' She added: 'And who you can have children with.'

'I've made my choice.'

'But –'

'I've made my choice. If you want to leave me because you no longer love me, then I have to accept that. But if you want to leave me because you love me and it scares you, I won't accept it.'

'Listen to me.'

'No.'

'Sandy –'

'No.' He propped himself up on one arm and leaned over her. 'Trust me. Let me trust you. I'll come into the underworld with you if you want. I'll wait for you at its entrance. But I won't be sent away.'

'You're a very stubborn man.'

Limb against limb; mouth against mouth; bodies losing their boundaries. Light spilling into darkness and dawn returning.

A few hours later, Frieda packed her toothbrush, checked her passport, said goodbye as if she was going round the corner to the newsagent. She'd always hated farewells.

TWENTY-TWO

It was the weekend and Karlsson had cancelled all arrangements so that he could spend two clear days with Mikey and Bella. His chest ached with the knowledge that in a few days they would be gone, far away from him, just photographs on his desk that he would stare at, tinny voices at the end of the phone, jerky images on Skype. Every minute with them felt precious. He had to stop himself holding Bella too close, stroking Mikey's hair until he squirmed away from him. They mustn't know how much he minded them going or feel anxious and guilty for him.

He took them to the pool at Archway, where there was a twisting slide into the deep end and wave machines that made them shriek with gleeful fear. He threw them up into the air, let them duck him, ride on his shoulders. He dived under the turquoise water, his eyes open, and saw their white legs thrashing around among all the other legs. He watched them as they raced into the shallow end, two squealing figures, their eyes pink from the chlorine.

They went to the playground and he pushed them on the swings, spun the roundabout until he was dizzy, crawled through a long plastic tube behind them and climbed up a pile of rubber tyres. My children, he thought, my boy and girl. He held their smiles in his mind for later. They ate ice creams and went to lunch at a Pizza Express.

Everywhere he looked, he seemed to see single fathers. He had made mistakes, he had always put work first, thinking he had no choice, and he had missed the bedtime rituals and the morning chaos. There had often been several days in a row when he hadn't seen his children at all, out before they woke and home after they slept, and had once flown home from holiday early. He had let his wife take up the slack and he hadn't understood the consequences until it was far too late, and there was no way back. Was this the price he had to pay?

They played a board game that he made sure he lost and he showed them a very simple magic trick he'd learned with cards, and they shouted at him as if he was a wizard. Then he put on a video and the three of them sat on the sofa together, him in the middle, warm and full of sadness.

When the phone rang, he ignored it and at last it stopped. Then it rang again. Mikey and Bella looked at him expectantly and moved away, so he reluctantly stood up, went over to it and picked it up from its holster.

'Yes?'

'It's Yvette.'

'It's Sunday.'

'I know, but . . .'

'I'm with my kids.' He hadn't told her they were leaving. He didn't want anyone at work to know and pity him. They'd start inviting him out for drinks after work, stop thinking of him as the boss and think of him as a poor sap instead.

'Yes.' She sounded flustered. 'I just wanted to keep you in the loop. You told me I should.'

'Go on.'

'Ruth Lennox went somewhere before she went home: a flat near Elephant and Castle. We've managed to trace the landlord; he was away so it took a bit of time. He seemed relieved to find that we were only contacting him about a murder,' she added drily. 'He confirmed that the flat was rented to a Mr Paul Kerrigan, a building surveyor.'

'And?'

'I talked to Mr Kerrigan. And there's something up. I don't know what. He didn't want to talk over the phone. We're meeting him tomorrow morning.'

There was a silence. Yvette waited, then said forlornly: 'I thought you'd like to know.'

'What time?'

'Half past eight, at the building site he's currently working on. The Crossrail development, down on Tottenham Court Road.'

'I'll be there.'

'Do you think –'

'I said I'll be there.'

Karlsson put the phone back in its holster, already regretting his sharpness. It wasn't Yvette's fault.

Later, after Mikey and Bella had been collected by their mother and he'd gone for a run, he paced the garden with one of his illicit cigarettes. Birds were singing in the dusk, but that just made him feel sourer and more defeated. He went indoors and picked up the phone, then sat on the sofa where his children had been just a couple of hours previously. He held the phone and stared at it as if it could tell him something. At last, before he could change his mind, he called Frieda's number. He had to talk to someone and she was the only person he could bear to unburden himself to. The phone rang and rang; he could almost hear it echoing in her tidy, empty house. She wasn't there. He called her mobile, although he knew that she almost never turned it on or even listened to messages left there – sure enough, it went straight to voicemail.

He closed his tired, sore eyes and waited for the feeling to recede. The thought of work was a relief from the thought of life.

'What was it like?' said Sasha, later that evening.

'When I got out of the tube,' said Frieda, 'on the way back from the airport, it was quite strange. For just a moment, London seemed different. It looked grubby and stunted and quite poor. It was like moving to the Third World.'

'I was really asking you about New York.'

'You've seen the movies,' said Frieda. 'You've probably been there several times. You know what it's like.'

'When I was asking you about New York, I was really asking you about Sandy.'

'He thinks I should move there,' said Frieda. 'He says I should be somewhere that's less dangerous.'

'And be with him.'

'Yes. That too.'

'Are you tempted?'

'I said no before,' said Frieda. 'Now – I don't know. I miss him. But I've got things to do here. Things that need finishing. Now, when am I going to meet this new man of yours?'

Frieda, my dearest heart, it all feels like a dream. You here in this city, this flat, this bed. Everything feels different now. Thank you for being here and remember everything I said. We've come too far together to stop now. We're on a journey together.
Sandy xxxx

TWENTY-THREE

At twenty past eight, Karlsson was standing on the edge of a vast crater in the heart of the city, looking at the activity in front of him: small diggers trundled across mashed earth, cranes lowered huge pipes into trenches, men in yellow jackets and hard hats gathered in groups, or sat on top of machines operating their articulated metal arms. Around the site were several Portakabins, some of them seeming almost as permanent as the buildings they were next to.

He saw Yvette walking towards him. She looked solid and competent to him, with her robust shoes and her brown hair tied tightly back. He wondered what he looked like to her: he felt fragile, incomplete. His head banged from the three whiskies he'd drunk last night, and his stomach felt hollow.

'Morning,' she said cheerfully.

'Hi.'

'He said he'd meet us in the office.' Yvette jerked her head towards the main Portakabin, a few yards away, with wooden steps leading up to the door.

They made their way over the rutted ground and up the steps, then Yvette knocked at the door, which was opened almost at once. The man in front of them was also wearing a yellow jacket, although his was over a pair of brown corduroy trousers and a grey-striped shirt. He was solidly built, with a creased face and brown eyes. Although he could only have been in his mid-forties, his hair was a thick silver-grey.

'Paul Kerrigan?'

'That's me.'

Yvette held up her ID. 'I'm DC Yvette Long,' she said. 'We spoke on the phone. And this is DCI Malcolm Karlsson.'

Karlsson looked into the man's soft brown eyes and felt a tremor of anticipation. He nodded at him.

'You'd better come in.'

They entered the Portakabin, which smelt of wood and coffee. There was a desk in there, a trestle table and several chairs. Karlsson sat to one side and let Yvette ask the questions. He already knew that they had reached a watershed: he could feel the inquiry shifting under their feet, turning into something altogether different and unexpected.

'We were given your name by Michael Reader.'

'Yes.' It wasn't a question.

'He said you rented thirty-seven A Shawcross Road from him and had done for almost ten years.'

Kerrigan's eyes flickered. Karlsson looked at him closely.

'That's right. Since June 2001.' He looked down at his large, calloused hands.

'The reason we're asking you is because we want to trace the last movements of Ruth Lennox, who was murdered twelve days ago. A taxi driver delivered her to that address on the day she died.'

'Yes,' he said again. He seemed passive and defenceless.

He was simply waiting for the truth to emerge, lie in front of the three of them.

'Were you there?'

'Yes.'

'You knew Ruth Lennox?'

There was a silence in the room. Karlsson listened to the sounds coming from the building site: the roar of engines and the shouts of the men.

'Yes,' said Paul Kerrigan, very softly. They could hear the sound he made when he swallowed. 'I'm sorry I didn't come before. I should have done. But I didn't see the point. She was dead. It was finished. I thought I could stop the hurt spreading.'

'Were you having a relationship?'

He glanced from Yvette to Karlsson, then put both hands on the table in front of him. 'I have a wife,' he said. 'I have two sons who are proud of me.'

'You understand this is a murder inquiry,' said Yvette. Her eyes were bright.

'Yes, we were having a relationship.' He blinked, folded his hands together. 'I find it hard to say that out loud.'

'And you saw her on the day she was killed?'

'Yes.'

Karlsson spoke at last. 'I think perhaps you'd better tell us the whole story.'

Paul nodded slowly. 'Yes,' he said. 'But I . . .' He stopped.

'What?'

'I don't want anyone to know.' He paused. 'I don't know how to do this.'

'Perhaps you can just tell us in chronological order what happened. Begin at the beginning.'

He stared out of the window, as if he couldn't start while looking at them. 'I met Ruth ten years ago. We live quite near each other. We met at fundraising events for the mothers and toddlers.' He smiled. 'She was selling falafels and I was helping with the lottery tickets on the next-door stall. We got on. She was very easy to get on with – everyone liked her. She was kind and practical and made you feel everything was going to be all right. I didn't know that at the time, of course. I just thought she was nice. You probably think that *nice* isn't a very romantic word. It wasn't that kind of affair.' He made a visible effort and went on with the story: 'We met after, for coffee. It just felt natural.'

'Are you saying,' interrupted Yvette, 'that you and Ruth Lennox were lovers for ten years?'

'Yes. We got the flat after a few months. We chose that area because it wasn't somewhere we'd bump into anyone we knew. We never went to each other's houses. We met on Wednesday afternoons.'

Yvette leaned forward. 'You're saying that every Wednesday afternoon, for ten years, you and Ruth Lennox met at this flat?'

'Except when we were on holiday. Sometimes we couldn't make it.'

'And no one knew?'

'Well, as a matter of fact my partner knows. I mean, my work partner. At least, he knows that every Wednesday I'm not available. He turns a blind eye. He probably thinks it's funny –' He stopped abruptly. 'Nobody else knew anything. We were careful. Once or twice we'd see each other on the streets near our homes and we'd ignore each other.

Not even a smile. Nothing. We never phoned each other or sent each other messages.'

'What if one of you had to cancel?'

'We'd tell each other the week before, if we could. If one of us went to the flat and the other hadn't turned up after fifteen minutes, we'd know something had happened.'

'That all sounds very neat,' Yvette said. 'A bit cold-blooded.'

He unplaited his hands. 'I don't expect you to understand, but I love my wife and Ruth loved her husband. We wouldn't have hurt them for the world. Or our kids. This was separate. Nobody would be affected. We never even talked about our families when we were together.' He turned back to the window. 'I can't believe I'll never see her again,' he said. 'I can't believe I won't go to the door and open it and she'll be standing there with her smiling face. I dream about her, and when I wake I feel so calm, and then I remember.'

'We need you to tell us about that last Wednesday,' said Yvette.

'It was the same as always. She came about half past twelve. I was already there. I always get there before her. I'd bought some bread and cheese for lunch and some flowers, which I'd put in a vase she'd bought the year before, and I'd put the heating on because although it was a warm day the flat felt a bit chilly.'

'Go on.'

'So.' He seemed to find it hard to speak now. 'She came and – do you need to know everything?'

'Just the bare facts for now. You had sex, I take it.' Yvette sounded harsh, even to herself.

'We made love. Yes. Then we had a bath together before we ate the food. Then she left and I locked up and left about half an hour after her.'

'What time would this be?'

'She left at about three, maybe a touch earlier, ten to three or something. Like she always did. So I left at three thirty or a quarter to four.'

'Did anyone see you?'

'I don't think so. We never met the other people in the building.'

'Do you know where she was going?'

'She always went home straight away.'

'And you?'

'Sometimes I went back to work. That day I went home.'

'Was your wife there?'

'No. She arrived at about six, I think.'

'So you saw no one between leaving Shawcross Street and your wife arriving home two hours or so later?'

'Not that I remember.'

'When did you hear about Ruth Lennox's death?' asked Karlsson.

'It was in the papers the next day. Elaine – my wife – showed me. Her photo was there, and she was smiling. At first I had this stupid idea that it was about us – that someone had discovered and put it in the papers. I couldn't speak. She said: "Isn't this terrible? Did we ever meet her?"'

'And what did you say?'

'I don't know. Elaine said, "Doesn't she have a nice face? Poor children." Things like that. I don't know what I said.

It's all a blur now. I don't know how I got through the evening. The boys were there and there was a general noise and bustle and they had their homework, and Elaine made a meal. Shepherd's pie. And I put it in my mouth and swallowed it. And I had a shower and just stood there for ages and nothing seemed real.'

'Did you feel guilty?'

'What about?'

'About having an affair for ten years.'

'No.'

'Although you're married.'

'I never felt guilty,' he repeated. 'I knew Elaine and the boys would never know. It wasn't hurting anyone.'

'Did Ruth feel guilty?'

'I don't know. She never said she did.'

'You are certain your wife didn't know?'

'I'd know if she knew.'

'And Ruth's husband, Russell Lennox? Did he know anything or have suspicions?'

'No.'

'Did Ruth Lennox tell you that?'

'She would have told me if he'd suspected, I'm sure.' He sounded uncertain, though.

'And that day, did she seem any different?'

'No. She was the same as always.'

'And how was that?'

'Calm. Cheerful. Nice.'

'She was always calm and always cheerful and nice? For ten years?'

'She had ups and downs, like anyone.'

'And was she up or down on that Wednesday?'

'Neither.'

'Just in the middle, you mean?'

'I mean she was fine.'

Yvette looked at Karlsson to see if he had any further questions. 'Mr Kerrigan,' said Karlsson. 'Your relationship with Ruth Lennox sounds oddly like a marriage to me, rather than an affair. Domestic, calm, safe.' Placid, he thought, almost dull.

'What are you saying?' Now he looked angry. His hands curled into fists.

'I don't know.' Karlsson thought of Frieda: what would she ask this man, who was sitting passively in front of them, his shoulders slumped and his big hands restless? 'You do understand this alters everything?'

'What do you mean?'

'You aren't stupid. Ruth Lennox had a secret. A great big secret.'

'But nobody knew.'

'You knew.'

'Yes. But I didn't kill her! If you think that – look, I swear to you, I didn't kill her. I loved her. We loved each other.'

'Secrets are difficult to keep,' said Karlsson.

'We were careful. Nobody knew.'

Karlsson took in Kerrigan's sad, uneasy face. 'Is it possible that she was going to end it?'

'No. It's not possible.'

'So nothing had changed.'

'No' His face was swollen with misery. 'Will they have to know?'

'You mean her husband? Your wife? We'll see. But it may be difficult.'

'How long?'

'For what?'

'How long do I have before I have to tell her?'

Karlsson didn't answer. He looked at Paul Kerrigan for a few moments, then said musingly, 'Everything has a consequence.'

Twenty-four

When Rajit Singh opened the door, he was wearing a heavy black jacket. 'It's the heating,' he said. 'Someone was meant to come today to fix it.'

'I'll only be a minute,' said Frieda. 'I won't even need to take my coat off.'

He led her through to a sitting room in which every piece of furniture, the chairs, a sofa, a table, seemed to jar with everything else. On the wall was a picture of the Eiffel Tower in brightly coloured velvet. He noticed her expression.

'When I was an undergraduate, I stayed in the residence that was right in the West End. Everything's sorted for you, where you sleep, where you eat, who you become friends with. But once you're doing your postgraduate work, you're left to fend for yourself. I was lucky to get this, believe it or not. I'm sharing it with a couple of Chinese engineering students who I never see.'

'You live all over the place,' said Frieda.

'Me?' said Singh. 'I just live here.'

'No, I mean you and the rest of you. Seamus Dunne, the one who came to see me, he lives in Stockwell. I saw Duncan Bailey at his flat in Romford. Later I'm going to Waterloo to see Ian Yardley.'

Singh sat in the armchair and gestured at the sofa. Frieda preferred to stand up so she could move around. Even though it was sunny in the street outside, it was icy in the house.

'We're not a gang,' he said. 'We don't exactly hang out together.'

'You're just Professor Bradshaw's students.'

'That's right. We're the ones who volunteered for his clever experiment. The one that seems to have got under your skin.'

'Which therapist did you see?'

Singh's face tightened. 'Are you trying to trap me?' he said. 'Are you going to sue us?'

'No,' said Frieda. 'This is all for my benefit. Let's just say I'm curious.'

'Look,' said Singh, 'we didn't have anything to do with that stuff in the newspaper. I thought it would appear in a psychology journal that no one would read and that would be the end of it. I don't know how that happened.'

'It doesn't matter,' said Frieda. 'I'm not bothered with that. Just tell me about your part in it.'

'I ended up with the therapist who passed the test. She's a woman called Geraldine Fliess. Apparently she wrote some book about how we're all really psychopaths, or something like that. Anyway, I went and saw her, gave the spiel about having been cruel to animals and that I had fantasies of hurting women. Later she got back in touch with me, asking me who my doctor was and other things like that.'

'What did you tell her?'

'Professor Bradshaw told us that if anyone took us up on what we had said, if they really picked up on the danger, we should just refer them to him and he would tell them about the experiment. You know, to avoid us getting arrested.'

'What would you have been arrested for?' Frieda asked.

'All right, all right,' said Singh, irritably. 'She got it right and you didn't. It's not the end of the world. Just let it go.'

'But I'm interested in the story you all told. How was that done?'

'There was nothing clever about it. Bradshaw gave us the things on the psychopath checklist and we just had to agree on a story, rehearse it and perform it.'

'I don't care about the checklist,' said Frieda. 'I'm more interested in the other details. Where did all the bits that had nothing to do with the checklist come from? Things like that story about cutting hair. What was that about?'

'What does it matter?'

Frieda thought for a moment and looked around her. The room wasn't just cold. There was a smell of damp. There didn't seem to be a single object that hadn't been left there by the landlord and that was the sort of stuff – abandoned, unloved – you'd pick up in car-boot sales, house clearances.

'I think it's difficult to pretend to be a patient,' Frieda said. 'For most people, the difficult bit is to ask for help in the first place. Once they're sitting in a room with me, they've already made a painful decision. I think it's just as difficult to pretend to ask for help.'

'I don't know what you're talking about.'

'When I came in, you apologized about the house.'

'I didn't apologize about it. I said I was lucky to get it.'

'You said that when you were an undergraduate

everything was arranged for you, but now you were left to fend for yourself. You told me that you never see your housemates.'

'I meant that as a good thing.'

'You probably don't want to hear this from me . . .'

'You know, I've got a feeling you're about to say something about me that isn't complimentary.'

'Not at all. But I wonder if when you volunteered for this experiment, the chance to go to a therapist but not *really* go to a therapist, it gave you an opportunity to express something. A kind of sadness, a feeling of not being cared for.'

'That is absolute crap. That's exactly what therapists like you do. You read things into what people say in order to give you power over them. And then if they deny it, it makes them look weak. What you're objecting to is the fact that you got involved in an experiment that showed you up. From what I've heard, you and Dr Bradshaw have some kind of history, and if I've played some part in that, then I'm sorry. But don't suck me into your mind games.'

'It doesn't look as if you live here,' said Frieda. 'You haven't hung up a picture, or put a rug down, or even left a book lying around. You're even dressed like you're outside.'

'As you can feel for yourself, it's cold in here. When the man fixes the boiler, I promise you I'll take my jacket off.'

Frieda took a notebook from her pocket, scribbled on a page, tore it out and handed it to Singh. 'If you want to tell me anything about what you said – I mean anything apart from the stupid Hare checklist – you can reach me at that number.'

'I don't know what you want from me,' said Singh, angrily, as Frieda left the house.

Ian Yardley's flat was in a little alley just off a street market. It was down from the Thames but far enough away that the river couldn't be seen. Frieda pressed a buzzer and heard an unintelligible noise from a speaker, then a rattling sound. She pulled at the door but it was still locked. More noise came from the speaker, then more electronic rattling, a click and the door was unlocked. Frieda walked up some carpeted stairs to a landing with two separate doors, labelled one and two. Door one opened and a dark-haired woman peered out.

'I'm here to see –'

'I know,' said the woman. 'I don't know what this is about. You'd better come in. Just for a minute, though.'

Frieda followed her inside. Yardley was sitting at a table, reading the evening paper and drinking beer. He had long curly hair and glasses with square, transparent frames. He was dressed in a college sweatshirt and dark trousers. His feet were bare. He turned and smiled at her.

'I hear you've been hassling people,' he said.

'I think you called on my old friend Reuben.'

'The famous Reuben McGill,' he said. 'I must say I was a bit disappointed by him. When I met him, he looked like someone who'd lost his mojo. He didn't seem to respond to what I was saying at all.'

'Did you want him to respond?' said Frieda.

'What rubbish,' said the woman, from behind her.

'Oh, sorry,' said Ian. 'I'm not being a proper host. This is my friend, Polly. She thinks I shouldn't have let you in. She's more suspicious than I am. Can I offer you a drink? A beer? There's some white wine open in the fridge.'

'No, thanks.'

'Not while you're on duty?'

Frieda began to ask some of the same questions she'd asked Rajit Singh, but she didn't get very far because Polly kept interrupting her, asking what the point of all this was, while Ian just continued to smile, as if he was enjoying the spectacle. Suddenly he stopped smiling.

'Shall I make things clear?' he said. 'If you're here out of some faintly pathetic attempt at revenge, then you're wasting your time. This was all cleared by the ethics committee in advance and we were indemnified. I can show you the small print, if you're interested in reading it. I know it's embarrassing when it's demonstrated that the emperor has no clothes. If you're the emperor. Or the empress.'

'As I've tried to explain,' said Frieda, 'I'm not here to argue about the experiment, I'm –'

'Oh, give us a fucking break,' said Polly.

'If you'll just let me finish a sentence, I'll ask a couple of questions and then I'll leave.'

'What do you mean, and then you'll leave? As if you had any right to be here in the first place! I've got another idea.' Polly prodded Frieda on the shoulder. It was close to where she was still bandaged and made her flinch slightly. 'You've been made a fool of. So deal with it. And just leave, because Ian has nothing to say and you're starting to harass him and to get on my nerves.' She started shoving at Frieda as if she wanted to push her out of the flat.

'Stop that,' said Frieda, raising her hands in defence.

'Time for you to go,' shouted Polly, and pushed even harder.

Frieda put her hand on the woman's chest and pressed her back against the wall and held her there. She leaned close so that their faces were only inches apart and she spoke in a quiet, slow tone. 'I said "stop".'

Yardley stood up. 'What the hell's going on?' he said.

Frieda turned, and as she turned, she took her hand away, then stepped back. She wasn't clear what happened next. She felt a flurry to the side of her. She sensed Polly flying at her and then stumbling over a low stool and falling heavily across it.

'I can't believe this,' said Yardley to Frieda. 'You come here and you start a fight.'

Polly started to struggle to her feet but Frieda stood over her. 'Don't you even think about it,' she said. 'Just stay where you are.' Then she turned to Yardley. 'I think Reuben understood you pretty well.'

'You're threatening me,' he said. 'You've come here to attack me and to threaten me.'

'That hair story had nothing to do with you, did it?' said Frieda.

'What hair story?'

'You're too much of a narcissist,' said Frieda. 'You wanted to impress Reuben and he didn't go for it.'

'What the fuck are you talking about?'

'It's all right,' said Frieda. 'I've got what I came for.'

And she left.

Jim Fearby brought out a large map of Great Britain. There wasn't room for it on the wall so he laid it out on the floor of the living room, with objects (a mug, a tin of beans, a book and a can of beer) on each corner. He took off his shoes and walked across the map, staring down at it and frowning. Then he stuck a flagged pin-tack to the spot where Hazel Barton's body had been found; another where Vanessa Dale had been approached by the man in a car that had perhaps been silver.

He skewered her photograph onto the big cork notice-board, next to Hazel Barton's picture. Two doesn't make a pattern – but it's a start.

TWENTY-FIVE

The only patient Frieda still saw was Joe Franklin. Many of the rest were waiting for her to return, sending her emails asking when she thought she would be well enough. Some she worried about. They jostled at the edge of her consciousness, with their pain and their problems. A few she thought perhaps she would never see again. She had said that in two weeks, at the start of May, she would resume her old duties whatever her doctor might advise, but in the meantime, twice a week and often more, she went to her rooms in the mansion block in Bloomsbury. Today she had been grateful for the opportunity to leave her house because, at a quarter to eight that morning, Josef had arrived. Frieda had left him trudging back and forth from the van, his face beaming at her behind piles of boxes.

After her session with Joe, Frieda stood with her back to the neat room, the red armchair where she always sat, the muted charcoal drawing of a landscape on the wall, staring into the tangled space outside where foxes lurked, shrubs and wild flowers forcing their way up through the cracked earth. She was thinking or at least letting thoughts run through her mind. Her old life seemed far away, a ghost of itself. The woman who had sat in the armchair hour after hour and day after day receded as she pictured her. She had always thought that the centre of her life was in this room, but now it seemed to have shifted: Hal Bradshaw and his four researchers, Karlsson and his cases of death and disappearance, Dean Reeve somewhere out there watching her – all these had pulled her out of it.

She thought now about the four psychology students and their stunt, trying to separate the actual story from the fact of having been tricked and the humiliation of this being made public. She didn't know why she couldn't lay it to one side. It prickled in her mind, shifted and changed in its meaning. There was something that wouldn't let her go, like a piece of string twitching in her hands. Sometimes at night, lying awake with the darkness pressing down on her, she would think of the four of them and what they had said to her. The blades opening and closing; the image of tenderness and dangerous power.

Her mobile rang in her pocket and she took it out.

'Frieda.'

'Karlsson.'

'You turned your phone on.'

'I can see why you became a detective.'

He laughed, then said: 'You were right.'

'Oh, good. What about?'

'Ruth Lennox. She was too good to be true.'

'I don't think I said that. I said she was like an actress performing her life.'

'Exactly. We've found out that she was having an affair. For ten years. Every Wednesday. What do you say to that?'

'That it's a long time.'

'There's more, but I can't talk about that now. I've got to go and see the husband.'

216

'Did he know?'

'He must have done.'

'Why are you telling me?'

'I thought you'd like to know. Was I wrong?'

'I don't know.'

'Can I come round for a drink later? I can fill you in. It can help to talk things through with someone on the outside.'

Something in his voice, the nearest he had ever come to pleading, stopped Frieda refusing.

'Maybe,' she said cautiously.

'I'll be there at seven.'

'Karlsson –'

'I'll call if I'm running late.'

The Lennox family had moved back into their home. The carpet had been removed; the walls had been washed, though the bloodstains were still visible; the broken glass and scattered objects had been taken away.

When Karlsson and Yvette arrived, the door was opened for them by a woman wearing an apron. He could smell baking.

'We've met before,' said the woman, noticing Karlsson's expression, 'but you've forgotten who I am, haven't you?'

'No, I remember you.' He recalled the baby in a sling, the little boy at her side, ashen with exhaustion, the girl pushing her buggy, as if she was trying to copy her mother.

'I'm Louise Weller. Ruth's sister. I was here on the day it all happened.' She ushered them inside.

'Are you staying here?' said Karlsson.

'I'm looking after the family, as much as I can,' she said. 'Someone's got to. It won't get done by itself.'

'But you have children of your own.'

'Well, of course Baby's always here. My sister-in-law is helping out with the other two when they're not at their nursery. This is an emergency,' she added reprovingly, as if he had forgotten that. She regarded him critically. 'I suppose you're here to see Russell.'

'You must have been close to your sister,' said Karlsson.

'Why do you say that?'

'You're here helping her family, even though you have small children of your own. Not everyone would do that.'

'It's my duty,' she said. 'It's not hard to do one's duty.'

Karlsson gave her a closer look. He felt she was telling him who was in charge. 'Did you see much of your sister?'

'We live over in Fulham. My hands are full with my family and we have very different lives. We saw each other when we could. And Christmas, of course. Easter.'

'Did she seem happy?'

'What does that have to do with anything? She was killed by a burglar, wasn't she?'

'We're just trying to build up a picture of your sister's life. I was interested in her frame of mind. As you saw it.'

'She was fine,' said Louise, shortly. 'There was nothing wrong with my sister.'

'And she was happy in her family life?'

'Haven't we suffered enough?' she said, looking at Yvette and then back at Karlsson. 'Are you digging around trying to find something nasty?'

Yvette opened her mouth to say something but Karlsson

flashed her an urgent look and she stopped herself. Somewhere out of sight, the baby began to cry.

'I'd just got him to sleep.' Louise gave a long-suffering sigh. 'You'll find my brother-in-law upstairs. He has his own room at the top.'

Russell Lennox's room was a little den at the back of the house that looked over the garden. Karlsson and Yvette could barely squeeze inside. Yvette leaned on the wall to one side, next to a poster of Steve McQueen clutching a baseball glove. Lennox was sitting at a small pinewood desk, on which was a computer. The screensaver was a family group. They were posing by a blue sea, all wearing sunglasses. Karlsson reckoned it must have been taken a few years earlier. The children were smaller than he remembered.

Before speaking, he examined Lennox, assessing his condition. He seemed in control, clean-shaven, in an ironed blue shirt, evidently the work of his sister-in-law.

'How are you doing?' said Karlsson.

'Haven't you heard?' said Lennox. 'My wife's been murdered.'

'And I was expressing concern. I want to know how you are. I want to know how your children are.'

Lennox replied in an angry tone, but without meeting Karlsson's eyes. He just stared down at the carpet. 'If you really want to know, Dora is scared to go to school, Judith cries all the time and I can't talk to Ted at all. He just won't communicate with me. But I don't want your concern. I want all this brought to an end.' Now he looked up at Karlsson. 'Have you come to tell me about the progress of the investigation?'

'In a way,' said Karlsson. 'But I also need to ask you a few questions as well.' He waited for a moment. He wanted to do this gradually but Lennox didn't speak. 'We're trying to build up a fuller picture of your wife's world.' He glanced at Yvette. 'Some of it may feel intrusive.'

Lennox rubbed his eyes, like someone trying to wake himself up. 'I'm beyond all that,' he said. 'Ask me anything you want. Do anything you want.'

'Good,' said Karlsson. 'Good. So. Well, one question: would you describe your relationship with your wife as happy?'

Lennox started slightly, narrowing his eyes. 'Why would you even ask that?' he said. 'You were here when it happened. On the same day. You saw us all. You saw what it did to us. Are you making some kind of insane accusation?'

'I'm asking a question.'

'Then I'll give you a simple answer, which is, yes, we were happy. Satisfied? And now I'll ask you a simple question. What's going on?'

'We've had an unexpected development in the inquiry,' said Karlsson. As he spoke, he was aware of listening to himself and being repelled by what he heard. He was talking like a machine because he was nervous about what was going to happen.

Frieda handed him a mug of tea and he took several sips before putting the mug on the table.

'Christ, I needed that,' he said. 'Just before I told him, I felt as though I was in a dream. It was as if I was standing in front of a large plate-glass window, holding a stone in my hand, round and solid like a cricket ball. I was about to throw it at the window and I was looking at the glass, smooth and straight, knowing that in a few seconds it would be lying on the ground in jagged pieces.' He stopped. Frieda was sitting down again with her own mug of tea, still untouched. 'You can see that I'm getting better. I didn't tell you not to analyse the image, not to read hidden meaning into it. Except that I have now. But you know what I mean.'

'How did he react?' said Frieda.

'You mean what happened when the stone hit the glass? It shattered, that's what. He was devastated. He'd lost his wife and it was as if I was taking her away from him all over again. At least he'd had the memory of her and there I was contaminating it.'

'You're sounding too much like a therapist,' said Frieda.

'That's rich coming from you. How can anyone be too much like a therapist?' He took another sip of tea. 'The more like a therapist everyone is, the more they're in touch with their feelings, the better.'

'The only people who should be like therapists are therapists,' said Frieda. 'And then only when they're at work. Policemen should be like policemen. So, to get back to my question, did he react in any way that was relevant to the investigation?'

Karlsson put his mug down.

'At first he denied it absolutely and said how much he trusted her and that we'd made a mistake. Then Yvette spelled out in detail what we'd learned about Paul Kerrigan, about the flat, about the days when they met, about how long it had been going on. In the end, he saw reason. He didn't cry, he didn't shout. He just looked almost empty.'

'But did you get the impression that he knew?'

'I don't know. I just don't know. How could it be possible? Ten years, eleven years. She was seeing this man, having sex with him. How did he not smell him on her? How did he not see it in her eyes?'

'You think he must have suspected, at least?'

'Frieda, you sit there day after day with people telling you their dark secrets. Do you ever just think that the clichés about relationships turn out to be true? What it's like to fall in love, what it's like to have a child, and then what it's like to break up. The old cliché, you can live with someone for years and you realize you don't know them.'

'Who are we talking about now?' Frieda asked.

'Well, that was a bit of me, but it's mainly about Russell Lennox. What I hoped for, obviously, was that we'd tell him about the affair, he'd break down, confess everything, case closed.'

'But he didn't.'

'I should have brought you.'

'You make me sound like a dog.'

'I should have invited you to come. As a favour. I'd like you to have been there to see his face at the moment I told him. You notice these things.'

'But Yvette was there.'

'She's worse than I am and I'm bloody awful. You should ask my ex-wife. She'd say that I didn't know what she was feeling, and I'd say that if she wanted me to know what she was feeling, she ought to tell me and . . . Well, you get the idea.'

'If he could sit with you on the day of the murder,' Frieda said, 'and not break down, then today would be no problem for him. And I wouldn't have been any help to you.'

'Do you miss it?' asked Karlsson. 'Be honest.'

Frieda was silent for a long time.

'I don't know,' she said. 'Maybe. Sometimes I catch myself, like when I heard about Ruth Lennox's secret life. But I tried to stop myself.'

'Oh, God,' said Karlsson, with a stab of alarm. 'You're meant to be recovering and here I am, trying to drag you back into what nearly killed you.'

'No! It's not like that at all. It's good to see you. It feels like a visit from the outside world. Some of the visits I have from the outside world are bad but this is one of the good ones.'

'Yes,' said Karlsson. 'Listen, Frieda. I've only just discovered about that bloody scam. I'd like to wring Hal Bradshaw's pompous neck.'

'That probably wouldn't help my cause.'

'He's got it in for you, hasn't he? You made him look bad, and he can't bear that and he won't ever forget it. No wonder he's had such a smirk on his face recently.'

'Are you saying he set the whole thing up just to get at me?'

'He's capable of it. If I had my way, I'd never have to listen to his drivel about the art of crime again. Unfortunately, the commissioner is a fan.' He hesitated, then added:

'Perhaps I shouldn't tell you this, but I'm going to anyway. At the beginning of the Lennox inquiry, I told the commissioner that I didn't want us to use Bradshaw any more. I thought I was making an informal suggestion, but Crawford hauled Bradshaw in and made me repeat what I'd said in front of him. There's nothing he loves more than playing one person off against another.'

'What's this got to do with me?'

'Bradshaw started slagging you off so I defended you and said he was jealous of you because you'd made him look stupid. It's probably my fault for taunting him. I wish there was something I could do.'

'There isn't. And if you think of something, please don't do it.'

'I'm not going to have him getting his hands on the Lennox children, though.'

'Are you going to tell them?'

'Yes. Although perhaps their dad will do it for me. Poor kids. First their mother gets murdered, and then their whole past gets demolished. You know the son already, don't you?'

'I've met him. Why are you looking at me like that?'

'I've got a proposition.'

'The answer's no.'

It was Riley who discovered all the bottles. They were in the small shed in the garden, which was full of the tiny lawnmower, spades, rakes, secateurs, a large ripped tarpaulin, a wheelbarrow, a stack of empty plastic flowerpots, old jam jars, a box of bathroom tiles. Somebody had wanted them to remain hidden, for they were pushed into a corner behind the half-used tins of paint and had been carefully covered with a dust sheet. He looked at them for a while, then went to get Yvette.

Yvette pulled them out one by one and inspected them. Vodka, white cider, cheap whisky: alcohol to get drunk on, not to give pleasure. Were they the children's or the parents', old bottles or recent? They looked new. They looked secret.

TWENTY-SIX

Karlsson needed to find an appropriate adult. Often an appropriate adult for a juvenile is a parent, but in the case of the Lennox children, one of their parents was dead and the other was not at all appropriate in the circumstances. He thought about asking Louise Weller, Ruth's sister, to be present instead – but Judith Lennox said that she would prefer to *die* than talk about her mother in front of her aunt, and Ted had muttered about Louise getting off on the whole thing.

'She can't keep away,' he said. 'We don't want her or her cakes or her religion. Or her bloody baby.'

So the appropriate adult was a woman nominated by Social Services, who turned up at the police station prompt and eager. She was in her early sixties, thin as a bird, bright-eyed and glittering with nervous excitement. It turned out that this was her first interview ever. She'd done the training, of course, she'd read everything she could lay her hands on and, what was more, she prided herself on her gift for getting on well with young people. Teenagers were so frequently misunderstood, weren't they? Often, all they needed was someone to listen to them and be on their side, which was why she was here. She smiled, her cheeks slightly flushed.

'Very well,' said Karlsson, doubtfully. 'You understand that we will conduct three interviews, one after the other, with each of the Lennox children. The eldest, Ted, isn't strictly juvenile – he's just eighteen. As you know, you're simply there to make sure they're properly treated, and if you feel they need anything, you should say so.'

'Such a painful and difficult age,' said Amanda Thorne. 'Half child and half adult.'

'I'll conduct the interviews, and my colleague, Dr Frieda Klein, will also be present.'

When he had told Yvette that he was taking Frieda to talk to Ted, Judith and Dora, not her, she had stared at him with such a reproachful expression that he had almost changed his mind. He could deal with her anger, not her distress. Her cheeks burned and she mumbled that it was fine, perfectly all right, it was up to him and she understood.

Ted was first. He shuffled into the room, laces trailing, hair straggling, hems fraying, all rips and loose ends. His cheeks were unshaven and there was a rash on his neck; he looked unwashed and malnourished. He refused to sit, and stood by the window instead. Spring had come to the garden. There were daffodils in the borders and blossom on the fruit tree.

'Remember me?' said Frieda.

'I didn't know you were with them,' he said.

'Thanks for agreeing to see us like this,' said Karlsson. 'Before we begin, this is Amanda Thorne. She's what is known as an appropriate adult. It means –'

'I know what it means. And I'm not a child. I don't need her here.'

'No, dear,' said Amanda, rising to her feet and crossing

the room to him. 'You're not a child. You're a young man who's been through a terrible, terrible event.'

Ted gazed at her with contempt. She didn't seem to notice.

'I'm here to support you,' she continued. 'If there's anything you don't understand, you must tell me and I can explain. If you feel upset or confused, you can tell me.'

Ted looked down at her tilted, smiling face. 'Shut up.'

'What?'

'Shall we start?' Karlsson interrupted.

Ted folded his arms, stared jeeringly out of the window and wouldn't meet their eyes. 'Go on, then. Are you going to ask me if I know about my mum and her other life?'

'Do you?'

'I do now. My dad told me. Well, he started to tell me and then he was crying and then he told me the rest.'

'So you know your mother was seeing someone else?'

'No. I just know that's what you think.'

'You don't believe it?'

Ted unfolded his arms and turned towards them. 'You know what I think? I think you'll get your hands on every bit of her life and make it ugly, dirty.'

'Ted, I'm very sorry but this is about a murder,' said Karlsson. 'You must see that we have to conduct a full investigation.'

'Ten years!' The words were a shout, his face contorted with fury. 'Since I was eight, and Dora was three. Did I know? No. How does it make me feel that it's all been a lie, a charade? How do you think?' He turned wildly to Amanda Thorne. 'Come on, Appropriate Adult. Tell me what I must be feeling. Or you.' He waved a dirty-nailed hand at Frieda. 'You're a therapist. Tell me about it.'

'Ted,' said Frieda. 'You need to answer the questions.'

'You know what? Some of my friends used to say that they wished she was *their* mother. They won't say that now.'

'Are you saying you had absolutely no idea?'

'Do you want to take a break?' Amanda Thorne asked.

'No, he doesn't,' Karlsson said sharply.

'Of course I had no idea. She was the good mother, the good wife, the good neighbour. Mrs fucking Perfect.'

'But does it make sense to you now?'

Ted turned to Frieda. He seemed bony and brittle, as if he might crumble into a pile of sharp fragments if anyone touched him, tried to hold him. 'What d'you mean?'

'You're suddenly and painfully having to see your mother in a new way – not the person everyone seems to describe as safe and calm and unselfish. Someone with another, radically different, side to her, with needs and desires of her own and a whole life she was leading in secret, separate from all of you – and I'm asking if in retrospect that makes any sense to you.'

'No. I don't know. I don't want to think about it. She was my mum. She was . . .' he closed his eyes for a moment '. . . comfy.'

'Exactly. Not a sexual being.'

'I don't want to think about it,' he repeated. 'I don't want the pictures in my head. Everything's poisoned.'

He wrenched his body sharply away from them once more. Frieda sensed he was on the verge of tears.

'So,' Karlsson's voice broke into the silence, 'you're saying you never suspected anything.'

'She was a terrible actor, useless at things like charades. And she couldn't lie to save her life. She'd go red and we'd all laugh at her. It was a family joke. But it turns out she was a pretty fantastic actor and liar after all, doesn't it?'

'Can you tell us about the day she was killed, Wednesday, the sixth of April?'

'Tell you what?'

'When you left home, what you did during the day, what time you returned. That kind of thing.'

Ted gave Frieda a wild stare, then said: 'OK. My alibi, you mean. I left home at the usual kind of time. Half eight, something like that. I had to be early at school, which is only a few minutes away, because I had my mock art exam. For which I just heard I got an A star, by the way.' He gave a savage grin. 'Brilliant, wasn't it? Then I was at school for the rest of the day. Then I met Judith, we hung about for a bit and came home together. And found police everywhere. Good enough for you?'

'Good enough.'

Judith Lennox was next. She came through the door quietly as a ghost, staring at each of them in turn with her pale blue eyes. She had coppery curls and freckles over the bridge of her nose. Although her hair needed washing and she was dressed in old jogging pants, with a baggy green jersey that probably belonged to her father, down almost to her knees and with long sleeves covering her hands, she was obviously lovely, with the peachy bloom of youth that days of crying couldn't entirely conceal.

'I've nothing to say,' she announced.

'That's quite all right, dear,' murmured Amanda Thorne. 'You don't need to say anything at all.'

'If you think it was Dad, you're just stupid.'

'What makes you say that?'

'It's obvious. Mum was cheating on him so you think he must have found out and killed her. But Dad adored her, and anyway, he didn't know a thing, not a thing. You can't make something true just by thinking it.'

'Of course not,' said Karlsson.

Frieda considered the girl. She was fifteen, on the edge of womanhood. She had lost her mother and lost the meaning of her mother; now she must fear that she could lose her father as well. 'When you found out about your mother –' she began.

'I came home with Ted,' said Judith. 'We held hands when we found out.' She gave a small sob. 'Poor Ted. He thought Mum was perfect.'

'And you didn't?'

'It's different for daughters.'

'What do you mean?'

'He was her darling boy. Dora was her sweet baby. I stole her lipstick – well, I didn't, really. She didn't go in much for makeup or stuff. But you know what I mean. Anyway, I'm the middle child.'

'But you're sure that no one knew?'

'That she was cheating on Dad all that time? No. I still don't really believe it.' She rubbed her face hard. 'It's like a film or something, not like real life. It's not the kind of thing she would do. It's just stupid. She's a middle-aged woman and she's not even that attractive –' She broke off, her face twisting. 'I don't mean it like that, but you know what I'm saying. Her hair's going grey and she has sensible underwear and she doesn't bother with what she looks like.' She seemed suddenly to realize that she was talking about her mother in the present tense. She wiped her eyes. 'Dad didn't know anything, I promise,' she said urgently. 'I swear Dad didn't suspect a thing. He's gutted. Leave him alone. Leave us alone.'

The interview with Dora Lennox wasn't really an interview. She was scrawny and limp and exhausted, smudged from all her weeping. Her father had grown years older in the days since his wife had died, but Dora had become like a tiny child again. She needed her mother. She needed someone to gather her up and cradle her in their arms, make all the horror go away. Frieda laid a hand on her damp, hot head. Amanda Thorne cooed and told her everything was going to be all right, seeming not to grasp the idiocy of her words. Karlsson stared at the girl, his brow furrowed. He didn't know where to start. The house was too full of pain. You could feel it prickling against your skin. Outside, the daffodils glowed in the warm brightness of spring.

When Yvette asked Russell Lennox about the bottles he just stared at her as if he hadn't understood a word.

'Do you know who put them there?'

He shrugged. 'What's that got to do with anything?'

'Perhaps nothing, but I need to ask. There were dozens of bottles hidden in the shed. There might be a harmless explanation, but it suggests that someone was drinking secretly.'

'I don't see why. The shed's full of junk.'

'Who uses the shed?'

'What do you mean?'

'Who goes into it? Did your wife?'

'It wasn't Ruth.'

'Or perhaps your son and his friends –'

'No. Not Ted.'

'Did you put the bottles there?'

The room filled with silence.

'Mr Lennox?'

'Yes.' His voice rose, and he looked away from her as though he couldn't bear to meet her gaze.

'Would you say –' Yvette stopped. She was no good at this. She asked questions too harshly. She didn't know how to sound clear yet unjudgemental. She tried to imagine Karlsson asking the questions. 'Do you have a drink problem?' she asked abruptly.

Russell Lennox jerked his head up. 'No, I don't.'

'But those bottles . . .' She thought about the white cider: nobody would drink that if they didn't have a problem.

'People think that because you drink, you have a drink problem, and they think if you have a drink problem you have a larger problem underneath.' He spoke rapidly, his words running together. 'It was just a stupid phase. To help me through. I put them in the shed because I knew everyone would say what you're saying now. Make it shameful. It was simpler to hide it. That's all. I was going to throw them away when I got the chance.'

Yvette tried to separate out his sentences. 'To help you through what?' she asked.

'It. Stuff.' He sounded like his son.

'When did you go through this phase?'

'Why?'

'Recently?'

Russell Lennox put his hand to his face, half covering his mouth. He made an indistinct sound through his fingers.

'Are you still drinking?'

'Are you my GP now?' His words were muffled. 'Do you want to tell me it's not good for me? Do you think I don't know that? Perhaps you want to tell me about liver damage, addiction, the need to acknowledge what I'm doing and seek help.'

'Were you drinking because of problems in your marriage?'

He stood up. 'Everything is evidence to you, isn't it? My wife's private life, my drinking too much.'

'A murder victim doesn't have a private life,' said Yvette. 'They both seem relevant to me.'

'What do you want me to say? I drank too much for a bit. It was stupid. I didn't want my kids to know so I hid it. I'm not proud of it.'

'And you say it wasn't for any particular reason?'

Russell Lennox was grey with weariness. He sat down again opposite Yvette, slumping in his chair. 'You're asking me to make everything neat. It wasn't like that. I'm getting older, my life felt stale. Nothing changing. No excitement. Maybe Ruth was feeling the same thing.'

'Perhaps,' said Yvette. 'But did your wife know you were drinking?'

'What's that got to do with her being dead? Do you

think I killed her because she found out my guilty secret?'

'Did she?'

'She suspected. She had a nose for people's weaknesses.'

'So she knew.'

'She smelled it on me. She was pretty contemptuous – that's a bit rich, isn't it, with what she was doing at the same time?'

'Which you still claim you had no knowledge of.'

'I don't *claim*. I had no knowledge.'

'And you still say you had a good marriage?'

'Are you married?'

Yvette felt a violent blush heat her neck and face. She saw herself through his eyes – a solid, brown-haired, clumsy, lonely woman with big feet and large, ringless hands. 'No,' she replied shortly.

'No marriage looks good when you start searching for the fault lines. Until now, I would have said that, although we sometimes wrangled and sometimes took each other for granted, we had a good, solid marriage.'

'And now?'

'Now it doesn't make sense. It's been smashed apart and I can't even ask her why.'

Frieda had only just arrived home when there was a ring at the door. She opened it to find two police officers, a man and a woman.

'Are you Dr Frieda Klein?' said the man.

'Did Karlsson send you?'

The two officers looked at each other.

'I'm sorry,' said the man. 'I don't know what you mean.'

'Well, what are you here for?'

'Can you confirm that you are Dr Frieda Klein?'

'Yes, I can. Is something wrong?'

The officer frowned. 'I have to inform you that we need to interview you in connection with an alleged case of assault causing actual bodily harm.'

'What case? Is this something I'm supposed to have witnessed?'

He shook his head. 'We're responding to a complaint that names you as the perpetrator.'

'What on earth are you talking about?'

The female officer looked down at her notebook. 'Were you present at flat four, number two Marsh Side on the seventeenth of April?'

'What?'

'It is currently occupied by Mr Ian Yardley.'

'Oh, for God's sake,' said Frieda.

'You admit you were present?'

'Yes, I admit I was present but –'

'We need to talk to you about this,' said the man. 'But we can't do it on the doorstep. If you wish, we can take you to an interview room.'

'Can't you just come in so that we can sort it out?'

'We can come in and put a few questions to you,' said the man.

In their bulky uniforms, the two of them made Frieda's house seem smaller. They sat down awkwardly, as if they were unused to being inside. Frieda sat opposite them. She waited for them to speak. The man took off his hat and laid it on the arm of the chair. He had curly red hair and pale skin.

'It's been reported that there was an incident,' he said. He took a notebook from the side pocket of his jacket, slowly opened it and inspected it, as if he was seeing it for the first time. 'I need to inform you from the outset that we are investigating a case of common assault and also a case of assault causing actual bodily harm.'

'What actual bodily harm?' said Frieda, trying to remain calm. At the same time she tried to remember the event. Could the woman have hit her head when she fell? The officer looked back down at his notebook.

'A complaint has been made by Mr Ian Yardley, the owner of the flat, and by Polly Welsh. Now, at this point I need to warn you that you are not under arrest and that you are free to stop the interview at any time. And I also need to tell you that you do not have to say anything but it may harm your defence if you do not mention when questioned something that you later rely on in court. Anything you do say may be given in evidence.' When he had finished this small speech, the officer's pale skin reddened. Frieda was reminded of a small boy reciting a speech at a school assembly. 'We always have to say that.'

'And that I'm entitled to a lawyer.'

'You've not been arrested, Dr Klein.'

'What was the "actual bodily harm"?' said Frieda. 'Was she injured?'

'I believe there was bruising and some medical attention was needed.'

'Does that count as actual bodily harm?' said Frieda.

'It is alleged,' said the woman, 'that psychological harm was caused. Sleep problems. Distress.'

'Psychological harm,' said Frieda. 'Is it possible that Dr Hal Bradshaw was connected with the assessment?'

'I can't comment on that,' said the man. 'But you admit that you were present at the incident.'

'Yes,' said Frieda. 'Haven't they waited rather a long time to report it?'

'From what I've heard,' said the man, 'Miss Welsh was at first too traumatized to talk about it. She needed re-assurance and treatment before she was able to come forward. We're trying to be more sensitive in our response to women who suffer violence.'

'Well, that's a good thing,' said Frieda. 'Do you want to know what happened?'

'We would be interested in your version of events, yes,' said the man.

'I arranged to see Ian Yardley to ask him some questions,' said Frieda.

'You were angry with him, I understand. You felt humiliated by him.'

'Is that what he said?'

'That's what our enquiries suggest.'

'I wasn't angry with him. But his friend . . .'

'Miss Welsh.'

'She was aggressive as soon as I arrived. She jabbed at me and tried to push me out of the flat. I pushed back. When she tried to retaliate, I think she fell over a chair. It all happened very quickly. And then I left. End of story.'

The man looked down at his notebook.

'One report claims that you pushed Miss Welsh against a wall and held her there. Is that accurate?'

'Yes, that's right. She started pushing at me. I told her

to stop, and when she wouldn't, I pushed her against the wall. But not roughly. Just to make her stop. Then I let her go and she came at me and fell over. I wasn't even touching her.'

'She just fell,' said the woman.

'That's right.'

The man looked back at his notes. 'Do you have a history of fighting in public?'

'What do you mean?'

He turned a page. 'You know a man called James Rundell?' he said. 'We've heard something about a fight in a restaurant, significant damage done. And it ended with you being arrested.'

'Where did you hear about that?'

'It's information we've received.'

'What's the relevance?'

'We're just trying to establish a pattern. And isn't James Rundell involved in this case as well?'

'That's right,' said Frieda. 'Rundell is one of the other therapists who were targeted in this . . .' She stopped, trying to think of an appropriate word. 'Project,' she said finally.

'"Targeted". That sounds like you're angry about it.'

'No, it doesn't,' said Frieda.

The man wrote something in his notebook. 'You get angry with Rundell and you confront him in a restaurant and attack him. You get angry with Ian Yardley and you confront him in his home and a fight ensues. Do you see a pattern?'

'The two cases have nothing in common,' said Frieda. 'And there was no fight in Ian Yardley's flat.'

Suddenly the man glanced round, like a dog that had caught a scent. 'What's that?' he said.

It was the banging from upstairs in the bathroom. It had become so much a part of Frieda's life that she had almost stopped hearing it. 'Do you really need to know?' she said. 'After all, I've got an alibi. I'm down here with you.'

The female officer frowned at her. 'There's nothing funny about violence against women,' she said.

'That's it,' said Frieda. 'I'm done. If you want to charge me, then go ahead. Otherwise, we have nothing left to talk about.'

With a grimace of concentration, the man wrote several lines of notes, then closed his book and stood up. 'Between ourselves,' he said, 'if I were you, I would talk to a solicitor. We've put weaker cases than this one in front of a jury. But even if we don't, you might well be facing a civil case.'

'What if I need to reach you?' Frieda asked.

'I was about to tell you,' said the man. He wrote in his notebook, tore a page out and handed it to Frieda. 'If you've anything more to say. But we'll be in touch anyway.'

When they were gone, Frieda sat for several minutes staring in front of her. Then she looked through her address book and dialled a number. 'Yvette,' she said. 'Sorry, it's Frieda. Have you got a moment?'

Thank you for your letter. I carry it around with me. It's so like you to write a real letter – on good-quality paper, in ink, with proper grammar and no abbreviations. I can't remember the last time anyone sent me a letter. My mother, maybe, years ago. She used to write to me on very thin airmail paper, gummed down. I could never read her tiny, cramped handwriting.

My mother; yours. All the things we've never told each other yet. I think we need to spend a month in a lighthouse, with rough seas all round us, and enough food and drink never to have to leave. We could talk and read and sleep and make love and share secrets. Make up for all the lost time. Sandy xxxx

Twenty-seven

Yvette and Karlsson walked together from the Lennoxes' house to the Kerrigans'. It took less than ten minutes. Yvette struggled to keep pace with his long stride. She had a bad cold: her throat was sore, her glands ached and her head throbbed. Her clothes felt tight and itchy.

The house was smaller than Ruth and Russell's, a red-brick terraced building up a narrow side-street, with a tiny front garden that had been gravelled over. Elaine Kerrigan opened the door before the chime had died away. She stood before them, a tall woman with a long, pale face and fading hair caught up in a loose bun; glasses hung round her neck on a chain. She was wearing an oversized checked shirt over loose cotton trousers. The sun caught her as she gazed at them, and she raised her hand – wedding ring and engagement ring on the fourth finger – to shield her from its dazzle.

She knows, Yvette thought. Her husband must have sat her down and told her.

She led them into the living room. Sun streamed through the large window and lay across the green carpet and the striped sofa. There were daffodils on the mantelpiece, doubled by the mirror. Yvette caught a glimpse of her own face there – flushed and heavy, with dry lips. She licked them. Elaine Kerrigan took a seat and gestured for them to do the same. She laid her long, delicate hands in her lap and sat up straight.

'I've been thinking about how to behave,' she said, in a voice that was low and pleasant, with a faint burr of an accent that Yvette couldn't place. 'It all seems unreal. I know I'm the wronged wife, but I can't feel that yet. It's just so . . .' She looked down at her hands, lifted her eyes again. 'Paul doesn't seem the sort of man someone would choose to have an affair with.'

'When did he tell you?' asked Yvette.

'When he came back yesterday. He waited till his tea was on the table and blurted it out. I thought he was joking at first.' She grimaced. 'It's mad, isn't it? It can't be happening to me. And this woman's dead. Did he say that I was the one who told him about it? I saw the story in the paper? I thought she had a nice face. I wonder if she thought about me when it was all happening.'

'We know it must be a shock,' said Yvette. 'Obviously we need to establish people's movements on the day that Ruth Lennox died.'

'You mean my husband? I can't remember. I've looked in the diary but the page is blank. It was just another Wednesday. Paul says he was definitely here at the time but I don't remember if I came home from work first or if he did. I can't remember if he was later than usual. If something unusual had happened, I suppose it would have stuck in my mind.'

'What about your sons?'

She turned her head. Following her gaze, Karlsson and Yvette saw the photograph next to the daffodils of two boys, young men even, both with dark hair and their father's broad face. One had a scar above his lip that pulled his smile slightly awry.

'Josh is at university in Cardiff. He hadn't come back for Easter by then. The other, Ben, he's eighteen and he takes his A levels this year. He lives at home. He's a bit vague about dates. And everything else. I haven't told them yet about the affair. After that I can tell them about the murder. That'll be fun. How long was it for?'

'Sorry?'

'How long had the affair been going on?'

'Your husband didn't tell you?'

'He said it was more than a fling, but he still loved me and he hoped I would forgive him.'

'Ten years,' said Yvette, calmly. 'They met on Wednesday afternoons. They rented a flat.'

Elaine Kerrigan sat up even straighter. Her face seemed to loosen, the skin grow slack. 'Ten years.' They could hear her swallow.

'And you didn't know?'

'Ten years, with a flat.'

'And we will also need to conduct a search here,' said Yvette.

'I understand.' Elaine Kerrigan's voice was still polite, but it had become faint.

'Have you noticed nothing unusual in his behaviour?'

'Over the last ten years?'

'Over the last few weeks, perhaps.'

'No.'

'He hasn't been upset or distracted?'

'I don't think so.'

'You didn't know that several hundreds of pounds have been disappearing monthly from your husband's bank account to pay for the rooms he rented?'

'No.'

'You never met her?'

'The other woman?' She gave them a tired half-smile. 'I don't think so. But she lived near here, didn't she? Maybe I did.'

'We would be grateful if you could try to find out exactly what time you and your husband came home on the Wednesday – ask colleagues at work, perhaps.'

'I'll do my best.'

'We'll see ourselves out.'

'Yes. Thank you.'

She didn't stand up as they left, but stayed sitting upright on the sofa, her long face blank.

'Do you want a drink?' Yvette asked Karlsson, trying to sound casual – as if she didn't care one way or the other. She heard her voice grate.

'I'm taking the rest of the day off and I won't be in tomorrow so I . . .'

'Fine. Just a suggestion. There was something I wanted to mention. Frieda rang me.'

'What about?'

As Yvette described the details of Frieda's police interview, Karlsson started to smile but finally he just looked weary.

'I said she should talk to you about it, but she said you'd probably had enough of her. You know, after that last time with Rundell.'

'What is it with her?' said Karlsson. 'There are night-club bouncers who get into fewer fights than she does.'

'She doesn't always choose them.'

'Yes, but they seem to happen wherever she goes. Anyway, she rang you. You'd better make a couple of calls.'

'I'm sorry. I didn't mean to bother you with it.'

Karlsson hesitated, looking at her flushed face. 'I didn't mean to snap. I'm spending the time with my kids,' he said gently. 'They're going away soon.'

'I didn't know – how long for?'

He found he couldn't tell her. 'Quite a long time,' was all he could manage. 'So I want to make the most of this.'

'Of course.'

Mikey had had his hair cut very short; it was like soft bristle; his scalp showed through and his ears stuck out. Bella's hair had been cut as well, so it was a mass of loose curls around her face. It made them seem younger and more defenceless. Karlsson felt too tall and solid beside them. His heart swelled in his chest and he stooped down and held them against him. But they squirmed free. They were excited; their bodies throbbed with impatience. They wanted to tell him about the flat they were going to live in, which had balconies on both sides and an orange tree in the courtyard. A fan in every room, because it was very hot in the summer. They'd got new summer clothes, shorts and dresses and flip-flops. It hardly ever rained there – the rain in Spain falls mainly on the plain. There was an outdoor pool a few streets away and at the weekends they could get a train to the coast. They would have to wear a uniform to their new school. They already knew some words. They could say, *Puedo tomar un helado, por favor?* And *gracias* and *mi nombre es Mikey, mi nombre es Bella.*

Karlsson smiled and smiled. He wanted them never to leave and he wanted them to be gone already, because waiting to say goodbye was the worst thing of all.

TWENTY-EIGHT

The following morning, when Frieda received Rajit Singh's call, she arranged to meet him in her rooms, which stood empty for so many hours of the week now, the red armchair abandoned. Later in the day she had to see Joe Franklin, so she could stay on for that, stand for a while at the window that overlooked the deserted and overgrown building site, sifting through the rubble of her thoughts. She walked as swiftly as her injured leg would allow through the narrow streets, the familiar clutter of shops. She had the sensation of following a thread, as thin as a spider's, through a dark and twisting labyrinth. She didn't know why she couldn't let go of the story: it had been a fake tale, crudely obvious, designed to trip her up and make her look foolish and incompetent. She should feel enraged, humiliated, exposed; instead, she felt troubled and compelled. She woke in the night and her thoughts, drifting up from the mud of her dreams, snagged on the story. There was a faint but insistent tug on the thread.

Singh arrived promptly. He was still wearing his thick black jacket – in fact, he seemed to be wearing the same clothes that Frieda had last seen him in. His face sagged with weariness and he sat heavily in the chair opposite her, as if this were indeed a therapy session.

'Thank you,' he said.

'What for?'

'For seeing me.'

'I think I was the one who asked you to contact me.'

'Yeah, but we fucked you over, didn't we?'

'Is that how it feels?'

'I don't know about the others, but I felt a bit crap about all the coverage.'

'Because you felt what you did was wrong?'

'It seemed a good idea at the time. I mean, how can therapists be checked? Teachers have inspectors, but therapists can do whatever damage they want in the privacy of their little rooms and no one's to know. And if patients don't like it, then the therapist can just turn it back on them: if you don't like it, it's because there's something wrong with you, not me. It's a self-justifying system.'

'That doesn't sound like you. It sounds like Hal Bradshaw speaking. Which doesn't mean it's wrong. There is a problem about checking up on therapists.'

'Yeah, well, but when it got all that attention, it felt wrong. Everyone found it funny, and then when I met you . . .' He stopped.

'I didn't seem quite as crazy as Bradshaw said I was?'

Singh shifted in his seat uncomfortably. 'He said you were a loose cannon. He said you – and people like you – could do a lot of damage.'

'So he set out to check us?'

'I suppose that's how he sees it. But that's not why I'm here. There's nothing I can do about that. You said I should get in touch if there was anything I wanted to say.'

'And there is?'

'Yeah. I guess. I'm, um, how do I put it? Not in the best place right now. As you noticed. I don't like my work as much as I thought I would – I thought it would be more seminars and discussions and research in groups and stuff, but mostly it's just me on my own, grubbing away in the library.'

'Alone.'

'Yeah.'

'And you're alone in your personal life as well?'

'You're probably wondering why this has anything to do with the story,' he said.

'Tell me.'

Singh looked down at the floor. He seemed to be pondering something.

'I was in a relationship,' he said at last. 'For a long time – well, a long time for me, anyway. I haven't had so much – well, anyway, that's irrelevant. We were together a year and a half, pretty much. Agnes, she was called. *Is* called. She hasn't died. But it didn't go well or end well or whatever. But that's not what I came here to say. The thing is, it was Agnes who gave me the detail about cutting the hair. I don't know why you're so interested in it. The whole thing was just a story. But I was writing up the notes for everybody and I thought it needed a touch of colour and it came into my mind. I've no idea why. So I put it in.'

'So your ex-girlfriend gave you the story about cutting her father's hair?'

'I wanted to tell you so that you'd see it's not a big deal. It was just a stupid story. And random – it just occurred to me and I used it. I could have used anything – or nothing.'

'Did you change any of the details?'

'I can't really remember.' He winced. 'We were lying in bed and she was stroking my hair and saying it had got really long and could do with a cut. And did I want her to cut it for me. Then she said this thing about her father – or I think it was about her father. I don't remember that bit. It could have been someone else. But she talked about holding the scissors and how that gave a feeling of power and tenderness at the same time. I suppose it stuck in my mind because it all felt so intimate. Though she never did cut my hair.'

'So the story was your ex-girlfriend's memory?'

'Yes.'

'Agnes.'

'Agnes Flint – why? Do you want to talk to *her* now?'

'I think so.'

'I don't get it. Why's it so important? We made a fool of you. I'm sorry. But why does any of this matter?'

'Can I have her number?'

'She'll just tell you the same as I have.'

'Or an email address would do.'

'Maybe Hal was right about you after all.'

Frieda opened her notebook and unscrewed the cap of her pen.

'I'll tell you if you tell her she's got to answer my calls.'

'She won't answer your calls just because someone else tells her to.'

Singh sighed heavily, took the notebook and scribbled down a mobile number and an email address. 'Satisfied?'

'Thanks. Do you want my advice?'

'No.'

'You should go for a run – I saw some running shoes in your living room – then have a shower and shave and put on different clothes and leave your cold little flat.'

'Is that it?'

'For a start.'

'I thought you were a psychotherapist.'

'I'm grateful to you, Rajit.'

'Will you tell Agnes I said –?'

'No.'

Jim Fearby had breakfast in the service station next to the hotel he had stayed in the night before: a mini-pack of corn flakes, a glass of orange juice from the tall plastic container in which a plastic orange bobbed unconvincingly, a mug of coffee. He returned to his room to collect his overnight bag and brush his teeth, watching breakfast TV as he did so. He left the room, as always, looking as if nobody had stayed there.

His car felt like home. After he had filled up with petrol, he made sure he had everything he needed: his notebook and several pens, his list of names, with numbers and addresses written neatly next to some of them, the folder of relevant information he had prepared the day before, the questions. He wound down the window and smoked a cigarette, his first of the day, then set the satnav. He was just nineteen minutes away.

Sarah Ingatestone lived in a village a few miles from Stafford. He had rung her two days ago and arranged to meet her at half past nine in the morning, after she had taken her two dogs for their walk. They were terriers, small, sharp, unfriendly, yapping creatures that tried to bite his ankles as he stepped from the car. He was tempted to knock them on their snouts with his briefcase, but Sarah Ingatestone was watching him from the front door so he forced a smile and made enthusiastic noises.

'They won't do any harm,' she called. 'Coffee?'

'Lovely.' He sidestepped a terrier and went towards her. 'Thanks for agreeing to see me.'

'I'm having second thoughts. I Googled you. You're the one who got that man George Conley out of prison.'

'I wouldn't say it was all me.'

'So he can go and do it again.'

'There's no evidence that –'

'Never mind. Come in and take a seat.'

They sat in the kitchen. Sarah Ingatestone made instant coffee while Fearby arranged his props in front of him: his spiral-bound notebook, which was identical to the one he'd had all those years ago as a junior reporter, his sheaf of papers in the pink folder, the three pens side by side, although he always used his pencil for shorthand. They didn't speak until she'd put the two mugs on the table and taken the chair opposite him. He looked at her properly for the first time: greying hair cut mannishly short, grey-blue eyes in a face that wasn't old yet had sharp creases and furrows in it. Worry lines, not laugh lines, thought Fearby. Her clothes were old and shabby, covered with dog hair. She was called Mrs Ingatestone, but there was no sign of a Mr in this house.

'You said this was about Roxanne.'

'Yes.'

'Why? It's been over nine years, nearly ten. No one asks about her any more.'

'I'm a journalist.' Best keep it vague. 'I'm following up some queries for a story I'm involved in.'

She folded her arms, not defensively but protectively, as if she was waiting for a series of blows to fall upon her. 'Ask away,' she said. 'I don't mind what it's for, really. I like saying her name out loud. It makes her feel alive.'

So it began, down the list of questions, pencil moving swiftly, making its hieroglyphic marks.

How old was Roxanne when she disappeared?

'Seventeen. Seventeen and three months. Her birthday was in March – a Pisces. Not that I believe in that. She would be – she is – twenty-seven years old now.'

When did you last see your daughter?

'The second of June 2001.'

What time?

'It would have been around half past six in the evening. She was going out to see a friend for a quick drink. She never came back.'

Did she go by car?

'No. It was just down the road, no more than ten or fifteen minutes' walk.'

By road?

'Yes. A quiet lane most of the way.'

So she wouldn't have taken a shortcut – over fields or anything?

'Not a chance. She was all dressed up – in a little skirt and high heels. That's what we argued about actually – I said she wouldn't be able to walk five yards, let alone a mile or so, in that garb.'

Did she ever arrive at the friend's?

'No.'

How long did the friend wait before alerting anyone?

'Apparently she tried phoning Roxanne's mobile after about forty-five minutes. I didn't know anything about it until the next morning. We – my husband and I – went to bed at about half past ten. We didn't wait up.' Her voice was flat. She laid down the answers like cards, face up on the table.

Were you living here when Roxanne disappeared?

'No. But nearby. We moved when – after – well, my husband and I separated three years after. We just couldn't – It wasn't his fault, more mine if anything. And Roxanne's sister, Marianne, went too, to university, but she doesn't come home much and I don't blame her. And, of course, Roxanne never came back. I waited as long as I could in a house that everyone else had left and at last I couldn't stand it any longer. I used to put hot-water bottles in her bed when it was cold, just in case. So I came here, and got my dogs.'

Can you please show me where you used to live on this map?

Fearby pulled it out from the folder and spread it on the table. Sarah Ingatestone put on her reading glasses, peered at it, then put her finger on a spot. Fearby took one of his pens and made a small ink cross.

You say you had argued?

'No. Yes. Not seriously. She was seventeen. She had a mind of her own. When I told them, the police thought – but that's not true. I know.' She pressed her hands tightly together, stared at him fiercely. 'She wasn't one to bear a grudge.'

Do the police believe she's dead?

'Everyone believes she's dead.'

Do you believe she's dead?

'I can't. I have to know she's coming home.' The face quivered, tightened again. 'Do you think I shouldn't have moved? Should I have stayed where we'd all lived together?'

Can you describe Roxanne? Do you have a photo?

'Here.' Glossy shoulder-length brown hair; dark eyebrows; her mother's grey-blue eyes but set wider in her narrow face, giving her a slightly startled look; a mole on her cheek; a large, slightly crooked smile – there was something asymmetrical and frail about her appearance. 'But it doesn't do her proper justice. She was little and skinny but so pretty and full of life.'

Boyfriend?

'No. Not that I knew of. She'd had boyfriends before but nothing serious. There was someone she liked.'

And her character? Was she shy or outgoing, for instance?

'Shy, Roxanne? She was ever so friendly – bold, you could even say. She always said what was on her mind and could have a bit of a temper – but she'd go out of her way to help people. She was a good girl, really. A bit wild, but she had a good heart.'

Would she have talked to a stranger?

'Yes.'

'*Would she have got into a car with a stranger?*

'No.'

When Fearby got up to go, she clutched his arm. 'Do you think she's alive?'

'Mrs Ingatestone, I couldn't possibly –'

'No. But do you? If you were me, would you think she was alive?'

'I don't know.'

'Not knowing is like being buried alive myself.'

Jim Fearby pulled over in a lay-by and took out his list of names. One was already crossed out. Next to Roxanne Ingatestone's name, however, he put a tick. No, he didn't think she was alive.

Twenty-nine

Joe Franklin had been more cheerful than for a long time but Frieda knew that he moved through repeating cycles of depression. For months he would be heavy, grey and defeated, barely able to go through the motions of living, often incapable of making it to her rooms or of uttering a word when he got there. The deathly numbness would lift and, for a while, he would emerge into a brighter world, exhausted and relieved. But he always got sucked back into the black hole of himself. Coming to see her was his way of holding on to a corner of life, but it was also his comfort blanket.

Frieda had often felt during her own therapy that she was standing in the desert, under the blowtorch of the sun, parched and bleached and unforgiven, with nowhere to hide. Joe, however, crept into her room like an animal into a lair. He hid from himself and perhaps she allowed him to do that in a way that wasn't necessarily helpful. Solace not self-knowledge. Yet how much should we face ourselves full on?

As she was thinking these things, making her notes after the session, with the spring sun slanting through the window and lying in a blade across the floor, her mobile vibrated in her pocket. She took it out: Sasha.

'I'm about to leave work. Are you free?'

'Yes.'

'Can I come and see you?'

'All right. I'll be home in about half an hour – is that good?'

'Perfect. I'll bring a bottle of wine. And Frank.'

'Frank?'

'Is that OK?'

'Of course.'

'I feel a bit nervous – as if I'm about to introduce him to my family. I want you to like him.'

Frieda walked to her house in the soft dying day. Petals of blossom lay on the pavement. She thought about Rajit Singh and the story he had told that was someone else's story; tonight she would send a message to Agnes Flint. And she thought about Joe and then about the happiness she had heard in Sasha's voice. As she unlocked her front door, she wondered how long it would be before she could have a hot bath again, with no dust swirling through her rooms.

The door stuck against something and she frowned, then squeezed through the narrow opening into her hall. There were two large bags there, blocking the entrance. There was a jacket lying on the floor beside them. There were voices and laughter coming from her kitchen. She could smell cigarette smoke. She pressed the light switch, but no light came on.

'Hello?' she called, and the voices ceased.

'Frieda!' Josef appeared in the kitchen doorway. He was in his work clothes, but held a brimming glass of vodka and he seemed to have trouble walking in a straight line. 'Come in and join.'

'What's going on? Whose are these bags?'

'Hello, Frieda.' Chloë appeared beside Josef. She was wearing what looked to Frieda like a jersey, but presumably was meant to be a dress, because there was no skirt underneath it. Her face was smeary with smudged makeup and she, too, was holding a glass of vodka. 'I'm so grateful to you. So, so grateful.'

'What do you mean, you're grateful? What have I done? Jack!' Jack was coming unsteadily down the stairs. 'What's going on? Is this a party?'"

'A gathering,' Jack said, looking sheepish. 'Chloë told me to come over.'

'Did she now? And why don't the lights work?'

'Ah.' Josef took a hasty swig of his vodka. 'Electrical problems.'

'What does that mean? Are these your bags, Chloë?'

'Frieda!' a voice roared cheerfully.

'Reuben? What's Reuben doing here?'

Frieda strode past Josef and Chloë into the kitchen. Lit candles had been placed on the windowsills and surfaces, and smoke hung in blue clouds. There was an open vodka bottle and an ashtray with several butts stubbed out in it. The cat clattered through the cat-flap and wound itself around Frieda's legs, mewing piteously for attention. Reuben, his shirt half unbuttoned and his feet up on the chair, raised his glass to her.

'I came to see my good friend Josef,' he said. 'And my good friend Frieda, of course.'

Frieda yanked open the back door to let the smoke out. 'Will someone tell me what's going on? First of all, why don't the lights work? What have you done?'

Josef looked at her with a wounded expression and put both palms upwards. 'The wires have been cut by a mistake.'

'You mean, "I cut the wires."'

'Complicated.'

'Why are your bags in the hall, Chloë? Are you going somewhere?'

Chloë gave a scared giggle, then a hiccup. 'It's more like I've arrived,' she said.

'What?'

'I've come to stay with you.'

'No, you have not.'

'Mum's on a rampage. She's booted poor Kieran out, too, and she hit me with a hairbrush. I can't live with her, Frieda. You can't make me.'

'You can't live here.'

'Why? I've nowhere else to go.'

'No.'

'I can sleep in your study.'

'I'll ring Olivia.'

'I'm not going back there. I'd prefer to be on the streets.'

'You can stay with us,' said Reuben, magnanimously. 'It'd be fun.'

'Or with me,' put in Jack. 'I've got a double bed.'

Frieda looked from Reuben to Josef to Jack, then back at Chloë. 'One night,' she said.

'I won't get in your way. I'll cook for us.'

'One night, so you won't need to cook. And there's no bath and no light anyway.'

The doorbell rang.

'That'll be Sasha,' said Frieda. 'Pour three large vodkas.'

Frank was quite short, solid, with his hair cut close to his scalp and dark melancholy eyes, with a slight cast in one so that he seemed to be both looking at Frieda and past her. His handshake was firm, his manner almost shy. He was wearing a beautifully cut suit and carrying a briefcase because he'd come straight from work.

'Come in,' said Frieda. 'But be warned – it's mayhem.'

Perhaps it was better that way, though. There was no room for self-consciousness. He took off his jacket, drank a shot of vodka and then was somehow persuaded by Reuben to cook omelettes for everyone, which he did very slowly and seriously. Chloë stood beside him in her absurd excuse for a dress, whisking eggs with a fork and gazing at him with an over-serious expression on her smeared face. She was tipsy and giggly and a bit weepy, and swayed as she whisked, slopping egg on to the floor. Reuben, Jack and Josef took Chloë's bags up to the study, making a lot of noise about it; they could be heard laughing and dropping things. Sasha and Frieda sat together at the table assembling a green salad, talking quietly. Sasha could feel that Frieda approved – or, at least, didn't disapprove – and happiness filled her.

THIRTY

'I think I should be present,' said Elaine Kerrigan.

'He's eighteen years old,' said Yvette, firmly. 'He counts as an adult.'

'That's ridiculous. You should see his bedroom.' There was a pause. 'You wait here. I'll get him.'

Yvette and Munster sat in the living room and waited. 'Do you ever think,' she asked, 'that we just go around and make things worse? In the great scheme of things. That in the end, when we're done, the general level of happiness is a bit less than it was before?'

'No, I don't,' said Munster.

'Well, I do.'

The door opened and Ben Kerrigan came in. Yvette first saw his stockinged feet, with odd socks, one red, one with green and amber stripes, a big toe poking through the end. Then she saw faded grey corduroy trousers, a flowery blue shirt, long floppy dark-brown hair. He sank on to the sofa, one leg pulled up beside him. He pushed his hair back off his face.

'You've heard about your father and this woman,' said Yvette, after they'd introduced themselves.

'A bit.'

'How did it make you feel?'

'What do you think?'

'You tell me.'

'I wasn't exactly happy about it. Does that surprise you?'

'No, it doesn't. Were you angry?'

'Why should I be?'

'Because your father was being unfaithful to your mother.'

'It doesn't matter what I feel.'

'Could you tell us where you were on Wednesday, the sixth of April?'

Ben looked puzzled, then grimly amused. 'Are you serious?'

'Yes.'

'All right, then. I'm a schoolboy. I was at school.'

'And you can prove that?'

He gave a shrug. 'I'm in the sixth form. We go out sometimes, if we've got a free. We might go for a coffee or, you know, a walk.'

'But not for the whole day,' said Yvette. 'And when you have coffee, you have it with someone. You have a walk with someone. And they can vouch for you?'

'I don't know. Maybe. Maybe not.'

'Hang on,' said Munster. 'What you need to do first is take this seriously. A woman has been killed. Some children have lost their mother. We don't want to waste our time chasing up false leads. So, what we want you to do is, first, to show us some respect, and second, pull your finger out, look through your diary or your phone, talk to your friends and put together a convincing story of what you were doing for every minute of that Wednesday. Because if we have to do it ourselves, we won't be very happy about it. Do you understand?'

'Whatever,' said Ben. 'So is it just me? Are you going to hassle Josh as well?'

'Your brother was a hundred and fifty miles away, so far as we know, but we'll check up with him.'

'Can I go now?' said Ben. 'I've got homework to do.'

When they were back in the car, Yvette asked if they could make a diversion via Warren Street.

'Is this about Frieda?' said Munster.

'Why shouldn't it be about Frieda?'

'I was just saying.'

When Frieda opened the door, Yvette noticed over her shoulder that there were people there. She recognized Josef but no one else. For a few seconds, the two women stared at each other, then Frieda stepped back and invited Yvette in. She shook her head.

'Why did you call me about the charge?' she asked.

'If it's a problem,' said Frieda, 'just say.'

'I didn't mean that.' Yvette glanced round to see if Munster was listening, but he was oblivious in the front seat of the car with his headphones on. 'Since your injury, we hadn't talked properly.'

'We hadn't talked at all.'

'Yes, well.' Yvette bit her lip. 'Anyway, I hadn't said things I meant to say. So when you rang, I didn't know how to interpret it.'

'You don't need to interpret it,' said Frieda. 'I told you about it on the phone. I thought Karlsson was sick of clearing up my messes.'

'And now it's my turn?'

'As I said, if it's a problem . . .'

'I called the police down at Waterloo. Look, Frieda, what

you did wasn't sensible. All right, that bastard Bradshaw set out to humiliate you. If it were me, I'd want to go and sort him out. But you can't do things like that. If you do, you leave yourself open to all kinds of trouble.'

'So you think I'm in trouble?'

'I talked to the officer you saw. I explained about our relationship with you, things you've done for us. So I think this will go away.'

'Yvette, this was all rubbish.'

'I'll take your word for it. But if these things get into court, you just never know which way they'll go. And another thing: you don't want to put yourself into the power of someone like Bradshaw.'

'Thank you,' said Frieda. 'Really. I hope you haven't gone out on a limb for me. But I just want you to know that when I went to see Ian Yardley it wasn't anything to do with Bradshaw.'

'Then what was it about?'

'I don't know,' said Frieda. 'Just a feeling.'

'I get worried about your feelings.'

Frieda began to close the door, then hesitated. 'What was it you wanted to say to me? I mean, apart from my so-called fight.'

Yvette looked at the people behind Frieda. 'Some other time,' she said.

Thirty-one

Josh Kerrigan was making roll-ups, adding thick tufts of tobacco to the Rizla paper, rolling it deftly between thumb and forefinger, licking the edge and laying the thin, straight tube beside the others he'd already assembled. He had six so far and was on to his seventh. Yvette was finding it hard to concentrate on what he was saying. Perhaps that was the point: he was making it quite clear that she was simply an interruption. She was getting a bit tired of these Kerrigan boys.

'Josh,' she said, 'I can understand why you might be upset –'

'Do I seem upset?' He passed the Rizla over the tip of his tongue.

'– but I'm afraid I'm not going until you've answered my questions.'

'No. You're fine.' He laid the seventh cigarette beside the others and tapped it into line with a finger, tipping his head on one side to examine them. He had a small vertical scar just above his lip that pulled it up slightly, giving him the suggestion of a perpetual smile.

'Where were you on Wednesday, the sixth of April?'

'Cardiff. Is that a good enough alibi?'

'It's not an alibi at all yet. How can you prove you were in Cardiff then?'

'Wednesday, the sixth of April?'

'Yes.'

'I have lectures on Wednesdays, until five. I don't think I could have got back to London in time to murder my father's lover, do you?'

'You didn't have lectures that Wednesday. Your term had ended.'

'Then I was probably out somewhere.'

'You need to take this more seriously.'

'What makes you think I'm not?'

He started on the next roll-up. At least there wasn't much tobacco left in the tin, only enough for one or two more.

'I want you to give proper thought to where you were on that Wednesday and who you were with.'

He lifted his head and Yvette saw the glint of his brown eyes. 'I was probably with my girlfriend, Shari. We got together at the end of term, so it was pretty intense. The things you're finding out about the sex life of the Kerrigan family.'

'You think or you know?'

'I'm a bit hazy on dates.'

'Don't you have a diary?'

'A diary?' He grinned as if she had said something unintentionally funny. 'No, I don't have a diary.'

'When did you return to London for the holidays?'

'When? At the end of that week, I think. Friday? Saturday? You'll have to ask Mum. I know I was back by the Saturday because there was a party. So it was probably the Friday.'

'Did you come back by train?'

'Yes.'

'So you can look at the ticket or your bank statement to confirm the date.'

'If I paid by card. Which I'm not sure about.'

He had finished the tobacco at last. One by one he delicately lifted the roll-ups and put them into the empty tin. Yvette thought his hands were trembling, but perhaps she was imagining things: his expression gave nothing away.

'Did you have any idea about your father's affair?'

'No.'

'What do you feel about it?'

'Do you mean, am I angry?' he asked mildly, one dark eyebrow lifting. 'Yes. Especially after all Mum's gone through. Am I angry enough to kill someone? I think if I was going to kill anyone, it'd be my dad.'

'I really don't think I can help you.'

Louise Weller was still wearing an apron. Maybe she lived in it, he thought. She must always be clearing up mess or cooking meals, scrubbing floors, helping her children splash paint on to sheets of paper. He saw that her shirtsleeves were rolled up.

'How old are your children?' he asked, following his train of thought.

'Benjy's thirteen weeks old.' She looked down at the baby asleep on the bouncy chair beside her, eyes twitching in dreams. 'Then Jackson is just two and Carmen is three and a bit.'

'You do have your hands full.' Karlsson felt tired just thinking of it and at the same time dizzy with a kind of nostalgia for those days of mess and tiredness. For one brief moment, he let himself think of Mikey and Bella in

Madrid, then blinked the image away. 'Does your husband help?'

'My husband is not a healthy man.'

'I'm sorry to hear that.'

'But they're good children,' said Louise Weller. 'They're brought up to behave well.'

'I'd like to ask you a few general questions about your sister.'

Louise Weller raised her eyebrows. 'I don't see why. Someone broke in and killed her. Now you have to find out who. You seem to be taking your time about it.'

'It might not be as simple as that.'

'Oh?'

Karlsson had spent years in the Met. He'd told mothers about children dying; he'd told wives about their husbands being murdered; he'd stood on countless doorsteps to deliver bad news, watching faces go blank with the first shock, then change, crumple. Yet he still felt queasy about telling Louise Weller that her sister had lived a double life. Ridiculous as it was, he felt that he was betraying the dead woman to the prim-mouthed living one.

'Your sister,' he said. 'It turns out that she had a complicated life.'

Louise Weller didn't move or speak. She just waited.

'You don't know about it?'

'I don't know what you're talking about.'

'Has Mr Lennox not said anything?'

'No, he hasn't.'

'So you had no idea that Ruth might have had a secret she was keeping from her family?'

'You're going to have to tell me what you're referring to.'

'She was having an affair.'

She made no response. Karlsson wondered if she'd even heard. Finally she spoke. 'Thank goodness our mother never lived to find out.'

'You didn't know anything about it?'

'Of course I didn't. She would have known how I would feel about it.'

'How would you have felt about it?'

'She's a married woman. She has three children. Look at this nice house. She never did know how lucky she was.'

'What do you mean by that?'

'People are very selfish nowadays. They put freedom before responsibility.'

'She's dead,' Karlsson said mildly. He suddenly felt the need to defend Ruth Lennox, though he wasn't sure why.

The baby woke, his face crinkled and he gave a piteous yelp. Louise Weller lifted him up and calmly unbuttoned her shirt, placing him at her breast and casting Karlsson a bright look, as if she wanted him to object.

'Can we talk about the specifics?' Karlsson said, trying to look neither at the naked breast nor away from it. 'Your sister, Ruth, who has been killed and who was having an affair. You say you had no idea?'

'No.'

'She never said anything to you that, now you think about it, might have suggested there was something going on?'

'No.'

'Does the name Paul Kerrigan mean anything to you?'

'Is that his name? No. I've never heard it.'

'Did you ever see any sign that there was a strain in her marriage?'

'Ruth and Russell were devoted to each other.'

'You never got the impression that there was any problem?'

'No.'

'Did you notice that he was drinking heavily?'

'What? Russell? Drinking?'

'Yes. You didn't see that?'

'No, I did not. I have never seen him drunk. But they say that it's the secret drinkers who are the problem.'

'And you had no sense at all, looking back, that he knew?'

'No.' Her eyes glittered. She wiped her hands down her apron. 'But I wonder why he didn't tell me when he discovered.'

'It's not something that's easy to say,' said Karlsson.

'Do his children know?'

'Yes.'

'And yet they haven't shared it with me. Poor things. To find that out about your mother.' She looked at Karlsson with distaste. 'Your job must be like lifting up a stone. I don't know how you have the stomach for it.'

'Someone's got to do it.'

'There are things it's better not to know about.'

'Like your sister's affair, you mean?'

'I suppose everyone will find out now.'

'I suppose they will.'

Back in his flat, Karlsson tidied away the last of the mess his children had made. He found it hard to believe he had ever been irritated by it. Now it simply filled him with nostalgic tenderness – the miniature plastic figures embedded in the sofa, the wet swimming things on the bathroom floor, the pastel crayons that had been trodden into the carpet. He stripped both their beds and pushed the sheets into the washing machine, and then, before he had time to stop himself, called Frieda's number. He didn't recognize the person who answered.

'Hello. Who's this?'

'Chloë.' There was a terrific banging going on in the background. He could barely make out her words. 'Who are you?' she asked.

'Malcolm Karlsson,' he said formally.

'The detective.'

'Yes.'

'Do you want me to call Frieda?'

'It's all right. It can wait.'

He put the phone down, feeling foolish, then called another number.

'Hello, Sadie here.'

'It's Mal.'

Sadie was the cousin of a friend of Karlsson whom he had met a few times over the years, with his wife, or with Sadie's current boyfriend. Their last meeting had been at a lunch a few weeks ago, both on their own, when, leaving at the same time, she had said that they ought to meet up, have a drink.

'Can I offer you that drink?' he said now.

'How lovely,' she said, and he was reminded of what he had always liked about her: her straightforward enthusiasm, her undisguised liking for him. 'When?'

'How about now?'

'Now?'

'But you're probably busy.'

'As it happens, I'm not. I was just worrying that my hair needs washing.'

He laughed, his spirits lifting. 'It's not a job interview.'

They met in a wine bar in Stoke Newington and drank a bottle of white wine between them. Everything was easy. Her hair looked fine to him, and so did the way she smiled at him, nodded in agreement. She wore bright, flimsy layers of clothes and had put lipstick on. He caught a whiff of her perfume. She put her hand on his arm when she spoke, leaned in close. Her breath was on his cheek and her pupils were large in the dimly lit room.

They went back to her flat because he didn't want to be in his, even though it was closer. She apologized for the mess, but he didn't mind that. He was a bit fuzzy from the wine and he was tired and all he wanted to do was to lose himself for a while.

She took an opened bottle of white wine from the fridge door and poured them each a glass. She looked up at him, expectant, and he leaned down and kissed her. As they undressed, he couldn't stop thinking what a long time it had been since he had done this. He closed his eyes and felt her against him, her soft skin, took in the smell of her. Could it really be this easy?

Paul Kerrigan wasn't exactly drunk, but after three pints and no food since the cheese sandwich he hadn't finished at lunch, he was blurry, hazy, a bit adrift. Theoretically he was on his way home, but he really didn't want to go there, to see his wife's thin, sad face, his sons' hostile, derisive stares. He was like a stranger in his own house, a hated impostor. So now he walked slowly, feeling the weight of his heavy body with each step he took, the thump of blood in his aching head. He needed to make sense of all that had happened, but this evening everything felt like an effort and thoughts were sludge in his brain.

One month ago, Ruth had been alive and Elaine had known nothing, and his boys had been full of teasing affection for him. Now, each morning when he woke, he had to realize all over again that the old life was over.

He reached the corner of his road and stopped. The pub was disgorging its drinkers on to the pavement in a burst of noise. He didn't hear the footsteps behind him, or turn in time to see who it was who brought something heavy down on the back of his head, so that he reeled, stumbled, fell in an ungainly heap on to the road. The blow came again, this time on his back. He thought how that would hurt later. And so would his cheek, which had scraped along the tarmac when he fell. He could taste blood, and there was also grit in his mouth. Through the roar in his head, he could hear the pubgoers, like distant static. He wanted to call out for help but his tongue was swollen and it was easier to close his eyes and wait for the footsteps to recede.

At last he struggled to his feet and blundered along the street to his front door. He couldn't make his fingers hold the key so he knocked and knocked until Elaine opened it. For a moment she stared at him, as if he was a monster standing in front of her, or a madman. Then her hand flew to her mouth in a cartoonish gesture of horror that he would have found funny in his safe old life.

'I didn't do it.' Russell Lennox's eyes were bloodshot. He had the sweet, stale smell of alcohol on him. Since the bottles had been found hidden in the garden shed, he seemed to have taken to drink in earnest – almost as if, now the secret was out, he had given himself permission.

'It would be understandable if . . .'

'I didn't do anything. I was here. Alone.'

'Can anyone confirm that?'

'I told you I was.'

'You seem to have had a fair bit to drink.'

'Is that illegal?'

'The man who was having an affair with your wife has been badly beaten up, not ten minutes from your house.'

'He had it coming to him. But I didn't do it.'

That was all he'd say, over and over, while Dora peered through the banisters at him, her face small and pale in the darkness.

Frieda lay in bed and tried to sleep. She lay quite straight, staring at the ceiling, and then she turned onto her side, rearranging the pillow, closing her eyes. The cat lay at her feet. She put an image in her mind, of a shallow river running over pebbles, but the water bubbled and the faces rose from the bottom. Thoughts stirred in the mud of her mind. Her body was sore.

It was no good. She could hear Chloë downstairs. She was talking to someone on Skype and had been for what seemed like hours, sometimes loudly and emphatically, with occasional bursts of laughter. Or was she crying? Frieda looked at the time. It was nearly one o'clock and tomorrow Chloë had school and she herself had a whole day to get through. She sighed and got out of bed, tweaking her curtains back to see the half-moon and then going down the stairs.

Chloë looked up from her computer guiltily. Frieda saw the image of Ted Lennox there, his peaky adolescent face staring out at her. She stepped back, out of range. 'I didn't know you were still awake.'

'I don't want to be.'

'I need to talk to Ted.'

'You were talking rather loudly. And I think it's time for you to go to bed.'

'I'm not sleepy.'

'Go to bed, Chloë. You have classes tomorrow.' Frieda stepped forward so that she could see Ted and Ted could see her. He looked dreadful. 'You too, Ted.'

'Can I have some tea first? With just a small amount of milk,' Chloë asked.

'This isn't a hotel.'

'Sorry.' Chloë didn't sound sorry. She grimaced into her computer screen and raised her eyebrows dramatically at Ted.

'Take your things up with you. And don't touch anything in my study.'

She returned to her room but for a long while she didn't get into her bed. Instead, she stood at the window, gazing out at the night.

THIRTY-TWO

When Karlsson woke, he wasn't sure where he was. He shifted in the bed and felt the warmth, saw the edge of a shoulder and thought, she's come back. And then he remembered and felt a lurch, and it was as if the colour had leached out of the world. He fumbled for his watch and found it still on his wrist. It was twenty to six. He lay back in the bed. There was a murmur of something he couldn't make out from Sadie beside him. Wasn't this what he had been wanting? Something uncomplicated, easy, affectionate, pleasurable? An ache started in his head and spread through his body. He felt an immense, disabling tiredness. Very cautiously, he edged himself out of the bed and started to dress.

'You don't have to run away,' said Sadie, from behind him.

She had pulled herself up and was leaning on one elbow. Her face was puffy from sleep. 'I could make you some breakfast,' she said. She looked kind and concerned.

'I've really got to go,' said Karlsson. 'I need to get back and get changed and go into work. I've really got to rush.'

'I can get you a tea or a coffee.'

'That's all right.'

Karlsson felt a sudden sense of panic, so that he was almost choking. He pulled his trousers on and fastened them. It all seemed to be taking a long time and he sensed Sadie watching him, a character in an unfunny farce. He pushed his shoes on. They felt too small for his feet. He picked up his jacket and turned to her. She was lying in the same position.

'Sadie, I'm sorry, I . . .' He couldn't think what else to say.

'Yes, all right.' She turned away from him and twisted the duvet around her so that he could see only the back of her head. He saw her bra draped over the end of the bed. He thought of her putting it on yesterday morning and then taking it off last night. He had an impulse to sit down, pull the duvet back and tell Sadie everything, explain what he was feeling, why this was all wrong, why they were wrong for each other and why he was wrong for anyone. But that wouldn't be fair on her. He'd already done enough.

He came out on to the quiet street. There was a hum of traffic but the main sound was birdsong all around him, with a blue sky and early-morning sunshine. It felt wrong. It should have been raining and grey and cold.

Frieda sat at her kitchen table while Josef boiled the kettle, ground coffee, washed up the remains of Chloë's breakfast. A good thing about Josef – and she had to hang on to the good things, in the middle of everything else – was that she didn't have to make conversation. So she could just sit at the table and stare in front of her. Finally he put the mug of coffee in front of her and sat down with his own mug.

'Is difficult to help,' he began. 'There is a Ukrainian joke about three people helping old lady across the road.

And a person say, why take three people? And they say because the old lady not want to cross the road.' He took a sip from his coffee. 'Is funny in Ukrainian.'

'So where are we?' said Frieda.

'It is finished today, even if I kill myself to finish it. This evening you will have a bath in your own beautiful bath.'

'Good,' said Frieda.

'And Chloë? She is staying here?'

'I don't know,' said Frieda. 'I need to find out what's going on. We'll see.'

Josef looked at Frieda with a concerned expression. 'You are not angry,' he said. 'You should be angry.'

'What do you mean?'

Josef gestured around him. 'I tried to make you better with your new bath but it is difficult to help. And I make things worse for you.'

'It wasn't your fault –'

'Stop. The bath didn't come, then came and went away again. And the electricity stopped.'

'Now that *was* irritating.'

'You need help and I make it worse for you and now Chloë is here. I saw upstairs and there is her things everywhere in your study.'

'Is there? Oh, God, I haven't been up there. Is it bad?'

'Is bad. There is girl things and clothes all over your things. Apple cores too. Wet towels. Mugs growing things inside. But I am saying, you should be angry. You should be hitting out. Fighting, no?'

'I'm not angry, Josef. Or maybe I'm too tired to be angry.' She relapsed into silence. 'But that bath had better be done by this evening or else –'

A ringtone went off and it took Frieda a moment to realize it was her own. It came from her jacket, which was draped over a chair. She fumbled through the pockets until she found it. She heard a woman's voice: 'Is that Frieda Klein?'

'Yes.'

'This is Agnes Flint. You left a message.'

As soon as Jim Fearby saw the photograph, he sensed he could cross her off his list. Clare Boyle was – had been – a round-faced girl, with frizzy blonde hair. Her mother had sat him down and brought him tea and cake, then had produced a handful of photographs from a drawer. Valerie Boyle settled down in the armchair opposite and talked about how her daughter had always been difficult.

'Did she ever run away?' Fearby asked.

'She got in with the wrong crowd,' Valerie said. 'Sometimes she'd stay out all night. Sometimes even for a few days. When I got upset she just flared up. There was nothing I could do.'

Fearby put his notebook down. Really, he could leave now, but he had to stay long enough to be polite. He looked at Valerie Boyle. He felt he could classify these mothers by now. Some of them had grief like a chronic illness; they were grey with it, had fine lines scratched in their faces, a deadness in the eyes as if there was nothing worth looking at. Then there were women like this one. Valerie Boyle had a quavering quality, a sense of flinching from a blow that might come at any moment, as if she were in the middle of an embarrassing scene that might turn nasty.

'Was there trouble at home?' Fearby asked.

'No, no,' she said quickly. 'She had some problems with her dad. He could turn a bit violent. But, like I said, she was difficult. Then she just disappeared. The police never did that much.'

Fearby wondered if it had just been violence, or whether it had been sex as well. And the woman in front of him; had she stood by and watched it happen? In the end there would have been nothing for the girl to do but escape. She was probably somewhere in London, one of the thousands of young people who'd had to escape, one way or another. Perhaps she was with one of the 'wrong crowd' her mother had talked about. Fearby silently wished her luck.

But when Fearby drove up to the little estate just outside Stafford, he knew he was onto something. The group of houses was just a few minutes' drive out of town but also semi-rural, surrounded by scrubby open spaces, playing fields, some woods. He saw signs for footpaths. This was more like it. Daisy Logan's mother was unwilling to let him in; she talked through the barely open door with the chain still attached. Fearby explained that he was a journalist, that he wanted to find out what had happened to her daughter, that he would only be a minute, but she was immovable. She said she didn't want to talk about it. It had been seven years. The police had given up. They'd put it behind them.

'Just a couple of minutes,' said Fearby. 'One minute.'

'What is it you want?'

Fearby got a glimpse of haunted dark eyes. He was

used to it by now, but sometimes he felt the odd pang, that he was hunting people down and opening up their old wounds. But what else could he do?

'I read about your daughter,' he said. 'It was a tragic case. I wanted to know whether you'd had any warning. Was she unhappy? Did she have trouble at school?'

'She loved school,' said the woman. 'She had just started the sixth form. She wanted to be a vet.'

'What was her mood like?'

'Are you asking me whether Daisy ran away from home? The week after she . . . well, she was going on a school trip. She'd done a part-time job for six months to pay for it. You know, my husband's at home here. He's on disability. It broke him. We keep going over that evening. She was walking over to see her best friend. She always took a shortcut across the common. If only we'd driven her. We just go over and over it.'

'You can't blame yourself,' said Fearby.

'Yes, you can.'

'I'm so sorry,' said Fearby. 'But have you got a photograph?'

'I can't give you one,' said the woman. 'We gave some to journalists at the time. And the police. We never got them back.'

'Just to look at.'

'Wait,' said the woman.

He stood on the doorstep and waited. After a few minutes, there was the sound of the chain being unfastened. The woman handed him a photograph. He looked at the girl, a young and eager face. He thought, as he always did, of what was to come, what that face would witness. He noted the dark hair, something about the eyes. They were like a family, like a gang. He took out his phone.

'Is that all right?' he said.

The woman shrugged. He took a picture with his phone and handed it back to the woman.

'So what are you going to do?' said the woman. 'What are you going to do about our Daisy?'

'I'm going to find out what I can,' said Fearby. 'If I find out anything, anything at all, I'll let you know.'

'Will you find Daisy?'

Fearby paused. 'No. No, I don't think so.'

'Then don't bother,' said the woman, and closed the door.

Frieda had been interested to meet the woman who had broken Rajit Singh's heart, but when Agnes Flint opened the door of her flat, she thought she must have come to the wrong door. The young woman had a smooth, round face, with coarse brown hair swept messily back. She wore a black sweater and jeans. But she was saved from being nondescript by her large dark eyes and a slightly ironic expression. Frieda had a sense of being appraised.

'I don't know what this is about,' she said.

'Just give me a minute,' said Frieda.

'You'd better come in. I'm on the top floor.'

Frieda followed her up the stairs.

'It looks a bit boring from the outside,' Agnes said, over her shoulder. 'But wait till you get inside.'

She opened the door and Frieda followed her in. They were in a living room with large windows on the far side.

'I see what you mean,' she said.

The flat looked over a network of railway tracks. On the other side was a warehouse and beyond that were some apartment buildings that marked the south bank of the Thames.

'Some people hate the idea of living by the railway,' said Agnes, 'but I like it. It's like living next to a river, with strange things flowing past. And the trains are far enough away. I don't get commuters staring in at me while I'm in bed.'

'I like it,' said Frieda. 'It's interesting.'

'Well, that makes two of us.' There was a pause. 'So you've been talking to poor old Rajit.'

'Why do you call him that?'

'You've met him. He wasn't much fun when we were together.'

'He was a bit depressed.'

'I'll say. Has he sent you to try to plead for him?'

'Didn't it end well?'

'Does it ever end well?' There was a rumble from outside and a train passed. 'They'll be in Brighton in an hour,' Agnes said. 'Do you mind if I ask you a question? I mean, since you've come all the way to my flat.'

'Go ahead.'

'What are you doing here? When you rang up, I was curious. Rajit probably told you that he had difficulty taking no for an answer. He rang. He came round. He even wrote me letters.'

'What did they say?'

'I threw them away without opening them. So when

you rang, I was kind of curious. I wondered whether he was sending women on his behalf. Like some kind of carrier pigeon. Are you a friend of his?'

'No. I've only met him twice.'

'So what are you?'

'I'm a psychotherapist.'

'Did he come to see you as a patient?'

'Not exactly.'

A smile of recognition spread across Agnes's face. 'Oh, I know who you are. You're *her*, aren't you?'

'It depends what you mean by "her".'

'What's this about? Is this some kind of complicated revenge?'

'No.'

'Don't get me wrong. I'm not judging you. If someone made a fool of me like that, I'd fucking crucify them.'

'But that's not why I'm here.'

'No? Then why?'

'There was something Rajit said.' Frieda saw herself from the outside, going from person to person reciting a fragment of a story that seemed increasingly detached from its context – an image that she couldn't shake off, but that glinted, sharp and bright, in the darkness of her mind. She should stop this, she told herself. Return to the life she'd been in before. She felt Agnes Flint waiting for her reply.

'Rajit wasn't actually the student who was sent to me; that was someone else. But all the four researchers told the same story, one that supposedly demonstrated they posed a clear threat.'

'Yeah, I read about it.'

'In this story, there was an arresting detail, which Rajit said actually came from you.'

'I don't understand.'

'About cutting his father's hair – well, I guess, your father's hair if it came from you originally and he changed it for his purpose.'

'Cutting my father's hair.'

'Yes. The feeling of power and tenderness you got from that.'

'This is freaking me out a bit.'

'He said you told him the story when you were lying in bed together, and you were stroking his hair and telling him it needed cutting.'

'Oh. Yes. Now what?'

Now what? Frieda didn't know the answer to that. She said wearily, 'So it was just a memory you had, a simple memory?'

'It wasn't my memory.'

'What do you mean?'

'It was something a friend once said to me. She told me this story about cutting hair. I don't think she said it was her father's, actually. Maybe it was her boyfriend's or her brother's or a friend's. I can't remember. I don't know why I even remember her saying it. It was just a little thing and it was ages ago. It just kind of stayed with me. Weird to think of Rajit writing it into his spiel. Passing it on.'

'Yes,' said Frieda, slowly. 'So your friend told you and you told Rajit.'

'A version of it.'

'Yes.'

Agnes looked quizzically at Frieda. 'Why on earth does it matter?'

'What's your friend's name?'

'I'm not going to tell you until you've answered my question. Why does it matter?'

'I don't know. It probably doesn't.' Frieda gazed into Agnes's bright, shrewd eyes: she liked her. 'The truth is, it bothers me and I don't know why, but I feel I have to follow the thread.'

'The thread?'

'Yes.'

'Lila Dawes. Her real name is Lily but no one calls her that.'

'Thank you. How do you know her?'

'I don't. I knew her. We were at school together. Best friends.' Again that ironic smile. 'She was a bit wild, but never malicious. We kept in touch after she dropped out, when she was just sixteen, but not for long. Our lives were so different. I was on one road and she – well, she wasn't on a road at all.'

'So you have no idea where she is now?'

'No.'

'Where were you at school?'

'Down near Croydon. John Hardy School.'

'Is Croydon where you both grew up?'

'Do you know the area?'

'No, not at all.'

'It's near Croydon. Next to it.'

'Do you remember her address?'

'It's funny. I can't remember what happened last week,

but I can remember everything about when I was young. Ledbury Close. Number eight. Are you going to try and find her?'

'I think so.'

Agnes nodded slowly. 'I should have tried myself,' she said. 'I often wonder about her – if she's OK.'

'You think she might not be?'

'She was in a bad way when I last saw her.' Frieda waited for Agnes to continue. 'She'd left home and she had a habit.' She gave a shiver. 'She looked pretty bad, thin, with spots on her forehead. I don't know how she was getting the money to pay for it. She didn't have a real job. I should have done more, don't you think?'

'I don't know.'

'She was in trouble, I could see that, and I just wanted to run a mile, as if it was contagious. I tried to put her out of my mind. Every so often I think of her and then I push her down again. Some friend.'

'Except you remembered that story, and passed it on.'

'Yeah. I can see her now, telling me. Grinning.'

'What did she look like when you knew her?'

'Little and thin, with long, dark hair that was always falling over her eyes, and a huge smile. It used to take over her whole face. Gorgeous, in an odd kind of way. Like a monkey. Like a waif. She wore eccentric clothes she picked up from vintage shops. Boys loved her.'

'Does she have family?'

'Her mum died when she was little. Maybe things would have turned out differently if she'd had a mother. Her dad, Lawrence, was lovely – he doted on her but he couldn't keep her in order, not even when she was small. And she has two brothers, Ricky and Steve, who are several years older than her.'

'Thank you, Agnes. I'll tell you if I find her.'

'I wonder what she's like now. Maybe she's settled down, become respectable. Kids, a husband, a job. It's hard to imagine. What would I say to her?'

'Say what's in your heart.'

'That I let her down. So odd, though, how it's all come back like this – just because of a silly story I told to poor Rajit.'

Frieda – you haven't answered my last phone calls or my emails.

Please let me know that everything's all right. Sandy xxxxx

THIRTY-THREE

Frieda walked home slowly. She could feel the warmth seeping into her body, hear her feet softly tapping on the pavement. People moved towards her and then flowed past, their faces blurred and indistinct. She saw herself from the outside; the thoughts that streamed through her brain seemed to belong to someone else. She knew that she was tired after all the nights of wakefulness and disordered dreams.

She did not go straight to her house but turned aside to sit awhile in Lincoln's Inn Fields. It was a small, green square, bright with blossom and new tulips. In the middle of the day it was often full of lawyers in their smart suits eating their lunch, but now it was quiet, except for a pair of young women playing tennis on the court at the far side. Frieda sat down with her back against one of the great old plane trees. Its girth was tremendous and its bark dappled. She closed her eyes and tipped her face to the sun that fell through its leaves. Perhaps she should do as Sandy said and go to New York, where she would be safe and with the man she loved, who loved her and who knew her in a way that no one else in the world ever had. But then she would no longer be able to sit in the shade of this beautiful old tree and let the day settle around her.

When she got up again, the sun was sinking lower and the air was beginning to feel cool. She thought wistfully of her bath. And she thought of Chloë, took out her mobile and made the call.

Olivia's voice was ragged. Frieda wondered if she'd been drinking. 'I suppose Chloë's been telling you all sorts of horrible lies about me.'

'No.'

'It's no good pretending. It's no good anyone pretending. I know what you all think.'

'I don't –'

'Bad mother. Fucked-up. Wash our hands of her.'

'Listen, Olivia, stop!' Frieda heard her own voice, harsh and stern. 'You need to talk about this, it's clear, but I'm not washing my hands of you. I'm ringing up to talk about Chloë.'

'She hates me.'

'She doesn't hate you. But it's probably a good thing if she stays with me for a few days while you sort things out.'

'You make me sound like a sock drawer.'

'Say, one week,' said Frieda. She thought of her tidy, secure house invaded by Chloë's mess and drama and experienced a feeling of near-panic. 'I'll come over tomorrow evening and we can talk about what you're going through and try to make some kind of plan to deal with it. Half past six.'

She turned off her phone and put it into her pocket. Her own plan was that she was going to go home, have a very long, very hot bath in her new and beautiful bathroom and climb into bed, pulling the duvet over her head, shutting out her thoughts. And hope that she wouldn't dream, or at least that she wouldn't remember her dreams.

She opened her front door. Several pairs of muddy shoes lay on the mat. A leather satchel. A jacket she didn't recognise. There was a nasty smell coming from the kitchen. Something was burning and an alarm was making a piercing sound that felt to Frieda as though it was coming from inside her head. For a moment she considered leaving her own house and simply walking away from everything that was going on in there. Instead, she went up to the alarm in the hall ceiling and pressed the button to turn it off, then called out for Chloë. There was no reply but the cat dashed past her and up the stairs

The kitchen was full of fumes. Frieda saw that the handle of her frying pan was blistered and twisted. That must be the nasty smell. There were beer bottles, empty glasses, a lovely bowl had been used as an ashtray and two dirty plates lay on the table, which was sticky and stained. She cursed under her breath and threw open the back door. Chloë was in the middle of the yard, and she saw that Ted was there as well, sitting with his back against the far wall and his knees drawn up to his chin. There were several cigarette butts scattered round him, and a beer bottle at his feet.

'Chloë.'

'I didn't hear you come in.'

'There's quite a mess in there.'

'We were going to clear it up.'

'I've been speaking to Olivia. You can stay here for one week.'

'Great.'

'But there are rules. This is my house and you have to respect it and me. You clear things up, for a start. Properly. You don't smoke inside. Hello, Ted.'

He raised his face and stared at her. His eyes were red-rimmed and his lips were bloodless. 'Hi,' he managed.

'How long have you been here?'

'I was just going.'

'Have you both been at school today?'

Chloë shrugged and gave her a defiant look. 'Some things are more important than school, you know. In case you forgot, Ted's mother was killed.'

'I know.'

'If you had to choose between double biology and helping your friend, which would you choose?'

'Helping friends is something you do after double biology.' She looked at Ted. 'When did you last eat?'

'We were going to have pancakes,' said Chloë, 'but they went wrong.'

'I'll make you some toast.'

'I don't want to talk to you about stuff, if that's what you're thinking.'

'It wasn't.'

'That's all everyone seems to want. For me to talk about my feelings and weep and then you can hug me and tell me everything will be OK in the end.'

'I'm just going to make toast. Does your father know you're here and skipping school, Ted?'

'No. I'm not a child.'

'I know you're not.'

'My dad's got his mind on other things. Mum was shagging another man.'

'That's a painful thing for you to find out.'

'Do you want to know how I feel about it? Because I'm not going to talk about that. Or anything else.'

There was a knocking at the door, hard and insistent, although Frieda wasn't expecting anyone.

'Come inside now,' she said, to the two of them. 'I'll see who's here.'

Judith stood on the doorstep. She was wearing a man's shirt over baggy jeans held up by rope, and broken flip-flops. There was a colourful bandanna wrapped round her chestnut curls. Her eyes, set wide in her face, seemed bluer than when Frieda had seen her at that awful interview, and there was vivid orange lipstick on her full mouth, which was turned down sullenly. 'I'm here for Ted. Is he here?'

'I'm making toast for him. Do you want some?'

'OK.'

'This way.'

Frieda led the girl into the kitchen. She gave a nod to Ted, who nodded back, then raised her hand in half-greeting to Chloë, whom she obviously knew.

'Louise is clearing out Mum's clothes.'

'She can't do that!' Ted's voice was sharp.

'She is.'

'Why can't she fuck off to her own house?'

'Dora's shut herself in her room and she's wailing. And Dad's shouting.'

'At you, or at Louise?'

'Everybody, really. Or nobody.'

'He's probably drunk.'

'Stop it!' She put her hands up as if to cover her ears.

'Face it, Judith. Mum was fucking another man and Dad's a drunk.'

'Don't! Don't be so cruel.'

'It's for your own good.' But he looked ashamed of himself.

'Will you come back with me?' his sister asked. 'It's better if we're there together.'

'Here's your toast,' said Frieda. 'Help yourself to the honey.'

'Just butter.'

'I'm very sorry about your mother.'

Judith shrugged her thin shoulders. Her blue eyes glittered in her freckled face.

'At least you've got Ted,' said Chloë, urgently. 'At least you two can help each other. Think if you were alone.'

'You were together when you found out, weren't you?' asked Frieda. 'But since then have you talked about it to each other?' Neither of them spoke. 'Have you talked to anyone?'

'You mean someone like you?'

'A friend or a relative or someone like me.'

'She's dead. Words don't change that. We're sad. Words won't change that.'

'There's this woman the police sent,' said Judith.

'Oh, yes.' Ted's voice was raw with contempt. 'Her. She nods all the time as if she has some deep understanding of our pain. It's crap. It makes me want to throw up.'

There were hectic blotches on his cheeks. He tipped himself back on his chair so he was balanced on only one of its legs and spun himself slowly.

'Mum hated it when he did that.' Judith waved at her brother. 'It was like a family thing.'

'Now I can do it as much as I want and no one will bother about it.'

'No,' said Frieda. 'I agree with your mother about that. It is very irritating. And dangerous.'

'Can we go home, please? I don't want to leave Dad on his own with Louise being all sad and disapproving.' She faltered. There were tears in her eyes and she blinked them away. 'I think we should go home,' she repeated.

Ted lowered his chair and stood up, a spindly, scruffy figure. 'OK, then. Thanks for the toast.'

'That's all right.'

'Bye,' said Judith.

'Goodbye.'

'Can we come again?' Judith's voice was suddenly tremulous.

'Yes.' Chloë's voice was loud and energetic. 'Any time, day or night. We're here for you – aren't we, Frieda?'

'Yes,' said Frieda, a little wearily.

She trudged upstairs to the bathroom. The bath was there in all its glory. She turned on the taps and they worked. But there was no plug. She looked under the bath and in the cupboard, but it wasn't there. The plug in the washbasin was too small, and the one in the kitchen was an irritating metal kind that didn't have a chain but twisted down. She couldn't have a bath, after all.

*

Karlsson and Yvette arrived at the Lennox house shortly after Judith had left. The shouting was over, and in its place there was a curdled silence, an air of unease. Russell Lennox was in his study, sitting at his desk and staring blindly out of the window; Dora was in her room, no longer sobbing but lying curled into a ball, her face still wet and swollen from tears. Louise Weller had been cleaning up. She had washed the kitchen floor, vacuumed the stairs, and was just about to make a start on some of her sister's clothes, when the doorbell rang.

'We need to look through Mrs Lennox's things one more time,' explained Yvette.

'I was making a start on her clothes.'

'Perhaps not just yet,' Karlsson told her. 'We'll tell you when you can do that.'

'Another thing. The family want to know when the funeral can be.'

'It won't be long. We should be able to tell you in the next day or so.'

'It's not right.'

Karlsson felt an impulse to say something rude back to her but he replied blandly that it was difficult for every-body.

They made their way upstairs, into the bedroom that the Lennoxes had shared for more than twenty years. There were signs of Louise Weller's work: there were several plastic bags full of shoes, and she seemed to have emptied most of the small amount of makeup Ruth had owned into the waste-paper bin.

'What are we looking for?' asked Yvette. 'They've been through all this.'

'I don't know. There's probably nothing. But this is a family full of secrets. What else don't we know about?'

'The trouble is, there's so much,' said Yvette. 'She kept everything. Should we look through all those boxes in the loft with her children's reports in? And what about the various computers? We've been through theirs, of course, but each child has a laptop and there are a few old ones that obviously don't work any more but haven't been thrown away.'

'Here's a woman who for ten years met her lover in their flat. Did she have a key? Or any documents at all that would shed light on this? Did she really never send or receive emails or texts? I've taken it for granted that this affair must have something to do with her death but perhaps there's something else.'

Yvette gave a sarcastic smile. 'As in, if she was capable of adultery, what else might she have done?'

'That's not exactly what I meant.'

Standing in the bedroom, Karlsson thought about how they knew so much about Ruth Lennox and yet didn't know her at all. They knew what toothpaste she used and which deodorant. What her bra size was and her knickers and her shoes. What books she read and what magazines. They knew what face cream she used, what recipes she turned to, what she put in her shopping trolley week after week, what tea she favoured, what wine she drank, what TV programmes she watched, what box-sets she owned. They were familiar with her handwriting, knew what biros and pencils she wrote with, saw the doodles she made on the sides of pads; they had studied her face in the photographs around the house and in the albums. They had read the postcards she'd received from dozens of friends over dozens of years from dozens of countries. Rifled through Mother's Day cards and birthday cards and Christmas cards. Checked and double-checked her email, and were sure she'd never used Facebook, LinkedIn or Twitter.

But they didn't know why or how she had managed to conduct a ten-year affair under the nose of her family. They didn't know if she'd felt guilty. They didn't know why she had had to die.

On an impulse, he pushed open the door to Dora's bedroom. It was very neat and quiet in there. Everything was put away and in its proper place: clothes neatly folded into drawers, paper stacked on the desk, homework books on the shelves above it, her pyjamas folded on the pillow. In the wardrobe, her clothes – the clothes of a girl who didn't want to become a teenager yet – hung above paired, sensible shoes. It made Karlsson feel sad just to look at the anxious order. A thin spindle of pink caught his eye on the top of the cupboard. He reached up his hand and pulled down a rag doll, then drew in his breath sharply. It had a flat pink face and droopy legs, red cotton hair in plaits, but its stomach had been cut away and the area between its legs snipped open. He held it for several moments, his face grim.

'Oh!' Yvette had come into the room. 'That's horrible.'

'Yes, isn't it?'

'Do you think she did that herself? Because of what she found out about her mother?'

'Probably.'

'Poor little thing.'

'But I'll have to ask her.'

'I think I've found something. Look.' She opened her hand to show a little dial of tablets. Karlsson squinted at them. 'This was in that long cupboard next to the bathroom – the one full of towels and flannels, body lotion, tampons and all sorts of bits and pieces they didn't know what to do with.'

'Well?'

'The Pill,' said Yvette. 'Inside a sock.'

'Funny place to keep your contraceptives.'

'Yes. Especially when Ruth Lennox had a coil.'

Karlsson's mobile rang. He took it out of his pocket and frowned when he saw who was calling. He had had two brief texts and one message from Sadie, asking him to get in touch. He was about to let it go to voicemail again. But then he hesitated: she clearly wasn't going to give up and he supposed he might as well get it over with.

'I'm sorry I didn't call you back. I've been busy and –'

'No. You didn't call me back because you didn't want to see me again and you thought if you ignored my calls I might just go away.'

'That's not fair.'

'Isn't it? I think it is.'

'I made a mistake, Sadie. I like you a lot and we had a nice evening, but it's the wrong time for me.'

'I'm not calling to ask you out, if that's what you're worried about. I got the message. But you need to meet me.'

'I don't think that's a good idea.'

'It's a very good idea. You need to sit down opposite me, look me in the eyes and explain yourself.'

'Sadie, listen –'

'No. You listen. You're behaving like an awkward teenager. You asked me out, we had a nice evening, we made love – that's what it felt like to me, anyway. And then you crept away, as if you were embarrassed. I deserve more than that.'

'I'm sorry.'

'I deserve an explanation. Meet me at the same wine bar at eight o'clock tomorrow. It'll only take half an hour, less. You can tell me why you behaved like that, then you can go home and I won't call you again.'

And she ended the call. Karlsson looked down at the mobile in his hand and raised his eyebrows. She was rather impressive, that Sadie.

THIRTY-FOUR

Frieda always felt a little strange when she went south of the river. But going to Croydon was like going to another country. She'd had to look it up on a map. She'd had to go to Victoria and get on an overground train. It had been full of commuters coming into London, but going out it was almost empty. London, this huge creature, sucked people in. It wouldn't be until late afternoon that it blew them out again. As the train crossed the river, Frieda recognized Battersea, the derelict power station. She even saw, or nearly saw, where Agnes Flint's flat must be, just near the huge market. After Clapham Junction and Wandsworth Common it gradually became vague and nameless for her, a succession of glimpsed parks, a graveyard, the backs of houses, a shopping centre, a breaker's yard, a flash of someone hanging out washing, a child bouncing on a blue trampoline. Even though the streets had become unfamiliar, she continued to stare out of the window. She couldn't stop herself. Houses and buildings didn't hide from trains the way they did from cars. You didn't see their smart façades but the bits behind that the owners didn't bother about, that they didn't think anyone would really notice: the broken fences, the piles of rubbish, abandoned machinery.

When she got out of the station, she had to use the street map to find her way and even that wasn't simple.

She rotated the map again and again to find which exit she had come out of. Even so, she walked in the wrong direction and had to look at the map again and orientate herself by seeing where Peel Way joined Clarence Avenue. She had to walk back past the station and then through a series of residential streets until she reached Ledbury Close. Number eight was a pebble-dashed detached house, indistinguishable from its neighbours, except that it was somehow more cared for – there was more precise attention to detail. Frieda noticed the new windows, the frames freshly painted in glossy white. On each side of the front door a purple ceramic pot contained a miniature bush, trimmed into a spiral. They were so neat, they looked as if they had been done with scissors.

Frieda pressed the doorbell. It didn't seem to make a sound, so she pressed it again and still heard nothing. She stood there, feeling irritated and uncertain. Either no one was in or the doorbell was broken and she was standing there pointlessly, or it wasn't broken and she was annoying someone even before she had met them. She wondered whether she should ring the bell again and possibly make the situation worse or bang on the door with her fist and make it worse still or just keep waiting and hope for the best. And she wondered why she was even worrying about something like that. Then she heard a sound from somewhere inside and saw a blurred shape through the frosted glass of the door. It opened, revealing a large man, not fat but big so that he seemed to fill the doorway. He was almost completely bald with messy grey hair around the fringes of his head. His face was flushed with the red of someone who spent time outside and he was dressed in bulky grey work trousers, a blue and white checked shirt and heavy dark leather boots that were yellow with dried mud.

'I wasn't sure if the bell was working,' said Frieda.

'Everyone says that,' said the man, his face crinkling around the eyes. 'It rings at the back of the house. I have it like that because I spend a lot of time in the garden. I've been out there all morning.' He gestured up at the blue sky. 'On a day like this.' He looked at Frieda questioningly.

'Are you Lawrence Dawes?'

'Yes, I am.'

'My name is Frieda Klein. I'm here because . . .' What was she going to say? 'I'm here because I'm trying to find your daughter, Lila.'

Dawes's smile faded. He suddenly seemed older and more frail.

'Lila? You're looking for my Lila?'

'Yes.'

'I don't know where she is,' he said. 'I lost touch with her.'

He raised his hands helplessly. Frieda saw his fingernails, dirty from the garden. Was that it? Had she come all the way to Croydon just for that?

'Can I talk to you about her?'

'What for?'

'I met someone who used to know her,' said Frieda. 'An old friend of hers called Agnes Flint.'

Dawes nodded slowly. 'I remember Agnes. Lila used to go around with this little gang of girls. She was one of them. Before things went wrong.'

'Can I come in?' said Frieda.

Dawes seemed to be thinking it over, then gave a shrug. 'Come through to the garden. I was just about to have some tea.'

He led Frieda through the house. It was clearly the home of a man – a very organized man – living alone. Through a door she saw a large flat-screen TV and rows of DVDs on shelves. There was a computer. Underfoot was a thick cream-coloured carpet, so that all the sounds were muffled.

Five minutes later they were standing on the back lawn, holding mugs of tea. The garden was much larger than Frieda had expected, going back thirty, maybe forty, metres from the house. There was a neat lawn with a curved gravel path snaking through it. There were bushes and flowerbeds and little flashes of colour: crocuses, primroses, early tulips. The far end of the garden was wilder and beyond it was a large, high wall.

'I've been trying to tidy things up,' said Dawes. 'After the winter.'

'It seems pretty tidy to me,' said Frieda.

'It's a constant struggle. Look over there.' He pointed to the garden next door. It was full of long grass, brambles, a ragged rhododendron, a couple of ancient fruit trees. 'It's some kind of council house. There'll be a family of Iraqis or Somalis. Nice enough people. Keep themselves to themselves. But they stay a few months and move on. A garden like this takes years. Do you hear anything?'

Frieda moved her head. 'Like what?'

'Follow me.'

Dawes walked along the path away from the house.

Now Frieda could hear a sound, a low murmuring that she couldn't make out, like a muttered conversation in another room. At the end of the garden, there was a fence and Frieda stood next to Dawes and looked over it. With an improbability that almost made her laugh, she saw that there was a dip on the other side and in the dip a small stream trickled along the end of the garden with a path on the other side, then the high wall she had already seen. She saw Dawes smiling at her surprise.

'It makes me think of the children,' he said. 'When they were small, we used to make little paper boats and put them on the stream and watch them float away. I used to tell them that in three hours' time those boats would reach the Thames and then, if the tide was right, they'd float out to sea.'

'What is it?' asked Frieda.

'Don't you know?'

'I'm from north London. Most of our rivers were buried long ago.'

'It's the Wandle,' said Dawes. 'You must know the Wandle.'

'I know the name.'

'It rises a mile or so back. From here it goes past old factories and rubbish dumps and under roads. I used to walk along the path beside it, years ago. The water was foamy and yellow and it stank back then. But we're all right here. I used to let the children paddle in it. That's the problem with a river, isn't it? You're at the mercy of everybody who's upstream from you. Whatever they do to their river, they do to your river. What people do downstream doesn't matter.'

'Except to the people *further* downstream,' said Frieda.

'That's not my problem,' said Dawes, and sipped his tea. 'But I've always liked the idea of living by a river. You never know what's going to float by. I can see you like it too.'

'I do,' Frieda admitted.

'So what do you do, when you're not looking for lost girls?'

'I'm a psychotherapist.'

'Is it your day off?'

'In a way.' They turned and walked back down the garden. 'What do you do?'

'I do this,' said Dawes. 'I do my garden. I do up the house. I do things with my hands. I find it restful.'

'What did you do before that?'

He gave a slow smile. 'I was the opposite, the complete opposite. I was a salesman for a company selling photocopiers. I spent my life on the road.' He gestured to Frieda to sit down on a wrought-iron bench. He sat on a chair close by. 'You know, there's an expression I never understood. When people say something's boring, they say, "It's like watching grass grow." Or "It's like watching paint dry." That's exactly what I enjoy. Watching my grass grow.'

'I'm really here,' said Frieda, 'because I'd like to find your daughter.'

Dawes put his mug down very carefully on the grass next to his foot. When he turned to Frieda, it was with a new intensity. 'I'd like to find her as well,' he said.

'When did you last see her?'

There was a long pause.

'Do you have children?'

'No.'

'It was all I wanted. All of that driving around, all that work, doing things I hated – what I wanted was to be a father and I was a father. I had a lovely wife and I had the two boys and then there was Lila. I loved the boys, kicking a ball with them, taking them fishing, everything you're supposed to do. But when I saw Lila, the moment she was born, I thought, You're my little . . .' He stopped and sniffed, and Frieda saw that his eyes were glistening. He coughed. 'She was the loveliest little girl, smart, funny, beautiful. And then, well, why do things happen? Her mum, my wife, she got ill and was ill for years and then she died. Lila was thirteen. Suddenly I couldn't get through to her. I'd thought we had a special bond and then it was like I was talking a foreign language. Her friends changed, she started going out more and more and then staying away from home. I should have done more but I was away so much.'

'What about her brothers?'

'They'd left by then. Ricky's in the army. Steve lives in Canada.'

'So what happened?'

Dawes spread his hands helplessly. 'I got it wrong,' he said. 'Whatever I did, it wasn't enough or it wasn't what she needed. When I tried to put my foot down, it just drove her away. If I tried to be nice, it felt like it was too late. The more I wanted her to be there, the more she rejected me. I was just her boring old dad. When she was seventeen, she was mainly living with friends. I'd see her every few days, then every few weeks. She treated me a bit like a stranger. Then I didn't see her at all. I tried to find her, but I couldn't. After a while, I stopped trying, although I never stopped thinking of her, missing her. My girl.'

'Do you know how she was supporting herself?'

Frieda saw his jaw flexing. His face had gone white.

'She was having problems. I think there may have been drugs. She hadn't been eating properly. Not for years.'

'These friends. Do you know their names?'

Dawes shook his head. 'I used to know her friends when they were younger. Like Agnes, the one you've met. They were lovely the way girls are together, laughing, going shopping, thinking they're more grown-up than they are. But she dropped them, took up with a new crowd. She never brought them back, never introduced me to them.'

'When she moved out for good, have you any idea where she lived?'

He shook his head again. 'It was somewhere in the area,' he said. 'But then I think she must have moved away.'

'Did you report her missing?'

'She was almost eighteen. One time I got so worried, I went to the police station. But when I mentioned her age, the policeman at the desk wouldn't even write a report.'

'When was this? I mean, the last time you saw her?'

He knitted his brow.

'Oh, God,' he said at last. 'It's more than a year now. It was November of the year before last. I can't believe it. But that's one of the things I think about when I'm working out here. That she'll walk through the door, the way she used to.'

Frieda sat for a moment, thinking.

'Are you all right?' Dawes asked.

'Why do you say that?'

'Maybe it takes one to know one, but you look tired and pale.'

'You don't know what I normally look like.'

'You said it's your day off. Is that right?'

'Yes. Basically.'

'You're an analyst. You talk to people.'

Frieda stood up, ready to go. 'That's right,' she said.

Dawes stood up as well. 'I should have found someone like you for Lila,' he said. 'It's not really my way. I'm not good at talking to people. What I do instead is to work at something, fix something. But you're easy to talk to.' He looked around awkwardly. 'Are you going to search for Lila?'

'I wouldn't know where to start.'

'If you hear anything, you'll let me know?'

On the way out, Dawes found a piece of paper, wrote his phone number on it and gave it to Frieda. As she took it, an idea occurred to her.

'Did she ever cut your hair?' she asked.

He touched his bald pate. 'I've never had much to cut.'

'Or you hers?'

'No. She had beautiful hair. She was proud of it.' He forced a smile. 'She'd never have let me anywhere near it. Why do you ask that?'

'Something Agnes said.'

Back on the street, Frieda looked at the map and set off, not back to the station she'd come from but the next one along. It was a couple of miles. That would be all right.

She needed the walk and she felt more alive now, alert to her surroundings in this part of the city she'd never seen. She found herself walking along a two-lane road, lorries rumbling by. On both sides there were housing estates, the sort that had been quickly knocked up after the war and were now crumbling. Some of the flats were boarded up, others had washing hanging from their little terraces. It didn't feel like a place for walking, but then she turned into a street of little Victorian terraced houses and it suddenly became quiet. Still she felt uncomfortable, miles from home.

As she approached the station, she passed a phone box and stopped. There wasn't even a phone in it. It had been ripped away. Then she looked more closely. On the glass walls there were dozens of little stickers: young model, language teacher, very strict teacher, escorts *de luxe*. Frieda took a notebook from her bag and wrote down the phone numbers. It took several minutes, and two teenage boys walking past giggled and shouted something but she pretended not to hear.

Back in her house, she made a phone call.

'Agnes?'

'Yes?'

'Frieda Klein.'

'Oh – did you find anything?'

'I didn't find Lila, if that's what you mean. She seems to have vanished. Her father can't find her. It's not good news, but I thought you'd want to know.'

'Yes. Yes, I do. Thank you.' There was a pause. 'I'm

going to the police to report her missing. I should have done it months ago.'

'It probably won't do any good,' Frieda said softly. 'She's an adult.'

'I have to do something. I can't just let it go.'

'I understand that.'

'I'll do it at once. Though now that I've waited all these years, I don't know what difference an hour will make.'

Jim Fearby was nearly three-fifths of the way through his list. There were twenty-three names on it, obtained from local newspapers and missing-person websites. Three he had already put a tick by; one he had put a query by; others he had crossed out. He had nine families left to visit – nine mothers who would look at him with stricken faces, haunted eyes. Nine more stories of missing and nine more sets of photos for him to add to the collection of young women's faces he had tacked up on his cork board in his study.

They stared down at him now as he sat back in his chair with his tumbler of whisky, no added water, and his cigarette. He never used to smoke inside the house, but now there was no one to care. He looked from face to face: there was the first girl, Hazel Barton, with her radiant smile – he felt he knew her well by now. Then there was Vanessa Dale, the one who had got away. Roxanne Ingatestone, her asymmetrical face and grey-green eyes. Daisy Crewe, eager and a little dimple on one cheek. Vanessa Dale was safe, Hazel Barton was dead. What about the other two? He stubbed out his cigarette and lit another at once, sucking smoke down into his lungs, staring at the faces until it almost seemed that they were alive under his gaze and were looking back at him, asking him to find them.

> That was a very enigmatic little email. What's going on? Tell me
> how you are, tell me how Reuben and Josef and Sasha are?
> What about Chloë? I miss hearing the details of your days. I miss
> you. Sandy xxx

THIRTY-FIVE

Frieda had arranged to meet Sasha at eight o'clock. Sasha had rung to say there was something she needed to tell her. Frieda hadn't known from her voice whether it was good or bad, but she did know it was important. Before then, as she had promised, she went to see Olivia.

She didn't know quite what to expect, but she was taken aback by Olivia's appearance. She came to the door in a pair of striped drawstring trousers, a stained camisole and plastic flip-flops. The varnish on her toenails was chipped, her hair was greasy – but, above all, her face, puffy and pale, was bare of any makeup. Frieda thought she had never seen Olivia without it. As soon as she got out of bed in the mornings, she would carefully apply foundation, eyeliner, thick mascara, bold red lipstick. Without it, she looked vulnerable and defeated. It was hard to feel angry with her.

'Did you forget I was coming?'

'Not really. I didn't know what time it was.'

'It's six thirty.'

'God. Time flies when you're asleep.' She made an attempt at a laugh.

'Are you ill?'

'I had a late night. I was just having a nap.'

'Shall I make us some tea?'

'Tea?'

'Yes.'

'I could do with a drink.'

'Tea first. There are things we need to discuss.'

'Like me being a crap mother, you mean.'

'No.'

They went into the kitchen together, which was as bad as Frieda had ever seen it. It was a bit like the disorder Chloë had created in Frieda's kitchen, with glasses and bottles everywhere, rubbish spilling out of bin bags on to the sticky tiles, puddles of wax over the table, a sour smell in the air. Frieda started stacking things in the sink to create a space.

'She ran away from me, you know,' Olivia said, who seemed not to notice the state of the room. 'She might have told you I threw her out, but I didn't. She said terrible things to me and then ran off.'

'She says you hit her with a hairbrush.'

'If I did, it was only a soft-bristled one. My mother used to hit me with a wooden spoon.'

Frieda dropped teabags into the pot and picked two mugs out of the sink to wash. 'Things have got a bit out of control here,' Frieda said. 'You need to sort them out before Chloë comes back.'

'We're not all like you. Everything in its proper place. That doesn't mean I'm not coping.'

'You look ill. You've spent the afternoon in bed. The house is in a dreadful state. Chloë's left. I gather Kieran's left too.'

'He's a fool. I told him to get out but I didn't think he'd take me literally.'

'How much are you drinking?'

'You can't tell me how to live my life, you know.'

'Chloë's in my house and we need to talk about how long she's going to be there, and when you'll be ready for her to come home. She can't come home at the moment, can she?'

'I don't see why not.'

'Olivia, she's still a child. She needs boundaries and she needs order.'

'I knew you were going to tell me I was a crap mother.'

'I'm saying that Chloë needs to be woken in the morning, talked to in the evening. She needs a clean kitchen and food in the fridge, a room where she can do her schoolwork, a sense of stability.'

'What about me? What about what I need?'

For a few minutes, there was silence. Olivia sipped her tea and Frieda made piles of dishes and pans and put bin bags out into the hall. After a while, Oliva said in a small voice: 'Does she hate me?'

'No. But she feels angry and neglected.'

'I didn't mean to hit her. I didn't mean to tell Kieran to get lost. I wasn't thinking straight. I just felt wretched.'

'And maybe you'd had too much to drink.'

'You're like a stuck record.'

Frieda didn't say anything to that, and a few moments later, Olivia spoke again: 'I can hear myself saying these terrible things. I can hear my voice screeching obscenities. I can't seem to stop myself, though. I know I'll regret it later.'

Frieda attacked the pans with a scouring pad. She felt terribly tired, defeated by the disorder of Olivia's days. 'You need to take control of your own life,' she said.

'That's all very well to say. Where do I start?'

'Take one thing at a time. Clear up the house from top to bottom. Drink a little less. Or nothing at all. You might feel better just by doing that. Wash your hair, weed the garden.'

'Is that what you tell your patients? Wash your hair and weed the bloody garden?'

'Sometimes.'

'This wasn't how I imagined my life would turn out, you know.'

'No, but I think –' Frieda began.

'It's like the man said, we all need to be loved.'

'What man?'

'Oh, just a man.' Olivia was beginning to cheer up. 'It was a bit embarrassing, actually. I met him last night when I was a tiny bit the worse for wear. I was so upset by everything and I went to that nice wine bar and had a few drinks, and it was when I was going home that I bumped into him.' She gave a small yelp of laughter – a mixture of shame and exultation. 'The kindness of strangers, you know what they say.'

'What happened?'

'Happened? Nothing like that, Frieda. Don't give me one of your looks. I tripped over on the street and there he was. My Good Samaritan. He helped me up and dusted me down, then said he'd make sure I got home safely.'

'That was kind of him,' said Frieda, drily. 'Did he want to come in?'

'I couldn't just turn him away. We had another glass together. And then after a bit he went.'

'Good.'

'He seemed to know you.'

'Me?'

'Yes. I think he sent his regards. Or his love.'

'What was his name?'

'I don't know. I asked him and he said that names weren't important. He said he'd had several names, and it was easy to change them. He said you could change names the way you change clothes, and I should try it myself one day. I said I wanted to be called Jemima!' She gave another of her raucous bursts of laughter.

But the air had cooled around Frieda. She sat down opposite Olivia and leaned across the table towards her, speaking with quiet urgency. 'What did this man look like, Olivia?'

'Look like? Well. I don't know. Nothing to write home about.'

'No, really,' said Frieda. 'Tell me.'

Olivia made the face of a sulky schoolgirl. 'He had grey hair, cut very short. He was solid, I suppose. Not tall. Not short.'

'What colour were his eyes?'

'His eyes? You are strange, Frieda. I can't think. Brown. Yes, he had brown eyes. I told him he had eyes like a dog we once had so they must have been, mustn't they?'

'Did he say what he did?'

'No, I don't think so. Why?'

'You are sure he said he knew me?'

'He said he'd helped you recently. He said you'd remember.'

Frieda shut her eyes for a moment. She saw Mary Orton gazing at her as she lay dying. She saw a knife raised towards her – and then, like a flutter at the margins of her vision, she saw, or sensed, a shape, a figure in the shadows. Someone had saved her.

'What else did he say?'

'I think I talked more than he did,' said Olivia.

'Tell me anything you remember.'

'You're scaring me a bit.'

'Please.'

'He knew I had a daughter called Chloë and that she was staying with you.'

'Go on.'

'There's nothing else. You're giving me a headache.'

'He didn't mention Terry or Joanna or Carrie.'

'No.'

'Or send any message.'

'Just his regards or love. Oh, and something about daffodils.'

'Daffodils – what about daffodils?'

'I think he said he'd once given you daffodils.'

Yes. Dean had sent a little girl across the park to her, bearing a bunch of daffodils and a message. Four words that Frieda had carried with her: 'It wasn't your time.'

She stood up. 'Did you leave him alone at all?'

'No! Well, I went to the loo, but apart from that – he didn't steal anything, if that's what you mean. He was just being kind to me.'

'How many spare keys do you have?'

'What? This is stupid. Anyway, I don't know. I've got keys and so has Chloë and there are a few others knocking around, but I've no idea where they are.'

'Listen, Olivia. I'm going to get Josef to come round

and change all the locks in the house and fit proper safety devices on your windows.'

'Have you gone mad?'

'I hope so. He'll come tomorrow first thing, so make sure you're up in good time.'

'What's going on?'

'Nothing, I hope. It's just a precaution.'

'Are you going?'

'I'm meeting Sasha. But, Olivia, don't go letting any more strange men into your house.'

THIRTY-SIX

Before his appointment with Sadie, Karlsson spent twenty minutes with Dora Lennox. They sat in the kitchen together, while Louise made loud clearing-up noises in the living room and hall. Karlsson thought that everything about Dora was pale – her thin white face, her bloodless lips, her small, delicate hands, which kept fiddling with the salt cellar. She seemed insubstantial. Her blue veins showed under her milky skin. He felt brutal as he took out the rag doll, hearing the suppressed whimper she gave on seeing it. 'I'm sorry to distress you, Dora, but we found this in your room.'

She stared at it, then away.

'Is it yours?'

'It's horrible.'

'Did you do this, Dora?'

'No!'

'It doesn't matter if you did. No one's going to be angry with you. I just need to know if you did this yourself?'

'I just wanted to hide it.'

'Who from?'

'I don't know. Anyone. I didn't want to see it.'

'So you cut it up a bit and then wanted to hide it?' Karlsson asked. 'That's OK.'

'No. I didn't do it! It's not mine. I wanted to put it in the dustbin but then I thought someone would see it.'

'If it's not yours, whose is it?'

'I don't know. Why are you asking?' Her voice rose hysterically.

'Dora. Listen. You haven't done anything wrong, but I just need to know how this came to be in your room, if it's not yours.'

'I found it,' she said, in a whisper.

'Found it where?'

'I was at home one day on my own, ill. I had a temperature and had the day off school. No one else was there. Mum said she'd come back from work early and she left me a sandwich by my bed. I couldn't read because my head hurt, but I couldn't sleep either, and I just lay there listening to sounds in the street. Then there was a clatter and someone pushed something through the letterbox but I thought it would be junk mail or something. Then later, when I needed the bathroom, I saw it from the top of the stairs and I went down and picked it up and saw –' She gave a small shudder and came to a halt, staring up at Karlsson.

'You're saying that someone pushed this through the letterbox?'

'Yes.'

'Cut up like this?'

'Yes. It scared me. I don't know why, but I just had to hide it.'

'And it was done during the day, when normally no one would have been there?'

'I had the flu,' she said defensively.

Karlsson nodded. He was thinking that on any ordinary day it would have been Ruth Lennox who found the mutilated doll. A message. A warning.

*

323

This time Sadie had not put on any makeup or perfume. She had arrived early and ordered a tomato juice, and greeted Karlsson as if he was a business colleague. He bent down to kiss her cheek, which she turned away from him so he kissed her ear instead.

'Get yourself a drink if you want. Then we can talk.'

He went and bought himself half a pint of beer, then took the chair opposite her. 'I don't know what there is to say,' he began. 'I behaved like an idiot. I've always liked you, Sadie, and I didn't want to mess you around.'

'But you did mess me around. If I'd known you just wanted one quick fuck on your night off, I wouldn't have let you near me.'

'I'm sorry.' There was a silence and she regarded him coolly. He found himself talking, to fill it and to bring some warmth back into her unyielding face. 'The thing is,' he said, 'I've been a bit wretched.'

'Lots of us are a bit wretched.'

'I know. It's not an excuse. My children – Mikey and Bella, you met them when they were younger – they've gone away with their mother.'

'Gone away – for a holiday, you mean?'

'No. She's got this new man – she's going to marry him, I guess, so he's really their stepfather – and he got a job in Madrid and they've gone there. The four of them, the happy family.' He heard and hated the bitterness in his voice. 'So they've gone away for two years. I'll see them, but it won't be the same. Well, it hasn't been the same since they moved out, of course. I kind of lost them then, but now I feel I've really lost them. And now that they've gone, I . . .'

He stopped dead. He suddenly found he couldn't continue, couldn't tell Sadie that he didn't really know what his life was about any more. That he woke each morning and had to make an effort to face the world.

'I thought I could fill the gap a bit,' he said lamely. 'Just to get through.'

'Fill the gap with me?'

'I suppose so. I feel detached from everything, as if everything is happening to someone else and I'm watching it, like in a film. So when I woke that morning and saw you lying next to me, I just – well, I knew I'd made a mistake and I wasn't ready for you or anyone.'

'So that's it?'

'Yes.'

'You should have thought about it before.'

'You're right.'

'I'm a person, me. Someone you used to call a friend.'

'I know.'

'I'm sorry about the way you're feeling. It must be hard.' She stood up, her tomato juice unfinished on the table.

'Thank you for being honest with me, in the end. If you ever feel in need of comfort again, call someone else.'

Frieda arrived back at her house just before Sasha. She called Josef, who said he would go round to Olivia's immediately, put bolts on the front and back doors and change all the locks the next morning. Then she called Karlsson, but only got his voicemail. She didn't leave a message – what would she say? 'I think Dean Reeve was in my sister-in-law's house last night'? He wouldn't believe her. She didn't even know if she believed herself, but dread washed through her.

Sasha arrived just after eight, bearing a takeaway, steam rising from the bag. She was wearing a loose orange dress and her hair was soft around her face. Frieda saw that her cheeks were slightly flushed and her eyes bright. She pulled naan bread out of a damp brown paper bag and laid it on a plate. Frieda lit candles and pulled a bottle of wine out of the fridge. She thought how strange it was that even in front of Sasha she could so successfully conceal her distress and fear. Her voice sounded steady; her hands as she poured wine were steady.

'Is Chloë still here?'

'Yes. But she's seeing her father tonight so I have the house to myself for once.'

'Do you mind?'

'I don't think I had a choice.'

'That wasn't the question.'

'Sometimes I come in,' Frieda said, 'and she's made herself completely at home. Mess everywhere. School stuff slung every which way. Dirty dishes in the sink. Sometimes her friends are here as well. Not to mention Josef. There's noise and chaos and even the smell is different. And I feel like an intruder in my own home. Nothing belongs to me in the same way. It's all I can do not to run away.'

'At least it'll soon be over. She's only here for a week, isn't she?'

'That was the agreement. This looks good. Wine?'

'Half a glass. So I can clink it against yours.'

They sat at the table facing each other and Frieda lifted her glass. 'So, tell me.'

Sasha didn't lift hers, just smiled radiantly. 'Do you know, Frieda, the world seems sharper and brighter. I can feel energy pumping through me. Every morning I wake up and the spring outside is inside my body as well. I know you're anxious that I'll let myself get hurt again – but you've met Frank. He's not like that. And, anyway, isn't that partly what falling in love is? Opening yourself up to the possibility of feeling joy and being hurt? Letting yourself trust? I know I've made mistakes in the past. But this feels different. I'm stronger than I used to be, less pliable.'

'I'm very glad,' said Frieda. 'Really.'

'Good! I know you'll like each other. He thinks you're terrific. But I'm not just here to gush about Frank, like a teenager. I've got something else I need to say. I haven't told anyone else but –'

The doorbell rang.

'Who can that be? It's too early for it to be Chloë and, anyway, she has a key.'

The bell rang once more, and then someone knocked. Frieda wiped her mouth on the paper napkin, took a gulp of wine and stood up. 'Whoever it is, I'll send them away,' she said.

Judith Lennox was standing at the door. She was wearing an oversized man's jacket and what looked to Frieda like jodhpurs. Dora was beside her, her long brown hair in a French plait, her face pinched and pale.

'Hello,' Judith said, in a small voice. 'You said I could come.'

'Judith.'

'I didn't want to leave Dora alone. I thought you wouldn't mind.'

Frieda looked from one face to the other.

'My dad's gone out drinking,' said Judith. 'And I don't know where Ted is. I can't spend any more time in the house with Aunt Louise. There'll be a second murder.'

Dora gave a strangled sob.

'You'd better come in,' said Frieda. She didn't know which feeling was stronger – pity for the two girls on her doorstep or a stifling sense of anger that she had to look after them.

'Sasha, this is Judith and Dora.' Sasha looked up, startled. 'They are friends of Chloë's.'

'Not really,' put in Judith. 'Ted's a friend of Chloë's. I know her a bit. Dora's never met her, have you, Dora?'

'No.' Dora's voice was a whisper. She was almost translucent, thought Frieda – blue veins under pale skin, blue shadows under eyes, neck that seemed almost too thin to hold up her head, bony knees, skinny legs with a big bruise on one shin. She'd been the one who'd found her mother dead, she remembered.

'Sit down,' she said. 'Have you had anything to eat?'

'I'm not hungry,' said Dora.

'Not since breakfast,' said Judith. 'And you didn't eat any breakfast, Dora.'

'Here.' Frieda got out two extra plates and pushed them in front of the girls. 'We've got plenty to go round.' She glanced at Sasha's bemused face. 'Judith and Dora's mother died very recently.'

Sasha leaned towards them, her face soft in the guttering candlelight. 'I'm so sorry.'

'Someone killed her,' said Judith, harshly. 'In our house.'

'No! That's dreadful.'

'Ted and I think it was her lover.'

'Don't,' said Dora, piteously.

Frieda noticed how in Ted's absence Judith took on his anger, his corrosive bitterness.

'Can I have some wine?'

'How old are you?'

'Fifteen. You're not going to tell me that I shouldn't drink wine because I'm only fifteen?' She gave an ugly snort. Her blue eyes glittered and her voice scratched.

'This is a school night and I hardly know you. I'll give you some water.'

Judith shrugged. 'Whatever. I don't really feel like it actually.'

'Dora, have some rice,' said Sasha. She had a cooing note to her voice. She's broody, thought Frieda. She's fallen in love and she wants babies.

Dora put a teaspoon of rice onto her plate and pushed listlessly at it. Sasha put her hand over the young girl's, at which she put her head on the table and started crying, her thin shoulders shaking, her whole starved body shuddering.

'Oh dear,' said Sasha. 'Oh, you poor thing.' She knelt beside the girl and cradled her. After a few moments, Dora turned urgently towards her, pressing her wet face into Sasha's shoulder, holding on to her like a drowning person.

Judith stared at them, her expression blank.

'Can I speak to you?' she hissed to Frieda, above the hiccuping sobs.

'Of course.'

'Out there.' Judith jerked her head towards the yard.

Frieda rose and opened the back door. The air was still quite gentle after the warmth of the day and she could smell the herbs she had planted in their tubs. 'What is it?' she asked.

Judith looked at her, then away. She seemed both older than her years, and younger: an adult and a child at once. Frieda waited. Her curry would be a congealing oily mass.

'I'm not feeling well,' said Judith.

The air seemed to cool around them. Frieda knew what she was going to say. This was the kind of thing she should be telling her mother.

'In what way?' she asked.

'I'm feeling a bit sick.'

'In the morning?'

'Mostly.'

'Are you pregnant, Judith?'

'I don't know. Maybe.' Her voice was a sullen mumble.

'Have you done a test?'

'No.'

'You ought to do one as soon as possible. They're very reliable.' She tried to make out the expression on the girl's face. 'You can buy them across the counter at a chemist's,' she added.

'I know that.'

'But you're scared because then you'd know for certain.'

'I guess.'

'If you were pregnant, do you know how far gone you are?'

Judith shrugged. 'I'm just a few days late.'

'Is it just from one sexual encounter?'

'No.'

'You have a boyfriend?'

'If that's the right word.'

'Have you told him?'

'No.'

'Nor your father?'

She gave her laughing snort – derisive and unhappy. 'No!'

'Listen. You must find out if you're pregnant first of all, and if you are, you have to decide what you want to do. There are people you can speak to. You won't have to deal with it alone. Are there other adults you could speak to? A family member, a teacher?'

'No.'

Frieda half closed her eyes. She let the weight settle on her. 'OK. You can do the test here, if you want, and then we'll talk about it.'

'Really?'

'Really.'

'And maybe you should think about talking to your father.'

'You don't understand.'

'He might not react the way you think.'

'I'm his little girl. He doesn't want me to wear makeup! I know how he'll react. Mum dying, police everywhere, and now this. It'll *kill* him. As for Zach –' She stopped and grimaced. Her small face worked with her emotions.

'Is Zach your boyfriend?'

'He'll be furious with me.'

'Why? It takes two, you know, and you're the one who has to deal with the consequences.'

'I'm supposed to be on the Pill. I *am* on the Pill. I just forgot for a bit.'

'Is Zach at your school?'

She pulled a face.

'What does that mean?'

'It means no.'

Frieda stared at her and Judith stared back.

'How old is Zach?'

'What's that got to do with anything?'

'Judith?'

'Twenty-eight.'

'I see. And you're fifteen. That's a big age gap.'

'Thanks. I can do the maths.'

'You're underage.'

'That's just a stupid rule old people make up to stop young people doing what they did when they were young themselves. I'm not a child.'

'Tell me something, Judith. Did your mother know about Zach?'

'I never told her. I knew what she'd say.'

'So she had no idea?'

'Why would she?' Judith gazed back into the lit kitchen. Dora was sitting with her head propped on her hand, talking; Sasha was listening intently. 'Except,' she added.

'Except?'

'I think she may have discovered I was on the Pill.'

'What makes you think that?'

'I knew she'd find them if I put them anywhere obvious. She had a talent for it – sniffing out other people's secret things. If I'd put them in my underwear drawer or in my makeup bag or under the mattress, she'd have dug them out

332

at once. Like Ted's weed. So I put them in a sock in the cupboard next to the bathroom, which nobody opens from one year to the next except to chuck stuff in. But I think she found them. Maybe I'm being paranoid, but I think she changed the dial so the arrow was pointing to the right day. I just used to take one and not bother about the day matching up, but someone changed it. Twice. I'm sure they did.'

'Perhaps it was her way of telling you she knew.'

'I dunno. It seems a bit stupid to me. Why wouldn't she just say?'

'Because she knew you'd be angry with her and clam up?'

'Maybe.' Judith turned. 'So you think she knew?'

'Perhaps.'

'And she was waiting for me to confide in her?'

'It's a possibility.'

'But I never did.'

'No.'

'I feel like she's someone I never knew. I can't remember her face properly.'

'It's very hard.' Frieda made up her mind. 'Listen, Judith. There's a late-night chemist a couple of minutes away. If I can, I'm going to buy you a Predictor kit, and then you can do it here, at once.'

'Now?'

'Yes.'

'I don't think I can.'

'At least you'll know. The worst thing is not knowing.' Her old mantra. Wearing a bit thin now. The girl's strained face glimmered in the darkness. Frieda put a hand on her shoulder and steered her into the kitchen.

'Your curry's all cold,' said Sasha, coming over to her and putting a comforting hand on her arm.

'Yes, well. We'll go to a restaurant next time. I've just got to go out for a few minutes.'

'Where?'

'Just to the chemist's to get a few things.'

'She thinks she's pregnant, doesn't she?' Sasha asked, in a low voice.

'How on earth do you know that?'

'Are you going to get a Predictor?'

'Yes. If it's open.'

Sasha said, turning away and speaking in a casual voice: 'I've got one in my bag she can use.'

'Oh, Sasha!' Images flashed through Frieda's mind – Sasha not lifting her glass, Sasha talking to Dora in a new voice of maternal tenderness, Sasha's hesitation earlier that evening, as if she was about to tell her something. 'That's what you wanted to tell me!'

'Yes.'

'Are you?'

'Let's talk later.'

Judith wasn't pregnant. Her sickness and her lateness were, Frieda told her, probably to do with shock and grief. But she needed to think about this properly, she said, not simply continue as she had been doing. She was fifteen and in a relationship with a man who was more than thirteen years older than her. 'You need to talk to someone,' she said.

'I'm talking to you, aren't I?'

Frieda sighed. Tiredness was making her head pound. 'Someone who's not me,' she replied.

She made Judith a mug of tea, and Dora, who was limp from crying, some hot chocolate. 'I'll order you a cab,' she said. 'Your father and aunt will be worried.'

Judith snorted.

Then the doorbell rang again.

'That'll be Chloë,' said Frieda.

'I'll go.' Sasha rose and put a hand on Frieda's shoulder, then went to the door.

It wasn't Chloë, it was Ted. He was clearly stoned.

'Isn't Chloë back yet?' he asked.

'No. I'm just ordering a cab,' Frieda told him, putting her hand over the receiver. 'You can all go home together.' She gave the taxi company her address and put the phone down.

'No way. No way in the world. Dad's drunk out of his head and Aunt Louise is very, very angry in a stomping kind of way. I'm not staying there tonight.'

'Well, then, I'm not either,' said Judith. Her blue eyes blazed with a kind of scared excitement. 'Nor will Dora. Will you, Dora?'

Dora stared at her. She looked stricken.

'The cab will be here in about five minutes. You're all going home.'

'No,' said Ted. 'I can't go there.'

'You can't make us,' added Judith. Dora put her head on the kitchen table again and closed her eyes. Her lids seemed transparent.

'No. I can't. Where are you going, then?'

'Does it matter?'

'Yes. You're eighteen now, I think, and a boy, and you can look after yourself – theoretically at least. Judith is fifteen and Dora thirteen. Look at her. Have you got a friend you can stay with?'

'Can't we stay here?' Dora said suddenly. 'Can't we be in your house for a night? It feels safe here.'

'No,' said Frieda. She could feel Sasha's eyes on her.

She considered picking up a plate and throwing it against the wall; she imagined taking a chair and smashing it against the window so that clean air streamed into this hot kitchen, with its smell of curry and sweat and grief. Or better still, just running out of her house, shutting the door behind her – she'd be free, in the April night, with stars and a moon and the wind soft in her face, and they could deal with their own chaotic sadness without her.

'Please,' said Dora. 'We'll be very quiet and we won't make a mess.'

Ted and Judith were silent, just gazing at her and waiting.

'Frieda,' said Sasha, warningly. 'No. This isn't fair on you.'

'One night,' said Frieda. 'One night only. Do you hear? And you have to ring home and tell your aunt and your father, if he's in a state to understand.'

'Yes!'

'And when the cab arrives I'll send it away but tell them to come back first thing tomorrow to take you home. You are all going to school. Yes?'

'We promise.'

'Where can we sleep?' asked Dora.

Frieda thought of her lovely calm study at the top of the house that was now strewn with Chloë's mess. She thought of her living room, with the books on the shelves, the sofa by the grate, the chess table by the window. Everything just so. Her refuge against the world and all its troubles.

'Through there,' she said, pointing up the hall.

'Have you got sleeping bags?'

'No.' She stood up. Her body felt so heavy it took an enormous effort of will to move at all. Her head thudded. 'I'll get some duvets and sheets, and you can use the cushions from the sofa and chair.'

'I'll sort all of that.' Sasha sounded urgent. She looked at Frieda with an expression of concern, even alarm.

'Can I have a bath?' asked Ted.

Frieda stared at him. The new plug was in her bag. 'No! You can't. You mustn't! Just the washbasin.'

The bell rang again and Sasha went to cancel the cab. Then, almost immediately, Chloë came in, in her usual high pitch of angry excitement after seeing her father. She threw her arms around Ted, around Frieda, around Sasha.

'Out of here,' said Frieda. 'I'm going to clean the kitchen, then go to bed.'

'We'll tidy,' Chloë shouted gaily. 'Leave it to us.'

'No. Go into the other room and I'll do it. You're all to go to sleep now – you're getting up at seven and leaving shortly after that. Don't make a noise. And if anyone uses my toothbrush I'll throw them out whatever time of night it is.'

You seem to have gone off radar. Where are you? Talk to me!
Sandy xxxxx

THIRTY-SEVEN

'It's fun, isn't it?' said Riley.

'In what way?' asked Yvette.

'We're looking through people's things, opening their drawers, reading through their diaries. It's all the stuff you want to do, but you're not meant to. I wish I could do this at my girlfriend's flat.'

'No, it's not fun,' said Yvette. 'And don't say that aloud, even to me.'

Riley was going through the filing cabinet in the Kerrigans' living room. They'd searched the main bedroom and the kitchen already. Paul Kerrigan had stayed in hospital only one night after he was beaten up and now he was out, but his wife had let them in, tight-lipped and silent. She hadn't offered them coffee or tea, and as they searched among the couple's possessions, lifting up underwear, turning on computers, reading private letters, noticing the tidemark in the bath and the moth holes in some of Paul Kerrigan's jumpers, they could hear her slamming doors, banging pans. When Yvette had last met her, she had been dazed and wearily sad. Now she seemed angry.

'Here,' she said, coming into the room. 'You might not have found these. They were in his bike pannier in the cupboard under the stairs.'

She was holding a small square packet between forefinger and thumb, with an air of distaste. 'Condoms,' she said, and dropped them on to the table, as if they'd been used. 'For his Wednesday dates, I assume.'

Yvette tried to keep her expression neutral. She hoped Riley wouldn't say anything, wouldn't react. 'Thank you.' She picked up the packet to put in the evidence bag.

'He didn't use them with you?' said Riley, in a bright voice.

'I had cancer several years ago and the chemotherapy meant that I'm now infertile,' said Elaine Kerrigan. Briefly, her stiff expression changed to one of distress. 'So, no, he didn't.'

'So . . .' Yvette began.

'There's something else I should say. Paul didn't get home until quite late on that day.'

'We're talking about the sixth of April.'

'Yes. I was here a long time before him. I remember because I made a lemon meringue pie and I was worried it would spoil. Funny the things you worry about, isn't it? Anyway, he was late. It must have been gone eight.'

'Why didn't you tell us that before?''

'It's hard to remember everything at once.'

'Yes, I can see that,' said Yvette. 'We'll need you to make a new statement.'

She glanced at Riley. There was a gleam about him, almost as if he were suppressing a smile.

'He had a long shower when he came in,' continued Elaine, 'and put his clothes straight into the wash. He said he'd had a hard day on site and had to wash away the grime before supper.'

'It's important you tell us everything you know,' said Yvette. 'I know how angry you must be, but I want to be clear that there is no connection between you finding this and your new account of events. Which is quite damaging to your husband's situation.'

'I'm angry with Paul, if that's what you mean,' said Elaine. 'I'm quite glad someone beat him up. It feels like they were doing it for me. But I'm just telling you what I remember. That's my duty, isn't it?'

As they were leaving, they met the two Kerrigan sons. They had their father's face and their mother's eyes and they both stared at Yvette and Riley with what looked to Yvette like hatred.

Meanwhile, Chris Munster was searching the flat where Paul Kerrigan and Ruth Lennox had met every Wednesday afternoon for the past ten years, barring holidays. He was making an inventory. Dutifully, he wrote down everything he found: two pairs of slippers, his and hers; two towelling robes, ditto; a single shelf full of books in the bedroom – an anthology of poems about childhood, an anthology of writings about dogs, Winston Churchill's *History of the English-Speaking People*, a collection of humorous pieces, a volume of cartoons that Munster didn't find particularly amusing – all books that he supposed were meant to be read in snatches. The bedlinen had been removed for traces of bodily fluids, but there was a brightly patterned quilt thrown over the small chair and a woven strip of rug running along the floor. The curtains were yellow-checked, very cheery. The stripped-pine wardrobe was empty except for two shirts (his) and a sundress with a torn zip.

In the clean, bare bathroom: two toothbrushes; two

flannels; two towels, shaving cream, deodorant (his and hers), dental floss, mouthwash. He imagined the two of them carefully washing, cleaning their teeth, gargling with mouthwash, examining themselves in the mirror above the sink for traces of their activities, before getting back into their sensible clothes and going back to their other lives.

In the kitchen-living room there were four recipe books, along with a set of basic cooking utensils (pots, pans, wooden spoons, a couple of baking trays) and a small number of plates, bowls, glass tumblers. Four mugs that looked to Munster much like the mugs he had seen in the Lennox house. She might well have bought them at the same time. There was a bottle of white wine in the little fridge and two bottles of red wine on the surface. There was a dead hyacinth tilting in its dried-up soil. Two onions shrivelling on the windowsill. A striped tablecloth thrown over the wooden table in the centre of the room. Jigsaws on the side, several, of different levels of difficulty. A pack of cards. A digital radio. A wall calendar with nothing written on it. A red sequined cushion on the two-seater sofa.

Ten years of lying, he thought. Just for this.

'Kerrigan no longer has an alibi,' said Karlsson.

'Well, maybe he doesn't,' said Yvette. 'I'm not sure which of Mrs Kerrigan's stories I believe.'

'So you're taking his side.' There was a sound to his left, a sort of cackle. It came from Riley.

'Yvette's definitely not taking Kerrigan's side. She can't stand him.'

'And what did he need condoms for?' said Karlsson. 'Not for his wife.'

'And not for Mrs Lennox,' said Yvette. 'We know she had an IUD fitted.'

'He still could have worn a condom,' said Riley.

'What for?' said Karlsson.

Riley looked uneasy now. Karlsson shouldn't need to be told this.

'You know,' he said. 'To stop him catching something from Ruth Lennox. You know what they say, when you sleep with someone, you're sleeping with all their partners and their partners' partners and their partners' parners ...'

'Yes, we get the idea,' said Yvette.

Karlsson suddenly thought of Sadie. It had been bad enough already. It wasn't possible, was it? He suppressed the idea. It was too terrible to think about. 'Do you think so?' he asked.

'No,' said Yvette, firmly. 'If the condoms had been for Ruth Lennox, they would have been in the flat and Munster didn't find any there. There must have been someone else.'

'That sounds right,' said Karlsson. 'The question is, did Ruth Lennox know about that?'

'The other question is why she had that dial of pills in her cupboard.'

'Also,' said Yvette, 'I've been thinking about the doll.'

'Go on.'

'We're assuming it was sent to Ruth Lennox and it was a warning. Which would mean that someone was on to them.'

'Yes?'

'What if it was meant for Dora all the time? We know she was being badly bullied at school in the months leading up to her mother's death. Maybe kids who knew she was ill and would be alone in the house did it.'

'Why?' Riley sounded indignant.

'Because kids are cruel.'

'But that's just horrible.'

'They would think it was just a game,' said Yvette. Everyone noticed the note of bitterness in her voice and her colour rose.

'You may be right.' Karlsson spoke quickly to cover the awkwardness. 'We might be leaping to conclusions.'

'Poor thing,' said Riley. 'Whichever it was.'

'The pills belonged to Judith Lennox,' said Frieda.

She had come to the police station first thing that morning. Karlsson noticed the rings around her eyes, the strain in her face. She wouldn't sit down, but stood by the window.

'That clears up one mystery.'

'She's fifteen.'

'It's not so unusual for a fifteen-year-old to be sexually active,' said Karlsson. 'At least she's being careful.'

'Her boyfriend is much older, in his late twenties.'

'That's a big gap.'

'And Judith thinks perhaps her mother found out about them.'

'I see.'

'I thought you should know. I told Judith I would pass on the information.'

'Thank you.'

'His name is Zach Greene.' She watched Karlsson scribble the name on the pad in front of him.

'Do you want some coffee?'

'No.'

'Are you all right?'

She considered the question, wondering whether to tell him about Dean, and her fear that he had been in Olivia's house. 'It doesn't matter,' she answered at last.

'I think it does. '

'I have to go now.'

'You're not back at work yet, are you?'

'Barely.'

'So please sit down for a few minutes and tell me what's up.'

'I have to go. There are things I have to do.'

'What things?'

'You wouldn't understand. I don't understand.'

'Try me.'

'No.'

'I'm going to have it.'

Sasha and Frieda were sitting in a small café beside Regent's Canal. Ducks leading flotillas of ducklings steered through the litter and twigs that bobbed in the brown waters.

'You've decided.'

'*We've* decided.'

'It's been so quick,' said Frieda. 'A month ago, you barely knew him.'

'I know – but don't look so worried. I want you to be glad for me.'

'I am glad.'

'I've never been so certain of anything in my life, or so happy. If it had been only a week, I'd still be certain. I'm going to move in with Frank and I'm going to have a baby. My whole life is changing.'

'You deserve your happiness,' said Frieda, sincerely. And she thought of Sandy in America. He seemed very far off now. Sometimes she could barely remember his face or the sound of his voice.

'Thank you.'

'I can't knit.'

'You don't need to knit.'

'Or baby talk.'

'No, I can't imagine you baby-talking.'

They laughed, then grew serious again. Sasha took Frieda's hand in hers. 'You are my very dear friend,' she said, and her large eyes swam with tears.

'You're hormonal already.'

'No. Without you, I don't know what would have become of me.'

'You'd have been fine.'

'I don't think so. But, Frieda – are you all right?'

'Why wouldn't I be?'

'I worry about you. We all worry.'

'You don't need to.'

'Will you promise to tell me if there's anything wrong?'

But Frieda changed the subject. She couldn't make that promise.

THIRTY-EIGHT

Josef looked at the notebook Frieda handed him.

'And I've got some phone numbers,' said Frieda. 'From the stickers on the side of the phone box.'

'So I phone the number,' said Josef.

'I know it's a big thing to ask. But if I phoned, they'd get puzzled hearing a woman's voice and I'd have to explain things and it probably wouldn't work.'

'Frieda, you say that already.'

Frieda took a sip from her cup. The tea was cold. 'I suppose I feel guilty asking you to phone up a prostitute. In fact a number of prostitutes. I'm grateful to you for doing it. You've already done so much.'

'Too much, maybe,' said Josef, with a smile. 'So I call now?' Frieda pushed her mobile across the table. He took the phone. 'We take the French teacher.' He dialled the number and Frieda couldn't stop herself wondering whether he'd done this before. Over the years, several of her patients had talked of using prostitutes, or fantasizing about using prostitutes. At medical school, she had been at parties, once or twice, where a stripper had turned up. Was that the same thing or something completely different? 'Get over it,' she remembered a red-faced medical student shouting at her. 'Lighten up.' Josef was writing something in the notebook. The instructions sounded complicated. Finally he handed her the phone.

'Spenzer Court.'

'Spenser,' said Frieda.

'Yes. And it is by Carey Road.'

Frieda looked at the index of her *A – Z*. 'It's a few streets away,' she said. 'We can walk.'

A gateway at the end of Carey Road led into the council estate. The first block was called Wordsworth Court and they went along a ground-floor level, consisting of lock-up garages and giant steel bins. Frieda stopped for a moment. There were split bin bags strewn about, a supermarket trolley lying on its side, a broken TV that had probably been thrown from an upper level. A woman in a full veil was pushing a pram along the far side.

'You know, I never understood places like this,' she said, 'until, one time, I was in a hill town in Sicily and I suddenly did. That was the idea about this sort of estate. It was going to be like the little Italian town that the architect had spent his holiday in, full of squares where children would play, and there would be markets and jugglers, and hidden passageways where people could bump into each other and gossip and go for evening strolls. But it didn't quite work out.'

'Is like Kiev,' said Josef. 'But these not so good when is twenty degrees cold.'

They reached Spenser Court and walked up a staircase to the third floor, picking their way through old food cartons. They went along the balcony. Josef looked at the notebook and then at the flat in front of him. The window next to the door was barred, but also broken and blocked from the inside with plasterboard.

'Is here,' he said. 'Is difficult to be in mood for the sex.'

'That's the way it's always been. In London anyway.'

'In Kiev also.'

'We need to be calm with her,' said Frieda. 'Reassuring.'

She pressed the doorbell. There was a sound of movement from inside. Frieda glanced at Josef. Did he feel like she did? A strange nausea and guilt about what was going on in the city where she lived? Was she just being prim or naïve? She knew the ways of the world. Josef looked calmly expectant. There was a fumbling sound, then the door opened a few inches and Frieda caught a glimpse of a face behind the taut chain: young, very small, lipstick, bleached hair. Frieda started to say something but the door slammed shut. She waited for the chain to be unfastened, the door opened properly, but there was silence. She and Josef looked at each other. Frieda pressed the doorbell again but there was no response. She leaned down, pushed the letterbox open and peered through. Something was blocking her view.

'We just want to talk,' she said. There was no response. She handed her phone to Josef. 'Try calling her. Say who you are.'

He looked puzzled.

'Who I am really?'

'Say you're the man who made the appointment.'

He called and waited.

'Leave message?' he said.

'No, don't bother. She probably thought we were from Immigration or the police or someone who meant trouble.'

'Is you.'

'What?'

349

'Is you. She see woman, she think we do something to her.'

Frieda leaned on the balcony railing and looked down. 'You're right,' she said. 'This was a stupid plan. I'm so sorry I dragged you out here for nothing.'

'No. It's not nothing. I keep your phone. You give me the map. I walk you back to café, you sit have nice tea and a cake. I will come back in one hour.'

'I can't ask you to do that, Josef. It's not right. And it's not safe.'

Josef smiled at that. 'Not safe? With you not protecting me?'

'It feels wrong.'

'We go now.'

When they got back on to Carey Road, Frieda took some banknotes from her purse and gave them to him. 'You should ask them if they know a girl called Lily Dawes. Lila. That's what she mainly called herself, I think. I wish I had a picture to show them but I don't know how to get one. Give them twenty pounds anyway, and another twenty if they tell you anything. Does that seem enough? I don't know about these things.'

'Is OK, I think.'

'And be careful.'

'Always.'

Frieda left him there. After a few moments she glanced back and saw him talking on the phone. She went back into the café and ordered another cup of tea but didn't touch it. What she really wanted was just to rest her head on her hands and sleep. She felt she should read, or think about something. She took the sketch pad out of her bag and spent twenty minutes making a sketch of the great plane trees in Lincoln's Inn Fields. She couldn't get them right and told herself that she would go back there soon and do it from life. She put the pad away and looked around the café. There was a couple sitting at a table by the door. She met the eye of the man, who gave her a hostile look, so from then on she just stared in front of her. When she felt a touch on her shoulder she started as if she had been asleep but she was sure she couldn't have been. It was Josef.

'Is it an hour already?' she said.

He looked down at the phone before handing it to her. 'An hour and a half,' he said.

'What happened? Did you find anything out?'

'Not here,' said Josef. 'We go to pub. You buy me drink.'

They could see a pub as soon as they were back on the pavement and they walked to it in silence. Inside there was noise from a games machine, with several teenage boys clustered around it.

'What do you want?' said Frieda.

'Vodka. Big vodka. And cigarettes.'

Frieda bought a double vodka, a packet of cigarettes, a box of matches, and a glass of tap water for herself. Josef looked at his drink disapprovingly.

'Is warm like the bathwater,' he said. 'But *budmo*.'

'What?'

'It means we shall live always.'

'We won't, you know.'

'I believe you will,' he said sternly, and drank his vodka in a single gulp.

'Can I get you another?' she said.

'Now we go for the cigarette.'

They stepped outside. Josef lit one and inhaled deeply. Frieda thought of long-ago days outside the school gates at lunchtime. He offered the packet to her and she shook her head. 'So?' she said.

His expression was sad, as he answered: 'I talk to four women. There is one from Africa, I think maybe from Somalia. She speak English like me but much, much worse. I understand little. Man there also. He want more than twenty for her. Much more. Angry man.'

'Oh, my God, Josef. What happened?'

'Is normal. I explain.'

'He could have had a gun.'

'Gun would be problem. But no gun. I explain to him and I go. But no use. And then I see a girl from Russia and then one girl I don't know where from. Romania, maybe. The last girl, the girl I just see, she say a few words and I have a strong feeling and I talk to her in Ukrainian. She have big shock.' He gave a smile but there was harshness in his eyes.

'Josef, I'm so sorry.'

He stubbed out his cigarette on the pub wall and lit another. 'Ah. It's not so big a thing. You expect me to say, "Oh, it's little girl from my own village." I'm not a child, Frieda. It's not just the plumbers and the haircutters who come here from my country.'

'I don't know what to say.'

'I do not say that it is a good job. I see her apartment. It is dirty and damp and I see the signs of drugs. That is not good.'

'Do you want us to do something to help?'

'Ah,' he said again, dismissively. 'You start there and you finish nowhere. I know this. It is bad to see but I know it.'

'I should have been the one doing all of this. It's my problem not yours.'

Josef looked at her with concern. 'Not good for you to do right now,' he said. 'You not well. We are both sad about her, about Mary. But you were damaged too. Not all better.'

'I'm fine.'

Josef gave a laugh. 'That is what everybody says and it means nothing. "How are you?" "I'm fine."'

'It means you don't need to worry. And I also want to say that I'm sorry I wasted your time.'

'Waste?'

'Yes. I'm sorry I dragged you all the way down here.'

'No. Not wasted. The one woman, the Romanian. I think Romanian. She also have the drugs, I think. You see it in the eyes.'

'Well, not always . . .'

'I see it. I talk to her of your Lily. I think she know her.'

'What do you mean you think?'

'She know a Lila.'

'What did she say about her?'

'She know her a bit. But this Lila, she was not completely . . . What do you say when someone is a bit part of it but not complete?'

'A hanger-on?'

'Hanger-on?' Josef considered the phrase. 'Yes, maybe. This girl Maria knew Lila a bit. Lila also with the drugs, I think.'

Frieda tried to digest what Josef had said. 'Does she know where we can find her?'

Josef shrugged. 'She not see her for a while. For two months or three months. Or less or more. They are not like us with the time.'

'Did she know where Lila had gone?'

'She did not.'

'She must have moved away,' said Frieda. 'I wouldn't even know where to start. That's fantastic, Josef. But I guess it's the end of the trail.' Then she noticed a faint smile on his face. 'What is it?'

'This Lila,' he said. 'She have a friend. Maybe a friend with the drugs or the sex.'

'Who was it?'

'Shane. A man called Shane.'

'Shane,' said Frieda. 'Does she have a number for him? Or an address?'

'No.'

'Did she know his second name?'

'Shane, she said. Only Shane.'

She thought hard and murmured something to herself. 'What you say?'

'Nothing, nothing much. That's good, Josef. It's amazing you found that out. I never thought we'd get anything. But what do we do with it?'

Josef gazed at her with his brown, sad eyes. 'Nothing.'

'Nothing?'

'I know you need to rescue this girl. But you cannot do this. Is over.'

'Is over,' repeated Frieda, dully. 'Yes. Perhaps you're right.'

That evening, Frieda put the plug in her bath. She had bought oil to pour in and a candle that she would light. For a long time now, she had imagined lying in the hot foamy water in the dark, just the guttering candle and the moon through the window to give light. But now it came to it, she found she wasn't in the right mood. It would just be a bath. She pulled out the plug and stood under the shower instead, briefly washing away the day. The bath would have to wait. It would be her reward, her prize.

Thirty-nine

Before interviewing Paul Kerrigan, Karlsson Skyped Bella and Mikey, sitting in his office and looking at their photographs in frames on his desk, and at their jerky images on the screen. They were excitable, distracted. They didn't really want to be talking to him and their eyes kept wandering away to something out of sight. Bella told him about a new friend called Pia who had a dog. She had a large sweet bulging in her cheek and it was hard to hear what she was saying. Mikey kept twisting his head to mouth something urgently at whoever was in the room. Karlsson couldn't think of anything to talk about. He felt strangely self-conscious. He told them about the weather and asked them about school, like some elderly uncle they'd barely ever met. He tried to make a funny face at them but they didn't laugh. He ended the call early and went to the interview room.

Kerrigan's face was swollen from his attack. There was a purple and yellow bruise on one cheek and his lip was cut. There were also pouches of fatigue under his eyes and deep grooves bracketing his mouth, which was slack, like that of an old man. He was unshaven, the collar of his shirt grimy, and one of the buttons was undone so that his stomach showed through, shockingly white and soft. Sitting in the interview room, he had a lumpy, defeated air.

The skin under his nostrils was red and he kept sneezing, coughing, blowing his nose. Karlsson asked him once more about his movements on Wednesday, 6 April, when Ruth Lennox had been murdered. He had a large white handkerchief that he buried his entire battered face in.

'Sorry,' he spluttered. 'I don't understand why you're asking me this again. I've just been in hospital, you know.'

'I'm asking because I want to get things clear. Which they are not. What did you do when you left Ruth Lennox?'

'I've told you. I went back home.'

'What time?'

'Late afternoon, early evening. I had dinner with Elaine.' He wrinkled his jowly face. 'She made a pudding,' he said slowly and clearly, as if his meal was his alibi.

'You weren't there until quite late that evening, Mr Kerrigan.'

'What do you mean?'

'Your wife has told us that you didn't return home until nearly eight o'clock.'

'Elaine said that?'

'Yes. And that you had a shower and put your clothes in the wash.'

Paul Kerrigan nodded slowly. 'That's not right,' he said.

'We just want to know what you did between the time that Ruth Lennox left the flat and the time that you returned home several hours later.'

'She's angry with me. She wants to punish me. You must see that.'

'Are you saying she's lying about the time you came back?'

'Everything's ruined,' he said. 'Ruth's dead and my wife hates me and my sons have contempt for me. And she wants to punish me.'

'Do you know what contraceptive Ruth Lennox used?' Karlsson asked.

Paul Kerrigan blinked. 'Contraceptive? What are you talking about?'

'You were sleeping with her for ten years. You must have known.'

'Yes. She had the coil fitted.'

'You're telling me you knew she was using contraception.'

'That's what I just said.'

'Yet your wife found condoms in your bicycle pannier.' Karlsson looked closely at Kerrigan's swollen, flushed face. 'If your wife is no longer fertile and Ruth Lennox had an IUD, why would you have condoms?'

Now there was a long silence. Karlsson waited patiently, impassively.

'It's complicated,' said Kerrigan, finally.

'Then you'd better explain it to me.'

'I love my wife. You won't believe that. And we've had a good marriage, until now. Ruth didn't alter that. I had two parallel lives and they didn't touch. If Elaine hadn't found out, none of this would have mattered. I just wanted to keep my marriage safe from harm.'

'You were going to explain about the condoms.'

'I don't know how to say this out loud.'

'But you're going to have to.'

'I have needs that my wife can't meet.'

Karlsson was starting to feel almost queasy but he had to proceed.

'Which was what Ruth Lennox was for, I suppose.'

Kerrigan made a hopeless gesture. 'She was at first. But then it became like another marriage. I liked it, in a way. But I needed something else.'

'And?'

'There's been someone else. For a while.'

'Who?'

'Do you need to know?'

'Mr Kerrigan, you don't need to worry about what I need to know. Just answer my questions.'

'Her name's Sammie Kemp. Samantha. She's done some casual admin work for my company. That's how we met. It was just fun.'

'Did Ruth Lennox know of your relationship with Samantha Kemp?'

'It wasn't exactly a relationship.'

'Did she know?'

'She may have suspected.'

'You should have told us this before.'

'It's got nothing to do with anything.'

'Did she confront you about it?'

'What did she expect? She knew I was being unfaithful. She knew I was sleeping with my wife. So . . .'

Karlsson almost laughed at that. 'That's really quite a clever way of almost convincing yourself. But Ruth Lennox didn't see it like that?'

'It's not as if she didn't know things had run their course.'

'You were going to leave her?'

'Not according to her,' Paul Kerrigan said bitterly, before he could stop himself. A flush spread over his face.

'Let me get this clear. You were having an affair with another woman, Samantha Kemp, and you wanted to end your relationship with Ruth Lennox but she wouldn't accept that.'

'I wanted it to be mutual. No recriminations. Ten good years. Not many people manage that.'

'But Ruth Lennox didn't see it that way. Was she angry? Did she even threaten to tell your wife?'

'She wouldn't have behaved like that.'

'Shall we stick for the moment to what you actually did, rather than what you're claiming she would have done if she hadn't been murdered?'

'I was with Sam that Wednesday.'

'With Samantha Kemp?'

'Yes.'

'It's a pity you didn't tell us this before.'

'I'm telling you now.'

'So you went from your Wednesday afternoon with Ruth Lennox to another assignation with Samantha Kemp.'

'Yes.'

'Where?'

'At her flat.'

'I'll need her contact details.'

'She's got nothing to do with any of this.'

'She has now.'

'She won't be pleased.'

'You realize this changes everything? You had a secret

360

that only one other person knew. You and Ruth Lennox had to trust each other. That was probably easy as long as you both wanted to continue your affair. For ten years you protected each other from being discovered. The problem arose when one of you wanted to leave.'

'That's not how it was.'

'She had power over you.'

'You're making a mistake. She didn't threaten to expose me and I was with Samantha Kemp from the moment I left the flat until the time I came back home. Check it if you don't believe me.'

'Don't worry, we will.'

'If that's all, I have things to do.'

He stood up from the chair, scraping it across the floor. Karlsson stared at him and waited, and eventually he lowered himself once more.

'I haven't done anything except be stupid,' he said.

'You've lied to us.'

'Not because I killed Ruth. I loved her.'

'But you were planning to leave?'

'Not planning in the way you mean. Just aware things were coming to an end.'

'She could have wrecked your marriage.'

'She has anyway, hasn't she? From beyond the grave.'

'How was she going to make you stay with her?'

'I've already said that she wasn't. She was just angry. You're twisting words to suit your suspicions.'

'I think you're still withholding information. We will find it out in the end.'

'There's nothing to find out.'

'We'll see.'

'I tell you there's nothing. Under the mess is just more mess.'

Further along the corridor, Yvette was interviewing Zach Greene, Judith Lennox's boyfriend. He worked part time for a software firm based in a converted warehouse just off Shoreditch High Street. He was a tall, skinny man with small pupils in eyes that were almost yellow. He had bony wrists, long, nicotine-stained fingers, and his brown hair was shaved close to his skull in a soft bristle. Yvette could see a V-shaped scar running from his crown to just above his delicate left ear. He had rosebud lips and shapely eyebrows, like a woman's, a nose stud and a tattoo just visible above his shirt. Everything about him contradicted everything else: he looked soft and rugged, feeble and aggressive, older than his years and much younger. He smelt of flowers and tobacco. His shirt was a pastel-green and on his feet were stout army boots. He was oddly attractive and a bit creepy, and he made Yvette feel dowdy and deeply unsure of herself.

'I know that theoretically it's against the law.'

'No, it's definitely against the law.'

'But why do you assume we were actually having sex?'

'Judith Lennox says you were. If she's lying, then say so.'

'Why do you assume I knew her age?'

'How old are *you*?'

'I'm twenty-eight.'

'Judith Lennox is fifteen.'

'She looks older.'

'That's a large age difference.'

'Jude is a young woman. She knows her own mind.'

'She's a girl.'

He gave a tiny, almost invisible shrug with one shoulder. 'Power is what matters, don't you think?' he said. 'The law is there to prevent the abuse of power. In our case, it's irrelevant. As far as I'm concerned we're both consenting adults.'

'The fact remains that she's a minor. You're guilty of a criminal offence.'

For a brief moment, anxiety broke the surface. His face puckered. 'Is that why I'm here?'

'You're here because her mother was killed.'

'Look. I'm really sorry about that but I don't see the connection.'

'Did you ever meet Mrs Lennox?'

'I *saw* her. I didn't meet her.'

'She didn't know about you?'

'Jude thought she wouldn't understand. And I wasn't going to argue.'

'You're quite sure you never met?'

'I think I'd remember.'

'And you think that Mrs Lennox wasn't aware of your existence.'

'Not that I know of.'

'Did she suspect that Judith was involved with someone?'

'I never met the woman. Why don't you ask Jude?'

'I'm asking you,' said Yvette, curtly. She saw him give his tiny smile.

'As far as I know, she didn't suspect. But mothers have a way of sensing things, don't they? So maybe she noticed something was up.'

'Where were you on the evening she was murdered – Wednesday, the sixth of April?'

'What? Do you really think I would have killed someone because I didn't want them to find out about a relationship with their daughter?'

'It's a criminal offence. You could go to prison.'

'This is all crap. She's nearly sixteen. She's not a little kid in pigtails with scabby knees. You've seen her. Drop-dead gorgeous. I met her at a club. Where you have to be eighteen to get in, by the way. And show your ID.'

'How long have you been involved with her?'

'What do you mean by *involved*?'

'Oh, please, just give me an answer.'

He closed his eyes. Yvette wondered if he could feel the pulse of her hostility from where he was sitting.

'I met her nine weeks ago,' he said. 'Not long, is it?'

'And she's on the Pill?'

'You'll have to ask Jude about things like that.'

'Are you still with her?'

'I don't know.'

'You don't know?'

'No. That's the truth.' For a moment, his mask seemed to slip. 'She couldn't bear to touch me. She wouldn't even let me hug her. I think she feels responsible for it all. Does that make sense?'

'Yes.'

'Which somehow makes *me* responsible too.'

'I see.'

'Not really responsible,' he added hastily.

'No.'

'So, really, I think it's over. You should be pleased. I'm legal again.'

'I wouldn't say that,' said Yvette.

That evening, there was a ring at the doorbell of the Lennox house. Russell Lennox heard it from the top of the house and waited for someone else to answer it. But Ted was out and he thought that Judith was too – that was something he ought to know, of course. Ruth would have known. Dora was in her room and already in bed. And, for once, Louise wasn't in the house, vacuuming with her bloody baby strapped round her, or doing her endless baking. The doorbell rang once more and Russell sighed. He went heavily down the stairs.

He didn't recognize the woman on the doorstep and she didn't immediately introduce herself, just stared at him as though she was searching for someone. She was tall and bony rather than thin, with long hair tied loosely back and glasses hanging round her neck on a cord. She was wearing a long patchwork skirt with a muddy hem.

'I thought I should come.'

'I'm sorry – who are you?'

She didn't answer, just raised her eyebrows, almost as though she was amused. 'You should recognize me,' she said at last. 'I'm your partner in humiliation.'

'Oh! You mean . . .'

'Elaine Kerrigan,' she said, and held out her long slim hand, which Russell took, then didn't know how to let it go.

'But why are you here?' he asked. 'What do you want?'

'Want? To see you, I suppose. I mean, see what you look like.'

'What do I look like?'

'You look done in,' she said, and suddenly tears welled in Russell's eyes.

'I am.'

'But really I came to thank you.'

'What for?'

'For beating up my husband.'

'I don't know what you're talking about.'

'You gave him a lovely black eye.'

'You're on the wrong track.'

'And a swollen lip so he can't talk properly. And I don't have to listen to his lies.'

'Mrs Kerrigan –'

'Elaine. You did what I wanted to. I'm grateful.'

Russell was about to protest again, then his face softened in a smile. 'It was my pleasure,' he said. 'You'd better come in. Maybe you're the only person in the world I want to talk to.'

FORTY

This time Frieda didn't need to ring the doorbell. Lawrence Dawes was at the front of the house with another man. Dawes was up a stepladder and the other man was holding it. When Frieda announced herself, he looked round, smiled and descended the steps with care.

'I'm sorry,' he said. 'I've forgotten the name.'

Frieda told him and he nodded in recognition. 'I'm terrible with names. I do apologize. I remember you very clearly. This is my friend, Gerry. He helps me with my garden, I help him with his and then we have a drink to celebrate. And this woman is a psychiatrist, so be careful what you say.'

Gerry was a similar age to Dawes, but looked entirely different. He was dressed in checked shorts that reached his knees and a short-sleeved shirt that was also checked, but of a different kind, so that he almost shimmered. His legs and arms were thin, wiry and deeply tanned. He had a small grey moustache that was very slightly uneven.

'You're neighbours?' said Frieda.

'Almost,' said Gerry. 'We share the same river.'

'Gerry's a few houses upstream from me,' said Dawes. 'He can pollute my stream but I can't pollute his.'

'Cheeky sod,' said Gerry.

'We've been giving my roses some attention,' said

Dawes. 'They've really started growing and we're trying to train them. You know, roses round the door. Do you like roses?'

'Yes, I suppose so,' said Frieda.

'We were about to have some tea,' said Dawes.

'Were we?' said Gerry.

'We're always about to have tea. We've either just had it or we're about to have it, or both. Would you like to join us?'

'Just for a few minutes,' said Frieda. 'I don't want to keep you from your work.'

Dawes stowed his stepladder away – 'Kids'll nick anything that moves,' he said – and they went through the house to the back lawn. Frieda sat on the bench and the two men came out, carrying mugs, a teapot, a jug of milk and a plate of chocolate biscuits. They laid them out on a small wooden table. Dawes poured the tea and handed a mug to Frieda.

'I know what you're thinking,' he said.

'What?' said Frieda.

'You're a psychiatrist.'

'Well, a psychotherapist.'

'Every time you come, I'm doing up the house. I'm digging the garden, I'm making the roses look nice. What you're thinking is that I have this feeling that if I make my house nice enough my daughter will want to come back to it.' He sipped his tea. 'I suppose that's one of the problems doing your job.'

'What's that?'

'You can never just sit in a garden and have a nice cup of tea and a normal conversation. People think, Well, if I say this, she'll think that, and if I say that, she'll think this. It must be difficult for you to stop working.'

'I wasn't thinking anything like that. I really was just drinking the tea and wasn't thinking about you at all.'

'Oh, that's nice,' said Dawes. 'So what were you thinking about?'

'I was thinking about the little river at the bottom of your garden. I was wondering if I could hear it, but I can't.'

'When there's been more rain, then you can hear it, even inside the house. Have a biscuit.'

He pushed the plate across to Frieda, who shook her head. 'I'm fine.'

'You don't look fine,' said Dawes. 'You look like you need feeding up. What do you think, Gerry?'

'Don't let him tease you,' said Gerry. 'He's like my old mother. Always wanting everyone to clear their plate.'

They sat in silence for a few minutes. Frieda thought she could just hear the soft murmur of the stream.

'So what brings you here?' asked Dawes, eventually. 'Have you got another day off?'

'I'm not exactly working at the moment. I'm taking some time off.'

Dawes poured some more tea and milk into her mug. 'You know what I think?' he said. 'I think you've taken time off work because you're supposed to be resting. And instead you're chasing around.'

'I'm a bit worried about your daughter,' said Frieda. 'Does that make sense to you?'

The smile faded from Dawes's face. 'I've been worried about her since she was born. I can remember the first time I saw her: she was lying in a cot next to my wife's bed in the ward. I looked down at her and she had a little dimple in her chin, like me. Look.' He touched the end of his chin. 'And I said to her, or to myself, that I was going to protect her for ever. I was going to make sure that no harm ever came to her. And I failed. I suppose you never can protect a child like that, not once they get older. But I failed as badly as it's possible to fail.'

Frieda looked at the two men. Gerry was staring into his tea. Maybe he'd never heard his friend talk so openly and emotionally before.

'The reason I'm here,' said Frieda, 'is that I wanted to tell you what I've done. I'd hoped I could find your daughter but I haven't got very far. I've heard from someone who knew her slightly.'

'Who?'

'A girl called Maria. I didn't even meet her so it's second-hand. But apparently she mentioned a man called Shane, who was some sort of friend of your daughter. Or, at least, he had some kind of connection with her. I don't have a second name and I don't know anything about him. I wondered if the name rang any bells with you.'

'Shane?' said Dawes. 'Was he a boyfriend?'

'I don't know. I only have the name. He might have been a friend, or some sort of associate. Or it may all be a misunderstanding. This woman was quite vague, I think.'

Dawes shook his head slowly. 'I don't know anyone by that name. But as I told you when we met before, in the last years I didn't know anything about my daughter's friends. I think she lived in different worlds. The only names I have are of schoolfriends and she'd lost touch with all of them.'

'Mr Dawes . . .'

'Please, call me Larry.'

'Larry, I was hoping you could give me the names of her friends. If I talked to them, I might be able to get some information.'

Dawes glanced at his friend. 'I'm sorry,' he said. 'I'm sure you're a good person and I'm touched by anyone who cares about my daughter. God knows, most people have already forgotten her. But if you have suspicions, why don't you go to the police?'

'Because that's all I've got: suspicions, feelings. I know people in the police and that won't be enough for them.'

'Yet you've come all the way down here twice, just because of your feelings.'

'I know,' said Frieda. 'It sounds stupid, but I can't stop myself.'

'I'm sorry,' said Dawes. 'I can't help you.'

'I'd just like some numbers.'

'No. I've been through this too often. I spent months looking and worrying and getting false hope. If you get any real information, then just tell the police, or come and see me and I'll do what I can. But I can't stir it all up again – I just can't.'

Frieda put her mug on the table and stood up. 'I understand. It's funny. It should be easy to find a missing person nowadays.'

'Sometimes,' said Dawes. 'But if someone really wants to get lost, then they can stay lost.'

'You're right. Perhaps I was really coming to see you to say sorry.'

Dawes seemed puzzled. 'Sorry? What for?'

'Various things. I tried to look for your daughter and I haven't succeeded. And I blundered into your personal grief. I've got a habit of doing that.'

'Maybe that's your job, Frieda.'

'Yes, but they're usually supposed to ask me before I do it.'

Dawes's expression turned bleak. 'You're just realizing what I realized some time ago. You think you can protect people, care for them, but sometimes they just get away from you.'

Frieda looked at the two men, sitting there like a comfortable old couple. 'And I interrupted your work as well,' she said.

'He needs interrupting,' said Gerry, with a smile. 'Otherwise he never stops with his gardening and his building and his mending and his painting.'

'Thank you for the tea. It's been nice, sitting in the garden with you both.'

'Are you going to the station?' asked Gerry.

'Yes.'

'I'm going that way so I'll walk with you.'

Together they left the house. Gerry insisted on carrying Frieda's bag, though she really didn't want him to. He strode along beside her, in his mismatching, multicoloured checks, with his lopsided moustache, a woman's leather bag slung incongruously from his shoulder, and for a few minutes they didn't speak.

'Do you have a garden?' asked Gerry, eventually.

'Not really. A bit of a yard.'

'Soil's the thing – getting your hands dirty. The pleasure of eating your own produce. Do you like broad beans?'

'I do,' said Frieda.

'From the plant to the pan. Nothing like it. Lawrence gardens so he doesn't have to brood.'

'About his daughter, you mean?'

'He doted on her.'

'I'm sorry if I've stirred up painful memories.'

'No. It's not as if he ever forgets. He's always waiting for her, and always wondering where he went wrong. But it's better to be active. Digging and mending, sowing and picking.'

'I understand.'

'I suppose you do. But don't go bringing hope into his life if it comes to nothing.'

'I don't mean to do that.'

'Hope's the thing that will destroy him. Remember that, and be a bit careful.'

On the train back, Frieda stared out of the window but saw nothing. She felt an ache of incompletion, of failure and, above all, of tiredness.

She made one last phone call. Then she would have done everything she could, she told herself, to rescue a girl she'd never met and to whom she had no connection, yet whose story had sunk its hooks into her mind.

'Agnes?' she said, when the woman answered. 'This is Frieda Klein.'

'You've found something?'

'Nothing at all. I just wanted to ask you something.'

'What?'

'Apparently Lila knew a man called Shane. Does that ring a bell?'

'Shane? No. I don't think so. I met several of her new friends. Mostly at this grotty pub, the Anchor. They used to hang out there. Maybe there was someone called Shane but I don't remember him. I don't remember any of their names.'

'Thanks.'

'You're not going to find her, are you?'

'No. I don't think I am.'

'Poor Lila. I don't know why you tried so hard. You tried harder than anyone who knew her. As if your life depended on it.'

Frieda was painfully struck by those last words. For a moment, she was silent. Then she said, 'Shall we give it one last try? Together?'

Perhaps Chloë told you that I rang your house and spoke to her. She said you were OK. But she seemed a bit distracted. There were lots of noises going on in the background. You may not know that I also rang Reuben and he said that you were not OK. That everyone's worried about you but that no one can really get through to you. What the fuck is going on, Frieda? Or shall I just fly over and hammer at your door until at last you have to answer me? Sandy

FORTY-ONE

'I don't get it.'

Agnes, dressed in baggy jogging trousers and a grey hoodie with fraying sleeves, was sitting beside Frieda in a cab. She looked tired. It was raining, and through the dark, wet windows they could see only the glimmering lights of cars and the massed shapes of buildings. Frieda thought of how she could have been in her house now, empty after so many weeks of disruption. She could have been lying in her new bath, or playing chess, or sitting in her study, drawing and thinking and looking out into the wet night.

'Get what?' she asked mildly.

'I was in bed with a novel and a cup of tea, all cosy. And then you ring up out of the blue and all of a sudden I'm on my way to some dingy little pub full of girls off their heads on who-knows-what and men with tattoos and dead eyes, just because Lila used to hang out there. Why?'

'Why are you going?'

'No. I know why I'm going. Lila was my mate. If there's some chance I can find her, I have to. But why are *you* going? Why do you even care?'

Frieda was tired of asking herself the same question. She closed her eyes and pressed her cool fingertips against her hot, aching eyeballs. She could see Ted Lennox's white face, like a petal on dark water, and Chloë's fierce, accusing gaze.

'Anyway, here we are,' said Agnes, with a sigh. 'I certainly never thought I'd set foot in this place again.'

Frieda told the cab driver to wait for them, and they both stepped out into the rain. They could hear the beat of music coming from the Anchor, and there was a huddle of smokers around the door. The tips of their cigarettes glowed and a miasma of smoke hung around them.

'Let's get this over with. You want me to look for anyone I think I might have seen hanging out with Lila.'

'Yes.'

'Two years ago.'

'Right.'

'Because we need to find someone called Shane.'

'Yes.'

'Do you think you're quite right in the head?'

They shouldered their way through the smokers and into the pub, if that was what it was. Frieda rarely went to pubs: she hated the smell of beer and the jangling music, the lights of the jukebox. Now she felt dozens of eyes on them as they entered: it didn't feel like a place where outsiders came casually for a pint. It was a dark room that stretched back out of view, where crowds of people, mostly men, were sitting at tables or standing at the bar and in corners. A few women straggled on the outskirts of the groups; Frieda saw their short skirts and cold white thighs, their shoes with dagger heels and their makeup; she heard their high, frantic laughter. The long dim room was hot and smelt stale. A man stumbled and almost fell in front of them, short and squat with spittle shining on his cheek, the drink he was holding splashing on to the floor.

'Should we buy drinks?' asked Agnes.

'No.'

Together they inched their way through the crowd, Agnes peering from face to face, her eyes flickering, a frown of concentration on her face.

'Well?' asked Frieda.

'I don't know. Maybe him.'

She hunched her shoulder towards a small table at the end of a room. A woman was sitting on the man's lap and they were kissing and unabashedly feeling each other, and beside them another man was watching them impassively, as if they were animals in a zoo. He was rail-thin, with peroxide blond hair, pale skin and a line of tiny red spots running like stitches along his forehead.

'Right.'

Frieda stepped forward and tapped him on the shoulder. He looked at her. His pupils were enormous, giving him an otherworldly appearance.

'Can I have a word?' she asked.

'Who are you?'

'I'm looking for Shane.'

'Shane.' It wasn't a question, just an echo. 'Shane who?'

The pair beside him stopped kissing and disentangled themselves. The woman leaned forward and took a swig from the glass on the table. Her face was empty of expression.

'Shane who knew Lila Dawes.'

'I dunno about any Lila.'

'But you know Shane?'

'I knew a Shane once, but I haven't seen him. He doesn't come here any more.'

'He went to prison,' the woman beside him said, in a flat voice. She was buttoning her blouse – wrongly, Frieda saw. The man whose lap she was sitting on tried to pull her back into him but she pushed him away.

'You know him?'

'Do you know Lila?' added Agnes, eagerly, almost imploringly.

'Was she one of the girls who hung around with Shane?'

'Why did Shane go to prison?'

'I think he hit someone,' the blonde said. 'With a bottle.'

'Is he still there?'

'I don't know. You could ask Stevie. He knows Shane.'

'Where can I find Stevie?'

'Right behind you,' said a voice. Frieda and Agnes turned to find a thickset man with a shaved head and an oddly soft, girlish face behind them. 'What do you want with Shane?'

'Just to find him.'

'Why?'

'He knew my friend,' said Agnes, whose voice trembled slightly. Frieda put a hand on her arm in reassurance.

'Which friend was that?'

'Lila. Lila Dawes.'

'Lila? Shane had so many friends.'

'Was he a pimp?' asked Frieda, her voice cool and clear in the overheated room.

'You should be careful what you call people,' said Stevie.

'Is he still in prison?'

'No, he only did a couple of months. Good behaviour.'

'Do you know where I can find him now?'

Stevie smiled, not at Frieda but at the blond man sitting at the table. 'You know what our Shane's doing now? He's working at a horse sanctuary in Essex. He's feeding ponies whose owners haven't treated them right. Lucky ponies.'

'Where in Essex?'

'Why do you want to know? Got a horse you don't want?'

'I want to talk to him.'

'Somewhere by a big road.'

'Which big road?'

'The A12. It's got a stupid name. Daisy. Or Sunflower.'

'Which?'

'Sunflower.'

'Thank you,' said Frieda.

'And fuck you, too.'

Jim Fearby was nearly at the end of his list: Sharon Gibbs was from the south of London, nineteen years old, and last seen approximately one month ago. Her parents hadn't reported her missing immediately – according to the police report he had in front of him, she was something of a drifter; perhaps one of those who go intentionally missing. Even in the bureaucratic language, Fearby sensed indifference, hopelessness. She looked like another dead end.

But when he stood in front of his large map and peered again at the small flags he'd pinned to it, he felt the surge of excitement that had kept him going through this strange one-man investigation. For it seemed clear to him that there was a pattern before his eyes. But then – at the end of a day, when he sat in this room with his whisky, his fags, fugging up the window, surrounded by crumpled balls of paper, overflowing ashtrays, cartons of takeaways, half-finished mugs of coffee, piles of books thumbed through and then discarded – it faded away.

He looked around him, for a moment seeing things as a stranger would see them. It was a mess, no doubt about it, but an obsessive mess. The walls were covered with maps, photographs of girls and young women, Post-it stickers with numbers scribbled on to them. It made him seem like a stalker, a psychopath. If his wife walked in now, or his children . . . He could picture their expressions of dismay and disgust. He was wearing shabby clothes, his face needed shaving, his hair needed cutting, he reeked of tobacco and drink. But if he was right, if these faces that stared at him from his walls had all been killed by the same person, then all of that would be justified and he would be a hero. Of course, if he was wrong, he would be a lonely fool and a pathetic failure.

It was no good thinking like that: he'd come too far and done too much. He just had to hold on to his original instinct and keep going, holding his doubts at bay. He sighed and picked up his overnight bag, his car keys, his cigarettes, and shut the door on his stale, untidy house with relief.

Brian and Tracey Gibbs lived in a first-floor flat in south London, at the point where the density of the city was petering out into suburbia. They were poor, Fearby could tell that at once. Their flat was small and the living room they showed him into needed a fresh coat of paint. He knew from the cutting that they were in their forties, but they looked older – and he felt a surge of anger. The comfortable middle classes can cheat time, while people like the Gibbses are worn down by it, rubbed away. Brian Gibbs was thin and apologetic. Tracey Gibbs was larger and at first more aggressive. She wanted to tell Fearby that they'd done their best, been good parents, never done anything to deserve this. Their only child. It wasn't their fault. All the while, her husband sat mute and thin beside her.

'When did you last see her?' asked Fearby.

'Six weeks ago. Give or take a few days.'

'And when did you report her missing?'

'Three and a half weeks ago. We didn't know,' she added quickly, defensively. 'She's an adult. She lives with us but she comes and goes as she pleases. Days could go by . . .' She faltered. 'You know how it is.'

Fearby nodded. He did.

'Could I see a picture of her?'

'There.' Tracey Gibbs pointed and he saw a framed photograph of Sharon: a round, pale face; dark hair in a neat, glossy bob; small mouth smiling for the camera. Fearby had seen too many young women smiling for the camera recently.

'Is she going to be all right?' Brian Gibbs asked, as if Fearby was God.

'I hope so,' he replied. 'Do you think she went of her own accord?'

'The police think so.' This, bitterly, from the mother.

'You don't?'

'She got into bad company.'

'What company was that?'

'The worst was this Mick Doherty. I told her what I thought of him but she wouldn't listen.'

She plaited her hands tightly together; Fearby saw that the wedding ring was biting into her finger and that the varnish on her nails was chipped. She looked uncared-for. There were moth holes in Brian Gibbs's ancient pullover. There was a hairline crack running up the mug of tea they had given him and a chip on its rim.

'I see,' he said, trying to sound neutrally cheerful.

'I know where he works. The police weren't bothered but I can tell you where to find him.'

'All right.'

He took the address. It wouldn't do any harm, he thought, and there was nothing else left for him to do, nowhere else to go.

FORTY-TWO

Karlsson opened the file. Yvette was writing in her note-book. Riley and Munster looked bored. Hal Bradshaw was sending a text. He noticed Karlsson's fierce glance and put the phone down on the table but continued to steal glances at it. Karlsson took his watch off and laid it next to the file.

'We're going to talk about this for five minutes,' he said, 'because that's about all I can stand and then we should go our separate ways and try to solve this case. Do you know what I wish? I wish Billy Hunt had killed her and that he was safely in prison and that we hadn't lifted the rock and found out about all the adultery and drink and drugs and underage sex.'

'Maybe Billy Hunt really did it after all,' said Riley.

'Billy Hunt didn't do it.'

'Maybe his alibi is flawed. Maybe the timing on the CCTV wasn't right.'

'Fine,' said Karlsson. 'Check it out. If you can break his alibi, you'll be a hero. Now, back in the real world. Remember when we first saw the body, all those days ago? I wondered who would kill this nice mother of three. Now the queue goes out the door. Who shall we start with? There's Russell Lennox: betrayed husband, drink problem, tendency to violence.'

'We don't know it was him who beat up Paul Kerrigan.'

'No, but I'd lay a bet on it.'

'And he didn't know about his wife's affair,' said Munster.

'You mean he *said* he didn't.'

'His print was on the cog along with Billy's,' put in Yvette.

'Because he owned it. But, still, that sounds most likely. Confronts his wife, picks up that cog thing. There's the awkward matter of his alibi, of course. So let's keep leaning on him. Their children were at school and they're children. But now we've got Judith and her every-parent's-nightmare boyfriend. Ruth discovers about him. Arranges a meeting at their house. Threatens him with the law. He picks up the cog. I don't like Zach Greene. I don't like him at all. Which unfortunately isn't evidence. Any comments?' He looked around. 'Thought not. But we should lean on him some more. Where did he say he was that afternoon, Yvette?'

Yvette turned pink. 'He didn't actually say,' she muttered.

'What do you mean?'

'I asked him. But, now you mention it, he didn't give me an answer. He went on about them being consenting adults or something. He distracted me. '

Karlsson stared at her. 'Distracted you?' he repeated pleasantly, coldly.

'Sorry. It was stupid of me. I'll get back to him.'

He stared down at his papers for a moment. He didn't want to shout at her in front of Riley and Bradshaw but it took an effort.

'Moving on. We have the Kerrigans. He wants to break off with her. Or she discovers about his office affair. Confronts him. He picks up the cog.'

'Would she do it at her house?' said Yvette. 'Wouldn't the flat be more logical?'

'She might have threatened him at the flat,' said Bradshaw. 'She could have said she would inform his wife. For him to confront and kill her in her own home would be a tit for tat. Exposing her in her own family home.'

Karlsson frowned at Bradshaw. 'I thought your theory was that the murderer was a loner, of no fixed abode, that he had no family connections, that the murder was a kind of love.'

'Ah, yes,' said Bradshaw. 'But in a real sense Kerrigan was a loner, estranged from his family, and because of this rented flat, he actually was of no fixed abode and the murder was, arguably, a last, desperate expression of love, the end of love.'

What Karlsson really wanted to do was to lean across, take Bradshaw's smartphone and hit him over the head with it repeatedly. But he said nothing.

'And then there's Kerrigan's wife, Elaine. Humiliated wife. Finds out about Ruth, confronts her, picks up cog.'

'But she didn't know about the affair,' said Yvette. 'Or Ruth's name. Or where she lived.'

'Maybe she did know,' said Munster. 'They always do.'

'What do you mean, *they*?' Yvette glared at him.

'Women.' Munster was wary at Yvette's sharp tone. 'You know, when their husbands are unfaithful. They know. Deep down. At least, that's what some people say.'

'Crap,' said Yvette, decisively.

'Anyway, we suspect that someone knew,' said Karlsson. 'Someone might have pushed that cut-up doll through the Lennox letterbox as a warning.'

'That could just be coincidence.'

'In my world,' announced Bradshaw with a modest smile, 'coincidence is another word for –'

'You're right,' cut in Karlsson, decisively. 'It could be coincidence. It might have been Dora's charming school-friends persecuting her. Did you talk to her again, Yvette?'

Yvette nodded. 'She said she'd assumed it was for her. And she thinks it arrived around lunchtime. She got distressed. But she didn't want to talk about it really – apparently things are better at school since her mother was killed. Everyone wants to be her friend suddenly.' She made a grimace of disgust.

'OK. So, the doll's either a clue or it isn't. Maybe we can talk to the head teacher and see if she can throw any light on it. Moving on, what about the sons?'

'Josh and Ben Kerrigan?' Yvette wrinkled up her face. 'They're both pretty contemptuous and angry. But Josh seems to have been in Cardiff – although he hasn't been able to come up with any concrete alibi apart from being in bed with his girlfriend, who confirms that was probably the case. No sign on his bank statements that he used his card for a train ticket or anything. But that doesn't mean much – as he himself pointed out, he could have used cash. His younger brother Ben was in a lesson. Apparently. His teacher can't remember his being there, but she can't remember his *not* being there and she thinks she would have noticed.'

'Brilliant.'

'What about Louise Weller?' asked Yvette. 'She was on the scene pretty quickly.'

'On the scene?' Karlsson shook his head. 'She came round to help.'

'It's a common expression of guilt,' Bradshaw explained comfortably. 'Perpetrators like to involve themselves in the inquiry.'

'What? Mother of three kills sister?'

'You can't rule it out,' said Bradshaw.

'I'm the one who rules people in or out.' Karlsson spoke quickly. 'But you're right. We'll talk to her again. And the Kerrigan boys. Anything else?'

'Samantha Kemp,' said Riley.

'What?'

'The woman Kerrigan had his affair with.'

'Yes, I know who she is, but . . .' Karlsson paused. 'You've got to talk to her anyway, to check Kerrigan's claim he was with her that afternoon. Maybe it'll turn out she has a jealous boyfriend.' He slammed the file shut. 'Right, that's it. Yvette, check that alibi. Chris, you talk to this Samantha Kemp. Now, for God's sake, one of you go out and get me something.'

FORTY-THREE

Yvette was still smarting as she left the room. She could feel Chris Munster looking at her sympathetically, which made it worse. She snapped at him when he asked her if she wanted a coffee and slammed herself down at her desk.

First, she rang Zach at his workplace in Shoreditch, but the woman who answered the phone said he wasn't in that day – he didn't work full time and as a matter of fact he wasn't the most reliable of employees. So she rang his mobile and went straight to voicemail, then his landline, which rang and rang. She sighed and pulled on her jacket.

On her way out, she met Munster once more.

'Where are you going?' she asked.

'To see Samantha Kemp. You?'

'To see bloody Zach Greene.'

'Would you like me to – '

'No, I would not.'

Samantha Kemp was doing some work for a digital-camera company just off Marble Arch. She met Munster in the small room set aside for visitors on the first floor; its window overlooked a sari shop.

When she came into the room, Munster was surprised by how young she was. Paul Kerrigan was a plump, greying, middle-aged man, but Samantha Kemp was in her twenties, neatly dressed in a black skirt and a crisply ironed white shirt. A ladder ran up her tights, from her ankle to her shapely knee. She had fluffy silver-blonde hair that framed her round pale face.

'Thank you for seeing me. This won't take long.'

'What's it about?'

Munster saw she was nervous: she kept sliding her palms down her skirt.

'Is it true that you know Paul Kerrigan?'

'Yes. I do work for his company sometimes. Why?' A flush spread over her fair skin, and even when the colour receded it left faint blotches on her cheeks. 'What's this about?'

'Can you remember what you were doing on Wednesday, the sixth of April?' She didn't answer. 'Well?'

'I heard you. I just don't know what you're getting at. Why should I tell you anything about my private life?'

'Mr Kerrigan says that you were with him on the afternoon and evening of Wednesday, the sixth of April.'

'With him?'

'Yes.'

'Is that a problem?'

'You tell me.'

'He might be married, but that's his lookout, not mine.'

'Wednesday, the sixth of April.'

'He's not happy, you know.'

'It doesn't matter.'

'He's not.' To his horror, Munster saw that she was about to start crying: tears stood in her grey-blue eyes. 'And I comfort him. I'm not going to be made to feel bad about that.'

'The point is, did you comfort him on Wednesday, the sixth of April?'

'Is he in trouble?'

'Do you have a diary?'

'Yes,' she said. 'Yes. I was with him on that Wednesday.'

'You're sure?'

'Yes. It was the day after my birthday. He bought me a bottle of champagne.'

'What time?'

'He arrived in the afternoon, about four. And we drank some champagne and then . . .' Her face was flaming again. 'He left at about seven or eight. He said he had to go back for his dinner.'

'Is there anyone who can confirm this?'

'My flatmate, Lynn. She came back at about six and had a bit of the champagne. I suppose you need her details as well.'

'Please.'

'Does she know about us? His wife, I mean? Is he in trouble?'

Munster looked at her. Surely she must know about Ruth Lennox. But it was impossible to tell, and he didn't want to be the one to break it to her. Paul Kerrigan should do his own dirty work.

Zach Greene lived near Waterloo, a few roads south of the station on a road that was clogged with midday traffic: cabs and cars and vans and buses. Cyclists wove in and out of the queues, heads down against a strengthening wind. An ambulance blared past.

Number 232 was a small terraced house set slightly

back from the road, with steps leading up to a cracked green door. Yvette rang the bell, then knocked hard as well. She already knew he wouldn't be in, so she was surprised when she heard footsteps and the rattling of a chain. A woman stood in front of her, clutching a baby in a striped all-in-one.

'Yes?'

'I'm looking for Zach Greene,' said Yvette. 'Does he live here?'

'He's our tenant. He lives in the flat. You have to go through the garden.' She came out in her slippers and took Yvette down the steps, pointing. 'That little road takes you round the back and there's a small garden with a gate that doesn't shut properly. If you go through there, his flat's to the side.'

'Thank you.' Yvette smiled at the baby, who stared at her in terror, then started to bawl. She'd never been good with babies.

'Tell him to keep the noise down, will you? He was making a hell of a racket last night, just after I'd got this one off to sleep at last.'

Yvette found her way in through the rickety back gate. Wooden stairs led from the house she'd just been in, down to the small garden, where a child's plastic tricycle lay tipped on its side. Tucked under the stairs was the door to the flat. Yvette rang the bell and waited. Then she knocked on the door and it creaked open a few inches.

For a moment, Yvette stood quite still, listening intently. Outside, she could hear the clamour of traffic. From within, there was nothing.

'Hello,' she called. 'Zach? Mr Greene? It's Detective Long here.'

Nothing. The wind blew a flurry of white blossom down on her where she stood. For a moment she thought it was snow. Snow in April: but stranger things happen. She pushed the door wider and stepped inside, onto a balding doormat. Zach Greene was not a tidy man. There were shoes on the floor, piles of junk mail, a couple of empty pizza boxes, a tangle of phone chargers and computer cords, a cotton scarf with tassels.

She took a few more cautious steps.

'Zach? Are you here?' Her voice rang out in the small space. To her right, a tiny kitchen, a hob encrusted with ancient food, an army of mugs, granules of instant coffee. Two shirts hanging to dry on the radiator. A smell of something going off somewhere.

It's odd, she thought. How you know when there's something wrong. You get a feel for it. Not just the open door, the smell. Something about the silence, as if it hummed with the aftermath of violence. Her skin prickled.

Another shoe, a brown canvas one with yellow laces, on the floor, in the barely opened door that presumably led to Zach's bedroom. She pushed the door with the tips of her fingers. The shoe was on a foot. The beginnings of the leg could be seen, encased in dark trousers and riding up to expose a striped sock, but everything else was covered with a patterned quilt. She took in the pattern: birds and swirling flowers; it looked Oriental, brightening up the grey and brown pokiness of the dingy flat.

She looked at her watch and noted the time, then

squatted down and very carefully drew off the quilt, feeling how damply sticky it was, seeing now that she was close up to it how its vivid pattern had obscured the stains.

It must be Zach lying in front of her at the foot of his bed, but the narrow face, the golden eyes, the rosebud lips that had given her the creeps were all gone – smashed into a pulp. Yvette made herself look properly, not squint in a reflex of horror. She could still make out the delicate ear lobes in his wrecked face. There was blood everywhere. People didn't know how much blood they had flowing through them, warm and fast – only when you saw it pooled around a body did you realize. Puddles of dark, sweet-smelling blood, thickening now. She laid one finger against his back, under his purple shirt; the skin was white and hard and cold.

She stood up, hearing her knees creak, and thought of Karlsson when he arrived at a crime scene: she tried to make herself into a camera. The muddy streaks in the passageway, the tipped picture above the bed, the thickening blood, the rigid flesh, the way his arms were flung out as if he was falling through the air. She remembered the noise the woman upstairs had said she'd heard last night.

And then she took out her phone. From upstairs, she could make out the sounds of the baby, still howling. They arrived so quickly, the ambulances and the police cars. It seemed only minutes before the flat had been transformed into a makeshift laboratory, bright lights shining, with Zach's body at the centre. Paper shoes, plastic gloves, brushes to dust for the fingerprints, bottles of chemicals, tweezers and evidence bags, tape measures, thermome-ters. Riley was talking to the woman upstairs. Munster, standing by the door and taking gulps of air, was talking into his phone. Zach was just an object now, a specimen.

Above the hubbub, Karlsson said to her: 'Chris is speaking to Greene's parents. Do you think you could be the one to tell Judith Lennox?'

She felt beads of sweat on her forehead as she thought of the fierce, desolate daughter. 'Sure.'

'Thanks. As soon as possible, I think.'

Yvette knew it would be bad and it was. She stood and listened to herself say the words and watched Judith Lennox's very young, very vulnerable face crumple. She spun round the small room, her slender figure twitching, all the separate parts of her apparently disconnected – hands fluttering, face tweaked in strange grimaces, head bobbing on thin neck, feet slipping in her frantic urge to move. They were in a room that the head teacher had put aside for them. There was a desk by the plate-glass win-dow and shelves full of folders in different colours. Outside, two teenagers – a boy and a girl – walked past and glanced without obvious interest into the large win-dow.

Yvette felt helpless. Should she go and wrap her arms round the girl's fragile bones, hold her still for an instant? This time it was a shriek that must surely fill the whole school, empty classrooms and bring teachers running. She banged against the desk and was sent in another direction. Yvette was reminded of a moth bruising its soft powdery wings against harsh surfaces.

She put out a hand and caught Judith by the hem of her shirt, heard it rip slightly. The girl stopped and stared wildly at her. She was still wearing dark orange lipstick, but the rest of her face was like a small child's. Suddenly, she sat, not on the chair, but in a heap on the uncarpeted floor.

'What happened?' she whispered.

'We're trying to find out exactly. All I can tell you at present is that he has been killed.' She thought of the mashed face and swallowed hard. 'In his flat.'

'When? *When?*'

'We haven't established the time of his death.' Stiff, pompous, she was embarrassed by her own awkwardness.

'Recently, though?'

'Yes. I'm sorry to have to ask but I'm sure you'll understand. Can you tell me when you last saw him?'

'Go away.' Judith covered her ears with her hands and rocked back and forwards on the floor. 'Just go away now.'

'I know it's very painful.'

'Go away. Go away. Go away. Leave me alone. Leave all of us alone. Get out. Why is this happening? Why? Please please please please.'

Yvette had only once been to Frieda's house and never to her consulting rooms until now. She tried not to seem curious; she didn't want to look too intently at Frieda herself, partly because Frieda's steady gaze had always made her uncomfortable and partly because she was shocked by Frieda's appearance. Perhaps she was thinner, Yvette couldn't tell, but she was certainly tauter. She seemed stretched tight. There were dark smudges under her eyes, almost violet. Her skin was pale and her eyes very dark, with a smokiness to them that was different from their usual glitter. She didn't look well, Yvette decided.

She watched Frieda walk towards her red armchair with a limp that she tried to disguise but couldn't, and thought: *This is my fault.* For a moment, she let herself remember Frieda lying in Mary Orton's house, unmoving, the sight of the blood. Then she saw young Judith Lennox flying around the schoolroom, like a broken moth, shouting at her to get out, to leave. Perhaps the simple truth is that I'm a hopeless detective, she thought. She hadn't even been able to get an alibi from Zach Greene.

Frieda gestured to the chair opposite and Yvette sat down. So this was where Frieda's patients sat. She imagined closing her eyes and saying: *Please help me. I don't know what's wrong with me. Please tell me what's wrong with me . . .*

'Thank you for agreeing to see me,' she said.

'I owe you a favour.' Frieda was smiling at her.

'Oh, no! It's me . . .'

'You made the complaint against me go away.'

'That was nothing. Idiots.'

'Still, I'm grateful.'

'I didn't want to meet at the station. I thought this would be better. I don't know if you've heard. Zach Greene was murdered. He was Judith Lennox's boyfriend.'

Frieda seemed to become even more still. She shook her head slightly. 'No. I hadn't heard. I'm sorry,' she said softly, as though to herself.

'She's in a dreadful state,' Yvette continued. 'I've just left her. The school counsellor was there and the head. I'm worried for her.'

'Why are you telling me this?'

'You've met her. I know about your behind-the-scenes dealings with the Lennox family.' She held up a hand. 'That sounded wrong. I didn't mean it grumpily.'

'Go on.'

'I wondered if you could go and see her. Call on her. Just to see how she is.'

'She's not my patient.'

'I understand that.'

'I hardly know her. Her brother is a friend of my niece. That's the only connection. I've met the poor girl a few times.'

'I didn't know how to deal with her. There are things they don't teach you. I could call up one of our people, I suppose.' She wrinkled her nose dubiously at the thought. 'Hal fucking Bradshaw would be only too pleased to tell her what she was feeling and why. But I – well, I guess I thought you could help.'

'For old times' sake?' Frieda asked ironically.

'You mean you won't?'

'I didn't say that.'

OK. I won't fly over and hammer at your door and I will trust you. But you make it very hard, Frieda. Sandy

FORTY-FOUR

In the morning Jim Fearby called on the family of Philippa Lewis. They lived on a new estate in a village a few miles south of Oxford. A middle-aged woman – she must have been Philippa's mother, Sue – slammed the door as soon as he identified himself. He had read about the case in the local paper, the usual story of walking home after staying late at school and not arriving; he had seen the blurry photo. She had seemed a plausible candidate. He put a tick after her name, followed by a question mark.

Up towards Warwick, Cathy Birkin's mother gave him tea and cake, and before the first mouthful he knew that this was a name he'd be crossing off the list. She'd run away twice before. The cake was quite nice, though. Ginger. Slightly spicy. Fearby had started to notice another sort of pattern. The mothers of the runaway girls were the ones who would invite him in and give him tea and cake. He could almost remember the houses and the girls by the cake he'd been served. The one up near Crewe, Claire Boyle, had been carrot cake. High Wycombe, Maria Horsley: chocolate. Was it as if they were still trying to prove that they had done their best, that they weren't bad parents? The ginger cake was slightly dry and stuck to the roof of his mouth. He had to wash it down with his cooling tea. As he chewed, he felt his own pang of conscience. He'd been putting it off and putting it off. It was on the way and would only be a small diversion.

He almost hoped that George Conley would be out, but he wasn't. The small block where he had moved to was neat enough. When Conley opened the door, he gave only the smallest flicker of recognition, but Fearby was used to that. When Conley had talked to him over the years, he had never seemed comfortable looking at him directly. Even when he talked, it was as if he was addressing someone slightly to the side of Fearby and behind him. As soon as Fearby stepped inside he was hit by the warmth and the smell, which seemed part of each other. It wasn't really identifiable and Fearby didn't want to identify it: there was sweat, dampness. He suddenly thought of the sour smell you get behind garbage vans in summer.

Fearby had lived alone for years and he knew about life with surfaces that never got properly wiped, dishes that piled up, food that was left out, clothes on the floor, but this was something different. In the dark, hot living room, he had to step around dirty plates and glasses. He saw opened cans half filled with things he couldn't recognize, white and green with mould. Almost everything, plates, glasses, tins, had stubs of cigarettes on or in it. Fearby wondered whether there was someone he could call. Did someone somewhere have a legal responsibility to deal with this?

The television was on and Conley sat down opposite it. He wasn't exactly watching the screen. It looked more like he was just sitting in front of it.

'How did you get this place?' said Fearby.

'The council,' said Conley.

'Does anyone come round to help you? I know it must be difficult. You've been inside so long. It's hard to adjust.' Conley just looked blank, so Fearby tried again. 'Does anyone come to check up? Maybe do some cleaning?'

'A woman comes sometimes. To check on me.'

'Is she helpful?'

'She's all right.'

'What about your compensation? How's it going?'

'I don't know. I saw Diana.'

'Your lawyer,' said Fearby. He had to speak almost in a shout to be heard above the television. 'What did she say?'

'She said it'd take time. A long time.'

'I've heard that. You'll have to be patient.' There was a pause. 'Do you get out much?'

'I walk a bit. There's a park.'

'That's nice.'

'There's ducks. I take bread. And seeds.'

'That's nice, George. Is there anyone you'd like me to call for you? If you give me a number, I could call the people at the council. They could come and help you clear up.'

'There's just a woman. She comes sometimes.'

Fearby had been sitting right on the edge of a sofa that looked as if it had been brought in from outside. His back was starting to ache. He stood up. 'I've got to head off,' he said.

'I was having tea.'

Fearby looked at an open carton of milk on the table. The milk inside was yellow. 'I had some earlier. But I'll pop back soon and we can go out for a drink or a walk. How's that sound?'

'All right.'

'I'm trying to find out who killed Hazel Barton. I've been busy.'

Conley didn't respond.

'I know it's a terrible memory for you,' said Fearby. 'But when you found her, I know you bent down and tried to help her. You touched her. That was the evidence that was used against you. But did you see anything else? Did you see a person? Or a car? George. Did you hear what I said?'

Conley looked round but he still didn't say anything.

'Right,' said Fearby. 'Well, it's been good to see you. We'll do this again.'

He picked his way carefully out of the room.

When Fearby got home, he went online to find the number of the social services department. He dialled it but the office was closed for the day. He looked at his watch. He had thought of calling Diana McKerrow about Conley's situation, but her office would be closed as well by now. He knew about these compensation cases. They took years.

He went to the sink, found a glass, rinsed it and poured himself some whisky. He took a sip and felt the warmth spreading down through his chest. He'd needed that. He felt the staleness of the day in his mouth, on his tongue, and the whisky scoured all that away. He walked through the rooms with his drink. It wasn't like Conley's flat, but it was a distant relation. Men adrift, living alone. Two men still trapped in their different ways by the Hazel Barton case. The police had no other suspects. That was what they'd said. Only George Conley and he knew different.

Suddenly the dirty glasses and bits of clothing, the piles of papers and envelopes scared him. People hardly ever came to the house, but the thought of anyone coming into this room and feeling some part of what he had felt in George Conley's flat made him flush with a sort of shame. For the next hour he picked clothes up, washed glasses and plates, wiped surfaces, vacuumed. At the end, he felt it was closer to some sort of normality. It needed more. He could see that. He would buy a picture. He could put flowers in a vase. Maybe he would even paint the walls.

He took a lasagne from the freezer and put it into the oven. The back of the packet said fifty minutes from frozen. That would give him time. He went to his study. This was the one part of the house that had always been tidy, clean and organized. He took the map from the desk, unfolded it and laid it out on the floor. He opened the top drawer of his desk and took out the card covered with red stickers. He peeled off one sticker and carefully placed it on the village of Denham, just south of Oxford. He stood back. There were seven of them now and a pattern was clearly forming.

Fearby took a sip of whisky and asked himself the question he'd asked himself many times before: was he fooling himself? He'd read about murderers and their habits. How they were like predatory animals that operated in territories where they felt comfortable. But he'd also read about the dangers of seeing patterns in random collections of data. You fire arbitrary shots at a wall, then draw a target around the marks that are closest together and it looks as if you were aiming at it. He examined the map. Five of them were close to the M40 and three to the M1, no more then twenty minutes' drive from a motorway exit. It seemed completely obvious and compelling. But there was a problem. As he'd read through newspapers, checked online, for missing teenage girls, one of his main criteria in weeding them out was looking for families near motorways, so maybe he was creating the pattern himself. But he thought of the girls' faces, the stories. It felt right to him. It smelled right. But what good was that?

FORTY-FIVE

Karlsson sat down opposite Russell Lennox. Yvette started the recorder and sat to one side.

'You know you're still under caution,' Karlsson said, 'and that you're entitled to legal representation.' Lennox gave a faint nod. He seemed dazed, barely responsive. 'You need to say it aloud. For the tape, or chip, or whatever it is.'

'Yes,' said Lennox. 'I understand. I'm fine.'

'You're quite a family,' said Karlsson. Lennox looked blank. 'You seem to do damage to everyone you come into contact with.'

'We're a family in which the wife and mother was killed,' said Lennox, hoarsely. 'Is that what you mean?'

'And now your daughter's boyfriend.'

'I didn't know about that, until I heard about the death.'

'The murder. Zach Greene was hit with a blunt instrument. Like your wife.' There was a pause. 'How did you feel about him?'

'What do you mean?'

'About your fifteen-year-old daughter's relationship with a twenty-eight-year-old man.'

'As I said, I didn't know about it. Now that I do, I feel concern for my daughter. For her welfare.'

'Mr Greene died some time during the day yesterday. Can you tell us where you were?'

'I was at home. I've been at home a lot lately.'

'Was anyone with you?'

'The children were at school. I was there when Dora came home at about ten past four.'

'What did you do at home?'

Lennox seemed terribly tired, as if even talking was a great effort. 'Why don't you just ask me if I killed that man? That must be why you brought me in here.'

'Did you kill him?'

'No, I didn't.'

'All right, so what did you do at home?'

'I pottered around. Sorted through some things.'

'Maybe you can help us by coming up with something we can check. Did someone call round? Did you make any calls? Did you go online?'

'Nobody came round. I probably made some calls and went online.'

'We can check that.'

'I watched a bit of TV.'

'What did you watch?'

'The usual rubbish. Probably something to do with antiques.'

'Probably something to do with antiques,' said Karlsson, slowly, as if he was thinking about it as he repeated it. 'I'm going to stop this now.' He leaned forward and pressed a button on the recorder. 'You're going to go away and have a think, maybe talk to a lawyer and come up with something better than what you've said. And meanwhile we'll make our own checks on who you were phoning and where you were.' He stood up. 'You need to think of your children, your family. How much more of this are they meant to take?'

Lennox rubbed his face, like a man checking whether he'd shaved. 'I think about them every minute of every day,' he said.

Chris Munster was waiting for Karlsson in his office. He had just returned from Cardiff where he had been interviewing Josh Kerrigan's girlfriend, Shari Hollander.

'Well?'

'She just repeated what Josh Kerrigan said: that he'd probably been with her, they'd spent practically every minute of the day together since they'd started going out, she couldn't quite remember. But she was pretty sure that there wasn't a time when he was away for a large chunk of the day or night.'

'It's a bit vague.'

'He didn't use his credit card to buy any kind of transport to London on that day. But he did take a hundred pounds out in cash a couple of days before, so he could have used that.'

'But he's not looking very likely, is he? Not that he ever was.'

'I wouldn't say that.'

Karlsson looked at Munster more attentively. 'What do you mean?'

'There was something his girlfriend mentioned that I thought might interest you.'

'Go on.'

'She said Josh was furious with his father. Spitting mad, she said. She said he'd had a letter, telling him his dad was not the happy family man he set himself up as.'

'So he knew.'

'That's what she said.'

'Good work, Chris. We need another talk with him. Right now. And his little brother while we're at it.'

Josh Kerrigan had got himself a haircut – or maybe, thought Karlsson, looking at the uneven tufts, he'd done it himself with clippers. It made his face seem rounder and younger. He sat in the interview room and couldn't keep still, but drummed his fingers on the table, twisted in his chair, tapped his feet.

'What now?' he asked. 'More questions about my whereabouts?'

'We spoke to Shari Hollander.'

'Did she say I was with her, like I said?'

'She said you probably were.'

'There you go, then.'

'She also said that you knew about your father's affair.'

'What?'

He suddenly looked scared.

'Is that true? Did you receive a letter telling you about the affair?'

Josh stared at Karlsson, then away. A heaviness settled on his young face, making him resemble his father. 'Yes. I got a letter sent to me, care of my physics department.'

'Anonymous?'

'That's right. So whoever sent it didn't even have the courage to admit who they were.'

'Who do you think it was?'

Josh gazed darkly at Karlsson. 'Her, of course. Who else?'

'You mean Ruth Lennox?'

'That's right. Though I didn't know that at the time.'

'Do you still have the letter?'

'I tore it into little bits and threw it in the bin.'

'What else did you do?'

'I tried to put it out of my mind.'

'Nothing at all?'

'I didn't get on a train to London, if that's what you mean.'

'Did you speak to your father about it?'

'No.'

'Or your mother?'

'No.'

'Are you close to your mother?'

'I'm her son.' He looked down, as if he was embarrassed about meeting Karlsson's eye.' She's always put me and Ben before anything else – even when she had cancer, we were all she thought about. And Dad,' he added viciously. 'She put him first, too.'

'But you didn't tell her about this letter?'

'No.'

'Did you tell your brother?'

'Ben's a kid doing his A levels in a few weeks' time. Why would I tell him?'

'Did you?'

Josh pulled at a tuft of newly cut hair. 'No.' But he sounded stiff and uneasy.

'Listen to me, Josh. We're going to talk to your brother, and if his account doesn't agree with yours, you're going to be in even more trouble than you are right now. It's better to tell us the truth at once. Better for Ben, as well.'

'All right, I told him. I had to tell someone.'

'Did you tell him over the phone?'

'Yes.'

'How did he react?'

'Like me. Like anyone would. He was shocked, angry.'

'Is that all?'

'He thought we should tell Mum. I didn't.'

'How did it end?'

'We agreed we'd wait until I came back for Easter, that we'd talk about it then.'

'And did you?'

He gave a wide, sarcastic smile. 'We sort of got over-taken by events.'

'And you didn't tell your mother?'

'Like I said.'

'And Ben didn't either?'

'He wouldn't without telling me.'

'And you're telling me that neither of you confronted your father, however angry you were with him.'

'I said, no.'

'Why were you both so quick to believe what the letter said?'

Josh seemed taken aback. 'I dunno,' he said. 'We just did. Why would anyone make up something like that?'

'And there's nothing else you want to tell me?'

'No.'

'You're sticking to your story that you didn't know who the mystery writer was?'

'Yes.'

Karlsson waited. Josh Kerrigan's eyes flickered towards him, then away again. There was a knock at the door and Yvette put her head around it. 'I need a word,' she said.

'We're done here anyway. For now.' Karlsson stood up. 'We'll speak to your brother.'

Josh shrugged. But his eyes were anxious.

'No,' said Ben Kerrigan. 'No, no and no. I did not tell my mother. I wish I had. But we decided to wait till we were together. I had to look at her over the breakfast table and not say anything. And him.' His face twisted.

'Yes?'

'I didn't say anything to him either. I wanted to. I wanted to punch him in his stupid fat face. I'm glad he's got beaten up. He's just a wanker. It's such a fucking cliché, isn't it? Except the other woman wasn't some bimbo. What did he think he was doing? Ten years. He was cheating on Mum for ten years.'

'But you never confronted him or told your mother about the letter.'

'Like I said.'

'And you never got the impression that your father knew about the letter.'

'He didn't know anything.' Ben's voice rang with scorn. 'He thought he could get away with it, and no price to pay.'

'Or your mother?'

'No. She trusted him. I know Mum. She thinks that once you trust someone, it's unconditional.'

'Why did you hide this information from us?'

'Why do you think? We're not stupid, you know – we do realize that you're all thinking this murder is some kind of revenge.' His voice rose in distress.

'All right.' Karlsson tried to hold his eyes. 'Let's take it slowly, from the beginning. You were here, living with your parents, when Josh told you.'

'Yes.'

'What did you do when you found out?'

'Nothing.'

'Nothing at all?'

'I keep telling you.'

'You didn't talk to anyone apart from Josh?'

'No.'

'But you believed it was true?'

'I *knew* it was true!'

'How?'

'I just did.'

'How did you know, Ben? What made you so sure?' He waited, then asked: 'Did you find out anything else?' He saw Ben flinch involuntarily before he shook his head. 'Ben, I'm asking you one more time: did you try to find anything out?' He stopped and let silence fill the space between them. 'Did you go through your father's things, looking for evidence? It would only be natural. Ben?'

'No.'

'Alone in the house, with this new and horrible suspicion, and you didn't do anything?'

'Stop it.'

'We will find out.'

'OK. I may have.'

'You may have?'

'I poked around a bit.'

'Where?'

'You know. Pockets.'

'Yes.'

'And his phone. His papers.'

'His computer?'

'That too.'

'And what did you find?'

'Nothing much.'

'You do understand how serious this is, Ben?'

The boy turned to him. Karlsson could hear his ragged breathing. 'All right. I looked fucking everywhere. Of course I did. What would you have done? Me and Josh agreed that I would do a search, and then I went through all his grubby tissues and his receipts and his emails and nicked his mobile phone to look at texts and calls. We – me and Josh – rang a few numbers I didn't recognize, just to check. There wasn't anything. But I couldn't stop. If I hadn't found something, I could have gone on for the rest of my life, trying to find the evidence that he was cheating on my mum. It's like that thing they teach in science, you can only prove something is true, not that it isn't.'

'But you did find something?' Karlsson said gently.

'I went through his history.'

'On his computer, you mean?'

'I don't really know what I was looking for. There was a search he'd done on Google images for Ruth Lennox. And I just knew. It's the way you look up someone you know, just to see if there's a picture of them somewhere.'

'So. You and Josh knew your father was having an affair with someone called Ruth Lennox.'

'Yes. Then of course I did a search for her name. He thought he was being so clever. He doesn't understand computers.'

'What did you find?'

'An email from her. Hidden in a folder called something boring like "Household Insurance". Just one email.' He snorted derisively.

'What did it say?'

'It didn't say, "Darling Paul, I like fucking you", if that's what you mean,' Ben said savagely. 'It said that yes, she would like to see him again and that he wasn't to worry, everything was going to be all right.' He grimaced violently. 'It was kind of tender and practical. I thought of Mum being so ill and weak and still looking after us, and then this other woman loving Dad as well, and it seemed so fucking unfair.'

'When was it sent?'

'The twenty-ninth of April 2001.'

'And you still insist you didn't tell your mother?'

'I didn't.'

'But you did push a mutilated doll through the Lennoxes' letterbox.'

Ben turned a deep red. 'Yeah. I didn't plan to. But I saw this stupid doll stuffed in a big basket of toys at a friend's house – it was his kid sister's. And I just took it on a whim and cut it up a bit to show her what we thought of her. I had to do something.'

'She never got your little message, though. Her ill daughter picked it up and thought it was meant for her.'

'Oh, shit.'

'So you and Josh knew where she lived?'

'Yes.'

'Did you go there at other times?'

'No. Not really.'

'Not really?'

413

'I might have stood outside every so often. To see her.'

'Did you see her?'

'No. I saw her kids, I think. It all made me feel a bit sick, if you want to know. Poisoned.'

'Is there anything you haven't told me?'

Ben shook his head miserably. 'Josh is going to be mad at me. He made me swear not to say anything.'

'That's what happens when you start breaking the law. People get mad at you.'

FORTY-SIX

Frieda had got Judith's email address from Chloë, and sent her a short message, saying she would be waiting for her at four o'clock the next afternoon at Primrose Hill, by the entrance just minutes from Judith's school. The weather had changed: it was blustery and the clouds were low and grey, threatening rain.

She saw Judith long before Judith saw her. She was in a knot of friends, which loosened and dispersed as they went, and finally it was just the girl making her way slowly towards the gate. She was wearing her clumpy boots, which made her legs seem thinner than ever, and she had an orange scarf tied several times round her head, like a turban from which wild tendrils of hair escaped. Even her walk was unsteady, her feet in their heavy boots tripping on the pavement. She looked hunted, her eyes darting from side to side, and she kept putting her hand to her mouth, as if she was stopping herself saying anything.

As she came into the park, she noticed Frieda sitting on the bench and her step quickened. A series of expressions flickered on her face: bewilderment, anger, fear. Then it hardened into a mask of hostility. The blue eyes glittered.

'Why is *she* here?'

'Because it's not me you need to speak to. It's DC Long. Yvette.'

'I don't know what you're talking about. I don't need to

talk to either of you. I don't want to. I want everyone to fuck off. Leave me alone, all of you.' Her voice cracked. A hoarse sob forced its way out of her mouth and she lurched where she stood, as if she would fall.

Frieda stood up and gestured to the bench. 'You've been under terrible pressure. You must feel as if you're about to explode with it.'

'I don't know what you're going on about. I don't want to be here. I want to go home. Or somewhere,' she added.

But she didn't move, and for a moment she looked so young and so full of uncertainty and terror that Frieda thought she would burst into tears. Then, as if her legs would no longer hold her, she crumpled on to the bench beside Yvette and pulled her knees up, wrapping her arms around them, hunching her body up protectively.

'Tell Yvette why you're so scared.'

'What do you mean?' whispered Judith.

'You can't protect him.'

'Who?'

'Your father.'

Judith closed her eyes. Her face became slack, suddenly like that of a middle-aged woman, defeated by tiredness.

'I sometimes think I'm going to wake up and this will be just a dream. Mum will still be there and we'll be arguing about stupid stuff, like staying out late and makeup and homework, and all the horrible things won't have happened. I wish I'd never had a boyfriend. I wish I'd never met Zach. I feel sick when I think about him. I want to be like I was before all of this.' She opened her eyes and looked at Frieda. 'Is it because of me he's dead?'

'You tell me.'

And then Judith did at last burst into tears. She leaned forward and covered her face with her hands and rocked her body to and fro and wept. Tears dripped through the lattice of her fingers and snorts and groans and gasps shook her.

Yvette stared at her, then tentatively put out one hand and touched her on the shoulder, but Judith reacted violently, lashing out and pushing her away. It was several minutes before the sobs got quieter, and at last they ceased. She lifted her face from the sieve of her hands; she was blotchy with weeping; there were streaks of mascara running down her cheeks. She was barely recognizable. Frieda took a tissue from her bag and, without a word, handed it over. Judith dabbed at her sodden face, still making sniffling sounds.

'I told him about Zach,' she said at last, in a whisper.

'Yes.'

'Did he kill him?'

'I don't know that.' Frieda handed her another tissue.

'But you did right to tell us,' added Yvette, decisively. 'We would have found out anyway. You're not to feel responsible.'

'Why? Why shouldn't I? It's my fault. I had sex with him.' Her face puckered. 'And then I told my dad. He just wanted to protect me. What's going to happen to him? What's going to happen to us? Dora's just a little girl.'

'Yvette's right, Judith: you're not responsible.'

'He'll know it was me who told you.'

'He should never have put you in this position,' Yvette said.

'Why is this happening to us? I just want to go back to when it was all right.'

'We should take you home,' said Frieda.

'I can't see him, not now. I just can't. My poor darling dad. Oh, God.' And she ended on a juddering sob.

Frieda made up her mind. 'You'll come to my house,' she said, thinking of how her calm, orderly home had become like a circus for other people's grief and chaos. 'You and Ted and Dora. We'll call them now.' She nodded at Yvette. 'And you'll have to speak to Karlsson.'

When Yvette told Karlsson what she'd learned from Judith, he just stared at her for a moment.

'Stupid, fucking idiot,' he said finally. 'Who's going to look after his family now? What a mess. Russell Lennox knew about Judith and Zach. Josh and Ben Kerrigan knew about their father and Ruth Lennox. All those secrets. Where's this going to end?' His phone rang and he snatched it up, listened, said, 'We'll be there,' then put it down again.

'That was Tate in forensics. He's invited us for a guided tour of Zach's flat.'

'But –'

'Have you got anything better to do?'

James Tate was a small, stocky, dark-skinned and peppery-haired man with a peremptory manner and sarcastic sense of humour. Karlsson had known him for years. He was meticulous and dispassionate, very good at his job. He was waiting for them and when they arrived he gave them a small nod and handed them both paper shoes and thin latex gloves to put on, before they stepped into the scene of the crime.

'You couldn't have just told me on the phone?' Karlsson asked.

'I thought you'd like to see it for yourself. Like this, for example.'

He pointed at the doorbell. 'Nice clear prints.'

'Do they match –'

'Don't be in such a hurry.' He opened the door into the little entrance hall. 'Exhibit number two.' He pointed at the muddy footprints on the floor. 'Size forty-one shoes. We've got a clear image. And three: signs of some kind of struggle. This picture has been dislodged.'

Karlsson nodded. Yvette, following them past the disordered kitchenette into the bedroom, had the strange sensation that she would find the body all over again.

'Four. Blood splash. Here, here and here. And substantially more there, of course, where the body was. Exhibit four, or should that be five: in that bin there,' he pointed, 'we found a very dirty kitchen towel covered with more blood. We took it away for DNA testing. Somebody had used it to clean himself up.'

'And that would be . . .'

'Exhibit six: fingerprints, containing traces of the victim's blood, all against that wall. There. What do you think?'

'What do I think? What do you *know*?'

'We can construct a very plausible scenario. Someone – a man wearing size forty-one shoes – entered. Presumably he was let in by the victim, but we can't be sure. There was no sign of a forced entrance. They had some kind of a struggle in the hall, then went into the bedroom where the victim was bludgeoned to death with a weapon as yet unfound. The perpetrator must have got splashed with the victim's blood and he wiped himself with the cloth and flung it into the bin. I take it he was feeling unsteady by then. He leaned against that wall, leaving several very satisfactory fingerprints. Then he left.' Tate beamed at them. 'There.'

'And the fingerprints belonged to?'

'Russell Lennox.' Tate's triumphant smile faded. 'Aren't you impressed?'

'No, I'm sorry. I really am. But there's being careless and there's being really careless.'

'You know all about that, Mal. Murderers are almost always in an almost psychotic state because of the stress. They suffer memory loss. I've found wallets, jackets at crime scenes.'

'You're right,' said Karlsson. 'I'm not going to say no to a clear result.'

'You're welcome,' said Tate.

FORTY-SEVEN

When Frieda and the Lennox children had arrived at her
flat, it was far from the calm place of refuge she had
wanted for them. Instead, it felt like a battle zone. Shoes
of all shapes and sizes lay in the hall, with coats piled up
by the banisters; bags and satchels, spilling their contents,
led into the living room. Music was playing loudly. The air
was thick with the smell of cooking: onions, garlic, herbs.
She had to pause for a moment and take a few deep
breaths. She felt as if she had led them all on stage. She
heard loud voices, the rattle of glasses, like a party. As she
stepped into the living room, Josef and Chloë looked up.
She saw the bottle of wine on the table, the glasses, a bowl
of nuts.

'It's all right,' said Chloë. 'Reuben's making supper. I
thought it would be nice for you not to think about it for
once. He says it's his speciality. Oh, hi, Ted!' She blushed
and smiled.

Then the door opened and Reuben peered round, his
face flushed and beaming. Drunk, thought Frieda. Drunk
as a lord.

'Hello, Frieda. I thought we all needed a slap-up meal
and since you won't come to me I thought –' He noticed
the Lennoxes bunched in a corner, dazed and scared.
'Sorry. I didn't realize. You must be the poor kids whose
mother died.'

'Yes,' said Judith, faintly. Dora started to snivel.

'Very tough,' said Reuben. 'Very very very tough.' He lurched a bit. 'I'm so sorry.'

'Thank you.'

'But for now, I've made enough for an army. The more the merrier. And the food is ready.' He gave a sweeping bow and winked at Judith.

'I don't think it's the right night,' Frieda said firmly. 'We need to have a bit of quiet here. I'm sorry.'

His expression curdled. He glared at her and raised his eyebrows, ready to pick a fight.

'Don't be mean, Frieda!' Chloë was indignant. 'He's been working for *hours* on this. You don't mind, do you, Ted?' She put a hand on his shoulder and he stared at her with stupefied eyes.

'Nah. It's OK,' he said listlessly. 'It doesn't really matter one way or another.'

'I don't think –' began Frieda.

'Great!'

Josef had already laid the table with unfamiliar plates that Frieda never used. He must have found them at the back of a cupboard. But when he laid them out on the table, it added to her impression that she was a guest in her own house and a stranger in her own life. He filled tumblers with water from a jug. Then Reuben drew a large blue casserole dish from the oven, his hands swathed in two tea-towels. Frieda already knew what it was. Reuben's speciality, his fallback dish, his comfort food, ever since she had known him, was a particularly hot, spicy and meaty chilli con carne. When he triumphantly lifted the lid, the sight of the meat and the purple kidney beans almost made her gag.

'This was the meal I used to cook as a student,' he said to Chloë. 'You'll need to build up a few dishes for when you go to college. And you're a bit peaky, if I may say so,' he told Judith. 'Red meat is what you need!'

'You didn't make a salad as well, did you?' Frieda asked.

Reuben left the room and returned with a fairly small green salad. He ladled the chilli on to the plates and passed them round. When he had finished, he poured wine into the glasses.

Chloë took a mouthful of chilli, flinched and coughed. 'It's really hot,' she said, with a gasp. She took a gulp of water.

'Water only makes it worse,' Reuben said. 'Wine's better.'

Josef took a large forkful and munched. 'Good,' he said. 'Feel it in the chest.'

Frieda toyed with the food. She took a salad leaf in her fingers and put it into her mouth. Ted drank a glass of wine as if it was water and, without asking, poured himself another. Dora simply stared at her plate and then at Frieda with her huge beseeching eyes.

Judith prodded the greasy pile in front of her. 'It's very nice, but I think I'm going to go and lie down,' she said. 'Can I lie on your bed for a bit?'

'Of course.'

'I've been having revenge fantasies about that bastard Hal Bradshaw,' said Reuben, loudly and cheerily, as Judith left the room.

'Who's he?' asked Chloë, looking anxiously at Ted.

'He's the bastard that conned me and Frieda and set us up to public ridicule. I keep imagining different scenarios.

Like I'm walking past a lake and I see Bradshaw drowning and I just watch him as he sinks below the surface. Or I come across the scene of a car accident and Bradshaw is lying on the road and I just stand and watch him bleed out. I know what you're going to say, Frieda.'

'I'm going to tell you to be quiet right now.'

'You're going to tell me that fantasies like that aren't very healthy. They're not *therapeutic*.' He stressed the last word as if there was something disgusting about it. 'So what do you think?'

'I think it might be a better revenge fantasy if you rescued Bradshaw from drowning. Or staunched his bleeding. And I think you've had too much wine and this is not the night.'

'That's not much fun,' said Reuben.

'No,' chimed in Ted. His cheeks were blotchy and his eyes bright. 'Not fun at all. Revenge should be bloody.'

'A dish served cold,' announced Chloë. 'We're doing it for GCSE.'

'Staunched?' said Josef. 'Served cold?' He was drunk too, decided Frieda.

'I've been planning a real revenge with Josef,' said Reuben.

Frieda looked at Josef, who had just taken a mouthful. He made an effort to chew and swallow it.

'Not the planning so much,' Josef said. 'The talking.'

'There are things builders know how to do,' Reuben continued, apparently unaware of the tangible air of distress in the room. 'Josef can gain entry. You hide shrimps inside the curtain rails and behind the radiators. When they start to rot, the smell will be staggering. Bradshaw won't be able to live in his own house. Then there's more subtle things you can do. You can loosen a water-pipe connector beneath the floorboards, just a little, just so there's a drip of water. That can cause some serious damage.'

'That's awesome,' said Ted, in a loud, harsh voice. His eyes glittered dangerously.

'This is just a fantasy you're talking about,' said Frieda. 'Right?'

'Or I could do worse than that,' said Reuben. 'I could tamper with the brakes on his car – with Josef's help, of course. Or torch his office. Or threaten his wife.'

'You'd go to prison. Josef would be sent to prison and then deported.'

Reuben opened another bottle of wine and started to fill the glasses again.

'I'm going to take Dora to her bed,' said Frieda. 'And when I come back, I think you should go. You and Josef are going home.'

'I'm having a second helping,' said Reuben. 'More, Ted?

'Reuben, you've gone far enough.'

But a few minutes later, when she came back into the room, Reuben began again. She knew him in this mood – petulant and dangerous, like a sore-headed bull.

'I think you're being pious about this, Frieda. I'm an advocate for revenge. I think it's healthy. I want to go round the table and everyone has got to say the person that they would like to take revenge on. And what the revenge would be. I've already named Hal Bradshaw. I'd like him to be tied to a mountain top naked for all eternity and then every day a vulture would come and eat his liver.' He grinned wolfishly. 'Or something.'

'But what about when it had finished?' said Chloë.

'It would grow back every day. What about you?'

Chloë looked at Reuben, suddenly serious. 'When I was nine, there was a girl called Cath Winstanley. In year four and the first half of year five, she spent the whole of every day trying to stop people talking to me or playing with me. And when a new girl arrived, Cath would become her friend straight away to stop her playing with me.'

'I didn't know that,' said Frieda.

'Mum knew. She just told me it would pass. It did. In the end.'

'What would you like to do to her?' said Reuben. 'You're allowed to do anything. This is fantasy revenge.'

'I'd just like her to go through what I went through,' said Chloë. 'Then at the end I would appear out of a puff of smoke and say: "That's what it was like."'

'That's what revenge should be like,' said Frieda, softly.

'But you survived,' said Reuben. 'What about you, Josef?'

Josef gave a sad smile. 'I don't say his name. The man with my wife. Him I want to punish.'

'Excellent,' said Reuben. 'So what punishments would you like to devise for him? Something medieval?'

'I don't know,' said Josef. 'If my wife is with him like me, how do you say it? Talk, talk, talk to him . . .'

'Nagging,' said Reuben.

'Yes, the nagging,'

'Oh, for Christ's sake, Reuben,' said Frieda. 'And you, Josef.'

'What's problem?' said Josef.

'Forget it,' said Frieda.

'What about you, Ted? If you could track down your mother's killer? You must think about it.'

'Out. Go home now,' said Frieda.

'No.' Ted said loudly, almost in a yell. 'Of course I think about it. If I could find my mother's killer, I'd – I'd –' He gazed around the table, his fist clenched around his wine glass. 'I hate him,' he said softly. 'What do you do to the people you hate?'

'It's OK, Ted,' said Chloë. She was trying to hold the hand that was clasping his glass.

'Attaboy,' said Reuben. 'Let it out. That's the way. Now you, Frieda. Who's going to be the object of your implacable revenge?'

Frieda felt a lurch of nausea in her stomach, rising in her chest. She felt as if she was standing on the edge of a chasm, with just her heels on the ground, her toes poking into the darkness and the temptation, always that temptation, to let herself fall forward into the deep darkness towards – well, towards what?

'No,' she said. 'I'm not good at these sorts of games.'

'Oh, come on, Frieda, this isn't Monopoly.'

But Frieda's expression hardened with a kind of anger and Reuben let it go.

'The bath,' said Josef, trying to make everything all right in his clumsy way. 'Is OK?'

'It's very good, Josef. It was worth it.' She didn't tell him she hadn't yet used it.

'Finally I help,' he said. He was swaying on his feet.

At last they had left. The soft spring dusk was darkening to real night. The clouds had blown away and the ghost of a moon was visible above the rooftops. Inside, an air of anticipation and dread filled the rooms. Even Chloë's animation had petered out. Judith, who had come downstairs when she heard the front door slam, sat in a chair in the living room, her knees drawn up, her head pressed down on them, her hair wild. If anyone spoke to her and tried to comfort her, she would simply shake her head vehemently. Dora lay on a camp bed in Frieda's study with a mug of cocoa beside her, which had cooled to form a wrinkled skin on its surface. She was playing a game of Snakes on her phone. Her thin plaits lay across her face. Frieda sat beside her for a few moments, without speaking. She turned her head and said, in a voice that sounded almost querulous: 'I knew about Judith and that older man.'

'Did you?'

'A few days ago, when Dad was drunk, I heard him shouting at Aunt Louise about it. Is Judith going to be OK?'

'In time.'

'Did Dad . . .?'

'I don't know.'

Frieda went downstairs. Outside on the patio, Ted was smoking and pacing to and fro, his unkempt head enclosed in his giant pair of headphones. None of them could help the others, or be helped by them. They were just waiting, while Chloë barged around the house with cups of tea or firm, encouraging pats on a bowed shoulder.

Frieda had asked Ted if there was anyone she should call and he had turned his sullen gaze on her. 'Like who?'

'Like your aunt.'

'You've got to be joking.'

'Don't you have other relatives?'

'You mean like our uncle in the States? He's not much use, is he? No, it's us and it's Dad, and if he's not there, there's no one at all.'

She sat with him for a while, relishing the cool night air. Nothing in her life felt rational or controlled any more: not her house, which used to be her refuge from the violent mess of the world, not her relationship with these young people, who had turned to her as if she knew answers that didn't exist, not her creeping involvement with the police again, not her unshakeable preoccupation with the shadowy world of the missing girl Lila. Above all, not her sense that she was following a voice that only she could hear, an echo of an echo of an echo. And Dean Reeve, keeping watch. She thought of Sandy, only halfway through his day, and wished that this day was over.

FORTY-EIGHT

The following morning Frieda woke everyone early and took them all to Number 9 for breakfast – a raggle-taggle crew of bleary-eyed, anxious teenagers, who seemed closer today to childhood than adulthood. Their mother had been murdered, their father was in a police cell and they were waiting for the sentence to fall.

She saw them all on to the bus, waiting till it drew away, then returned home. She felt drained and subdued, but she had things to do. Josef was building a garden wall in Primrose Hill; Sasha was at work. So Frieda took the train out from Liverpool Street, through the nearly completed stadiums and sports halls of the Olympic Park. They looked like toys abandoned by a giant child. Coming out of the station at Denham, she climbed into a taxi waiting at the rank.

A horse refuge named after a flower. Frieda had imagined rolling meadows and woodland. The taxi passed a large, semi-demolished set of warehouses, then a housing estate. When the taxi stopped and the driver announced that they had arrived, Frieda thought she must have come to the wrong place, but then she saw the sign: 'The Sunflower Horse and Donkey Refuge'. The driver asked if she wanted him to wait for her. Frieda said she might be some time so he wrote his number on a card and gave it to her.

As the car drove away, she looked around. By the entrance, there was a pebbledash house. There were deep cracks in the façade and an upper window was covered with cardboard. It seemed deserted. On the wall, to the side of the entrance, there was another sign, stencilled: 'Visitors Report to Reception'. She walked into a yard lined with stable buildings made out of breeze blocks and concrete but no Reception that she could see. There were piles of horse manure and straw bales, and off to the side a rusting tractor with no tyres on the front wheels. Frieda stepped delicately across the yard, making her way between brown muddy puddles.

'Is there anyone here?' she called out.

She heard a scraping sound and a teenage girl carrying a spade emerged from one of the stable doorways. She was dressed in rubber boots and jeans and a bright red T-shirt. She wiped her nose with the back of her hand. 'Yeah?'

'I'm looking for someone called Shane.'

The girl just gave a shrug.

'I heard that a man called Shane works here.'

The girl shook her head. 'No.'

'Maybe he used to work here.'

'I don't know nobody called Shane.'

'How long have you been working here?'

'A few years. On and off.'

'And you know everyone who works here?'

The girl rolled her eyes. 'Course I do,' she said, and disappeared back into the stable. Frieda heard the spade scraping on the concrete floor. She walked out of the yard on to the road where she had come in, looked at her watch and wondered what to do. She thought back to the conversation in the pub. Had she misunderstood somehow? Were they just trying to get her to go away? She started to walk along the road. There was no pavement, just a grass verge, and she felt vulnerable to the cars that were passing her with a rush of air and noise. As she got beyond the buildings, she reached a rough wooden fence that separated the field from the road.

She leaned on the fence and looked across. The field was large, maybe a quarter of a mile across, bordered on the far side by the busy A12, cars and lorries rumbling along it. The field itself was scrubby and abandoned, broken only by occasional clumps of gorse and, in the middle, a large, dead oak tree. And then there were horses, and a few donkeys, scattered around. They were old and mangy but they seemed contented enough, heads down, nibbling at the grass, and Frieda found it relaxing just watching them. It wasn't much, perhaps, but better here than anywhere else. It was a strange scene, neither town nor country but something messily in between. It looked like land that had been neglected, unloved, half forgotten about. Maybe some buildings had been there, had been demolished and the grass and the gorse had grown back. One day someone would notice it again, next to the motorway, close to London, and they'd build an industrial estate or a service station, but until then it would struggle on. Frieda rather liked it.

She rummaged in her pocket and found the card that the taxi driver had given her. It was probably time to give up, return to London and to her normal life and her work. The impulse brought an immediate feeling of relief. She was just reaching for her phone when a car pulled up at the entrance to the refuge. A man got out. He was tall, slightly stooped, with unkempt hair that was nearly white and a beaked nose. He wore dark trousers and a rumpled jacket, a thin dark tie pulled loose over his shirt. He had a watchful, unsmiling air, and she saw the blare of his pale, hooded eyes. They stared at each other. They were thirty or more yards apart, too far to talk comfortably. Frieda stood back from the fence. She walked a few steps towards him and he walked towards her. The expression on his face didn't alter: it was as though he was looking not at but through her.

'Do you work here?' the man asked.

'No. I was trying to find someone, but he's not here.' A thought occurred to her. 'You aren't called Shane, are you?'

'No,' said the man. 'I'm not.' And he walked past Frieda into the yard. Suddenly he stopped and turned. 'Why do you want him?'

'It's difficult to explain.'

The man came back towards her. 'Tell me anyway.'

'I'm searching for a girl,' said Frieda, 'and I thought that someone called Shane might help me. I was told he was here but they haven't heard of him.'

'Shane,' said the man, reflectively. 'I haven't heard of him. Still, you may as well come along.'

Frieda raised her eyebrows in surprise. 'Why should I do that?'

'I'm trying to find someone as well.' He spoke slowly and sombrely.

'I'm sorry, but I don't know you. You're a stranger to

me, and I don't know who you're meeting or why you're here. I've finished and I'm going home.'

'It'll just take a minute.' He scrutinized her. 'My name's Fearby, by the way. Jim Fearby. I'm a journalist.'

The sun passed behind a cloud and the landscape in front of them darkened. Frieda had the feeling of being in a dream, where everything made sense but was senseless. 'I'm Frieda Klein.'

'And who *are* you?'

'I don't know.' She stopped, hearing the words. 'I'm just someone trying to help someone.'

'Yes. What's the name of your missing girl?'

'Lila Dawes.'

'Lila Dawes?' He frowned. 'No, I haven't heard of her. But come with me.'

They walked into the yard where the girl was now sweeping. She was obviously puzzled to see Frieda again.

'I'm looking for a man called Mick Doherty,' said Fearby.

'He's over the other side,' said the girl. 'Doing the fence.'

'Where?'

The girl sighed. She led them through the yard to the field and pointed across. They could see signs of someone moving on the far side, right by the main road.

'Is it safe to walk across?' asked Fearby.

'They don't bite.'

A small gate opened into the field. Fearby and Frieda walked across it in silence. Two horses came to them and Fearby glanced at Frieda.

'They think we've got food,' said Frieda.

'What will they do when they find we haven't?'

A small ragged horse nuzzled against Frieda. She stroked it between the eyes. How long was it since she had been that close to a horse? Twenty years? Longer? She felt the warmth of its breath on her. Comforting. It smelt sweet, musty, earthy. As they got closer to the far side, they saw a man fastening the fence to a new post, twisting wire with pliers. He looked at them. He was tall, with very long reddish-brown hair, tied back in a ponytail. He wore jeans and a black T-shirt. At first the T-shirt appeared to have long sleeves, but then Frieda saw his arms were covered with a network of tattoos. He had earrings in both ears.

'Are you Mick Doherty?' asked Fearby.

The man frowned at them. 'Who are you?'

'We're not police. I'm looking for a young girl called Sharon Gibbs. She's missing. Your name came up as someone who knew her.'

'I've never heard of her.'

'I think you have. You are Mick Doherty?'

'That's right.'

'We just want to find her.' Frieda heard the 'we', but didn't protest. This odd man spoke wearily but with a tone of authority. 'However, if we don't find anything, we'll have to turn over what we know to the police. I'm sure that's not a problem, but . . .' Fearby paused and waited.

'I'm clean. You've got nothing on me.'

Still Fearby waited.

'I don't know what you want.' His eyes slid to Frieda. 'You're wasting your time here.'

'Sharon Gibbs.'

'OK. I know her a bit. So what?'

'When did you last see her?'

'You say she's missing?'

'That's right.'

'When did she go missing?'

'Just over three weeks ago.'

Doherty finished twisting a wire fastening on the fence. 'I haven't seen her for months. Maybe more. I've been away.'

'You've been away.'

'That's right.'

'Where?'

'In prison. Just for a bit. Bloody set up, I was. I went in in January. I got out last week. They let me out and they got me a job. Shovelling fucking dung for fucking donkeys.'

'And have you seen Sharon since getting out?'

'Why would I have? She's not my girlfriend or anything, if that's what you're getting at. Just a squirmy little kid.'

'A squirmy little kid who got into the wrong company, Mr Doherty.' Fearby fastened his unnerving eyes on the man. 'And whose parents are very anxious about her.'

'That's not my problem. You're talking to the wrong person.'

A thought struck Frieda. 'Do people call you Shane?'

'What do you mean?'

'Reddish hair, Irish name.'

'I'm from Chelmsford.'

'But they call you Shane.'

Doherty gave a faint, sarcastic smile. 'Sometimes they do. You know. Begorrah.'

'Tell me about Lila Dawes.'

'What?'

'You knew a girl called Lila Dawes. Also missing.' She felt Fearby stiffen beside her, as if a current of electricity had passed through him.

'Two missing girls,' he said softly. 'And you knew them both.'

'Who says I knew Lila?'

'Lila. Crack addict. Spent time with you, Shane – Mr Doherty – around the time she went missing. Two years ago.'

'You say you're not the police, so I don't have to say anything to you. Except . . .' He put the wire down. Frieda could see the spittle on his mouth and the broken blood vessels on his skin. He clenched and unclenched his fists so that the tattoos on his arm rippled, and his eyes wandered round her, as if he was trying to see something behind her. 'Except piss off back to where you came from.'

'Hazel Barton, Roxanne Ingatestone, Daisy Crewe, Philippa Lewis, Maria Horsley, Lila Dawes, Sharon Gibbs.'

It sounded like a chant, an incantation. Frieda felt the breath go out of her body. She stood absolutely still and quiet. For a moment, it was as if she'd entered a dark tunnel that was leading towards a still darker place.

'What the fuck are you talking about, old man?'

'Missing girls,' Fearby said. 'I'm talking about missing girls.'

'OK. I knew Lila.' He gave a smirk of recollection. 'I don't know where she went.'

'I think you do,' said Frieda. 'And if you do, you should tell me, because I'm going to find out.'

'People come and go. She was always more trouble than she was worth.'

'She was just a teenage girl who had the terrible bad luck of meeting you.'

'My heart bleeds. And, yeah, I knew Sharon a bit. Not those others.'

'Was this the first time you'd been in prison?' Fearby asked.

'I think I've had enough of your questions.'

'Dates, Mr Doherty.'

Something in his voice made the man's expression waver for a moment, the sneer replaced by a kind of wariness. 'Eighteen months ago I was in Maidstone.'

'What for?'

'There was a thing with a girl.'

'A thing.' Fearby repeated the words as if tasting them. 'What did you get?'

Doherty just shrugged.

'How long?'

'Four months, give or take.'

Frieda could sense Fearby working something out. His face was ravelled with concentration, deep furrows lining his forehead.

'OK,' he said at last. 'We're done.'

Fearby and Frieda walked back across the field. Two horses followed them; Frieda could hear their hoofs on the dried earth, like a drum.

'We need to talk,' Fearby said, as they reached his car. She simply nodded. 'Is there somewhere we can go? Do you live nearby?'

'No. Do you?'

'No. How did you get here?'

'I got a taxi from the station.'

'We can find a café.'

Frieda got in beside him; the seatbelt didn't work; the car smelt of cigarettes. On the back seat there were several folders. Only when they were seated at a table by the window of a small, dingy café on Denham High Street, with mugs of too-milky tea in front of them untouched, did they exchange another word.

'You begin,' said Fearby. He put a Dictaphone in front of him, then opened a spiral-bound notebook and took a pen out of his jacket pocket.

'What are you doing?'

'Making notes. Is that OK?'

'I don't think so. And turn that off.'

Fearby looked at her as if he was seeing her properly for the first time. Then a faint smile appeared on his weathered face. He turned off the machine and laid his pen down.

'Tell me why you're here.'

So Frieda told her story. At first, she was conscious of its irrationality: just a paranoid instinct in the wake of her own trauma that had led her on a fruitless and inexplicable search for a girl she had never known. She heard herself talking about the tiny vivid anecdote that had sparked off her quest, of the dead ends, the sad encounters with Lila's father and with the woman from Josef's homeland, who had pointed her in the direction of Shane. But bit by bit she realized that Fearby wasn't responding with incredulity, as if she had gone slightly mad, the way that others had. He nodded in recognition, leaned forward; his eyes seemed to grow brighter and his granite face softer.

'There,' she said, when she had finished. 'What do you think?'

'It sounds like the same man.'

'You're going to have to explain.'

'Well. I suppose it all began with George Conley.'

'Why does that name sound familiar?'

'He was found guilty of murdering a girl called Hazel Barton. You'll probably have heard of him because he was released a few weeks ago, after spending years in the nick for a crime he never committed. Poor sod, he'd almost have been better off staying inside. But that's a whole other story. Hazel was the first girl, and the only one whose body was found. I believe Conley interrupted the crime, whereas all the others – but I'm getting ahead of myself. And, in fact, Hazel wasn't really the first – there were others. Vanessa Dale, for a start, and I just didn't realize that at the time, because Vanessa was the one who got away. I tracked her down, though. I should have done it sooner, when she had a fresher memory, or any memory, but I didn't know. I didn't understand for many years what the story was really about, what a long, dark shadow it cast. Back in the day, I was just a hack, with a wife and kids, covering local news. Anyway –'

'Stop,' said Frieda. Fearby looked up at her, blinking. 'I'm sorry, but I don't understand a word you're saying.'

'I'm trying to explain. Listen. It all links up, but you have to follow the connections.'

'But you're not making any connections.'

He sat back, rattled his teaspoon in his cooling tea. 'I've lived with it too long, I guess.'

'Are you trying to tell me that the girls whose names you gave Doherty are all connected, and that Lila Dawes may be too?'

'Yes.'

'How?'

Fearby stood up abruptly. 'I can't tell you. I need to show you.'

'Show me?'

'Yes. It's all written down. I've got maps and charts and files. Everything's there.'

'Where?'

'At my house. Will you come and have a look?'

Frieda paused. 'All right,' she said at last.

'Good. Let's go.'

'Where do you live? London?'

'London? No. Birmingham.'

'Birmingham!'

'Yes. Is that a problem?'

Frieda thought of her house waiting for her, of her friends who didn't know where she was, of her cat whose bowl would be empty. She thought of Ted, Judith and Dora – but she couldn't resist the strangeness of the encounter, the pull of this strange old man. She would call Sasha, and tell her to hold the fort.

'No,' she said. 'Not a problem.'

FORTY-NINE

In the warmth of the car, Frieda felt herself sliding towards sleep. She had had several nights of insomnia, worse than usual, tormented in between by scraping, violent dreams, and was ragged and scorched-eyed with tiredness. But she struggled against sleeping in front of Fearby, this shabby bird of prey; she couldn't let herself be defenceless in front of him. Yet it was no good, she couldn't stay awake. Even as she let herself go at last, her eyes closing and her body softening, she was thinking how odd it was that she should trust someone she didn't know at all.

Fearby turned off the M25 and on to the M1. This was a road he knew; it seemed fitting they should be driving it together. He slid some Irish folk music into the CD player, turned the volume down so it was only just audible, and glanced at her. He couldn't make her out. She must be in her mid- to late-thirties – from a distance, she looked younger, with her slim upright body and her supple movement, but up close her face was gaunt; there were hollows under her eyes and a strained, almost haunted expression on her pale face. He hadn't asked her what she did. Frieda Klein: it sounded German, Jewish. He looked at her hands, lying half folded in her lap, and saw they were ringless, with unvarnished nails cut short. She wasn't wearing any jewellery or makeup. Even in sleep, her face was stern and troubled.

Nevertheless – and his heart lifted – he had a companion, a fellow-traveller, at least for a while. He was so used to working alone that it had become hard to tell where the outside world blurred with his private obsessions. She would be able to tell him: she had a good, clear gaze, and whatever motives she had for her own particular quest, he had felt her cool shrewdness. He smiled to himself: she didn't like being ordered around.

She murmured something and threw up one hand. Her eyes clicked open and, in a moment, she was sitting up straight, pushing her hair off her hot face.

'I fell asleep.'

'That's OK.'

'I never fall asleep.'

'You must have needed it.'

Then she sat back once more and gazed out of the windscreen at the cars streaming past in the opposite direction.

'Is this Birmingham?'

'I don't actually live in the city. I live in a village, or small town, really, a few miles away.'

'Why?'

'Sorry?'

'Why don't you live in the city?'

'It's where I lived with my wife and kids. When my wife left, I never got around to moving.'

'Not from choice, then?'

'Probably not. Don't you like the countryside?'

'People should think about where they live, make a deliberate choice.'

443

'I see,' said Fearby. 'I'm passive. And you've made a choice, I take it.'

'I live in the middle of London.'

'Because you want to?'

'It's somewhere I can be quiet and hidden. Life can carry on outside.'

'Maybe that's what I feel about my little house. It's invisible to me. I don't notice it any more. It's just a place to go. I'm an ex-journalist. What do you do?'

'I'm a psychotherapist.'

Fearby looked bemused. 'Now that I wouldn't have guessed.'

He didn't seem to understand just how wretched he had let his house become. There was a gravelled drive almost entirely grown over with ground elder, dandelions and tufts of grass. The windowsills were rotting and the panes were filthy. He might have cleared away the dirt, but a general air of neglect lay over everything. In the kitchen, piles of yellowing newspapers were stacked on the table, which clearly wasn't used for eating at. When Fearby opened the fridge door to look for milk that wasn't there, Frieda saw that, apart from beer cans, it was quite empty. It was a house for a man who lived alone and wasn't expecting company.

'No tea, then,' he said. 'How about whisky?'

'I don't drink in the day.'

'Today is different.'

He poured them both a couple of fingers into cloudy tumblers and handed one to Frieda.

'To our missing girls,' he said, chinking his glass against hers.

Frieda took the smallest stinging sip, to keep him company. 'You were going to show me what you've found.'

'It's all in my study.'

When he opened the door, she was speechless for a few seconds, her eyes trying to become accustomed to the combination of frenzy and order. Briefly, she was reminded of Michelle Doyce, the woman to whom Karlsson had introduced her, who had filled her rooms in Deptford with the debris of other people's lives, carefully categorizing litter.

Fearby's study was dimly lit, because the window was half blocked with teetering piles of paper on its sill: newspapers and magazines and printouts. There were piles of papers on the floor as well: it was almost impossible to make a path through them to the long table that acted as his desk, also disappearing under scraps of paper, old notebooks, two computers, a printer, an old-fashioned photocopying machine, a large camera with its lens off, a cordless phone. Also, two chipped saucers overflowing with cigarette stubs, several glasses and empty whisky bottles. On the rim of the table there were dozens of yellow and pink Post-it notes, with numbers or words scribbled on them.

When Fearby turned on the Anglepoise lamp, it illuminated a paper copy of a photograph of a young woman's smiling face. One chipped tooth. It made Frieda think of Karlsson, who also had a chipped tooth and who was many miles away.

It wasn't the mess of the room that arrested her, however: it was the contrast of the mess to the meticulous order. On the corkboards, neatly pinned into place, were dozens of young women's faces. They were obviously separated into two categories. On the left, there were about twenty faces; on the right, six. Between them was a large map of Britain, covered with flags that went in a crooked line from London towards the north-west. On the opposite wall, Frieda saw a huge time line, with dates and names running along it in neat, copperplate writing. Fearby was watching her. He pulled open the drawers of a filing cabinet, and she saw racks of folders inside, marked with names. He started pulling them out, putting them on top of the dangerous heap of things on his table.

Frieda wanted to sit but there was only one swivel chair and that was occupied by several books.

'Are they the girls?' she asked, pointing.

'Hazel Barton.' He touched her face gently, amost reverently. 'Roxanne Ingatestone. Daisy Crewe. Philippa Lewis. Maria Horsley. Sharon Gibbs.'

They smiled at Frieda, young faces smooth, eager.

'Do you think they're dead?'

'Yes.'

'And maybe Lila is too.'

'It can't be Doherty.'

'Why?'

'Look.' He directed her towards his timeline. 'This is when Daisy went, and Maria – he was in prison.'

'Why are you so sure it's the same person?'

Fearby pulled open the first folder. 'I'm going to show you everything,' he said. 'Then you can tell me what you think. It may take some time.'

*

446

At seven o'clock, Frieda called Sasha, who agreed to go round to her house and stay there until she returned. She sounded concerned, a note of panic in her voice, but Frieda cut the conversation short. She also called Josef to ask him to feed the cat and perhaps water the plants in her yard.

'Where are you, Frieda?'

'Near Birmingham.'

'What's this?'

'It's a place, Josef.'

'What for?'

'It would take too long to explain.'

'You have to come back, Frieda.'

'Why?'

'We all worry.'

'I'm not a child.'

'We all worry,' he repeated.

'Well, don't.'

'You are not well. We all agree. I come to collect you.'

'No.'

'I come now.'

'You can't.'

'Why can't?'

'Because I'm not telling you where I am.'

She ended the call but her mobile rang again almost immediately. Now Reuben was calling; presumably Josef was standing beside him with his tragic eyes. She sighed, turned the phone off and put it into her bag. She'd never wanted to have a mobile in the first place.

'Sharon Gibbs,' said Fearby, as if nothing had interrupted them.

*

At half past ten, they were done. Fearby went outside for a cigarette and Frieda went to look in his cupboards for some food. She wasn't hungry, but she felt hollow and couldn't remember when she had last eaten. Not today; not last night.

The cupboards, like the fridge, were almost empty. She found some quick-boil rice and vegetable stock cubes long past their sell-by date: that would have to do. As she was boiling the rice in the stock, Fearby came back in and stood watching her.

'So, what do you think?' he asked.

'I think either we're two deluded people who happen to have bumped into each other at a donkey sanctuary – or that you're right.'

He gave a grimace of relief.

'In which case, it's not Doherty or Shane or whatever he's called.'

'No. But it's odd, isn't it, that he knew them both? I don't like coincidences.'

'They lived the same kind of lifestyle – two young women who'd fallen off the track.'

'Perhaps they knew each other?' Frieda suggested, lifting the rice off the hob, letting the steam rise into her face, which felt grimy with toil and weariness.

'That's a thought. Who would know?'

'I have one idea.'

After they'd eaten the rice – Fearby had eaten most of it, Frieda had just picked at hers – Frieda said she should take the train back. But Fearby said it was too late. After some argument about hotels and trains, Fearby ended by getting an old sleeping bag out of a cupboard and Frieda made a sort of bed for herself on a sofa in the living room. She spent a strange, feverish night in which she didn't know when she was awake and when she was asleep, when her thoughts were like dreams and her dreams were like thoughts, all of them bad. She felt, or she thought, or she dreamed, that she was on a journey that was also a kind of obstacle race, and only when she had got past the obstacles, solved all the problems, would she finally be allowed to sleep. She thought of the photographs of the girls on Fearby's wall and their faces became mixed up with the faces of Ted, Judith and Dora Lennox, all staring down at her.

From about half past three she was starkly, bleakly awake, staring at the ceiling. At half past four, she got up. She went to the bathroom and ran herself a bath. She lay there and watched the edges of the window blind grow light. She dried herself with the towel that looked like the least used and dressed herself in yesterday's dirty clothes. When she emerged from the bathroom, Fearby was there pouring coffee into two mugs.

'I can't offer you much of a breakfast,' he said. 'I can go out at seven and get some bread and eggs.'

'Coffee will be fine,' said Frieda. 'And then we should go.'

Fearby put a notebook, a folder, a little digital recorder into a shoulder bag and within half an hour they were back on the motorway, heading south. For a long time, they drove in silence. Frieda looked out of the window, then at Fearby. 'Why are you doing this?' she said.

'I told you,' he said. 'At first, for George Conley.'

'But you got him out,' said Frieda. 'That's something most journalists wouldn't achieve in their whole career.'

'It didn't feel enough. He only got out on a technicality. When he got out and everyone was cheering and celebrating and the media were there, it felt incomplete. I needed to tell the whole story, to show that Conley was innocent.'

'Is that what Conley himself wants?'

'I've been to see him. He's a ruined man. I don't think he's capable of putting into words what he wants.'

'Some people who looked at your house would say that you were a ruined man.'

Frieda thought Fearby might flare up at that or say something defensive but he smiled. 'Would say? People have said it already. Starting with my wife and colleagues. My *ex*-colleagues.'

'Is it worth it?' said Frieda.

'I'm not asking for thanks. I just need to know. Don't you agree? When you saw those photographs of the girls, didn't you want to know what happened to them?'

'Did it ever occur to you that there may not be any link between the pictures on your wall, except that they're just poor, sad girls who went missing?'

Fearby glanced at her. 'I thought you were supposed to be on my side.'

'I'm not on anybody's side,' Frieda said, with a frown, and then she relaxed. 'Sometimes I think I'm not even on my own side. Our brains are constructed so that we find patterns. That's why we see animal shapes in clouds. But really they're just clouds.'

'Is that why you came all the way up to Birmingham? And why we're driving all the way back to London?'

'My job is listening to the patterns people make of their lives. Sometimes they're damaging patterns, or self-serving, or self-punishing, and sometimes they're just wrong. Do you ever worry what would happen if you discovered that you were wrong?'

'Maybe life isn't that complicated. George Conley was convicted of murdering Hazel Barton. But he didn't do it. Which means someone else did. So, where in London are we going?'

'I'll put the address into your satnav.'

'You'll like it,' said Fearby. 'It's got the voice of Marilyn Monroe. Well, someone imitating Marilyn Monroe. Of course, that might not appeal to a woman as much a man. I mean the idea of driving around with Marilyn Monroe. In fact, some women might find it quite annoying.'

Frieda punched in the address, and for the next hour and a half, the car was guided down the M1, round the M25, by a voice that didn't really sound like Marilyn Monroe's at all. But he was right about the other bit. She did find it annoying.

Lawrence Dawes was at home. Frieda wondered if he ever wasn't at home. At first he seemed surprised. 'I thought you'd given up,' he said.

'I've got news for you,' said Frieda. '*We've* got news for you.'

Dawes invited the two of them through, and once more Frieda found herself sitting at the table in Dawes's back garden being served tea.

'We found Shane,' she said.

'Who?'

'He was the man your daughter was associated with.'

'Associated with? What does that mean?'

'You knew that your daughter was involved with drugs. He was involved with drugs too. In a more professional way.' Dawes didn't react, but didn't seem like a man expecting good news. 'Shane was just a nickname. His real name is Mick Doherty.'

'Mick Doherty. Do you think he's connected with my daughter's disappearance?'

'It's possible. But I don't know how. It was when I went to see Doherty, out in Essex, that I met Jim. We were both looking for Doherty, but for different reasons.'

'How do you mean?'

'I was investigating the case of a young woman called Sharon Gibbs,' Fearby said. 'She had gone missing and I learned that she had known this man, Doherty. When I met Frieda, I discovered that we both wanted to talk to him about different missing women. It seemed an interesting coincidence.'

Dawes looked thoughtful and pained in a way that Frieda had never seen him before. 'Yes, yes, I can see that,' he said, almost to himself.

'You'd never heard of Shane,' said Frieda. 'But now that we know his real name – Mick Doherty – do you recognize it?'

Dawes shook his head slowly. 'I can't remember ever hearing that name.'

'What about Sharon Gibbs?'

'No, I'm sorry. It doesn't mean anything to me. I can't help you. I wish I could.' He looked in turn at Frieda and Fearby. 'I must seem like a bad father to you. You know, I always thought of myself as the sort of man who would move heaven and earth to find his daughter, if anyone had tried to harm her. But it wasn't like a five-year-old girl going missing. It was more like someone growing up, moving away and wanting to lead their own life. Bit by bit, she disappeared. Some days I think of her all the time and it hurts. It hurts here.' He pressed his hand to his heart. 'Others, I just get on with things. Gardening, mending. It stops me thinking, but perhaps I shouldn't stop thinking because that's a way of not caring so much.' He paused. 'This man, what's his name?'

'Doherty,' said Fearby.

'You think he's connected with Lila's disappearance?'

'We don't know,' said Fearby, then glanced at Frieda.

'There's some kind of link,' said Frieda. 'But he can't be responsible for both. Doherty was in prison when Sharon Gibbs disappeared. I can't make it out. Jim's been looking at some girls who've gone missing and Sharon Gibbs fits with that pattern. But the case of your daughter seems different. Yet she seems connected to them through Doherty. Somehow he's the hinge to all of this, but I don't know why.'

'Why is she different?' asked Dawes.

Frieda stood up. 'I'll take the tea things in and wash up and Jim can tell you what he's been up to. Maybe something will ring a bell with you. Otherwise, we've got through one brick wall only to run up against another.'

Dawes started to protest but Frieda ignored him. She picked up the patterned plastic tray that he had leaned against the leg of the table and put the mugs, the milk jug and the sugar bowl on to it. Then she walked into the house and turned right into the little kitchen. The window above the sink looked out on to the garden and Frieda watched the two men as she did the washing-up. She could see them talking but couldn't hear anything that was being said. Dawes was probably the sort of man who was more comfortable saying things to another man. They got up from the table and walked down the garden away from the house. She saw Dawes gesturing towards various plants and at the end of the garden where the little river flowed. The Wandle, shallow and clear, trickling its way towards the Thames.

There were four other mugs in the sink and some dirty plates and glasses on the Formica worktop. Frieda washed those as well, then rinsed and stacked them on the draining-board. She looked around the kitchen, wondering if men reacted to absence differently from women. The contrast with Fearby's house was sharp. Here, it was tidy, clean and well organized where Fearby's house was dirty and neglected. But there was something they had in common. Frieda thought that a woman would perhaps have turned the home into some sort of shrine to the missing person but Fearby and Dawes were the opposite. Their very different spaces were both like highly organized ways of keeping all those terrible thoughts and feelings of loss at bay. Fearby had filled his house with other missing faces. And this house? It seemed like a house where a man lived alone and had always lived alone. Even doing the washing-up, she felt like a female intruder.

She wiped her hands on a tea-towel, neatly hanging on

its own hook, then stepped outside to join the men. They turned at the same moment and gave a smile of recognition, as though in the few minutes she had been away, they had bonded.

'We've been comparing notes,' said Fearby.

'It feels like we've been doing the same sort of god-forsaken work,' said Dawes.

'But you were a salesman, not a journalist,' said Frieda.

Dawes smiled. 'Still too much time on the road.'

'I suppose you got out just in time?' said Fearby.

'What do you mean?'

'Do offices have photocopiers any more?'

'They certainly do,' said Dawes.

'I thought they'd gone paperless.'

'That's a myth. They use more than ever. No, Copycon are going strong. At least, my pension still arrives every month.' He smiled but then seemed to correct himself. 'Is there anything I can do for you?'

'No. I don't think so.'

'Tell me something, do you think my daughter is alive?'

'We don't know,' said Frieda, softly.

'It's the not knowing that's hard,' said Dawes.

'I'm sorry. I keep coming around and stirring up old feelings and it's not as if I've got much to report.'

'No,' said Dawes. 'I'm grateful anyone's trying to do anything for my daughter. You're welcome here whenever you want to come.'

After a few more exchanges, Frieda and Fearby were back out on the street.

'Poor man,' said Frieda.

'You came back out just in time, though. Dawes was just explaining in unnecessary detail how he and his neighbour were building a new wall.'

Frieda smiled. 'Speak of the devil,' she said, pointing. And there was Gerry, walking down the road, clasping two enormous bags of compost that almost obscured him. Frieda saw that one bag was leaking, leaving a thick brown trail in his wake.

'Hello, Gerry.'

He stopped, put the bags down, wiped a grimy hand across his forehead. His moustache was still uneven. 'I'm getting too old for this,' he said. 'Not to seem unfriendly, but why are you here again?'

'We came to ask Lawrence a couple of questions.'

'I hope you had good reason.'

'I thought so, but –'

'You mean well, I can see that. But he's had enough pain. You leave him be now.' He bent to lift up his bags again and stumbled away, his trail of soil behind him.

'He's right,' said Frieda, soberly.

Fearby unlocked his car. 'Can I drop you home?'

'There's a station round the corner. I can walk and take the train back. It's easier for both of us.'

'Tired of me already?'

'I'm thinking of your trip back. Look, Jim, I'm sorry for dragging you all the way down here. It didn't amount to much.'

He laughed. 'Don't be ridiculous. I've driven across the country for way less than this. And been glad to get it.' He got into his car. 'I'll be in touch.'

'Aren't you baffled by the way these girls can just dis-appear?'

'Not baffled,' he said. 'Tormented.'

He closed the door but opened it again.

'What?' asked Frieda.

'How will I get in touch? I don't have your phone number, your email, your address.'

They swapped numbers and he nodded to her. 'We'll speak soon.'

'Yes.'

'It's not over.'

FIFTY

Frieda walked to the station slowly. The day was grey but hot, almost oppressive, and she felt grimy in the clothes she'd worn yesterday. She allowed herself to think of her bath – Josef's gift to her – waiting in her clean, shaded house, empty at last of all people.

She turned on her mobile and at once messages pinged on to the screen: missed calls, voicemail, texts. Reuben had called six times, Josef even more. Jack had written her a very long text full of abbreviations she couldn't understand. Sasha had left two texts. Judith Lennox had phoned. There were also several missed calls from Karlsson. When she rang voicemail she heard his voice, grave and anxious, asking her to get in touch as soon as she got his message. She stared down at her phone, almost hearing a clamour of voices insisting she get in touch, scolding her and pleading with her and, worst of all, being in a state of distress about her. She didn't have the time for any of that now, or the energy or the will. Later.

When she eventually reached her house, letters lay on the doormat and, as she stooped to pick them up, she saw that a couple had been pushed through the letterbox rather than posted.

One was from Reuben; she recognized his writing at

once. 'Where the fuck are you, Frieda?' he wrote. 'Ring me NOW.' He didn't bother to sign it. The other was from Karlsson, and was more formal: 'Dear Frieda, I couldn't get you on your phone so came round on the off-chance. I really would like to see you – as your friend and as someone who is worried about you.'

Frieda grimaced and pushed both notes into her bag. She walked into her house. It felt cool and sheltered, almost like she was walking into a church. It had been so long since she had spent time there alone, gathering her thoughts, sitting in her study-garret, looking out over the lights of London, at the centre of the city but not trapped in its feverish rush, its mess and cruelty. She went from room to room, trying to feel at home again, waiting for a sense of calm to return to her. She felt that she had passed through a storm and her mind was still full of the faces she had dreamed about last night, or lain awake thinking of. All those lost girls.

The flap rattled and the tortoiseshell cat padded across to her and rubbed its body against her leg, purring. She scratched its chin and put some more food into its bowl, though Josef had obviously come in to feed it. She went upstairs, into her gleaming new bathroom, put in the plug and turned on the taps. She saw her reflection briefly in the mirror: hair damp on her forehead, face pale and tense. Sometimes she was a stranger to herself. She turned the taps off and pulled out the plug. She wouldn't use the bath today. She stepped under the shower instead, washed her hair, scrubbed her body, clipped her nails, but it was no use. A thought hissed in her head. Abruptly, she stepped out of the shower, wrapped herself in a towel, and went into her bedroom. The window was slightly open and the thin curtains flapped in the breeze. She could hear voices outside, and the hum of traffic.

Her mobile buzzed in her pocket and she fished it out, meaning to turn it off at once because she wasn't ready to deal with the world yet. But it was Karlsson, so she answered.

'Yes?'

'Frieda. Thank God. Where are you?'

'At home. I've just come in.'

'You've got to get over here now.'

'Is it the Lennox case?'

'No.' His voice was grim. 'I'll tell you when you come.'

'But –'

'For once in your life, don't ask questions.'

Karlsson met her outside. He was pacing up and down the pavement, openly smoking a cigarette. Not a good sign.

'What is it?'

'I wanted to get to you before bloody Crawford.'

The commissioner? What on earth –'

'Is there anything you need to tell me?'

'What?'

'Where were you last night?'

'I was in Birmingham. Why?'

'Do you have witnesses to that?'

'Yes. But I don't understand –'

'What about your friend, Dr McGill?'

'Reuben? I have no idea. What's going on?'

'I'll tell you what's going on.' He stubbed out his cigarette and lit another. 'Hal Bradshaw's house burned down last night. Someone set it on fire.'

'*What?* I don't know what to say. Was anyone inside?'

'He was at some conference. His wife and daughter were there, but they got out.'

'I didn't know he had a family.'

'Or you wouldn't have done it?' said Karlsson, with a faint smile.

'That's a terrible thing to say.'

'It surprised me as well. I mean that someone would marry him, not that someone would burn his house down.'

'Don't say that. Not even as a bad joke. But why have you made me come here to tell me this?'

'He's in a bad way, saying wild things. That it was you – or one of your friends.'

'That's ridiculous.'

'He claims that threats have been made against him.'

'By me?'

'By people close to you.'

Frieda remembered Reuben and Josef at that dreadful meal, Reuben's revenge fantasies and the look of hatred on his face, and her heart sank. 'They wouldn't,' she said firmly.

'It gets worse, Frieda. He's spoken to the press. He hasn't gone as far as naming names but it doesn't take a genius to put two and two together.'

'I see.'

'They're inside, waiting for you.' Briefly, he laid a hand

461

on her arm. 'But I'll be there as well. You're not on your own.'

The commissioner – a stocky man with beetling brows and a pink scalp showing through his thinning hair – was a deep shade of red. His uniform looked far too hot for the day. Bradshaw was in jeans and a T-shirt and hadn't shaved. When Frieda entered the room, he stared at her, then slowly shook his head from side to side, as if he was too full of pity and anger to trust himself to speak.

'I'm very sorry indeed about what happened,' said Frieda.

'Sit down,' said the commissioner, pointing to a small chair.

'I'd prefer to stand.'

'Suit yourself. I've been hearing your story from Dr Bradshaw. I'm bewildered, absolutely bewildered, as to why we ever had professional dealings with you.' Here he turned towards Karlsson. 'I must say I'm disappointed in you, Mal, turning a blind eye to your friend letting a possible psychopath loose.'

'But he wasn't a psychopath,' said Karlsson, mildly. 'It was a set-up.'

The commissioner ignored him.

'Punching a colleague. Attacking a young woman she'd never met before and forcing her to the floor, just because she stood up for her boyfriend. Stalking poor Hal here. Not to mention killing this schizophrenic young woman, of course.'

'In justified self-defence,' said Karlsson. 'Be careful what you say.'

Crawford looked at Frieda. 'What have you got to say in your defence?'

'What am I defending myself against? Arson?'

'Frieda, Frieda,' murmured Bradshaw. 'I think you need some professional help. I really do.'

'I had nothing to do with it.'

'My wife was in that house,' said Bradshaw. 'And my daughter.'

'Which makes it even worse,' said Frieda.

'Where were you?' said Crawford.

'I was in Birmingham. And I can put you in touch with someone who can confirm that.'

'What about your friends?' asked Bradshaw.

'What about them?'

'They've taken your side against me.'

'It is true that I have several friends who think you acted unprofessionally and unethically –'

'That's rich,' said the commissioner.

'– but they wouldn't do anything like this.'

Karlsson coughed loudly. 'I think this is getting us nowhere,' he said. 'Frieda has an alibi. There's not a shred of evidence, just Dr Bradshaw's claims, which some might believe to be motivated by malice. In the meantime, I have an interview to conduct with Mr Lennox, who is being charged with the murder of Zach Greene.'

Bradshaw rose and came close to Frieda. 'You won't get away with this,' he said, in a low voice.

'Leave her alone,' said Karlsson.

Frieda walked back home. She tried not to think, just put one foot in front of the other, moving steadily through the thickening crowds, feeling the warmth of the day on her. She needed to steady herself before she was with the Lennox family again. Soon they would have neither mother nor father to turn to.

FIFTY-ONE

'Are you ready?' said Karlsson. Yvette nodded. 'We've let him stew long enough and it looks cast-iron to me. You won't have to do much. Just keep an eye on me and make sure I don't do anything stupid. Even I couldn't fuck up this one, though.'

He nodded at her and they walked into the interview room. Russell Lennox was sitting at a table and next to him was his solicitor, a middle-aged woman in a dark suit. She was called Anne Beste. Karlsson didn't know her but he didn't give her much consideration. What could she do? Yvette started the recording machine, then stepped away from the table and stood to one side, leaning back against the wall. Karlsson reminded Lennox that he was still under caution, then opened the file and carefully went through the forensic evidence from Zach Greene's flat. As he talked, he glanced from time to time at Lennox and Anne Beste to see the effect he was having. Lennox's wearily impassive expression was unchanged. Anne Beste listened intently with a frown of concentration and occasionally looked sideways at her client. They never spoke.

When he had finished, Karlsson closed the file quietly. 'Can you give me some innocent explanation for the traces you seem to have left at the scene of the murder?' Russell Lennox shrugged. 'Sorry, you have to say something. For the benefit of the machine.'

'Do I have to explain it?' said Lennox. 'I thought you had to make the case against me.'

'I think we're doing that pretty well,' said Karlsson. 'One more question: have you any evidence about your whereabouts on the day of the murder?'

'No,' said Lennox. 'I've told you already.'

'Yes, you have.' Karlsson paused for a moment. Then, when he spoke, it was in a calm, almost soothing tone. 'Look, Mr Lennox, I know what you've been through, but haven't you put your family through enough? Your children need to put this behind them and move on.'

Lennox didn't speak, just stared at the table.

'All right,' said Karlsson. 'Let me tell you – both of you – what is going to happen. We're going to leave the room now, Mr Lennox, and give you five minutes to discuss various issues with your solicitor. Then I'm going to come back into this room and you will be charged with the murder of Zachary Greene. I need to caution you clearly that you don't have to say anything, but it may harm your defence if you do not mention now something that you later rely on in court. Anything you do say may be given in evidence. But what I'd really like to say to you is we all, but especially you, and even more especially your family, need to lay this to rest.'

When they were outside, Karlsson looked at Yvette and smiled grimly.

'Does it matter what he says?' she asked.

'It'll go a bit more quickly if he confesses,' said Karlsson. 'But it's not that big a deal.'

'Can I get you a coffee?'

'Let's just wait.'

After a couple of awkward minutes, Karlsson looked at his watch, then knocked on the door and stepped inside. Anne Beste held up her hand.

'We need more time.'

Karlsson stepped back outside and closed the door. 'What the hell's that about?' Had something gone wrong? Could they have made some mistake?

It was more like ten minutes when they were both back in the room. Anne Beste was briskly tapping the surface of the table with the fingers of her left hand. She glanced at Lennox and he gave the smallest of nods.

'Mr Lennox is willing to admit to the manslaughter of Zachary Greene.'

Karlsson looked at Lennox. 'What happened?' he asked.

'I went to see him,' said Lennox. 'After Judith told me. I had to. I was desperate. I was just going to talk to him, but we started arguing and I lost control. And then he was dead.'

Karlsson sighed. 'You fucking idiot. Do you realize what you've done?'

Lennox barely seemed to hear him. 'What about the children?' he said.

Yvette started to say something, but Karlsson stopped her with a look.

'Do you know where they are?' Karlsson asked.

Lennox leaned back in his chair. His face was dark with misery. 'They're all staying in that therapist woman's house.'

'With Frieda?' said Karlsson. 'What are they doing there?'

'I don't know.'

'Mr Lennox,' said Yvette. 'You do understand, don't you, that this isn't over?'

'What do you mean?'

'There have been two murders – Zach Greene's, to which you've confessed.'

'Manslaughter,' put in Anne Beste.

'And your wife's.'

Lennox lifted his eyes to her, then dropped them.

'My client has co-operated and now he has nothing further to say,' said Anne Beste.

Karlsson rose. 'We'll talk again tomorrow. As my colleague here says, this isn't over, Mr Lennox.'

FIFTY-TWO

Frieda opened her door to find Karlsson, Yvette and a woman she didn't recognize outside. The woman forced her way inside. Ted and Judith, Dora and Chloë were sitting around the table in the living room, with mugs and plates and phones and a laptop.

'Oh, my darlings, my poor, poor darlings,' said Louise. The three Lennoxes shrank from her, but she didn't seem to notice. Chloë put a hand on Ted's shoulder.

'What's going on?' Frieda asked Karlsson, who murmured a quick explanation to her. When she heard, she looked round at the young people. Her face became stern.

'We want to stay here.' Judith turned to Frieda. 'Please? Please, Frieda.'

'They're quite welcome,' Frieda said to Karlsson. 'If I can do anything to help.'

Louise put her hands on her hips, as if willing to square up to her. 'No. Absolutely not. They're coming home with me. That's what they need. Children, say thank you to this woman for everything she's done.' She looked back at Frieda with a fierce expression. 'They need to be with their family,' she said, in a sort of stage whisper. Then she turned back to the children. 'Now, we're going back to our house, I mean *my* house, and this policewoman is coming with us.'

'No!' said Chloë. 'Frieda, can't you stop this?'

469

'No. I can't.'

'But it's horrible and –'

'Chloë, quiet now.'

Karlsson turned to Yvette. 'Are you going to be all right dealing with this? It'll be difficult.'

'I'll be fine.' Yvette had paled. 'That's what female police officers are for, isn't it? To do the emotional stuff.'

'Not exactly,' said Karlsson.

There was a chaos of bags being picked up and jackets looked for and Chloë being hugged and the three Lennoxes making their way out to Louise's car. They got inside. It was a tight fit, with Yvette sitting in the front seat. Ted's face stared out through the window.

'This doesn't feel right,' said Frieda.

'It's the beginning of the rest of their lives,' said Karlsson. 'They'd better get used to it. Sorry. That came out wrong. But what can we do? They've lost their mother, and now they're losing their father, for the time being at least. They need a family. You can't be that for them.'

'But it's important how they hear about their father,' said Frieda. 'And how they're listened to afterwards.'

'You don't think Yvette can handle it? All right. You don't need to answer that. You'd probably be the person to do it.'

'I didn't say that.'

'I can't ask you,' said Karlsson. 'I'm sorry. Yvette may fuck it up. She probably will. But she'll do her very best, and at least she's on the payroll.' He frowned. 'Can I have a word?'

Frieda glanced at Chloë.

'What?' Chloë's voice was high and harsh.

'I'm going to have to tell you something in a minute,' said Frieda. 'It's about Ted and Judith's father. But, first, Karlsson and I are going out for a few minutes. Is that all right?'

'No! It isn't all right. They're my friends and I have a right to –'

'Chloë.' Frieda spoke in a quiet, warning tone that silenced her niece. She pulled on a jacket and stepped outside.

'You don't mind walking?' she said.

'I'm used to it,' said Karlsson.

Frieda led the way out of the cobbled mews and turned right. When they reached Tottenham Court Road, they stood for a moment and watched the buses and cars careering past them.

'You know,' said Frieda, 'that if you move from the countryside to a big city like London, you increase your chance of developing schizophrenia by five or six times.'

'Why?' said Karlsson.

'Nobody knows. But look at all this. It makes sense, doesn't it? If we abolished cities and went back to living in villages, we'd reduce the incidence of the disease by a third at a stroke.'

'That sounds a bit drastic.'

Frieda turned south, then took a small quiet road off to the right.

'I missed you today,' said Karlsson.

'But you saw me today. Remember? With Hal Bradshaw and your commissioner.'

'Oh, that,' Karlsson said dismissively. 'That was just a farce. No, when Lennox confessed, I actually expected to see you standing there with your beady-eyed expression.'

'But I wasn't. And you seem to have done all right. So what happened?'

As they headed west, Karlsson gave Frieda a brief account of the day's events.

'Will you charge him with manslaughter?'

'Probably. He hears about the relationship. Rushes round in a rage. A father's anger. A jury would probably be sympathetic to that.'

'I don't suppose it matters,' said Frieda, 'but he didn't find out just before he killed Zach. According to Dora, he'd known for some time.'

Karlsson frowned. 'Really? That's not what he said. I'm not sure I want to know that. Oh, well, it probably won't make much difference. He's still an angry father. And we've got the pattern of behaviour. An argument escalates into violence. It's the same thing.'

Frieda stopped. 'Yes. It is the same.'

'You've got a way of saying that that makes it sound suspicious.'

'No. I was just echoing what you were saying.'

'We know that Lennox has a habit of turning violent. Look at him with Paul Kerrigan, we're pretty sure that was him, and even that dealer in stolen goods. Why not his daughter's predatory boyfriend?'

The streetlight shone on Frieda's face, which seemed thin and sad.

'Poor kids,' she said softly. 'With that dreadful aunt.'

'Yes.'

'And what about their mother's murder?'

Karlsson shrugged. 'I'm going to have another go at Lennox,' he said. 'Everything points to him. But it's all so tangled. There's so much rage and grief swilling around the whole affair, so many people who knew or might have known. It was a leaky secret, after all, for all they thought they were being so careful.'

'Tell me.'

'The Kerrigan boys knew,' said Karlsson. 'It turns out that Ruth Lennox – this cheerful, kind woman – turned a bit nasty when she discovered that Paul Kerrigan was going to leave her and she must have sent them a poison-pen letter. Someone did, anyway.'

'Oh,' said Frieda. 'So that changes everything.'

'They knew about the relationship and they knew who it was with. They tracked her down – the younger one even posted a nasty little message through the Lennox letterbox.'

'What did it say?'

'It wasn't in words. It was a rag doll, with its genitals cut out.'

'So it was like a warning.'

'Perhaps – though the wrong person picked it up, as it happens. Also, once a secret's out, it spreads. You can't stop it. Who else did they tell? They swear they didn't mention it to Mrs Kerrigan – but I don't know if I believe them. Those boys adore their mother.'

FIFTY-THREE

She turned on her mobile once more and scrolled down her contacts.

'Agnes?'

'Yes.'

'Frieda here. Sorry to bother you.'

'I'm in a meeting. Is this –'

'It won't take long. Did you know Sharon Gibbs?'

'Sharon Gibbs? Yes. Not very well. We weren't friends – but she lived near us and she was a year below me at school. Lila knew her. I think they hung out with the same crowd after we'd lost touch.'

'Thanks. That's what I wanted to know.'

'But –'

'You go back to your meeting.'

Frieda sat on the bed, looking at the blowing curtain, hearing the sound of life outside. She thought of Sharon Gibbs's face, which had smiled at her from Fearby's crowded wall. His voice came back to her: *Hazel Barton, Roxanne Ingatestone, Daisy Crewe, Philippa Lewis, Maria Horsley, Lila Dawes, Sharon Gibbs.*

When her mobile rang, she reached out to turn it off, then saw it was Fearby calling.

'Sharon knew Lila,' she said.

There was a pause.

'That makes sense,' he said.

'What do you mean?'

'You know that conversation I had with Lawrence Dawes?'

'Yes. You seemed to be getting on pretty well.'

'About being in the same line of work.'

'Selling photocopiers and finding news. I can see the similarity."

'Come on, Frieda. Don't you get it? Being on the road.'

'Being on the road,' Frieda repeated dully. She felt suddenly and overwhelmingly tired. Her pillow looked plump and soft and welcoming.

'I'm a journalist. So what do I do? I go to Copycon – that's the company he worked for. Who'd call a company Copycon? I spoke to the area manager.'

'Did you say who you were?'

'You need to feel your way with these things,' he replied vaguely. 'Make people want to tell you stuff. And he did.'

'What?'

'He told me the area Lawrence Dawes covered until he retired a few months ago.'

Frieda felt clammy and sick. She could feel beads of sweat breaking out on her forehead.

'His own daughter?' she said. 'All those others? Is that possible?'

'Everything fits, Frieda.'

'Why didn't I know?'

'Why would you?'

'Because – are you sure?'

'I'm not sure. But I *know.*'

'Where are you?'

'Near Victoria.'

'Good. We've got to get hold of Karlsson.'

'Karlsson?'

'He's a police officer. Quite senior.'

'I'm not sure we're ready to go to the police yet, Frieda.'

'We can't wait. What if he does it again?'

'They'll need more than we've got. Believe me, I know them.'

'So do I,' said Frieda. 'Karlsson will listen. I can't explain – but he owes me. Anyway.' She remembered the note he'd pushed through her door. 'He's a friend.'

Fearby still sounded unsure. 'Where do you want to meet?'

'At the station.' She looked at her radio clock. 'In about forty-five minutes. Three o'clock. Is that good?'

'I'll get there as soon as I can.'

She gave him the address and ended the call. Her tiredness had lifted. She felt glitteringly awake and alert. Only her eyes throbbed, as if the migraines she had had as a teenager had reappeared. Lawrence Dawes. She had sat in his lovely, well-tended garden. She had drunk tea with him. Shaken his hand and looked into his weathered face. Heard the pain in his voice. How had she not known? She put her head into her hands, feeling the relief of darkness.

Then she swiftly pulled on baggy linen trousers and a soft cotton shirt, dropped her keys into her bag and left.

Fearby was waiting for her. Approaching him, Frieda was struck by how odd he looked, with his long white hair and those eyes that glared from his creviced face. He was more crumpled than ever, as if he'd been sleeping rough. He

476

seemed to be talking to himself and when he saw her he simply continued with the sentence.

'. . . so I have a few of the folders in my car but of course we can collect everything else later, and there are still some notes I haven't typed up –'

'Let's go in,' said Frieda. She put her arm under his sharp elbow and pulled him through the revolving door.

Karlsson was in a meeting, but when he heard that Dr Frieda Klein was downstairs he left it and bounded into Reception to meet her. She was standing very upright in the centre of the hall and her face was set in an expression of determination that he recognized from the old days. Beside her was a man who resembled a moth-eaten bird of prey. He was carrying several plastic bags bulging with folders and holding a tape recorder. Karlsson didn't connect him to Frieda. He looked like one of the obsessive people who wandered into the station to disclose lunatic conspiracies to the indifferent duty officer behind the desk.

'Come into my office,' he said.

'This is Jim Fearby. He's a journalist. Jim, this is DCI Malcolm Karlsson.'

Karlsson put out a hand but Fearby had none to spare. He simply nodded twice and stared fiercely into Karlsson's face.

'We need to speak to you,' Frieda said to Karlsson.

'Is this about Hal Bradshaw?'

'That's not important right now.'

'Actually, it is quite important.'

Karlsson ushered them into his room and pulled up

two chairs for them. Frieda sat but Fearby put his bags on the chair, then stood behind it.

'Hal Bradshaw has made it quite clear that –'

'No,' Fearby said harshly, the first word Karlsson had heard from him. 'Listen to her.'

'Mr Fearby –'

'You'll understand in a minute,' said Frieda. 'At least, I hope you will.'

'Go on, then.'

'We believe that a man called Lawrence Dawes, who lives down near Croydon, has abducted and murdered at least six young women, including his own daughter.'

There was silence. Karlsson didn't move. His face was expressionless.

'Karlsson? Did you hear?'

When he finally responded it was in a tone of deep dismay. 'Frieda. What have you been doing?'

'I've been trying to trace a missing girl,' said Frieda, steadily.

'Why don't I know about this? Is there an ongoing murder inquiry that I've somehow missed?'

'I told you they wouldn't believe you,' said Fearby.

'You have to listen to me.' Frieda fixed Karlsson with her bright gaze. 'There's no inquiry because no one has made the connection. Except Jim Fearby.'

'But how did you get involved?'

'It was something that that fake patient of Hal Bradshaw's told me.'

'The one who shafted you?'

'That's irrelevant. I don't care about it any more. There was a detail that stood out and I couldn't get it out of my mind. It haunted me. I had to find out what it meant.'

Karlsson looked at Frieda and the dishevelled character with her. He felt a lurch of pity.

'I know it sounds irrational,' she continued. 'At first I thought I was going crazy and it was just a projection of my own feelings. But I traced where the story came from. I went from the man who'd been sent to me by Hal to the other three researchers. I met Rajit, who had got the story from his girlfriend. I found her and she told me it had come from her old friend, Lila. And then I discovered that Lila had gone missing.'

Karlsson held up his hand. 'Why didn't you say anything? Why didn't you come to me, Frieda?'

'I knew what everyone says: people go missing all the time and they don't want to be found. But this felt different to me. I met Lila's friend and then this man Lila had spent time with just before she disappeared. Nasty character. Dodgy, violent, creepy. That was where I met Jim.'

'Who was also looking for Lila?' asked Karlsson.

'I was looking for Sharon.'

'Sharon?'

'Another missing girl.'

'I see.'

'And all the others, of course. But it was Sharon who led me there.' He smiled suddenly. 'And that was where I met Frieda.'

Karlsson looked at Fearby. He reminded him of the drunks who sometimes slept the night in the police cells. He smelt a bit like them too: the thick reek of whisky and stale tobacco. Frieda saw his expression.

479

'You should have heard of Jim Fearby,' she said. 'He was the journalist who got George Conley's murder conviction overturned.'

Karlsson turned to Fearby with new interest. 'That was you?'

'So you can see why I've mixed feelings about the police.'

'Why are you here now?'

'Frieda told me to come. She said you'd help.'

'I said you'd listen,' said Frieda.

'We think Lila's father is responsible.' Fearby walked round the desk and stood beside Karlsson, who could hear him breathing heavily. 'For his daughter and Sharon and the others.'

'Lawrence Dawes,' said Frieda.

'This is the man in Croydon?'

'Yes.'

'You're asking me to believe that the two of you have discovered that a man is responsible for several murders that the police didn't even know had been committed?'

'Yes.' Fearby glared at Karlsson.

'The girls went missing,' Frieda said. She was trying to speak as clearly and logically as she could. 'And because they lived in different places and no bodies were found, there was no connection made between them.'

Karlsson sighed. 'Why do you think this Lawrence Dawes is the killer?'

Fearby went back to the other side of the desk and started rummaging in the bags for something. 'The real maps are in my house, but I did this for you. So you'd see.'

He brandished a sheet of paper on which he'd drawn, very messily, a map of the route between London and Manchester, with asterisks where the various missing women had disappeared.

'It's all right, Mr Fearby.'

'You don't believe us.' Frieda spoke quietly.

'Look. Try to see it from my point of view. Or the commissioner's.'

'No. It doesn't matter. You don't believe us but I still want you to help me.'

'How?'

'I want you to go and interview Lawrence Dawes. And search his house, every room. And the cellar. I think there's a cellar. And his garden, too. You'll find something.'

'I can't just send a team of police officers to take a house apart on your suspicions.'

Frieda had been watching him attentively as he spoke. Now her expression closed; her face became a blank. 'You owe me,' she said.

'Sorry.'

'You owe me.' She heard her voice, cool and hard. It wasn't how she was feeling. 'I nearly died because of you. So you owe me. I'm calling in a favour.'

'I see.'

Karlsson stood up. He was trying to hide his angry distress and turned his back on Frieda and Fearby as he put on his jacket and slid his mobile into his pocket.

'You'll do it?' Frieda asked.

'I do owe you, Frieda. And, also, you're my friend. So I

trust you as well, in spite of the apparent wildness of this. But you understand this might backfire?'

'Yes.'

'On me, I mean.'

Frieda met his gaze. She could have wept at his expression. 'Yes, I understand.'

'All right.'

'I can't come with –'

'No.'

'Will you let me know?'

He let his eyes meet hers. 'Yes, Frieda. I'll let you know.'

As they left his room, a familiar figure approached them.

'Oh, shit,' Karlsson hissed.

'Malcolm,' said the commissioner. His face was red with anger. 'A word.'

'Yes? I'm on my way to see Mr Lennox. Can this wait?'

'No, it cannot wait. There was a report.' He pointed a quivering finger. 'Her contract was terminated. There's this scandal with Hal. You know what I think. What the flaming hell is she doing here?'

'She's been an important –'

'Do you realize what this looks like?'

Karlsson didn't reply.

'Have you paid her?' Crawford jabbed Karlsson and, for a terrible moment, Frieda thought there might be a fight between Karlsson and his boss. She winced with the fresh knowledge of how he had risked himself for her.

'Commissioner, as you must be aware, Dr Klein has been very helpful to us and –'

'*Have you paid her?*'

'No, I haven't been paid.' Frieda stepped forward. Her voice was cold. 'I'm just here as a member of the public.'

'What the hell are you doing, then?'

'I came to see DCI Karlsson on a purely private matter. As a friend.'

Crawford raised his eyebrows. 'Careful, Mal,' he said. 'I'm paying attention.' And he noticed Fearby. 'Who's *that*?'

'This is my colleague, Jim Fearby,' said Frieda. 'We were both leaving.'

'Don't let me stop you.'

At the entrance, Fearby turned to Frieda. 'That went well, after all.'

'It went terribly,' Frieda said dully. 'I abused my friendship with Karlsson and lied to the commissioner.'

'If we achieve what we're after,' said Fearby, 'none of that matters.'

'And if we don't?'

'Then it doesn't matter either.'

As they left, they met a woman coming in – middle-aged and tall, with long brown hair and wearing a long patchwork skirt. Frieda was struck by her expression of fierce purpose.

FIFTY-FOUR

'I'd like to see Malcolm Karlsson,' said the woman, speaking loud and fast.

'I think DCI Karlsson is rather busy at the moment. Do you have –'

'Or Yvette Long. Or that other one.'

'Can you tell me what it's about?'

'My name is Elaine Kerrigan. It's about the murder of Ruth Lennox. There is something I need to say.'

Yvette sat opposite Elaine Kerrigan. She saw the hectic blotches on the woman's normally pale cheeks and the brightness of her eyes. Her glasses, hanging round her neck on a chain, were smudged and her hair hadn't been brushed.

'You told the officer on the desk there was something you needed to say.'

'Yes.'

'About the murder of Ruth Lennox?'

'That's right. Can I have a glass of water first, please?'

Yvette left the room and bumped into Karlsson. He looked awful and she touched him on the elbow. 'Are you OK?'

'Why wouldn't I be?'

'No reason. I'm in there –' she jerked her head in the direction of the room '– with Elaine Kerrigan.'

'What for?'

'I don't know. I'm just going to get her some water. She seems agitated.'

'Does she indeed?'

'Have you finished with Russell Lennox?'

'I'm taking a break for an hour or so. It won't do him any harm to wait and worry.' His face grew grim. 'There's something I have to do.'

'What's that?'

'You wouldn't understand. You'd think I'd gone mad. Sometimes I think I've gone mad myself.'

There was nothing to do but wait. Fearby said he had people he needed to see while he was in London and drove off once more, leaving Frieda unsure of what to do with herself. In the end she did what she always did at times of uncertainty or distress, when dark thoughts filled her: she walked. She found herself going towards King's Cross, weaving along minor streets to avoid the roar of traffic, then took the road that led to Camden Town, which made her think again of the house where the Lennox family used to live, in clutter and a sort of happiness, but which now stood empty. Russell was in prison; Ted, Judith and Dora were at their aunt's house, many miles away. At least it was neat.

She turned on to the canal. The houseboats moored by the path had pot plants and herbs on their decks. On a couple of them dogs lay in the sunshine; on one, Frieda saw a parrot in a large cage, eyeing her. Some were open to the public, selling banana bread and tie-dye scarves, herbal tea and recycled jewellery. People passed her on bikes; runners pounded by. Summer was coming. She could feel it in the warm air, see it in the thin brightness of the light and the sappy greenness of unfolding leaves on the trees. Soon Sandy would be back and they would have weeks together, not days.

She thought these things but couldn't feel them. Indeed, the clear light and the happy people seemed unreal, far off, and she belonged to a different world – one in which young women had been dragged out of their lives by a man who had a smiling, sympathetic face. He had killed his daughter, Lila, Frieda was sure of it now – and yet he had seemed genuinely grief-struck by her absence. A piece of chalked graffiti on the wall showed a huge mouth full of sharp teeth, and she shuddered, suddenly cold in spite of the warmth of the afternoon.

She walked along the canal as far as Regent's Park. The houses on the other side were grand here, like small castles or mock châteaux. Who would live in such places? She walked through the park swiftly, scarcely noticing the gaggles of children, the courting couples, the young man with closed eyes doing some strange slow exercises on a roll-out mattress by the ornamental gardens.

At last, making her way through side streets, she was at home. The phone was ringing as she opened the door and she half ran to get it, in case it was Karlsson.

'Frieda? Thank God. Where the fuck –'

'Reuben, I can't talk now. I'm waiting for a call. I promise I'll phone you as soon as I can, all right?'

'Wait, did you hear about Bradshaw?'

'Sorry.'

She slammed the phone down. How long would it take

for Karlsson to go to Lawrence Dawes's house? When would he call? Now? This evening? Tomorrow?

She made herself some toast and marmalade and ate it in the living room, listening to the phone ringing over and over and the answering machine playing messages: Chloë, plaintive; Sasha, anxious; Reuben, furious; Sandy – oh, God, Sandy. She hadn't even told him what she was up to. She'd gone into a different world, of terror and darkness, and hadn't even thought to confide in him. She didn't pick up, but let him leave his message asking her, yet again, to contact him, *please*. Josef, drunk; Olivia, drunker.

The day darkened and still Karlsson hadn't called. Frieda went upstairs to her study and sat at the desk that looked out over the great sprawl of the city, now lit up and glittering under the clear sky. In the countryside, the sky tonight would be thick with stars. She picked up her pencil and opened her sketch pad, made a few indeterminate lines, like ripples. She thought of the stream at the bottom of Lawrence Dawes's garden.

Perhaps she should have that long-delayed bath now. She was as tired as she had ever been, but far from sleep. Indeed, it felt as though sleep would never come again and she was trapped for ever in this dry, hissing wakefulness where thoughts were knives.

And then the phone rang again.

'Yes?'

'Frieda.'

'Karlsson? What did you find?'

'Nothing.'

'That's not possible.'

'One very bewildered and distressed father, and a house

487

in which there is no evidence of any kind whatsoever that he has ever done anything wrong.'

'I don't understand.'

'Don't you? I felt very sorry for him.'

'Something's not right.'

'Frieda, I think you need help.'

'Are you sure there was nothing at all?'

'Listen to me. You have to walk away from all of this. And I need to placate the commissioner, who's not a happy man, I can tell you. He wants to drag me in front of some official hearing.'

'I'm sorry about that but –'

'Draw a line under everything.' His voice was horribly gentle. 'No more following your instincts. No more trying to rescue people who don't want to be rescued. No more teaming up with some mad old hack. Go back to the life we dragged you out of. Try and recover.'

He ended the call and Frieda sat for a long time in her garret room, staring at the kaleidoscope of lights spread out before her.

Dear Sandy, I think I am in trouble, in the world and in my head or my heart –

But she stared at the few words for a long time and then pressed the delete button.

Karlsson and Yvette sat in front of Elaine Kerrigan. Her face was unyielding and she repeated, in a wooden tone: 'I killed her.'

'Ruth Lennox?'

'Yes.'

'Tell me how it happened,' said Karlsson. 'When did you discover your husband's affair?'

'Why does it matter? I killed her.'

'Did your sons tell you?'

'Yes.' She took a sip of water. 'They told me and I went there and killed her.'

'With what?'

'An object,' she said. 'I can't remember. I can't remember anything except I killed her.'

'Take us through it,' said Yvette. 'We have plenty of time. Start from the beginning.'

'She's protecting her sons,' said Karlsson.

'So you think one of them did it?'

'She does, anyway.'

'And you?'

'Fuck knows. Maybe everyone joined up together to do it, like in that book.'

'I thought you believed it was Russell Lennox.'

'I'm sick of this case. It's too full of misery. Come on, let's get a coffee. Then you're going home. I don't know when you last had any sleep.'

FIFTY-FIVE

Frieda phoned Fearby and told him what had happened – or hadn't happened. There was a pause and then he said he was still in London and he was coming right over. Frieda gave him her address, then tried to tell him it wasn't necessary, that there was nothing more to say, but he had already rung off. In what seemed like a few minutes, there was a knock at the door and Fearby was sitting opposite her with a glass of whisky. He asked her to tell him exactly what Karlsson had said. Frieda reacted impatiently.

'It doesn't matter,' she said.

'What do you mean?'

'They went to Lawrence Dawes's house. They turned it upside down. They didn't find anything suspicious at all.'

'How did Dawes react?'

'You know what? I didn't ask. The police appeared out of the blue and searched his house and all but accused him of killing his daughter. I imagine he was shocked and distressed.' Frieda felt a tiredness that was actually painful. 'I can't believe it. I sat in his garden with him and he talked about what he'd been through and I set the police on him. Karlsson is furious with me as well. And rightly so.'

'So where do we go from here?' said Fearby.

'Where do we go? We go nowhere. I'm sorry, but are you incapable of seeing what's in front of your nose?'

'Have you stopped trusting your instincts?'

'It was my instinct that got us into this.'

'Not just your instinct,' said Fearby. 'I'd been following a trail and we found we were on the same trail. Doesn't that mean anything to you?'

Frieda sat back in her chair and sighed. 'Have you ever been out in the countryside and you were walking on a path and then you realized it wasn't really a path at all, it just looked like one, and you were lost?'

Fearby smiled and shook his head. 'I never was much for walking.'

'For all we know, Sharon Gibbs is somewhere reasonably happy, not wanting to be found. But, whatever the truth, I think we're done.'

Fearby shook his head again, but he didn't seem dismayed or angry. 'I've been doing this too long to get put off by something like this. I just need to go over my files again, make some more enquiries. I'm not going to give up now, not after all I've done.'

Frieda looked at him with a kind of horror. Was he a bit like her? Was this the way she appeared to other people? 'What would it take for you to give up?'

'Nothing,' said Fearby. 'Not after all this, after what George Conley suffered, after Hazel Barton's murder.'

'But what about what you've suffered? Your marriage, your career?'

'If I give up now, that won't bring my job back. Or my wife.'

Suddenly Frieda felt as if she was trapped in a disastrous therapy session where she couldn't find the right thing to say. Should she try to convince Fearby that everything he had sacrificed his life for had been an illusion?

Did she even believe it? 'You've already done so much,' she said. 'You got George Conley out of prison. That's enough.'

Fearby's expression hardened. 'I need to know the truth. Nothing else matters.' He caught Frieda's eye and gave a slightly embarrassed smile. 'Just think of it as my hobby. It's what I do instead of having an allotment or playing golf.'

When Fearby got up to go, Frieda felt as if she was someone he had sat next to on a train journey and struck up a conversation with and now they were arriving at the station and would part and never meet again. They shook hands at the door.

'I'll let you know how things progress,' he said. 'Even if you don't want me to.'

When Fearby was gone, Frieda leaned against her door for a few minutes. She felt as if she needed to catch her breath but couldn't, as if her lungs wouldn't work properly. She forced herself to concentrate and take long, slow breaths.

Then, at last, she went up to her bathroom. She'd been waiting for the right time but there was never a right time. There was always something left to do. She thought of Josef, her shambolic and eager friend, all the work he'd put into this for her. It was his act of friendship. She had good friends, but she hadn't turned to them, not even to Sandy. She could listen but she couldn't talk; give help but not ask for it. It was strange that in the last days she had felt closer to Fearby, with his neglected home, his huge filing system and his wreck of a life, than she had to anyone else.

The doorbell rang and for a moment she thought she wouldn't answer. But then, with a sigh, she turned away from the bath, and went to the front door.

'Delivery for you,' said the man, half obscured by a tall cardboard box. 'Frieda Klein?'

'Yes.'

'Sign here, please.'

Frieda signed and took the box into the living room, levering open its top. As she did so, she was hit by a smell whose powerful sweetness reminded her of funeral parlours and hotel lobbies. Carefully, she lifted out an enormous bouquet of white lilies, tied at the bottom with purple ribbon. She had always hated lilies: they were too opulent for her and their fragrance seemed to clog her airways. But who had sent them?

There was a miniature envelope with the flowers and she opened it and slid out the card.

We couldn't let him get away with it.

The world narrowed, the air cooled around her. *We couldn't let him get away with it.*

Bile rose in her throat and her forehead was clammy. She put out one hand to steady herself, made herself breathe deeply. She knew who had sent her these flowers. Dean Reeve. He had sent her daffodils before, telling her it wasn't her time, and now he had sent her these lush, pulpy lilies. He had set fire to Hal Bradshaw's house. For her. She pressed her hand hard against her furious heart. What could she do? Where could she turn? Who would believe her, and who would be able to help?

She had a sickening sense that she had to do something, or talk to someone. That was what she believed in, wasn't it? Talking to people. But who? Once it would have been Reuben. But their relationship wasn't like that any more. She couldn't talk to Sandy because he was in America and these weren't things to be put into words on the phone. What about Sasha? Or even Josef? Wasn't that what friends were for? No. It wouldn't work. She couldn't find the proper explanation, but she felt it would be a betrayal of their friendship. She needed someone outside everything.

Then she remembered someone. She went to the bin outside her house and thrust the flowers into it. Back inside, she rummaged through her shoulder bag but it wasn't there. She went upstairs to her study. She pulled open one of the drawers of her desk. When she cleared out her bag, she either threw things away or kept them here. She went through the old postcards, receipts, letters, photographs, invitations, and found it. A business card. When Frieda had faced a medical disciplinary panel, she had encountered one kindly face. Thelma Scott was a therapist herself and she had immediately seen something in Frieda that Frieda hadn't wanted to be seen. She had invited Frieda to come and talk to her any time she felt the need and given Frieda her card. Frieda had been sure that she would never take her up on the offer, almost angry at the suggestion, but still she had kept it. She dialled the number, her hands almost trembling.

'Hello? Yes? I'm sorry to call at this time. You probably won't remember me. My name is Frieda Klein.'

'Of course I remember you.' Her voice sounded firm, reassuring.

'This is really stupid, and you've probably forgotten

this as well, but you once came to see me and you said I could come and talk to you if I needed it. I was just wondering if at some point I could do that. But if that's not convenient, then it's completely all right. I can find someone else to talk to.'

'Can you come tomorrow?'

'Yes, yes, that would be possible. But there's no hurry. I don't want to force myself on you.'

'What about four o'clock, the day after tomorrow?'

'Four o'clock. Yes, that would be fine. Good. I'll see you then.'

Frieda got into bed. She spent most of the night not sleeping, besieged by faces and images, by fears and dark, pounding dread. But she must have slept a bit, because she was woken by a sound that at first she didn't recognize, then gradually realized was her mobile phone. She fumbled for it and saw the name Jim Fearby on it. She let it ring. She couldn't bear to talk to him. She lay back in the bed and thought of Fearby and had a sudden vivid, sickening, flashing sense of what it would be like to be mad, really mad, finding your own hidden meanings in a chaotic world. She thought of the troubled, sad people who came to her for help, and then the even more troubled, sadder people who were beyond anything she could do, the people who had voices in their heads telling them about conspiracies, how everything made horrible, terrifying sense.

Frieda looked at her clock. It was a couple of minutes after seven. Fearby must have waited for a permissible time to ring her. She got up and had a cold shower, so cold it made her ache. She pulled on some jeans and a shirt and made herself coffee. She couldn't face anything else. What if Fearby had left a message? She didn't even want to hear his voice, but now she'd thought of it, she couldn't stop herself. She retrieved the phone from upstairs and called her voicemail. He probably wouldn't have said anything. But he had.

The message began with a nervous cough, like someone starting a speech without knowing quite what to say.

'Erm. Frieda. It's me. Jim. Sorry about everything yesterday. I should have thanked you for all you've done. I know I come over as a bit of a nutter. And an obsessive. Anyway, I said I'd keep you in touch. Which is probably not what you want to hear. I'm in London. I've been going over things, the files on the girls. I've had a thought. We weren't thinking about them properly. We didn't hear the engine. I'm going out to have another look. Then I'll call round to you and fill you in. I'll be there at two. Let me know if that's no good. Sorry to go on so long. Cheers.'

Frieda almost wished she hadn't heard the message. She felt she was being sucked back in. It was clear that Fearby would never let go. Like those people obsessed with the Freemasons or the Kennedy assassination, he would never give up and nothing would change his mind. She was tempted to ring him back and tell him not to come but then she thought: No. He could come one last time and she would hear what he had to say and respond rationally and that would be that.

The day was almost as much of a blur as the night had been. Frieda thought she might read a book but she knew she couldn't concentrate. Normally at a time like this she would have done a drawing, of something simple, like a glass of water or a candle. She didn't even want to go out, not in the daytime, with the people and the traffic noise. She decided to clean her house. That would do. Something that required no thought. She filled bucket after bucket with hot water and cleaning fluid and took objects off shelves and wiped them down. She sprayed the windows. She mopped floors. She polished surfaces. The more she cleaned, the more she had a comforting sense that nobody lived in the house or had lived there or had ever been there.

The phone rang periodically, but she didn't answer. She didn't know whether it had been a surprisingly long time or a surprisingly short time, but she looked up at the clock and saw it was five to two. She sat in a chair and waited. There was going to be no coffee. Certainly no whisky. He could say what he had to say, she would respond, and he could go. Then it would be over, and she could go to talk to Thelma Scott and start to deal with all of this because it just couldn't go on.

One minute past two. Nothing. She actually went to the door and opened it and stepped out. As if that would help. She sat back down. Ten past, nothing. Quarter past, nothing. At twenty past, she called Fearby and went straight to his voicemail.

'I was wondering where you were. I need to go out soon. Well, not that soon. I'll be here until half past four.'

She thought he might be one of the people who had called during the day. There were fourteen messages on her answering machine. They were the usual suspects: Reuben, Josef, Sasha, someone about a possible patient, Paz, Karlsson, Yvette. She tried her voicemail. Nothing.

497

For the next half-hour she answered the phone three times. One was a fake survey, one was Reuben, one was Karlsson. Each time she said she couldn't talk. By three o'clock she was genuinely puzzled. Had she got the time wrong? She'd deleted Fearby's message as soon as she'd heard it. Was it possible she had misheard? God knew, she hadn't been thinking all that clearly. Was it really two o'clock? Yes, she was sure about that. He'd even said that if she couldn't make that time, she should ring back. Could he just be late? Caught in traffic? Or maybe he had decided not to come. He might have drawn a blank and headed home. Or he might have picked up on her scepticism. She phoned his number again. Nothing. He wasn't coming.

At last she gave up on Fearby. She put food in the cat's bowl and then she walked to Number 9 for coffee. As she was returning, she saw a figure walking towards her. Something about the heavy-footed purposeful stride was familiar.

'Yvette?' she said, as they drew close to each other. 'What is it? Why are you here?'

'I've got to talk to you.'

'What's happened?'

'Can we go inside?'

She led Yvette into the house. Yvette took off her jacket and sat down. She was wearing black jeans with a hole in the knee and a button-down man's shirt that had seen better days. Clearly, she wasn't on duty.

'So what is it? Is it something about the Lennoxes?'

'No, I'm taking a well-earned break from that bloody

circus. You wouldn't believe – but anyway. That's not why I'm here.'

'So why are you?'

'I had to tell you: I'm on your side.'

'What?'

'I'm on your side,' Yvette repeated. She seemed close to tears.

'Thank you. But on my side against who?'

'All of them. The commissioner. That wanker Hal Bradshaw.'

'Oh, that.'

'I needed you to know. I know you had nothing to do with it, but if you had – well, I'd still be on your side.' She gave a crooked, emotional smile. 'Off the record, of course.'

Frieda stared at her. 'You think I might have done it,' she said at last.

Yvete flushed. 'No! That's not what I was saying at all. But it's not a secret that you and Dr McGill were angry with him. You had every reason. He shafted you. He was just jealous.'

'I promise you,' Frieda said softly, 'that I haven't been near Hal Bradshaw's house.'

'Of course you haven't.'

'It was a monstrous thing to do. And I know that Reuben wouldn't do that, however angry he was.'

'Bradshaw said something else as well.'

'What?'

'You know what he's like, Frieda. Insinuating.'

'Just tell me.'

'He said that he had some dangerous enemies, even if they didn't do their own dirty work.'

'Meaning me?'

'Yes. But also that he has some powerful friends.'

'Good for him,' said Frieda.

'Don't you care?'

'Not so much,' said Frieda. 'But what I want to know is why you do.'

'You mean why should I care?'

She looked steadily at Yvette. 'You haven't always looked after my best interests.'

Yvette didn't look away. 'I have dreams about you,' she said, in a low voice. 'Not the kind of dreams you'd expect, not dreams where you're nearly killed or stuff like that. These are odder. Once I dreamed we were at school together – though we were our real age – and sitting next to each other in class, and I was trying to write neatly to impress you but I just kept smearing the ink and couldn't form the letters correctly. They were crooked and childish and kept sliding off the page, and yours were perfect and neat. Don't worry, I'm not asking you to interpret my dreams. I'm not so stupid I can't do that myself. In another dream, we were on holiday and were by a lake surrounded by mountains that looked like chimneys, and I was really nervous because we were about to dive in the water but I didn't know how to swim. Actually, I can't really swim – I don't like getting my head underwater. But I couldn't tell you because I thought you'd laugh at me. I was going to drown so I didn't look like a fool in front of you.'

Frieda was about to speak, but Yvette held up a hand. Her cheeks were crimson. 'You make me feel completely inadequate,' she said, 'and as if you can look into me and see through me and know all the things I don't want people to see. You know I'm lonely and you know I'm jealous of you and you know I'm crap at relationships. And you know . . .' Her cheeks burned. 'You know I've got a schoolgirl crush on the boss. The other night I got a bit drunk, and I kept imagining what you'd think of me if you could see me lurching around.'

'But, Yvette –'

'The fact is that I nearly let you get killed, and when I'm not having dreams I've been lying awake and wondering if I did it out of some pathetic anger. And how do you think that makes me feel about myself?'

'So you're making amends?' Frieda asked softly.

'I guess you could call it that.'

'Thank you.'

Frieda held out her hand and Yvette took it, and for a moment the two women sat across the table from each other, holding hands and gazing into the other's face.

FIFTY-SIX

Frieda was dreaming about Sandy. He was smiling at her and holding out his hand to her, and then Frieda, in her dream, realized it wasn't Sandy at all – that it was actually Dean's face, Dean's soft smile. She woke with a lurch and lay for several minutes, taking deep breaths and waiting for the dread to subside.

At last, she rose, showered, and went into the kitchen. Chloë was already sitting at the table. There was a mug of untouched tea and what looked like a large album in front of her. She was bedraggled, her hair unbrushed and her face grimy with yesterday's mascara. She looked as though she had hardly slept for nights. She was like an abandoned waif – her mother was going through a messy crisis and barely thought about her, her friends had been taken away from her, and her aunt had absented herself at her time of need. She lifted her smudged, tear-stained face and stared blindly at her.

Frieda took a seat opposite her. 'Are you OK?'

'I guess.'

'Can I get you some breakfast?'

'No. I'm not hungry. Oh, God, Frieda, I can't stop thinking about it all.'

'Of course not.'

'I didn't want to wake you.'

'How are you feeling?'

'I was lying in bed and I kept imagining what they were feeling at that very moment. They've lost everything. Their mother, their father, their belief in their past happiness. How do they ever get back to an ordinary kind of life after this?'

'I don't know.'

'What about you?'

'I didn't sleep so well either. I was thinking about things.' Frieda walked across the kitchen and filled the kettle. She looked at her niece, who had her head propped on her hand and was dreamily staring at the pages of the album in front of her.

'What is that?' she asked.

'Ted left his portfolio. I'll give it back to him but first I've been looking through it. He's an amazing artist. I wish I was just a tenth, a hundredth as good as he is. I wish –' She stopped and bit her lip.

'Chloë. This has been hard for you.'

'Don't worry,' she said harshly. 'I know he just thinks of me as a friend. A shoulder to cry on. Not that he does cry on it.'

'And probably,' said Frieda, 'your own feelings are rather complicated because of everything he's been through.'

'What d'you mean?'

'I mean there's something extremely attractive about a young man who's so surrounded by tragedy.'

'Like I'm a grief tourist?'

'Not exactly.'

'It's all over now,' said Chloë. Her eyes filled with tears and she went on staring at the book in front of her.

Frieda leaned over her shoulder as she turned the large pages. She saw a beautifully exact drawing of an apple, a bulbous self-portrait as reflected in a convex mirror, a painstakingly precise tree. 'He's good,' she said.

'Wait,' said Chloë. 'There's one I want to show you.' She leafed over page after page until she was almost at the end. 'Look.'

'What is it?'

'Look at the date. Wednesday, the sixth of April, nine thirty a.m. That's the still-life drawing he had to do for his mock A level. It's also the drawing he did on the day his mother was killed. It almost makes me cry just to look at it, to think of what was about to happen.'

'It's beautiful,' said Frieda, and then she frowned, turning her head slightly. She heard the kettle click behind her. The water had boiled. But she couldn't attend to it. Not now.

'It bloody is,' said Chloë, 'it –'

'Wait a moment,' said Frieda. 'Describe it to me. Tell me what's in it.'

'Why?'

'Just do it.'

'All right. There's a watch and a bunch of keys and a book and an electric plug thing and then . . .'

'Yes?'

'There's something leaning on the book.'

'What is it?'

'I can't tell.'

'Describe it.'

'It's sort of straight, and notched, like a sort of metal ruler.'

Frieda concentrated for a moment in silence, so hard that her head hurt.

'Is that what it is?' she said finally. 'Or what it looks like?'

'What do you mean?' said Chloe. 'What's the difference? It's just a drawing.' She slammed the portfolio shut. 'I need to take it into school,' she said. 'To give to Ted.'

'He won't be at school,' said Frieda. 'And, anyway. I need that book today.'

Karlsson stood in front of her but he didn't look at her. 'I wasn't expecting you,' he said at last.

'I know. This won't take long.'

'You don't understand, Frieda. You shouldn't be here. The commissioner doesn't want you here. And you'll not make your case any better with Hal Bradshaw if you start hanging round the station. He already thinks you're an arsonist and a stalker.'

'I know. I won't come again,' said Frieda, steadily. 'I want to see the murder weapon.'

'As a favour? But you've called in the favour, Frieda. And I'm in huge trouble now. I won't bother you with the details.'

'I'm very sorry,' said Frieda. 'But I need to see it. And then I'll go away.'

He stared at her, then shrugged and led her down the stairs into a basement room, where he opened a metal drawer.

'This is what you want,' he said. 'Don't put fingerprints on it, and let yourself out when you've finished.'

'Thank you.'

'By the way, Elaine Kerrigan has confessed to the murder of Ruth Lennox.'

'What?'

'Don't worry. I think Russell Lennox is about to confess as well. And the Kerrigan sons. The whole station will be full of people confessing and we still won't know.'

And he left.

Frieda pulled on plastic gloves and lifted out the large cog, placing it on the table in the centre of the room. It looked as if it should be in the machinery of a giant clock, but the Lennoxes had had it on their mantelpiece as a sort of sculpture.

She opened Ted's art book at the page dated Wednesday, 6 April and put it on the table as well. She stared from cog to drawing so hard that everything began to blur. She stood back. She walked round the table so that she could see the cog from every angle. She squatted on the floor and squinted up at it. Very delicately, she tipped the object, swivelled it, held it so that it flattened out in her view.

And then at last she had it. Viewed at a certain angle, levered back and twisted, the heft object looked like a straight notched line. The same straight and notched line that she could see among the items that Ted had drawn for his mock art A level, on the morning of Wednesday, 6 April.

Frieda's face became expressionless. At last she gave a small sigh, put the cog back into the metal drawer, which she slid shut, pulled off the gloves and left the room.

FIFTY-SEVEN

Louise Weller and her family lived in Fulham, in a narrow red-brick terraced house set slightly back from the long, straight road, lined with plane trees and regulated by speed humps. The bow windows downstairs had lace curtains, to prevent anyone looking in, and the door was dark blue with a brass knocker in the middle. Frieda rapped on it three times, then stood back. The spring weather had turned cooler, and she felt a few welcome drops of rain on her hot skin.

The door opened and Louise Weller stood in front of her, holding a baby to her chest. Behind her the hall was dark and clean. Frieda could smell drying clothes and detergent. She remembered Karlsson telling her about the sick husband and imagined him lying in one of the rooms upstairs, listening.

'Yes? Oh – it's you. What are you doing here?'

'Can I come in, please?'

'This is probably not a good time. I'm about to feed Benjy.'

'It's not you I've come to see.'

'They don't need to be disturbed. They need stability now, a bit of peace.'

'Just for a moment, then,' said Frieda, politely, and stepped past Louise Weller into the hall. 'Are they all here?'

'Where else would they be? It's a bit cramped, of course.'

'I mean, all here at the moment.'

'Yes. But I don't want them troubled.'

'I'd like a word with Ted.'

'Ted? Why? I'm not sure that's appropriate.'

'I'll be brief.'

Louse Weller stared at her, then shrugged. 'I'll call him,' she said stiffly. 'If he wants to see you. Come through into the drawing room.'

She opened the door beside them and Frieda stepped into the front room with the bow window. It was too hot and had too much furniture in it, too many little tables and straight-backed chairs. There was a doll's buggy parked by the radiator, with a flaxen-haired blue-eyed doll propped in it. She found it hard to breathe.

'Frieda?'

'Dora!'

The girl's face had a greeny pallor and there was a cold sore at the corner of her mouth. Her hair wasn't in its usual plaits but hung limply around her face. She was wearing an old-fashioned white blouse and looked, thought Frieda, like a figure in a Victorian melodrama: pitiable, abandoned, acutely distressed.

'Have you come to take us away?' Dora asked her.

'No. I've come to see Ted.'

'Please can we go to yours?'

'I'm sorry. It's not possible.' Frieda hesitated, taking in Dora's scrawny frame and her pinched, dejected face.

'Why?'

'Your aunt is your guardian. She'll take care of you now.'

'Please. Please don't let us stay here.'

'Sit down,' said Frieda. She took Dora's hand, a parcel of bones, between both hers and gazed into the girl's eyes. 'I'm so very sorry, Dora,' she said. 'I'm sorry about your mother, and I'm sorry about your father. I'm sorry you're here, not with people you love – though I'm sure your aunt loves you in her way.'

'No,' whispered Dora. 'No. She doesn't. She tells me off about mess and she makes me feel like I'm in her way all the time. I can't even cry in front of her. She just tuts at me.'

'One day,' said Frieda, slowly, feeling her way, 'one day I hope you'll be able to make sense of all of this. Now it must just feel like a terrible nightmare. But I want to tell you that these bad days will pass. I'm not telling you that it will cease to be painful, but the pain will become bearable.'

'When will Dad come back?'

'I don't know.'

'Her funeral's next Monday. Will you come to it?'

'Yes. I'll be there.'

'Will you sit with me?'

'Your aunt –'

'When Aunt Louise talks about her, she makes this horrible face. As if there's a bad taste in her mouth. And Ted and Judith are so angry about her. But –' She stopped.

'Go on,' said Frieda.

'I know she had an affair. I know she did wrong and cheated on Dad. I know she lied to us all. But that's not how I think of her.'

'Tell me how you think of her.'

509

'When I was ill, she used to sit on my bed and read to me for hours. And in the mornings, when she woke me up, she'd always bring me a cup of tea in my favourite mug and put her hand on my shoulder and wait till I was properly awake. Then she'd kiss me on my forehead. She always had a shower in the morning and she smelt clean and lemony.'

'That's a good memory,' said Frieda. 'What else do you remember?'

'When I was being bullied, she was the only person in the world I could talk to about it. She made me feel less ashamed. Once, when it was really bad, she let me stay home from school and she took the day off herself and we spent hours in the garden, dead-heading the roses together. I don't know why it made me feel better, but it did. She told me about how she was bullied at school. She said I had to go on being who I was, being kind and nice.'

Dora stopped. Tears stood in her eyes.

'I think she sounds like a lovely mother,' said Frieda. 'I wish I'd met her.'

'I miss her so much I want to die. I want to *die*.'

'I know,' said Frieda. 'I know, Dora.'

'So why did she –'

'Listen to me now. People are very complicated. They can be lots of different people at the same time. They can cause pain and yet still be kind, sympathetic, good. Don't lose your memories of your mother. That's who she was to you and that's real. She loved you. She may have been having an affair but that doesn't alter the way she felt about her children. Don't let anyone take her away from you.'

'Aunt Louise says —'

'Fuck Aunt Louise!'

Ted was standing in the doorway. His hair was greasy and lank and his face looked mushroomy in its unhealthy pallor; there were violet smudges under his eyes and a prickling rash on his neck. Small sprouts of a young man's beard were beginning to appear on his chin. He was wearing the same clothes as yesterday. Frieda wondered if he'd even been to bed, let alone slept. As he approached, she could smell sweat and tobacco, a yeasty unwashed aroma.

'What are you doing here? Couldn't keep away?'

'Hello, Ted.'

Ted jerked his head at Dora. 'Louise wants you.'

Dora got to her feet, still holding Frieda's hand. 'Will you come and see us?' she asked urgently.

'Yes.'

'Promise.'

'I promise.'

The girl left the room and Frieda was left with Ted. She held up his portfolio. 'I've brought you this.'

'You thought I might be worrying about where it was? I've had other things on my mind.'

'I know. DCI Karlsson told me that your father has confessed to the manslaughter of Zach Greene and he's under suspicion of murdering your mother.'

His face twisted violently and he turned away from her. His thin, dirty figure reeked of misery and wretchedness.

'I've also been told that Elaine Kerrigan has confessed, though I think she might be trying to protect her sons.'

'Jesus,' he muttered.

'I'd like to say something, but maybe we can get out of here for a bit,' suggested Frieda.

'There's nothing to say.'

'Please.'

They went outside together. Frieda thought she saw a face staring at them out of a high window, but perhaps she was imagining things. She waited until they turned off the road on to a narrower street, which ran along a deserted playground and then beside a small grey church, before speaking.

'I was looking at your art,' she said. 'You're good.'

'That's what my mum used to say. "Ted, you've got a gift." Is that what you've come to tell me?'

'I saw the still-life you did for your mock exam. On the morning your mother died.'

Ted said nothing. They continued walking in silence down the street. It felt like everybody had gone away and only they were left.

'There was a strange object I didn't recognize at first,' said Frieda. Her voice sounded dry and scratchy. She cleared her throat. 'You'd drawn it from an interesting angle, so it took me some time to see what it was. I went to the evidence room to check.'

Ted had slowed. He dragged his feet as though they were too heavy for him.

'You can only see the cog as it appears in your drawing if you tip it sideways and back. Then it flattens out, into what looks more like a ruler.'

'Yes,' said Ted, in what sounded more like a shudder than a word. 'We had riddle books like that when I was a boy. I used to love them. I Spy . . .'

Frieda put her hand on Ted's shoulder and he looked at her. 'Your father knew you'd taken the cog to school that morning. When it turned up as the murder weapon, he knew it couldn't have been there until you brought it back.'

'He never said.' Ted spoke in a dull voice. 'I thought it could be all right, that nobody would ever know.'

'You discovered about your mother's affair?'

'I'd suspected for ages,' Ted said drearily. 'I followed her that day, on my bike. I saw her go to the flat and a man open the door. I left her there and I wandered around for ages, in a kind of fog. I couldn't really think and I felt sick. I thought I would be sick. I went home and I was putting the fucking cog back on the mantelpiece when she came in.' He put one hand up to his face for a moment, touching his skin. 'When I was little, I thought she was the best person in the whole wide world. Safe and kind. She'd tuck me into bed every night and she always had the same smell. She looked at me and I looked at her, and I knew she knew that I'd found out. She didn't say anything at once, and then she gave me this odd little smile. So I swung the thing in my hand and it hit her, smack, on the side of her head. I can still hear the sound it made. Loud and dull. For one moment, it seemed like nothing had happened and she was still looking at me and I was looking at her and there was this funny smile on her face and then – she seemed to explode in front of my eyes. Blood everywhere and she didn't look like my mother any more. She was lying on the floor and her face was mashed up and I was still holding the cog and it was all . . .'

'So you ran away.'

'I went to the park and I was sick. I was so sick and I've

513

felt sick ever since. Every moment. Nothing takes the taste away.'

'And then Judith gave you an alibi?'

'I was going to confess. What else could I do? But then the murder weapon had gone and everyone was saying it was a burglary gone wrong and Judith was begging me to say I'd been with her that afternoon. So I went along with it. I didn't work anything out in advance.'

'You do understand that your father planned Zach's murder, don't you, Ted? It wasn't manslaughter. It was murder. Once Judith came to him and told him about her affair and that she'd been with Zach on the day your mother died, he knew your alibi would be broken. Zach would say he'd been with Judith that afternoon.'

'He killed Zach to save me,' said Ted, in a low voice.

'If he wasn't caught, your alibi was safe. If he was, he could say he did it in an argument.'

'What will happen to him now?'

'I don't know, Ted.'

'Is he going to say he killed Mum as well, to save me?'

'I think he will if he has to. It's all a bit of a muddle at the moment, because of Elaine Kerrigan's intervention.'

'Will you tell the police?'

'No,' said Frieda, thoughtfully. 'I don't think I will.'

'Why?'

Frieda stopped and turned to him. She looked at him with her dark eyes. 'Because you are going to.'

'No,' he whispered. 'I can't . . . I never meant to . . . I can't.'

'What's it been like?' said Frieda. 'These last weeks.'

'Like being in hell,' he said, the words barely audible.

'That's where you'll be for ever, unless you speak the truth.'

'How can I? My mother. I killed my mother.' He jerked to a pause, and then dragged the words back again. 'I killed my mother. I can see her face.' He repeated the words wildly: 'I can see her face, her smashed-in face. All the time.'

'This is the only way. It won't make things better. You will always be the person who killed his mother. You will always carry that with you, until the day you die. But you have to admit what you did.'

'Will I go to prison?'

'Does that matter?'

'I wish I could tell her –'

'What would you tell her?'

'That I love her. That I'm sorry.'

'You can tell her.'

The street had swung round in a crescent and now they were back on the road where Louise Weller lived. Ted stopped and drew a deep, unsteady breath.

'We don't need to go back in there,' said Frieda. 'We can just go to the station.'

He stared at her, his young face stricken with dread. 'Will you come with me?'

'Yes.'

'Because I don't think I can do it alone.'

Frieda had walked through London many times, but she couldn't remember a walk so ghostly and so strange. It felt that crowds separated as they passed, and their footsteps rang out in the fugitive grey light. After a while, she put her arm through Ted's and he drew closer to her, like a child with his mother. She thought of Judith and Dora in that dark, tidy, airless house, their father locked away, their brother too – this young, horror-struck man. Everyone alone in their own terror and grief.

At last they were there. Ted drew apart from her. Beads of sweat had sprung up on his forehead and there was a dazed expression on his face. Frieda put a hand on the small of his back.

'This is it,' she said. And they went inside together.

Karlsson had just gone back in to Russell Lennox when Yvette put her head round the door and beckoned him out again.

'What is it?'

'I thought you should know at once. Frieda's here, with the Lennox boy.'

'With Ted?'

'Yes. She says that he has something important to say to you.'

'OK. Tell them I'll come now.'

'And Elaine Kerrigan is still insisting she did it.'

Karlsson went back into the room. 'I'll be back shortly,' he said to Russell Lennox. 'But apparently your son's here to see me.'

'My son? Ted? No. No, he can't be. No –'

'Mr Lennox, what is it?'

'I did it. I'll tell you everything. I killed my wife. I killed Ruth. Sit down. Turn on the tape recorder. I want to confess. Don't go. I did it. No one else. It was me.

You have to believe me. I murdered my wife. I swear to God it was me.'

Ted lifted his burning eyes and stared at Karlsson full in the face. For the first time, Karlsson felt a stillness about him, a sense of concentrated purpose. The boy took a breath and then said in a clear and ringing voice: 'I am here to confess to the murder of my mother. Who I loved very much . . .'

Fifty-eight

Josef was sitting in the kitchen with Chloë, playing some card game that involved lots of shouting and slapping of cards one on top of another when Frieda returned. Even as she was considering how to break the news to her niece, she had time to wonder why Chloë was in her house when she should have been at school, and think of how, from being her secure retreat from the world, it had become a casual meeting place for everyone, a place of disorder and grief. Perhaps, she thought, she would replace all the locks when this was over. She looked at Josef. 'Could Chloë and I have a moment?' she asked.

Josef seemed puzzled. 'Moment?'

'Yes,' said Frieda. 'Could you go out of the room?'

'Yes, yes,' said Josef. 'I go to Reuben now anyway. Poker for the guys.'

He picked the cat off his lap and, holding it against his broad chest, backed out.

As Frieda told Chloë, she watched the succession of emotions on the young girl's pale face: confusion, shock, distress, disbelief, anger. When Frieda had finished, there was a silence. Chloë's eyes flickered from side to side.

'Is there anything you want to ask me?' she said.

'Where is he?'

'At the police station.'

'In a cell?'

'I don't know. They were going to take a statement, but they'll keep him in.'

'He's only a child.'

'He's eighteen. He's an adult.'

There was another pause. Frieda saw that Chloë's eyes were glistening. 'Tell me,' she said.

'You were supposed to look after him.'

'I think I *was* looking after him.'

'What do you mean?'

'He had to own up to what he did.'

'Even if it meant ruining his life.'

'It's his only hope of *not* ruining his life.'

'In your opinion,' said Chloë, bitterly. 'In your fucking professional opinion. I brought him to you. I brought him to you so that you could help him.'

'Helping people isn't simple. It's –'

'Shut up. Shut up shut up shut up. I don't want to hear you talk about taking responsibility and fucking autonomy. You've betrayed him and you've betrayed me. That's what you've done.'

'He killed his mother.'

'He didn't mean to!'

'And that will be taken into account.'

'I'm going.'

'Where?'

'Back home. Mum might be a head case and the house might be a slum, but at least she doesn't send my friends to prison.'

'Chloë –'

'I'll never forgive you.'

*

519

It was finished, she told herself. She had finished. The feverishness of the last few weeks could abate; the strangeness could fade, as a violent bruise fades until at last it is just a faint ache, invisible to anyone else. The Lennox murder was solved. The Lennox children had gone to their different kinds of prison. Chloë had gone. Frieda had betrayed her friendship with Karlsson. The wild quest for a girl she had never known was over and already it had the quality of a dream. She wondered if she would ever see Fearby again, with his staring eyes and his silver hair.

She started clearing up, putting objects back where they belonged, wiping stains off surfaces, rubbing beeswax polish on to the little chess table by the window. That afternoon she would go and see Thelma Scott and dip the bucket down into the dark well of thoughts, but perhaps later on she could play through an old chess game, let the wooden pieces click their way across the board while silence settled around her again. She would have to call Sandy too. In her tumult, she had let him go. The two days in New York seemed distant, unreal. Now at last she let herself dwell upon the way he'd held her that night and the words he had said. Remember.

Remember. Halfway up the stairs, Frieda stopped dead. Something had come into her mind, setting her heart racing. What was it? Fearby. Something about Fearby, and his last message to her, before he'd disappeared out of her life. Frieda sat down on the step and tried to recall exactly what he'd said in his message. Most of it wasn't important but he'd obviously had an idea that seemed worth following up. He'd said he'd looked over the files of the girls. She remembered that bit clearly enough. Then he'd said something else. That we'd been thinking about them in the wrong way. Yes, and that he was going out to take another look.

Was there anything else? Yes: they hadn't heard the engine – what did that mean, for God's sake? It sounded like a slightly mad metaphor for the way the mind works. Frieda thought so hard that it almost hurt. No, that was all, except that he'd said he'd come round and tell her what he found. So that was all. It didn't seem much. The files on the girls. We'd been thinking about them in the wrong way. What had he meant by that? How could it be the wrong way? Was there some sort of connection they'd missed? He'd said 'we'. In what way had Fearby and she been thinking together about the girls? She thought about the rest of the message. He was going to take another look. Another. What did that mean? Was he going to go back to one of the girls' families? It was possible.

But then Frieda thought: No. There had been three parts to what he'd said. The girls. 'We' had thought wrongly about them – and he hadn't heard the engine. And he was going to take another look. That must mean – mustn't it? – that he was going to a place the two of them had been together.

Was he going to the horse sanctuary to talk to Doherty? No, that didn't make sense. Then he would have said he was going to talk to someone. His message was about a place. That must mean he'd been going back to Croydon. To take another look. But what could be the point of that? The police had been to the house. They had searched it. What could there possibly be to take another look at? She thought again about the message, as if it was a machine she was taking apart and laying out on the table. The girls. We had the wrong idea about them. Taking another look. The first bit was clear enough. The girls. The third bit seemed obvious. Another look. That must be Croydon. The problem was the second bit, the middle. We had the wrong idea about them. We. That was clear enough: Fearby and Frieda. What did Fearby and Frieda have the wrong idea about? Them. The engine. They hadn't heard the engine. What bloody engine?

And then, quite suddenly, it was as if Frieda had walked out of a dark tunnel into light so dazzling that she could hardly see.

Them. What if 'them' wasn't the girls? What if the engine wasn't a metaphor at all – because, after all, Fearby didn't talk in metaphors. He made lists; he focused on objects, facts, details, dates. The engine was the one that Vanessa Dale had heard, the day she was attacked, just before Hazel Barton had been killed. Vanessa Dale, through her panic, when her attacker's hands were round her throat, had heard an engine revving.

That meant her attacker hadn't been acting alone. Someone else had been sitting in the car, revving the engine, waiting to drive them away. Not one person. Two. A pair of killers.

Fifty-nine

Everything had a steely clarity now, icy, hard-edged. She found Thelma Scott's number and dialled it.

'Dr Scott? This is Frieda Klein. I've got to cancel.'

There was a pause.

'Do you have a moment to talk?'

'Not really. I've got something to do. Something that can't wait.'

'Frieda, are you quite well?'

'Probably not, just at the moment. But there's something important. It overrides everything.'

'It's just that you don't sound quite well.'

'I'm so sorry. I've got to go.'

Frieda hung up. What did she need? Keys, jacket, her hated phone. That was all. She was just pulling on her jacket when the doorbell rang. It was Josef, dusty from work.

'I'm on my way out. I've got no time. Not even to talk.'

Josef took her by the arm. 'Frieda, what is happening? Everyone phoning everyone. Where is Frieda? What she doing? You never phoning. Never answering.'

'I know, I know. I'll explain. But not now. I've got to get to Croydon.'

'Croydon? The girls?'

'I don't know. Maybe.'

'Alone?'

'I'm a big girl.'

'I take you.'

'Don't be ridiculous.'

Josef looked stern. 'I take you or I hold you here and phone to Reuben.'

'You want to try it?' said Frieda, fiercely.

'Yes.'

'All right, drive me, then. Is this yours?'

Behind Josef was a battered white van.

'Is for work.'

'Then let's go.'

It was a long, long drive, first across to Park Lane, then Victoria and over Chelsea Bridge into south London. Frieda had the map open on her lap, guiding Josef and thinking about what she was going to do. Battersea. Clapham. Tooting. Should she be calling Karlsson? And saying what? Suspicions about a man whose name she didn't know? Whose address she didn't know? About a girl nobody was looking for? And after their last awful encounter? Now they were in parts of south London with names she barely recognized. The instructions got more complicated and then, finally, Frieda steered Josef just a little past Lawrence Dawes's house.

'So,' said Josef, expectantly.

Frieda thought for a moment. Lawrence and his friend, Gerry. Them. She didn't know Gerry's second name and she didn't know where he lived. But she knew something. Upstream. That was what Lawrence had said. He lived upstream, which meant he was on the same side of the road, and she remembered that when she had stood in the garden with her back to the house, the river flowed from right to left. So Gerry's house was up to the right. And it probably wasn't next door. Lawrence would have said 'my next-door neighbour'. And hadn't he talked about next door being used for refugees? She got out of the car. She would start with the house next door but one. Josef got out as well.

'I'm fine,' said Frieda.

'I come with you.'

Lawrence Dawes lived at number eight. Frieda and Josef walked up the path of number twelve. Frieda rang the bell. There was no response. She rang again.

'No people home,' said Josef.

They walked back on to the pavement and up to the door of number fourteen and rang the bell.

'This is for what?' said Josef, puzzled, but before Frieda could answer, the door was opened by a white-haired old woman.

Frieda was momentarily at a loss. She hadn't thought of what she was going to say. 'Good afternoon,' she said. 'I'm trying to drop something off for a friend of a friend. He's called Gerry. He's in his sixties. I know he lives in one of these houses but I'm not sure which one.'

'It might be Gerry Collier,' said the woman.

'Early sixties?' said Frieda. 'Brown hair going grey?'

'That sounds like him. He lives along there. Number eighteen.'

'Thanks so much,' said Frieda.

The woman closed the door. Frieda and Josef walked back to the van and got inside. Frieda looked at the house. A two-storey, semi-detached house, grey pebbledash exterior, aluminium window frames. Ornate front garden, with a little white brick wall, yellow, blue, red, white flowers spilling over.

'And now?' said Josef.

'Wait a moment,' said Frieda. 'I'm trying to think what to do. We can –'

'Stop,' said Josef, in a hiss. 'Look.'

The door of number eighteen opened and Gerry Collier stepped out. He was wearing a grey windcheater and carrying a plastic shopping bag. He walked out on to the pavement and set off along the road.

'I wonder if we should follow him,' said Frieda.

'Follow the man?' said Josef. 'Is no good.'

'You're right. He's probably going to the shops. We've got a few minutes. Josef, can you help me break inside?'

Josef looked bemused and then he grinned. 'Break into the house? You, Frieda?'

'Now, this minute.'

'This not a joke?'

'It's really, really not a joke.'

'OK, Frieda. You ask. Questions later.' He picked up his work bag, from which he grabbed a heavy wrench and two large screwdrivers. They left the van and walked up to the front door of number eighteen.

'We need to be quick,' said Frieda. 'And quiet. If you possibly can.'

Josef ran his fingers over the lock with a certain delicacy. 'Which is most important? Quick or quiet?'

'Quick.'

Josef pushed one screwdriver into the gap between the door and the frame. He flexed it, and the gap widened slightly. Then he pushed the other screwdriver into the gap about a foot further down. He looked at Frieda. 'All right?'

She nodded. She saw him silently mouth the words, one, two, *three*, and pull the two screwdrivers sharply towards him, at the same time leaning hard on the door. There was a splintering sound and the door swung inwards.

'Where now?' said Josef, in a hoarse whisper.

Frieda had seen Lawrence Dawes's house. Where was possible? She pointed downwards. Josef put down his bag, and they walked softly along the hallway, by the left side of the staircase, Josef in front. He stopped and nodded to the right. There was a door leading back under the stairs. Frieda nodded and Josef gently opened it. Frieda saw the beginning of stairs leading down into darkness. There was a smell, something slightly sweet that she couldn't quite identify. Josef fumbled along the wall and switched on a light.

With a start, Frieda saw that a figure was sitting at the bottom of the flight, on the floor, back against the brick wall, half lost in shadow. Whoever it was didn't look round. Josef hissed at Frieda to stop, but she walked decisively down the steps. She had only taken a few steps before she knew who it was. She recognized the jacket, the white hair, the bent frame. When she reached the cellar floor, Jim Fearby was looking up at her with open, unblinking, unseeing, yellow dead eyes. His mouth gaped open as well, as if in surprise, and there was a large brown stain extending from his scalp down one side of his face. Frieda was going to lean down and check if he was dead but she stopped herself. There was no point. She felt a jolt of nausea that was overtaken by an intense aching sadness as she gazed down at this abandoned, dear man, who had finally been proved right.

Josef was coming down the stairs and Frieda was turning to speak when she heard a sound, like the whimper of an animal, somewhere further in the cellar, where it went under the pavement. She looked and saw a movement. She stepped forward and in the semi-darkness a figure took shape. A person, female, young, propped upright against the wall, arms splayed, legs splayed. Frieda saw matted hair, staring blinking eyes, taped mouth. She stepped forward and saw that the woman was secured by wire around her wrists and ankles, waist and neck. She was whimpering. Frieda put her finger to her lips. She tried to pull at the wire around one wrist but then Josef was beside her. He took something from his jacket pocket. She heard a click of pliers and one hand was free. The other wrist, the neck, the waist and then the woman fell forward. Frieda supported her, fearing she might break her ankles. Josef knelt down and cut her free and the woman fell to her knees.

'Call for help,' said Frieda to Josef.

Josef took out his phone.

'Upstairs for signal,' he said.

'Nine, nine, nine,' said Frieda.

'I know it,' said Josef.

Frieda looked into the woman's face. 'Sharon?' There was another whimper. 'I'm going to pull the tape off. You'll be fine but keep quiet. Gerry has gone out but we have to move.' Another whimper. 'You'll be all right. But this will sting.' Frieda got some purchase on the tape and pulled it off. The skin underneath was pale and raw and smelt of decay. Sharon whimpered like an animal. 'It's all right,' said Frieda, soothingly. 'I told you. He's gone.'

'No,' said Sharon, shaking her head. 'Other man.'

'Fuck!' Frieda turned round and started to run up the stairs. 'Josef.'

As she ran she heard a clattering and banging, like furniture falling downstairs, and as she emerged from the cellar door she saw shapes moving and heard shouts. She couldn't make anything out clearly and her foot slipped. The floor was wet, sticky. Then there was a mess of impressions: the figures moving and flexing, flashes of metal, cries, splashes, bangs, impacts so that the floor shook under her feet. Her focus became narrow, as if she was looking at the world through a long thin tube. Her thoughts became narrow as well. They seemed slow and time seemed slow and she knew that she must not collapse because then it would all have been for nothing. She found something in her hand – she didn't know what it was or how it got there, but it was heavy and she was hitting with it, as hard as she possibly could, and then the scene became clearer, as if the light had gradually been turned up. Lawrence Dawes was lying face down on the hall floor and a dark red pool was spreading out from him, and Josef was leaning back against the wall, panting and groaning, and Frieda herself was leaning against the wall opposite and she realized that the wet sticky stuff on her hands and clothes was blood.

SIXTY

'Frieda? Frieda, *Frieda.*' Josef seemed to have lost his English; her name was all that he could say, over and over.

Frieda crossed to him. She felt suddenly clear and light and calm, a sense of purpose and energy coursing through her. She saw that he had a violent gash running down his face and neck and one of his arms was hanging in an odd way. His face was horribly pale under the grime.

'It's all right, Josef,' she said. 'Thank you, my very dear friend.'

Then she stooped down beside Lawrence Dawes. There was a matted red patch on his head where she had hit him but she could see that he was breathing. She looked at the heavy object she was still holding: it was one of Josef's heavy spanners, which must have tumbled from his bag, and it had red smeared across it.

'Take this,' she said to Josef. 'If he comes round, hit him again. I'll be back in a minute.'

She ran into the kitchen and started pulling drawers open. Gerry Collier was a very organised man: everything had its proper place. She found a drawer full of string, masking tape, pens, and took out a roll of washing line. That would do. She returned to the two men and, bending down, brought Lawrence Dawes's hands together and rapidly bound the line round them multiple times, before bringing it down and wrapping it round his ankles as well, until he was trussed.

She pulled her phone out of her pocket with fingers that were not trembling, and dialled the emergency services. She said she needed the police, lots of them, and ambulances and gave the address, repeating it to make sure they had it. She gave her name, and heard it as if it belonged to someone else. She told them they should be quick. Then she put her phone back into her pocket. She could hear Josef's laboured breathing beside her and, turning, saw the pain on his drawn face. She took the spanner out of his hand and touched him lightly on the shoulder.

'Wait there for one more minute,' she said, and kissed him on his clammy forehead.

She ran down the cellar stairs. At the bottom, she stopped briefly to put two thumbs on Fearby's lids, closing them. She smoothed his hair off his face, then went to where Sharon Gibbs was still on her knees, her head cradled on her arms. She was making guttural little cries, like those of an animal in pain. She was wearing a bra that barely covered her shallow breasts and some filthy drawstring trousers; her feet were bare and torn. Frieda could see in the dim light that she was covered with bruises and what looked like cigarette burns.

She squatted beside her and put a hand under her elbow. 'Can you get up?' she asked. 'Let me help. Here.' She took off her jacket and wrapped it around the girl's emaciated frame. Her ribs stood out starkly, and her collarbone. She smelt of rot and decay. 'Come with me,

Sharon,' Frieda said gently. 'It's over, and you're safe. Come out of here.'

She half led and half carried the girl, past Fearby and up out of the cellar that had been her torture chamber, into the light that was fading now. Sharon gave a little cry of pain at the dazzle and bent over, almost falling, coughing up dribbles of vomit. Frieda got her to the doorway, out of the accursed house and into the clean air, and sat her on the steps.

Josef shambled over. Frieda took off her cotton scarf and wrapped it around his neck, where blood was running thickly. He made to sit on the step, but Sharon shrank from him.

'It's OK,' Frieda said. 'This man is good. He rescued you, Sharon. We both owe him our lives.'

'I was coming to find Lila,' Sharon whimpered. 'I wanted to see Lila.'

'It's all right now. Don't talk yet.'

'Is she dead?'

'Yes. I'm certain she is. She must have found out about her father so he killed her. But you are alive, Sharon, and you're safe now.'

She stood beside the two of them. There was the smell of honeysuckle wafting over to them from the neighbouring garden, and three doors down Frieda could see the old woman watering her tiny front garden with a hose. It was a beautiful late-spring evening. She fixed her eyes on the road – looking not just for the flashing blue lights of the police and the ambulances, but also for the figure of Gerry Collier. It was only minutes since she and Josef had watched him leave, but it seemed like hours, days –

another world. Behind them, the door was wrenched off its hinges, and in the cellar lay Jim Fearby, his long task over.

At last they came, sirens and lights shattering the soft evening. She heard them before she saw them, blue arcs swinging over the street before the cars and ambulances arrived, a screech of brakes, a sudden rush of men and women, voices speaking urgently, orders and exclamations, people bending towards them, stretchers, oxygen masks. Neighbours gathering on the road, a sudden sense of being at the centre of a world closing in on them.

There was a man standing in front of her, asking her something. She couldn't make out his questions but she knew what she had to say.

'My name is Frieda Klein.' She heard her voice, calm and clear. 'I made the call. This is Josef, who is hurt. And Sharon Gibbs, who has been missing for weeks. She has been held in the cellar by the man tied up inside, Lawrence Dawes. Be careful with her. You can't know what she's been through. A second man is at large, Gerry Collier. You have to find him.'

'Gerry Collier, you say?'

'Yes. He owns this place. And a man called Jim Fearby is dead, inside the house. You're too late for him.'

Faces hovered above her, blurred, anonymous, mouths opening and stretching, eyes large and staring. Someone was saying something, but she pressed on.

'There will be bodies in the garden.' She could no longer tell if she was speaking quietly or shouting, as if from a pulpit. 'Or bodies in the cellar.'

Sharon Gibbs was lifted from her crouched position on the steps to a stretcher. Her huge eyes gazed imploringly at Frieda from her pinched, dirty face. Now Lawrence Dawes was carried from the house, still tangled in the washing line. His eyes were flickering and they opened briefly on Frieda. For a moment they stared at each other, into each other, and then he turned his head away.

'Please can someone tell Karlsson?' Frieda continued.

'Karlsson?'

'DCI Malcolm Karlsson.'

A woman was wrapping a blanket around Josef's shoulders, unwrapping Frieda's bloody scarf from his neck. He stood up, bulky and dazed, staggering slightly. Frieda put her arms round him, careful of his dangling arm, and pressed her head against his chest. She could feel his heart hammering and smell his sweat and his blood. 'You'll be fine now,' she said. 'You've done well, Josef.'

'I?'

'Yes. I will write to your sons to tell them. They will be very proud of you.'

'Proud?'

'Yes, proud.'

'But you –'

'I'll come and see you very soon.' She looked at the woman. 'Where are you taking him?'

'St George's.'

Now Josef was gone and Fearby's body was being carried out of the house. His face was covered, but Frieda could still see his fine white hair. His feet poked out of the blanket at the other end; the shoes were old and scuffed and on one the lace was undone.

The ambulances slid away, and suddenly she was alone. There were gathering crowds in the street, and in the house the light was unnaturally bright and full of noises, voices. But here, on this small patch of soil, she was by herself at last. The door gaped behind her, like a foul, hot mouth; she could smell its sickening stench.

'Frieda Klein?'

A man was in front of her, blocking out the light.

'Yes.'

'I need to talk to you urgently. I will be a few more minutes. Would you wait for me here, please?'

He left her again. Her mobile rang. She looked at it – Sandy – but didn't answer. Then she turned it off.

Without thinking what she was doing, she stood up and went into the house. No one stopped her or even seemed to notice. She stepped out of the back door into the garden. It was the same size and shape as Lawrence Dawes's garden, and was full of flowers. Bright, sweet, fragrant flowers, peonies and roses and foxgloves and tall lupins; perhaps they were feeding on the bodies, she thought. Perhaps that was why they were so strong and bright and colourful. She walked down the lawn, past a well-tended vegetable plot, until she was standing by the shallow brown River Wandle. She could see the pebbles on its bottom, and a few tiny dark fish. Behind her, there was the roar of the world, but here just the trickle of water; she could hear its faint gurgle. A swallow dipped past her, low and fast, then up into the evening sky.

She knew she had to go home. She thought of something she had read in a book when she was a child. If you're lost in the jungle, find a stream and follow it downhill and it will reach a larger river or the sea. This little brook would take her home.

She took off her sandals, rolled up her jeans and stepped into the water. It was cool, not cold, and rose to her ankles. She walked delicately along the stony bed until she was standing outside Lawrence Dawes's garden. They'd drunk tea together there, and he'd shown her this little river. She could hear his voice now, mild and amiable: . . . *we used to make little paper boats and put them on the stream and watch them float away. I used to tell them that in three hours' time, those boats would reach the Thames and then, if the tide was right, they'd float out to sea.*

Frieda crossed to the other side and stepped out on to a narrow, overgrown path, pulling her sandals back on to her wet feet. Here it was green, tangled and wild – a place of nettles and cow parsley, a smell of grass, mulched leaves and moisture. She started to walk.

The secret river narrowed to a ribbon of brown water. Frieda kept pace with its flow, watching the bubbles beading and bursting on its surface. She saw Jim Fearby's face. She saw his dead eyes staring at her. What had his last thoughts been? She wished so much that he had stayed alive long enough to know he had won. She saw Josef's face. He would lay down his life for her, but she would lay down hers for no reason at all, except that it seemed a cursed thing.

A short distance away in the opposite direction, the Wandle disappeared underground for ever, into a network of springs, burrowing its way under the earth.

Here it wound north, the path following it almost closed over now with nettles that stung her feet and hanging branches that stroked her cheeks, so that Frieda felt she was in a tunnel of green light. She smelt something sweet and nasty; there must be the carcass of an animal or bird rotting nearby. This little river had worked so hard in its time, and carried so much shit and poison and death, a sclerotic artery clogged with waste. There would have been water mills once, and tanning factories, lavender fields and watercress ponds, litter and chemicals and flowers. All gone now, demolished and lying buried under concrete and housing estates. To her left Frieda could see through the tangle of weeds a deserted warehouse, a rash of light industrial units, a deserted car park, a rubbish dump rising out of the dusk. But the little river flowed on, quick and clear, leading her out of the labyrinth.

The water widened again, slowed. There were faces she could see in its swirling course, rising up at her. Faces of young women. Weeds for hair. Calling out for help. Too late. Only Sharon Gibbs had been saved: Frieda could hear her animal cries and smell her dying flesh. In the darkness, rats with yellow teeth – what had been done to her and what had she felt? Drinking tea in the garden, smiling. Shaking his hand – what had that hand done? His daughter. Lily. Lila. Wild child. All those wild children. Lost young women. How many more were there, in their own underworlds?

She saw Ted's young face, then Dora's and Judith's – motherless, fatherless children, hungry for love and for safety. Lives wrecked. Homes torn apart. What had she done? How could she bear the damage she had caused and carry the burden through the rest of her days?

Now the river was channelled between concrete banks, tamed. And suddenly the path was a road that ran alongside a red-brick, buttressed wall. For a moment, she felt that she was in a country village long ago. There was a grey church beside her, surrounded by a huddle of graves. Frieda looked at one of the names, a teenage boy dead in the Great War. She thought she saw a shape rise up from the ground, but it was only a trick of the dying day. She didn't know what time it was. She didn't want to turn on her mobile to see. It didn't matter anyway. She could walk through the evening and into the night. She could walk for days and never stop. The pain in her legs and her lungs was good; better than pain in her heart.

But where was her river? It had disappeared. They had taken it away from her. She stumbled, feeling sharp pebbles under her soles. Ahead, a park stretched out, an avenue of great trees. She walked towards it and after a while saw a small stone bridge. She had found it again and it took her to a pond. Dragonflies in the dusk. A child's sandal on the bank. But it led her to a road and then disappeared, and a car sped by with the bass thump of music coming from it, and then a man in black leather crouched low on his motorbike, and Frieda was lost in a dingy corridor of houses and flats. But she walked in the direction it had been flowing and after a few minutes there it was, merry and leaping, as if it had been teasing her. Past buildings, cottages, an old mill, and once more she was on an overgrown path, leaving the road behind. The surface of the city dropped away as she walked along its hidden corridor.

You could stand ten feet away and not know it was there. You could hide there, seeing but unseen. Like a ghost.

Too many ghosts. Too many dead people in her life. Already a crowd of them behind her. The ghost of herself, young and eager. You start on your journey full of ignorance and hope. Her father. Sometimes she still saw him, not just in her dreams but among the faces she passed on the streets. There was something she wanted to tell him but she could no longer remember what it was. Darkness was gathering round her. Her head was filled with the colours of pain.

Past an old deserted warehouse, painted an ugly blue and covered with graffiti. Shattered windows. You could hide there. Perhaps it, too, was full of dead people, or of lost people. You couldn't look everywhere. There isn't an end, there are always others, and she was tired. Not a soft, blurred tiredness but one that was sharp and insistent. Tiredness like a knife, a millstone grinding. Sharon Gibbs was alive, but Lila was dead. The others were dead. Bones in the rich soil that fed a garden full of flowers.

The path broadened out into a wide track. The river was slow and brown. If she lay down here, would she ever get up? If Sandy were here, would she tell him? If Sasha were here, would she cry at last? Or sleep? When would she ever sleep? To sleep was to let go. Let go of the dead, let go of the ghosts, let go of the self.

Cranes. Great thistles. A deserted allotment with crazy little sheds toppling at the edge of the river. A fox, mangy, with a thin, grubby tail. Swift as a shadow into the shadows. She liked foxes. Foxes, crows, owls. A shape flitted by and she realized it must have been a bat. It was night at last. How long had it been? Her river was still showing her the way and a moon rose and everyone she knew stood a long way off. Reuben, Sasha, Olivia, Chloë, Josef, Sandy, Karlsson. Her patients were reduced to a crouched figure in a chair, asking her to rescue them from themselves. Dean Reeve stood in a corner; he looked in at a window; she heard his footsteps when no one was there; and he left behind him the sickly smell of lilies and death. He was more real than anyone.

It was hard to know any longer why she put one foot in front of the other, one foot in front of the other, and kept breathing in and out, as if her body had the willpower her spirit no longer possessed. She was spent. Her waters were run dry.

But then the river widened and the path opened out and there was a fence, an iron bell hanging in a metal cage. The Wandle had guided her and now it opened out into its own small estuary and poured itself at last into the great thoroughfare of the Thames. Frieda was standing on a stone walkway, looking out at the lights of the city. She wasn't lost any more, and somewhere in those pulsing lights lay home.

SIXTY-ONE

This was not a night for sleep. Thoughts burned in Frieda's brain; images pulsed behind her eyes. She sat upright in her armchair and stared into the empty grate, where she saw the well-tended garden in Croydon. Now they would be pushing spades into the loamy soil, pulling the house apart. She remembered the two of them, Dawes and Collier, sitting in the garden. She felt sick and closed her eyes, but the pictures wouldn't go away. She thought the stench of lilies still hung in the air.

At last she rose and went upstairs. She put the plug into the bath – Josef's bath – and turned the taps, poured in bath lotion until the water foamed. She peeled off her dirty clothes and cleaned her teeth, avoiding looking at herself in the little mirror over the basin. Her limbs felt heavy and her skin stung; she was all used up. At last she climbed into the fragrant, scorching water and let herself sink beneath the surface. Perhaps she could lie here until day, her hair floating on the surface and her blood pounding in her ears.

At last she got out. It was still dark but there was a faint band of light on the horizon. A new day was starting. She dressed and went downstairs. There were things she needed to do.

First, she made a phone call, one she should have made days ago. He didn't reply at once and when he did his voice was thick with sleep.

'Sandy?'

'Frieda? What? Are you all right?'

'I don't think so. I'm sorry.'

'Hang on.' There was a pause. She imagined him sitting up, turning on the light. 'Why are you sorry?'

'I'm just sorry. I'm so sorry. I should have told you.'

'Told me what?'

'Can you come over?'

'Yes. Of course.'

'I mean, now.'

'Yes.'

That was one of the things she loved about him – that he would make a decision like that, without hesitation or a flurry of anxious questions that she wouldn't be able to answer, knowing she would only ask out of extreme need. He would get up at once, book a flight, make arrangements with his colleagues, be with her before the day was out because she had turned to him at last.

'Thank you,' she said simply.

She made herself a bitterly strong cup of coffee and fed the cat, watered the plants in her backyard, breathing in the intense fragrance of hyacinths and herbs. Then she put on her jacket and left the house. It was a fresh, damp dawn; later it would be warm and bright. The sweetness of spring. The shops were all still shut, but she could smell bread baking in the little bakery on the corner. Lights were coming on in flats and houses; metal shutters rattled up in newsagents and corner shops; a bus lurched by with a single passenger staring out of the window. A postman pulling his red cart passed her. The great life of London starting up again.

Frieda reached Muswell Hill and consulted her *A-Z*, then turned off into a wide residential street full of handsome detached houses. Number twenty-seven. From the outside, the damage wasn't immediately obvious – just darkened bricks, some charred woodwork, a broken window on the first floor and, as she drew closer, the acrid smell that caught in the back of her throat. She hesitated, then stepped into the front garden with its gravelled pathway and its tub of red tulips that had survived the blaze. From here she could see through the large bay window into the front room, where the devastation was obvious. She pictured the fire raging through the orderly spaces, gobbling tables, chairs, pictures, doors; licking ashy blackness up the walls. Dean had done this – casually pushed a petrol-soaked rag through the letterbox, dropped a match after it. *We couldn't let him get away with it.* In a way, Bradshaw was right: this was her fault.

There was a side door to the left of the house, and when she pushed at it, it opened on to the garden at the back. She stepped through into a green space, and now she was looking in at what had once been a conservatory and kitchen but was now a ruin. She was about to turn away when she saw something that stopped her.

Hal Bradshaw was in there, stooped over the scorched remains. He squatted, pulled out what had obviously once been a book, held it up to examine, then dropped it again. He was wearing a crumpled suit and wellington boots and stepped softly through the silt of ashes that stirred as he walked, lifted in dark petals around him. Frieda saw his face, which was tired and defeated.

He seemed to sense her presence because he straightened up. Their eyes met and his expression tightened. He pulled himself back into the Hal Bradshaw she knew: controlled, knowing, defended.

'Well,' he said, coming towards her. 'Quite a sight, isn't it? Come to assess the damage?'

'Yes.'

'Why?'

'I needed to see it. What were you looking for?'

'Oh.' He smiled mirthlessly, lifted his sooty hands, then let them drop. 'My life, I suppose. You spend years collecting things and then – poof, they're gone. I wonder now what they all meant.'

Frieda stepped into the ruin and picked up the remains of a book that crumbled at her touch. She watched words dissolve into ash and dust.

'I'm very sorry,' she said.

'Is that an admission?'

'A regret.'

As she made her way towards the Underground, Frieda turned on her mobile and looked at all the messages. So many, from people she knew and people she didn't. She was walking towards uproar, questions and comments, the dazzle of attention that she dreaded, but for now she was alone. Nobody knew where she was.

But there was someone she did have to call.

'Karlsson. It's me.'

'Thank God. Where are you?'

'I'm on my way to Tooting, to the hospital.'

'I'll meet you there. But are you all right?'

'I don't know. Are you?'

*

He met her in the lobby, striding towards her as he came in through the revolving door, putting one hand briefly on her shoulder as he stared into her face, looking for something there.

'Listen –' he began.

'Can I say something first?'

'Typical.' He tried to smile, his mouth twisting. He looked exhausted and stricken.

'I'm sorry.'

'You're sorry!'

'Yes.'

'But you were right. Frieda, you were horribly right.'

'But I did wrong, too. To you. And I apologize.'

'Oh, Jesus, you don't need to –'

'I do.'

'OK.'

'Have you been there?'

'Yes.'

'Have they found the missing girls?'

'It'll take more than one night. But yes.'

'How many?'

'It's too early to say.' He swallowed hard. 'Several.'

'And have you found . . .'

'Of course we have. Gerald Collier isn't saying anything. Nothing at all. But we don't need him to. They were in his cellar.'

'Poor Fearby,' said Frieda, softly. 'It was him, you know, not me. I would have given up, but he never did.'

'An old drunk hack.' Karlsson's voice was bitter. 'And a traumatized therapist. And you solved a crime we didn't even know existed. We'll be tremendously efficient now, of course. Now that it's too late. We'll identify the remains and we'll inform the poor bloody relatives and we'll go back over their lives and we'll find out everything there is to be discovered about those two fucking bastards who got away with it for so many years. We'll update computers and conduct an inquiry as to how this could have happened. We'll learn from our mistakes, or that's what we'll tell the press.'

'His own daughter,' said Frieda. 'She was the one I was looking for.'

'Well, you found her.'

'Yes.'

'You'll need to answer a lot of questions, I'm afraid.'

'I know. I'll come to the station later. Is that all right? But first I'm going to see Josef. Have you seen him?'

'Josef?' A tiny smile broke through Karlsson's wintry expression. 'Oh, yes, I've seen him.'

Josef had a room to himself. He was sitting up in bed, wearing oversized pyjamas, with a bandage round his head and his arm encased in plaster. A nurse stood by his side with a clipboard. He was whispering something to her and she was laughing.

'Frieda!' he cried. 'My friend Frieda.'

'Josef, how are you?'

'My arm is broken,' he said. 'Bad break, they say. But clean snap so good recovery. Later you write on arm. Or draw one of your pictures maybe.'

'Does it hurt?'

'Drugs take away pain. I have eaten toast already. This is Rosalie and she is from Senegal. This is my good friend Frieda.'

546

'Your good friend who nearly got you killed.'

'Is nothing,' he said. 'A day's work.'

There was a knock at the door and Reuben came in, followed by Sasha, who was bearing a bunch of flowers.

'I'm afraid you aren't allowed flowers,' said Rosalie.

'He's a hero,' said Reuben, decisively. 'He has to have flowers.'

Sasha kissed Josef on his bristly cheek, then put her arm around Frieda, gazing at her with beseeching concern.

'Not now,' said Frieda.

'I've brought you some water.' Reuben drew a little bottle out of his pocket and gave Josef a meaningful look.

Josef took a gulp, flinched and offered it to Frieda. She shook her head, withdrew to the chair by the window, which looked out on to another wall and a narrow strip of pale blue sky. She could see the vapour trail of a plane, but it was too soon for it to be Sandy's. She was aware of Sasha's eyes on her, heard Reuben's voice and Josef's boisterous replies. A junior doctor came in and then left. A different nurse entered, wheeling a trolley; the creak of shoes on lino. Doors opening, doors closing. A pigeon perched on the narrow sill and stared in at her with a beady eye. Sasha said something to her and she replied. Reuben asked her a question. She said yes, no, that she would tell them everything later. Not now.

Sandy took her in his arms and held her against him. She could feel the steady beat of his heart and his breath in her hair. Warm, solid, strong. Then he drew away and looked at her. It was only when she saw the expression on his face that she began to understand what she had come through. It took a great effort not to turn away from his pity and horror.

'What have you done, Frieda?'

'That's the question.' She tried to laugh but it came out wrong. 'What *have* I done?'

SIXTY-TWO

Frieda had the strange feeling that she was on stage but that she was playing the wrong part. Thelma Scott was sitting in what should have been Frieda's chair and Frieda was pretending to be a patient. They were facing each other and Thelma was looking straight at her with a kind, sympathetic expression, an expression that said there was no pressure: anything could be said, anything was allowed. Frieda knew the expression because it was one she used herself. She felt almost embarrassed that Thelma was trying it out on her. Did she think she would be so easily fooled?

Frieda kept her own consulting room deliberately austere, with neutral colours, a few pictures deliberately chosen not to send out any precise signals. Thelma Scott's room was quite different. She had busy, patterned wallpaper, blue and green tendrils intertwined, here and there a bird perched on them. The surfaces were crowded with little objects, knick-knacks. There were miniature glass bottles, porcelain figurines, a glass vase with pink and yellow roses, pill boxes, china mugs, a set of plates decorated with wildflowers. But there was nothing personal, nothing that told you about Thelma Scott's life or personality, except that she liked little objects. Frieda hated little objects. They felt like clutter. She would have liked to sweep them all into a bin bag and put them out on the pavement for the binmen to take away.

Still Thelma looked at her with her kind, accepting expression. Frieda knew what it was to sit there, to wait for the first step that would mark the beginning of the journey. Sometimes Frieda had sat for the entire fifty minutes with a patient failing to say a single word. Sometimes they would just cry.

Why was she here? What, really, was there to talk about? She'd already gone through it all, all the choices, all the permutations, the roads she had taken and the roads she hadn't taken, while lying awake at two, three, four in the morning. Because of her intervention, Russell Lennox's attempt to protect his son had failed and Ted was now in custody. The thought of him in prison and all he might be going through was terrible, but he had committed a terrible act of violence, and against his own mother. His only hope was to acknowledge what he had done and take the consequences. The legal system might be merciful. With the right defence, he might escape a murder conviction.

Some people might think that Ted would have stood a better chance if he had remained free. Human beings have an ability to survive by burying the past, making themselves forget. Ted might have found his own way of atoning. But Frieda couldn't make herself believe that. You had to face the truth, however painful, and move on from there. Burying it didn't make it die, and in the end it would claw its way out of the earth and come for you. But was that just an opinion and was Ted paying the price for it?

And were Dora and Judith paying the price as well? As she thought of them, the image came into her mind of the funeral that she had attended just two days ago. There had been music and poems and hundreds of people, but what she had seen from her position at the back had been the two girls, one on either side of their grimly virtuous aunt. Both had had their hair cut for the occasion: Dora now had a severe fringe and Judith's wild curls had been shorn. They seemed limp and defeated, utterly wretched. Judith had seen Frieda; her remarkable eyes had blazed briefly and then she had turned away.

The truth: Jim Fearby had lived for it and sacrificed everything for it, his family, his career and his life. In those last moments, when Lawrence Dawes and Gerry Collier had killed him, did he briefly realize he had found the truth? Did he feel justified? And was it her fault? She had tried to help Fearby and he had died. She had travelled with him, talked with him, planned with him. She had abused her friendship with Karlsson to get him involved but she had failed Fearby. Fearby had made the connection with Dawes but should Frieda herself have realized that he couldn't have acted alone? He had gone ahead of her into that underworld and she hadn't been able to save him.

Sharon Gibbs had been rescued and restored to her family and that was something. If she and Josef hadn't burst in, Sharon Gibbs would have joined the others. They had found them buried in the cellar. Frieda was haunted by their names, and by their faces in the photographs Fearby had shown her. Happy family snapshots of young girls, who didn't know what was ahead of them. Hazel Barton and Roxanne Ingatestone and Daisy Crewe and Philippa Lewis and Maria Horsley and Lila Dawes. And there was a seventh. The police had found another body in the cellar, the skeletal remains of a young female. Unidentified. Fearby had missed her somehow and the police had the names of too many missing girls. Karlsson said they had a DNA sample and might strike lucky. All those lost girls, but Frieda couldn't stop thinking about the unknown one. It was like staring into an abyss and being lost there.

Frieda wanted to feel guilty about what she'd done to Josef as well, but that was harder. She suspected at first that his cheerful stoicism might be concealing post-traumatic stress. It could emerge much later, that was what the literature said. But really there was no sign of it at all. He was enjoying the attention, and when Karlsson had said there was some possibility of an award for bravery, he seemed to enjoy it even more. His account of the event seemed to become more embroidered with each retelling, but even Frieda couldn't detect signs of emotional distress.

And there was Dean Reeve. He was like an obscene kind of lover, someone who wanted to observe everything she did, feel everything she felt, accompany her to places no one else would go. The memory, the smell of the charred ruin, of Hal Bradshaw's house haunted her. Had Dean Reeve done it to punish Bradshaw or to punish her? Had he sensed, in a way nobody else could, her hostility towards Bradshaw, then acted it out in a way she never would have? This is you, he was telling her. This is who you really are and you and I are the only people who truly recognize that. I am your twin, your other self.

So much wreckage, so much damage she had left trailing behind her.

Frieda lifted her eyes. She had almost forgotten where she was. Thelma was looking at her, full in the face.

'I'm sorry,' said Frieda. 'I can't put this into words.'

Thelma gave a slow nod. 'That sounds like the place to begin.'

Can't wait for more? Turn the page for a taste of *Thursday's Children*, the next instalment in the Frieda Klein series, coming soon from Michael Joseph.

I

It started with a reunion and it ended with a reunion and Frieda Klein hated reunions. She was sitting in front of her fire, listening to its slow crackle. Beside her was Sasha, who was staring into the glow. Beside Sasha was a Moses basket. In the Moses basket was Sasha's ten-month-old son, Ethan, a blur of dark hair and soft snoring. A cat lay at Frieda's feet, faintly purring. They could hear the wind blowing outside. It had been a day of fog and swirling leaves and gusts of wind. Now it was dark and they were inside, hiding from the approaching winter.

'I've got to admit,' said Sasha, 'that I'm intrigued by the idea of meeting an old school friend of yours.'

'She wasn't a friend. She was in my class.'

'What does she want?'

'I don't know. She rang me up and said she needed to see me. She said it was important and that she'd be here at seven.'

'What time is it now?'

Frieda looked at her watch.

'Almost seven.'

'I don't know things like that any more. Since Ethan was born, I've forgotten what a night's sleep is like and my brain has turned into sludge. I don't even know what day it is. Is it Wednesday?'

'Thursday.'

'That's good. Almost the weekend.'

Frieda gazed back into the fire. 'Thursday's perhaps the worst day of the week. It's nothing in itself. It just reminds you that the week's been going on too long.'

Sasha pulled a face. 'That may be reading too much into it.' She leaned over the basket and stroked her son's hair. 'I love him so much but sometimes when he's asleep I feel relieved and grateful. Is that a terrible thing to say?'

Frieda turned to her friend. 'Is Frank helping out?'

'He does his best. But he's so busy with his work. As he says, helping the guilty walk free.'

'That's his job,' said Frieda. 'He's a defence barrister and –'

She was interrupted by a ring at the door. Frieda gave Sasha a rueful look.

'You are going to answer it, aren't you?' Sasha said.

'I was tempted to hide.'

Opening the door, she heard a voice that seemed to come out of the darkness and was immediately enfolded in a hug.

'Frieda Klein,' said the woman. 'I'd know you anywhere. You look just like your mother.'

'I didn't know you'd ever met my mother.' She gestured towards the fireplace. 'This is my friend Sasha. This is Madeleine Bucknall.'

'Maddie,' said the woman. 'Maddie Capel. I got married.'

Maddie Capel put down her large embossed bag and unwound a chequered scarf from her neck. She took off a heavy brown coat that she handed to Frieda. Underneath she was wearing a maroon crossover dress with wedge-heeled leather boots. There was a thick gold chain round her neck and small gold earrings in her lobes. She smelt of expensive perfume. She stepped towards the fire and looked into the basket.

'What a darling little baby,' she said. 'Frieda, is it yours?'

Frieda pointed at Sasha.

'Just the sight of it makes me want to have another,' said Maddie. 'I love them at that age, when they're like a little warm bundle. Is it a boy or a girl?'

'A boy.'

'So cute. Is he walking yet?'

'He's only ten months old.'

'You just need to be patient.'

Frieda pulled a chair up, close to the fire, and Maddie sat down. She had long brown hair, artfully styled into shagginess and streaked with blonde. Her face was carefully made up, but this only emphasized the tightness of the skin over the cheekbones, the little lines around the eyes and at the corners of the mouth. Frieda remembered her from school, cheerful, laughing, loud, but there was always an anxiety: being in the group or not in the group, having a boyfriend or not having a boyfriend.

'Should I give you some privacy?' said Sasha.

'No, no, it's lovely to meet a friend of Frieda's. Do you live here as well?'

Sasha gave a faint smile. 'No, I live with my partner. Somewhere else.'

'Yes, of course. Thank you, thank you,' she said, as Frieda handed her a mug of tea. She took a sip and looked around her. 'Such a sweet little place you have here. Cosy.' Another sip. 'I read about you in the newspaper, Frieda. About how you helped on that terrible, terrible case with all those girls. And you rescued one of them.'

'Only one,' said Frieda. 'And it wasn't just me.'

'How can people do things like that?'

There was a pause.

'What was it you wanted to talk to me about?'

A gulp of tea.

'I can't believe we've lost touch,' Maddie said. 'You know that I still live in Braxton. Do you ever come back?'

'No.'

'Some of the old lot are still there.' She gave a mischievous smile. 'I remember you and Jeremy. I used to be rather jealous of you. He was quite a catch. He left, of course. Do you keep in touch with him?'

'No.'

'I married Stephen. Stephen Capel. Did you know him? We had some good years but it went wrong. He's remarried, but he still lives nearby.'

'When you phoned, you said there was something you needed to talk to me about.'

Another gulp of tea. Maddie looked around. 'Is there somewhere I can put this?'

Frieda took the mug from her.

'I've read about you in the paper.'

'You said.'

'More than once,' Maddie said. 'You've attracted quite a lot of attention.'

'Not by choice.'

'Yes, it must be difficult sometimes. But they said that apart from solving crimes . . .'

'That's not really . . .' Frieda began, and Sasha smiled again.

'No, but the articles mentioned that you're a psychologist.'

'I'm a psychotherapist.'

'I'm not very good on all the jargon,' said Maddie. 'I'm sure there's a difference. I don't know all the details, but from what I understand, people talk to you and you help them. Is that right?'

Frieda leaned forward. 'What is it you want?'

'It's not me.' Maddie gave a little laugh. 'If that's what you're thinking. Not that I couldn't do with some help. When Stephen left, I was crying for days and days. Weeks, really. I didn't know who to turn to.'

There was another pause.

'I know things like that are terrible,' said Frieda, 'but, please, why have you come to see me?'

'It'll sound silly. It's probably a waste of your time, my coming up all the way from the country.'

'Should I leave?' asked Sasha, again.

'No,' said Maddie. 'We're just old friends talking.'

'Tell me what you want from me.'

Maddie hesitated. Frieda had experienced this moment dozens of times with her patients. One of the most difficult, precarious moments in therapy was that first naming of the patient's fear. It was like jumping off a cliff edge into darkness.

'It's my daughter, Becky,' said Maddie. 'Rebecca. But everyone calls her Becky. She's fifteen, almost sixteen.'

'Has something happened?'

'No, no, nothing like that. It's hard to put into words. Becky was such a sweet little girl. When I looked at this little boy in the basket, it reminded me of those days, when it was all so simple. I could just look after her. You know, when Becky was that age I thought I was going to have lots of children and I was going to be the best mother in the world and protect them from everything. I was so young when I had her, almost a child myself. And then . . .' she breathed deeply, as if she were trying to control herself '. . . I couldn't have another child. And then Stephen left. It was probably my fault. I tried to hide the way I felt from Becky but I didn't do a very good job. She was only six. Little thing. And I was still in my twenties and all over the place.' Her voice wavered and she stopped for a moment. 'It must have hit her hard but I thought we'd come through it. I suppose I'd always dreaded the teenage years.' She glanced at Frieda. 'Maybe I was thinking of our own teenage years. We got up to one or two things that we probably regret now, didn't we?'

A voice inside Frieda was saying, What do you mean 'we'? We weren't friends. We didn't get up to anything together. But she stayed silent and waited.

'In the last year or so she's changed. I know what you're going to say. She's just an adolescent. What am I worrying about? Well, I am worrying. To begin with, she was just withdrawn and moody and she wouldn't talk about anything. I wondered whether there were drugs or boys involved. Or drugs *and* boys. I tried to ask her about it. I tried to be sympathetic. Nothing worked.

'About a month ago, it got worse. She seemed different. She looked different. She stopped eating. She was on this stupid diet before, and was already rail-thin. Now I don't know how she's managing to stay alive. I've cooked everything I can think of, but she just moves it about on her plate. Even when she does eat, I think she makes herself sick. She misses school. She doesn't do homework.'

'Does she see her father?'

'Stephen's hopeless. He says it's just a phase. She'll get over it.'

'What do you want from me?' said Frieda.

'Can't you just talk to her? Isn't that what you do? Just have a word with her?'

'I'm not sure if you're clear about what I do. I see patients over extended periods of time in order to explore problems they have in their life. I wonder if your daughter ought to see a school counsellor or a teacher.'

'Becky won't accept it. I've tried everything. I'm completely desperate. I don't know who to turn to. Please. As a favour to an old school friend.'

Frieda looked at Maddie's pleading expression. She didn't like this woman from her past claiming to have been her friend and wanting something she couldn't really give. She felt bad about Sasha being there to witness it. 'I'm not sure I'm the right person for this,' she said, 'but if you bring your daughter here, I'll talk to her. I'll see if I can give you, or her, some advice. But I can't promise anything.'

'That's wonderful. I can be there too, if you want.'

'I'll need to talk to her alone. At least at first. She needs to know it's private and that she can say anything. That is, if she wants to say anything. She may not be ready to talk. Or, at least, ready to talk to me.'

'Oh, I'm sure she'll talk to you.'

Maddie stood up and fetched her coat as if she needed to get away before there was any possibility of Frieda withdrawing her offer. She pulled it on and wound the scarf back round her. Frieda felt she was watching someone put a shell on. In the doorway, after saying goodbye, Maddie suddenly turned round.

'You know, there's something in my daughter that frightens me,' she said. 'Isn't that terrible?'

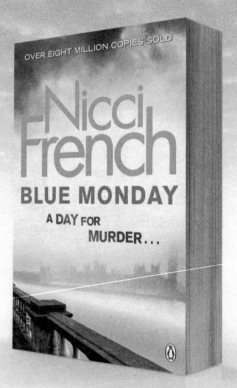

OVER EIGHT MILLION COPIES SOLD

Nicci French

BLUE MONDAY

A DAY FOR MURDER...

Book 1 in the Frieda Klein series

Monday: five-year-old Matthew Faraday is abducted. His face is splashed across newspaper front pages. His parents and the police are desperate. Can anyone help find their little boy before it is too late?

Psychotherapist Frieda Klein just might know something.

One of her patients describes dreams of seizing a boy who is the spitting image of Matthew. Convinced at first the police will dismiss her fears out of hand, Frieda reluctantly finds herself drawn into the heart of the case. A previous abduction, from twenty years ago, suggests a new lead - one that only Frieda, an expert on the minds of disturbed individuals, can uncover.

Struggling to make sense of this terrifying investigation, Frieda will face her darkest fears in the hunt for a clever and brutal killer . . .

'Nerve tingling and addictive'
Daily Express

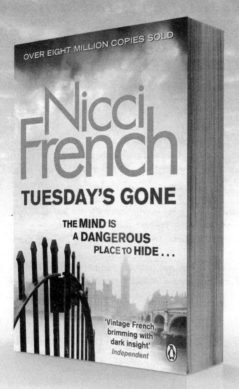

OVER EIGHT MILLION COPIES SOLD

Nicci French

TUESDAY'S GONE

THE **MIND** IS
A **DANGEROUS**
PLACE TO **HIDE**...

'Vintage French,
brimming with
dark insight'
Independent

Book 2 in the Frieda Klein series

For Frieda Klein the days get longer, the cases darker . . .

Psychotherapist Frieda Klein thought she was done with the police. But once more DCI Karlsson is knocking at her door.

A man's decomposed body has been found in the flat of Michelle Doyce, a woman trapped in a world of strange mental disorder. The police don't know who it is, how he got there or what happened – and Michelle can't tell them. But Karlsson hopes Frieda can get access to the truths buried beneath her confusion.

He just wanted a decent book to read ...

Not too much to ask, is it? It was in 1935 when Allen Lane, Managing Director of Bodley Head Publishers, stood on a platform at Exeter railway station looking for something good to read on his journey back to London. His choice was limited to popular magazines and poor-quality paperbacks – the same choice faced every day by the vast majority of readers, few of whom could afford hardbacks. Lane's disappointment and subsequent anger at the range of books generally available led him to found a company – and change the world.

'We believed in the existence in this country of a vast reading public for intelligent books at a low price, and staked everything on it'
Sir Allen Lane, 1902–1970, founder of Penguin Books

The quality paperback had arrived – and not just in bookshops. Lane was adamant that his Penguins should appear in chain stores and tobacconists, and should cost no more than a packet of cigarettes.

Reading habits (and cigarette prices) have changed since 1935, but Penguin still believes in publishing the best books for everybody to enjoy. We still believe that good design costs no more than bad design, and we still believe that quality books published passionately and responsibly make the world a better place.

So wherever you see the little bird – whether it's on a piece of prize-winning literary fiction or a celebrity autobiography, political tour de force or historical masterpiece, a serial-killer thriller, reference book, world classic or a piece of pure escapism – you can bet that it represents the very best that the genre has to offer.

Whatever you like to read – trust Penguin.